OUTCASTS

OUTCASTS

CrossWorld: Book II

Robert V. Aldrich

iUniverse, Inc.
New York Lincoln Shanghai

OUTCASTS
CrossWorld: Book II

iUniverse books may be ordered through booksellers or by contacting:

iUniverse
2021 Pine Lake Road, Suite 100
Lincoln, NE 68512
www.iuniverse.com
1-800-Authors (1-800-288-4677)

Cover at by Kathleen Morton
(www.nekopaw.com)

Interior artwork by Leslie Berry
(theinterloper.deviantart.com)

ISBN-13: 978-0-595-36874-7 (pbk)
ISBN-13: 978-0-595-81285-1 (ebk)
ISBN-10: 0-595-36874-3 (pbk)
ISBN-10: 0-595-81285-6 (ebk)

Printed in the United States of America

This book is dedicated to my grandmother, Dorothy Aldrich, who passed away just weeks before the release of the second edition of Crossworld.

This story is dedicated to the cast of the original 'Outcasts', whether or not you made it past the cutting-room floor. You were my audience, my inspiration, and my reason for writing.

Contents

I'd like to extend a very special thanks to the video game companies whose creations are referenced in this book. Specifically to Nintendo, Capcom, Midway, and Square Enix, as well as a host of other companies whose influence and inspiration was pivotal in the development of this story and book.

For Those Who Came In Late…

In early May, the interdimensional demon Pihc stopped time across the earth, freezing everyone in place except those with magic within their souls. With the help of his lieutenants, the alternates, he then began a systematic massacre of all the mystics on the earth.

Vincent Pierce, Dan Hardin, and Michelle Stone made their way to the site of the initial assault, teaming up with the bewildered high school friends Emily Peters, Jared Kresge, and Beth Phillips. But after the six barely survived a direct confrontation with Pihc, they were drafted by Chip Masters to join him in a counter-offensive on another world.

The rag-tag band traveled with Chip to Crossworld Castle, where they prepared to strike at Pihc's seat of power. However, the demon followed them and ultimately captured Vincent and Beth, alternating her and torturing Vincent in an effort to rejoin his soul with his alternate, Trebor.

Chip returned to earth and gathered Vincent's older brother Tim and his childhood friend Ben Poulson. However, when he returned, he found an old traitor, Jessica, in the midst of the group. Putting aside previous differences, the collected group launched out against Pihc, rescuing Vincent. But this incited Pihc's fully fury as he drove his forces against Crossworld Castle. An epic battle raged, but Chip and the group survived, giving them the chance to defeat Pihc and to buy time for the magic on earth.

That was six months ago…

Sophia

CHAPTER 1

New Beginnings

"Don't call it a comeback,
I been here for years,
Rockin' my peers and puttin' suckas in fear,
Makin' the tears rain down like a Monsoon,
Listen to the bass go boom,
Explosion, overpowerin',
Over the competition, I'm towerin',"

—LL Cool J, Mama Said Knock You Out

The birds scattered frantically, filling the gray sky with a living cloud of white fear.

The roar of the motorcycle preceded the sleek machine as it coasted down the street. Eyes and attention at the trendy café spot turned from the stylish block of upper-scale coffee shops to see the massive beast of black leather and chrome steel.

The giant motorcycle came to a halt at the edge of the pavement, its kick-stand scratching the dull gray cement of the sidewalk as it pushed down. Standing up from the bike was a large man, dressed in faded denim and aged black leather. His duster laid still against the wind, while his black cowboy hat rode low over his eyes.

He took a moment, standing at the edge of the street, looking over the densely-packed array of cafés and coffee houses with bored disapproval. Then with a cat-like step, he moved forward, making the sparse crowd of coffee-drinkers stiffen in fear.

He pushed through the white fence decoration that surrounded one café's outdoor seating, ignoring the stares that came from the patrons seated at the sidewalk tables. He strode with long steps through the glass door, taking off his black hat as he passed by the line of stylish patrons that stretched along the vineyard-decorated brick wall up to the counter. Passing by the collection of espresso and cappuccino machines, the biker came to stand over the glass case of imitation deserts as he towered over the gerbilish man behind the cash register.

"Hello…" The biker started, his hard voice making the man cower even more. "Darren." He said, leaning forward to read the man's nametag. "I'm Jon.", He said with a smile. Darren just stared back up at the wide man, petrified. "Now that we've been introduced," Jon went on with a casual tone and an intense gaze from behind his circular riding glasses. "Maybe you can help me out. I'm looking for someone." The biker reached inside his duster, producing a folded up piece of paper. He opened it with a whip of his hand and held it out for Darren to see. "I'm looking for a guy who looks kind of like this." He stated, leaning down on the glass case.

Darren, afraid to take his eyes off the biker, glanced at the picture, seeing a computerized image of a man with short, dirty blonde hair and intense eyes. The gaze was artificial and aimless, but the striking resemblance to the man holding the picture was unmistakable.

"Hey!" Came a shout.

The biker and Darren looked up from the paper in unison towards the door to the storage room as a bearded man's stomach led him towards the register, his round finger pointed at the biker. "You need to get in line like everyone else." The man called.

The biker looked at the man with a disinterested glance, not moving at all. He just waited for a moment, then looked at Darren's green apron. "Unlike everyone else, I'm not ordering."

"If you're not ordering then you need to leave." The manager demanded, keeping several feet away from the man. "Just get out of here."

The biker looked up at the middle-aged man. "I'll leave when I've got what I came for."

"I'm calling the cops."

The biker looked up, slowly taking off his black glasses, revealing a pair of hard blue eyes. "Fine." He said with utter indifference. He turned back towards Darren, away from the stunned manager. "Have you seen someone that looks like this?"

Darren swallowed hard, the sweat running off his chin, staining the burgundy collar of his shirt. "Um, you?" He whispered in a fearful voice.

The biker closed his eyes, sighing. "Yes, I know he looks like me. We're twins. That's why I'm trying to find him. Have you seen anyone ELSE that looks like this?" He finished with just a hint of annoyance in his patient tone. Darren just shook his head, the sweat from his frosted hair splattering on the paper and counter.

The biker stood up from the counter, his height once again becoming clear. He looked around the establishment, shaking his head in disgust at the new wealth mixed with the illusion of old-world style. He looked down at Darren, smiling politely. "Thanks." He said before turning around and heading out.

"Six months!"

Vincent Pierce stormed across the brick ground of the North Carolina State University courtyard, his eyes cast hatefully forward, hidden behind his wrap-around sunglasses. His black trench coat slapping against his legs as he stormed away from the mid-campus dining hall, his hands balled into tight fists. "Vincent!" Came a voice calling after him. In the late autumn day, surrounded by nearly-dead trees and dark gray skies, the stalwart figure didn't turn. He kept walking; his attention facing forward as he made his way through the spaciously arranged brick buildings that littered the university campus.

A strong hand grabbed Vincent's right shoulder, spinning him around. As Vincent turned, his left arm came up, swinging with a tight punch. The man he swung at ducked expertly beneath the blow, side-stepping it like a shadow. With a fast shove, he pushed Vincent off-balance and sent him stumbling a few steps away.

The clatter of Vincent's boots echoed off the brick walls as he turned. He spun around, his hands raised as Chip Masters stepped into the space he had been pushed from. The taller figure stood before Vincent, his hands kept relaxed but ready while his body was poised to move. Dressed in a black karate gi beneath a black jacket, the blonde fighter watched Vincent cautiously from behind his own black glasses.

"Six months." Vincent said without relaxing, his voice still filled with anger. He stood up tall, then settled his ice-cutting gaze on Chip. "You told me to wait six months. And it's been six months since we beat Pihc at Crossworld Castle. It's been six months. And Trebor's still out there."

"So is Cye." Chip said, struggling to stay calm in the face of Vincent's hurricane of hate. "We can't just go charging after them, Vincent." He implored with a calm tone. "They could be anywhere by now. You know Trebor, better than anyone." He said, braving the intensifying glare from Vincent at the sound of the name. "You know he's going to get as far away from Pihc's castle and Crossworld as he can."

"All the more reason we've got to go after him." Vincent insisted coldly, his fists tightening to the point his fingerless gloves began to groan from the tension. "He could be anywhere, yes. Imagine what kind of chaos he's not doubt been causing."

"Queen Titonus, January," Chip said, emphasizing the informal, familiar name. "Is looking for him." He continued, for the first time glancing around to make sure there were no other college students around. "Crossworld has access to the Council of Elders. They have an extensive intelligence network. They will find him."

"He'll move too fast." Vincent said with a softer voice, shaking his head, still glaring at Chip. "The only chance we have to catch him is a direct hunt."

"Vincent." Chip said calmingly, stepping closer to the darkly dressed fighter. "The VGM is not ready." He said succinctly and clearly. "We've been training four new people, two of whom just joined in the last couple of weeks. You know this. Emily's only now beginning to come around to the idea of belonging to a magical militia. We're still dealing with Dan and Michelle's parents about moving them out here from Salt Lake City. Michelle's still having trouble adjusting to being the only one in the Video Game Masters who's still in high school." Vincent turned, ready to protest. But Chip caught his left arm, just above his elbow. "Trebor can wait." He said softly, his voice a whisper. "He's not going anywhere."

"Jim! Go for the nads!"

Jessica Cameron leaned forward over the edge of the blue and red boxing ring, banging her hand on the edge of the apron. The violent thumping of her hand tossed her back-length black hair like a whip, while her intense eyes kept the lecherous perverts in the raucous crowd fearfully at bay.

Standing next to her, Tim Pierce looked around uncomfortably. His arms crossed nervously over his heavy white t-shirt, he looked around the converted bomb shelter as the standing-room only crowd roared from one side of the room to the other. The echoing din was unbearable as the crowd stamped on the bleachers, all while watching the fight in the center of the room.

Standing opposite each other in the boxing ring, two competitors squared off.

With his arms held next to his head, a large black man kept his muscled body rigid and tight, his hands kept in tight fists. He walked with high steps, his wide-cut satins shorts shimmering with the bright lights and the dripping sweat from his bruised body.

Opposite the man was Jim Ayers. Dressed in a Metallica T-shirt and baggy black jeans, he kept rolling his body from side to side. The slightly-rotund figure kept his hands moving in rhythm with his body. As if dancing to some mysterious beat only he could hear, he kept his sharp eyes locked on the man. As he moved, the three watches on each forearm jingled and slid, while his red bandana was soaked against his greasy almost-black hair.

The black man rushed in with a sudden sprint, swinging with a hard left hook. Jim slid down under it, bending low to keep the blow from connecting. He bent over so far, his body so close to the ground, he put his right hand on the canvas before bringing both his feet up. He snapped two fast kicks at the fighter, but the man absorbed both harmlessly with his rock-hard forearms.

Taking the kicks, the man bent down with a hard right elbow, catching Jim in the side of the body. The rubbery midsection took the hit, sending Jim's balance off course. Swinging on one arm, Jim's legs swept out of the ring then came back around like a gymnast on a pommel horse.

Slamming both of his legs into his opponent's side, Jim sent him collapsing to the ground. He swept his feet back onto the mat, then immediately leapt up onto the ropes, balancing for a single instant. He held up one hand, the crowd going crazy.

"He's gonna get killed." Jessica yelled over the crowd to Tim.

"He might not be the only one." Tim called over the cheering, still glancing nervously around.

"Oh, relax." The female kick boxer said, looking back at him. She flipped her head to throw her back-length pony-tail over her shoulder. "This place is cool." She said, looking around at the rowdy crowd of construction workers, fight fanatics, and business types. "They're getting caught up in it, but it's all in good fun."

"If you say so." Tim grumbled next to Jessica, looking away from the fight, his glasses flashing as if to protect his gaze. "But I don't like the idea of any of us competing in tournaments."

"If it makes you feel better," Jessica said, grimacing as the ring shook. "This isn't technically sanctioned by the VGM. This is just Jim doing what he does."

"And we're just here as the cheering section?" Tim asked with half a laugh.

Jessica looked up at him with a sympathetic smile. "Emily had class."

Jim bent forward, leaping off the top rope. Flipping over, he came down in a fast arc, giving the fighter beneath him just enough time to gasp before the Jim's body came slamming down on top of him, back first. Jim collided with his foe and the ground indiscriminately, then recoiled off the impact, coming up to his feet. He spun around, swaying as if he was still dancing, but his foe stayed on the ground.

Ding

Ding

Ding

Jim looked up at the sound of the bell, his eyes wide with shock. He looked down at his fighter, then his face exploded in joy. "Holy shit!" He exclaimed with delight. "I did it! I did it! I won!"

Tim looked over at Jessica as the crowd surged towards the ring, stuffing his hands unenthusiastically into his jean pants. "Hey." The woman said, shrugging. "It worked for Brazilian slaves, why not him?"

"Ah." Ben Poulson grinned, standing at the entrance to the massive grocery store, his hands held at his waist like a superhero while his prismed shirt cast multi-colored lights across the surrounding area. Holding his head high with his neon-green hair, the tautly built college student flashed an overly-wide at the store. "I love the smell of commerce in the morning."

"You know, I've seen Mallrats too." Dan Hardin said, strolling up next to Ben as he considered the erratic collection of pieces of paper of all shapes, sizes, and colors that he held. Dressed in blue jeans and a denim jacket, the t-shirt clad Dan stared over the collection, while blowing his eye-brow length brown hair away from his nose. "We've got some diverse tastes in the Video Game Masters." Dan observed, switching from one page to the next.

"Did Michelle ask for the blood of a virgin again?" Ben said, his façade dropped as he leaned in next to Dan, considering the pages.

"Worse." Dan grimaced, showing the page to Ben.

The flashy-dressed student read for a moment, then turned his head away in disgust. “That’s just nasty.” He winced.

“Yeah, I know.” Dan agreed. He looked over a few more pages, then shrugged. “Okay. First things first. Produce.” He announced, pointing off to the right of the store.

“You okay?”

Emily Peters looked up from her reflection and the dress she held on top of her cheerleading-built shoulders to glance back at Michelle Stone. “Yeah.” Emily said, going back to the blue dress she held over her front while the high school girl lounged in the store’s chair behind her. “I’m fine.”

“Fine, huh?” Michelle spurned on, playing with the tips of her dark brown hair that ran down to her ankles. She tossed the hair down, then looked over at Emily as she slid into a more socially-acceptable position. She shamelessly adjusted her bra under her black shirt and sat back.

Emily gave up on the dress and sat back roughly in the other chair across from Michelle. Moping in the corner of the ritzy university store, she sighed, her chin in her hands. “I need a boyfriend.” She said, staring off in her misery. Surrounded by imitation wood and imitation brass along with bright lights, she glanced back at her reflection, the image of a conscientious college student in hip-hugger jeans and an elbow-length t-shirt staring back.

She looked over at the chair across from her in the small cluster that surrounded the mirror, to see Michelle sitting with one leg hanging over the arm of the farthest-most chair. The dark-haired girl sat with her head dangling over the back of the chair, staring at the counter girl of the college clothes store. She smiled at the uniformed woman, making the girl giggle.

“I’m talking to you.” Emily sighed.

“And I’m ignoring you.” Michelle said, not even turning to glance back at her friend. “Look, you’re at least in college, so quite complaining. I don’t even know why you’d want a boyfriend. As much fun as boys can be, they’re so much trouble.”

“It’s not the boyfriend exactly so much as it’s…” Emily’s voice trailed off. She threw her hands up and sat back defeatedly. “I don’t know.” She finally said. She reached down into the crook of the seat and pulled out her bottle of fruit-flavored tea and undid the cap. She took a swig, then rescrewed the cap with one hand. “It’s just, everyone can see it, you know?”

“See what?” Michelle asked.

"It." Emily said, leaning forward now, her light brown hair falling down over her shoulder. "It. The fact that I helped save the world. But I'm not allowed to tell anyone about it, even the weirdoes. Not that it would matter, since everyone acts like I'm some kind of three-eyed bug because of it."

"Oh." Michelle groaned, sitting back. "That." She said, getting comfortable. "I know what's coming." She mumbled to herself.

"I mean, come on." Emily started harshly. "Doesn't that seem unfair? I had a life, a life I liked. I had a lot of friends. And my grades were really good." Michelle nodded with blatant sarcasm when Emily looked back at her. "Now," The girl continued, ignoring Michelle's lack of interest. "No one will return my phone calls. I was the captain of the Cheerleading squad at my high school, but NC State's cheer team won't even give me the time of day. Why? Cause I helped to save the world?"

"Quiet down." Michelle suddenly cautioned in a soft, but cautious voice as she sat up. "Like you said, not a lot of people know about that, remember?"

"Yeah, well, enough people seem to be avoiding me because of it." Emily said, turning away.

"You've got the VGM." The raven-haired beauty tried, smiling. "And, like I said, you're at least in college and not the only one still stuck in high school. Let me tell you how much that sucks."

"I know, Mich." Emily said, using her friend's nickname. "But you guys, it's just not that much of a substitute for actually having 'social' friends. You guys, well, you're more like my co-workers or something." She sighed. "Besides, I don't really even like video games."

"Comes with the territory." Michelle countered. "Besides, I didn't say the Video Game Masters was the grand prize. More like the parting gift."

"And that's supposed to make me feel better?" Emily sent back, without looking at Michelle.

"I don't care if it makes you feel better or not." The girl said, smiling. "I'm just a free psychiatrist. You're getting exactly what you paid for."

Emily almost cracked a smile "Yeah, well, I did pick you up after school and buy lunch, so it's not entirely free." The cheerleader pointed out.

"Don't worry, I'll put out." Michelle grinned. Emily laughed with a smile, uncomfortably trying to decide whether Michelle was kidding or not.

"We buy a lot of vegetables." Ben complained as he picked up entire mounds of cucumbers. He turned to Dan as the high school wrestler tried to tear the plastic bag off the roller. "What's the hold up?"

"I thought you liked holding lots of long, round, hard things." Dan mocked as he worked on the roll of plastic bags.

"Ha ha, smart ass." Ben said, dropping the cucumbers. "At least my god was seen by more than one person." He said, coming over to help Dan.

"Hey, Mormons are Christians." Dan protested. "Only we actually try to answer our questions."

"Blah blah blah." Ben discarded, taking the plastic bag Dan had and yanking hard. A long line of the bags came unraveling off the dispenser. Ben looked down at the untorn bag in his hand, then back at Dan. One eyebrow went up. "Got any ideas? Cause all mine involve dynamite."

"Mom! I'm off!" Came the wind-like voice as the girl raced down the steps. Dressed in baggy jeans and a black tank top, the blonde-haired girl ran down the steps, her blank eyes leading her to the heavy red oak door. She grabbed the curved brass handle and started to pull, just barely cracking the door.

"Wait, wait, wait!" Came a shout. Beth Phillips stopped, her eyes closed. Holding the left strap of her backpack, she sighed heavily, then turned. "Mom, Eric and Shane are waiting."

"I know, I know." Beth's mother called as she rushed into the cluttered foyer of their house, a large brown bag in her hand. "You told me this is Dan and Ben's turn to shop, so here's you some extra stuff. Dan will get nothing but healthy food and Ben will get nothing but snack food."

"Wouldn't that cancel each other out?" Beth asked, her voice draining of inflection.

"Or they might not buy anything at all." Her mother said. But as she spoke, her daughter's face slowly went blank. "Beth." She said plainly. "You're doing it again."

It took Beth a second to shake her head and snap out of it. "Oh. Right. Sorry."

"Go. The boys are waiting." She said, holding her daughter's head, kissing her forehead. "Say hi to Vincent for me, okay? And Chip too, if you're not too busy with him."

Beth turned around as she shut the door. "Mom!" She warned, shutting the door with embarrassed emphasis. Beth turned away from her door, shaking her head. Her hand still on the brass doorknob, she closed her eyes as the wind swept the edges of her almost-white hair across her shoulders. With a hard breath out, she pushed herself away from the door and the small porch around her. A quick skip down the brick stairs and she set off across the stone walkway through the dying yard.

Waiting for her in the sloped driveway was a small two-door sports car. Each door was a different color from the main frame which had long ago been bright red. The front bumper was missing, while the windshield cracks looked more like a torrential rainfall than damage done to glass.

She pulled the seat up to see the red-haired guy in the back with the light brown trench coat. She handed her book bag to him, then pushed the seat back and sat down with a huff. She looked over at the driver, her sigh sending her hair skating up from her eyes. The young sportster in the gray jacket zipped up to his neck and red baseball cap worn backwards looked back at her with a grin. "Let's go." Beth almost pleaded with another sigh, shutting the door.

"How's Mommy Phillips?" Shane asked as he shifted the purring car into gear. "Is she okay?"

"She's fine." Beth shrugged.

"She's better than fine. She's insane." Eric called from the backseat as he dug through the grocery bags Beth had tossed back to him. He pulled out a tray of cookies. "The woman gave us sweets."

"Oh hell." Shane said as he watched through the rearview mirror as Eric shoveled a mouthful of cookies into his face. He rolled his eyes and pulled out of the driveway, heading off. "Was your mom being mean again?" He half-chided towards Beth.

"She keeps making these insinuations about me and Chip." Beth said, her head propped against her hand as she leaned against the door's empty, glassless window.

Shane's car zipped along, the clean rumble of its engine at ends with the deteriorated and trashed all-black leather interior. "But you and Chip are sleeping together, right?" Came Eric's voice from the back.

"Where do you guys get this stuff?" Beth exclaimed, whirling back around at him.

"Well," Shane chimed in, focusing his attention on the car. "I have personally seen you go into Chip's room at the warehouse late at night, and seen you come out again in the morning. And then there's the fact that the walls at the warehouse are made out of cannibalized office material. So their insulation isn't exactly up to specs."

Beth's face went pale. She looked over at Shane, then back at Eric, her eyes wide with worry. "You…you could hear?"

"Could I hear?" The driver asked, checking both ways at a stop sign. "Woman, you were setting off car alarms."

Beth sat forward, her face by her knees. "Oh god." She moaned.

"Yep. That sounds about right." Shane grinned, laughing as Beth sat back up, hitting him on the shoulder. "Hey!" He exclaimed. "I'm driving."

"You know," Beth said indignantly, glaring at him. "I could conceivably demote you or something. You're only a novice, like Sophia. Since I'm an intermediate, I could, I don't know, give you kitchen duty or something."

"Hey." Eric grinned. "Me too. Kitchen duty's fine with me. Aria's garden is through the kitchen. I got no problems having to spend hours a day in there."

"Same here." Shane nodded contently.

"The kitchen or her garden?" Beth asked, her voice suddenly absent, her eyes confused.

"Well, if you assign me to the kitchen, I'll be in the garden." Eric looked forward, grinning. "With Aria." He sighed with delight.

Beth's detachment shook off at the mention of the name. She glared at Eric and Shane in tandem, then looked away. "Let's just get to Starcade. And please don't mention Aria." She said in a huff.

"One." Ben said, holding tight the edge of the plastic bag.

"Two." Dan said, holding the other end.

"Three!" The two shouted, pulling with all their might. With their legs braced against the bag dispenser, the two pulled as hard as they could, but the serrated edge of the bags didn't give.

Dan finally slowed his pull, both hesitantly giving up. "Geez." The wrestler said, out of breath as he scratched the back of his head.

"I…" Ben started. He looked down at the bags, but couldn't think of anything to say.

As the two stood there, considering the bags, an old woman in a walker came hobbling up between them. She smiled sweetly at Dan, but did at double-take at Ben. With wide eyes, she looked away from the deviant and grabbed the bag the two had been trying to tear off. With a quick yank of her wrist, she pulled the bag free and headed back towards the tomatoes.

Ben looked down at the bags, to the woman, the bags, then to the woman. He reached inside his pants, drawing out a special forces knife. Dan grabbed Ben's shoulders as he started towards the oblivious woman, wrestling him to the ground.

The cab pulled away, leaving Sophia Englert standing on the edge of the street, four big grocery store boxes stacked haphazardly next to her. Clinging to her book bag, she watched the cab disappear with a hopeless look on her face. With a hesitant step, she turned around, looking up at the large three-story brick warehouse that stared down at her. She sighed, squeezing the strap of her book bag even harder. She walked up to the door and glance around for a bell. When she didn't see one, she fumbled for a knocker. But at her slight touch, the door moved inward and swung open easily.

Sophia lingered in the dark doorway, then took a deep breath. "Okay." She said, stepping inside. "Hello?" She called into the open space.

The mousey girl hesitantly pushed through the small doorway, her bag knocking against her knees. Dressed in a gray sweater and blue jeans, she looked around with wide-eyes. "Chip?" She called to the giant room that spread out before her. The afternoon sun spilled in from the windows high above, casting a strong contrast of shadow and dusty light onto a house-sized wrestling mat with enough room around it for a respectable track. Along the far left wall, a variety of weight benches and cardio-trainers sat, paired off against the line of punching bags and other training implements lining the wall directly before Sophia.

At the far end of the warehouse, four sets of doors sat quietly. The far left set of double doors were stainless-steel and swung freely in the breeze. Next to those was a single, non-descript metal door, followed by an elevator gate, and then a set of industrial metal doors.

The small girl walked in, her blonde hair hanging loosely by her face. She walked carefully into the dusty air, looking from the single door she had entered to the line of doors at the far end of the warehouse. She looked around the entire space, seeing no one.

"Chip?" She called again. "Jessica? Tim?"

There was a sound behind her.

The girl turned her head just in time to see a knife's blade.

In a flash, a shadow circled around behind the girl, the blade of a knife coming to her throat. "Oh god!" She screamed, dropping her bag. A hand came around her shoulders from behind and grabbed her jaw, holding her still as the razor edge of the knife pressed against her skin. "Oh god, I'm sorry!" She begged, her eyes closed as her body went rigid with fear. "I've got the wrong warehouse. I'm sorry I'm sorry I'm sorry."

"Sophia."

The harsh, but familiar voice opened the girl's eyes. She blinked and gasped a hard breath, feeling the knife sudden absence. She turned around to look up at Vincent Pierce. Standing a head taller than her, the dark fighter slipped his bowie knife back into its sheath in the small of his back, hidden by his ever-present black trench coat.

"What the hell was that?" The terrified girl breathed.

"A test." Came the sound of Chip's voice. Sophia looked up from the floor as Chip Masters strolled up to the two, a pleasant grin on his face. "Hey." He said, holding out his hand. She hesitantly took it, unable to break her fearful gaze of Vincent. "Welcome to the warehouse of the Video Game Masters." Chip said, smiling broadly. "But I'd like to start by saying it's a really bad idea to just randomly walk into an unmarked warehouse. While I don't mean to deter your enthusiasm Sophia, this is hardly the neighborhood for a young girl such as yourself to just walk in off the street."

"But the door was open." She protested.

Chip looked up, his lips puckering as he stared at the door. "I really need to fix that." He mumbled to himself. But then he looked down at Sophia and smiled. "Come on. Let me give you the grand tour."

Sophia stood still as Vincent and Chip both headed towards the far end of the industrial-sized building. "You know," She said stalwartly, forcing herself to gather some nerve as she glared at Vincent. "Just because you're like Chip and Jessica and Tim, one of the Vgms, the video game masters or whatever they're called, doesn't mean you can just…"

Vincent stopped and turned back to her.

"Coming." She exclaimed, bolting towards Chip. She caught up next to him, keeping on the opposite side of the blonde Vgm from Vincent. She glanced up at the amused Chip, then smiled half-heartedly over at Vincent. "So, if that was a test, did I pass?" She asked to the stoic Vgm.

"No." Vincent said in his usual cold voice.

"Oh." Sophia swallowed.

Chip looked from her, then back to Vincent. "Anyway, just for the record, it's pronounced 'vee-gym', not V-G-M." Chip explained. "VGM is what we use to refer to the organization, the Video Game Masters. Vgm is used to refer to one of the four senior officers; me, Vincent, Vincent's brother Tim, and Jessica. Which, coincidentally, also stands for video game master."

"I know. I'm sorry." Sophia tried to defend. "And I did try to call you guys" She explained. "But no one was picking up." She said, holding her cell phone.

"We were probably training." Chip disregarded casually, looking at the bag she carried. "How much stuff do you have?" He asked.

"Four boxes." She answered quickly.

"Have at it." Chip said with a smile at Vincent. The dark Vgm said nothing as he pivoted in mid-step and headed off back towards the entrance. "Is that all you're bringing?" Chip said after Vincent was out of earshot.

"Yeah." Sophia said. "My mom wouldn't let me take any more. She said I was being a stupid, selfish little girl because I was moving into some dorm. She said college isn't about getting laid, it's about learning all I can so I can bring more glory to god."

"Ah." Chip said with a tight-lipped smile. "One of those moms."

"Yeah." Sophia nodded, as she embarrassedly pushed her blonde hair behind her ear. "But she was like that before my dad died so I'm used to it."

"I'm glad and sorry to hear that." Chip said, leading her towards the far wall. "That's the kitchen." He said, pointing to the swinging stainless-steel doors. "And past that, through the kitchen, is the garden. Which is where Aria spends most of her time, when she doesn't have classes. She's in there now, so keep your voice down." He knelt down next to Sophia. "I don't want her to hear us." He whispered loudly.

The doors to the kitchen parted and Sophia's jaw dropped. Out stepped a raven-haired woman with pale skin and a sultry presence. Like a full-sized porcelain doll, the woman's every move was seductive and alluring. She stayed partially-hidden from just behind the swinging doors of the kitchen as she stared at Chip with her intoxicating eyes. "You know I can hear you, Chip." She looked over at Sophia, her eyes flaring with delight like a wolf sighting a rabbit. "Hello, Sophia." She said, taking a step out of the kitchen.

"And that's been fun." Chip said, grabbing the small girl by her shoulders and spinning her away from Aria and the kitchen. Glancing back at the woman as he pushed Sophia forward, he pointed ahead vaguely at the other doors that lined the far wall. "That's the stairs, the elevator, and then the garage."

Sophia turned her head to look back at Aria, but the woman was already looking away, down the training hall as Vincent carried in all four of the heavy boxes. "I'm afraid we sort of have communal cars, and by communal I mean, you have to get real friendly with someone who has a car." Chip explained, still keeping subtle tabs on Aria. "And right now, that's just Shane, Tim, Emily, and Vincent."

"You don't have a car?" She asked as Chip led her to the elevator doors, hitting the call button. He just smiled, shaking his head. As they waited for the elevator, Sophia looked back, able to see better once she stood within the columns of light that cast down from the windows high near the roof. Like sheets of golden light, the late morning sun created dusty slates of visibility in the otherwise shadowed domain. From this vantage, she could see a variety of hanging bars and chains up near the roof, while the actual surface of the wall they had passed was remarkably empty and scarred as if burned repeatedly.

Chip pulled the elevator gate open, politely ushering Sophia into the wooden machine, then holding the door for Vincent. He shot Aria one quick sarcastic look, but she just smiled and winked. Chip turned back into the elevator and hit the button for the second floor, then leaned against the grating. The industrial elevator began to slowly move, the air coming alive as a cool breeze was sent down onto Sophia.

"As I think Shane explained to you at your initiations last week, this place is a converted warehouse." Chip explained, his hands stuffed into his jacket's pockets. "The second floor contains most of the sleeping chambers, which is where we set up your room." The elevator stopped and Chip pulled back the gate. Sophia stepped out into what looked almost like a shanty town.

The line of doors seemed thrown together, amalgamated from office furniture used to create cubicles. Rising from floor to ceiling, they managed to seal off the rooms, but their flimsy design didn't inspire confidence.

"We're working on improving the design." Chip explained with some embarrassment. "As we find more and hopefully better material to work with, we're going to renovate each room, starting with the girls first."

"Thank god." Sophia sighed, swallowing hard.

"Let me guess." Chip smiled, standing next to her. "You wouldn't have signed up to join with us if you'd seen the place first, right? Cause you can still back out."

"No, it's not that." She said her voice heavy with disappointment. She looked down at the floor, her own hands stuck in her pockets. "It's just; I needed to join a society in order to get into State. And when I saw there was a video game society, I went nuts." She looked up at Chip, her head tilting in confusion. "But why aren't you guys on Greek row, over on the other side of campus?"

"We have special needs." He smiled, as if to himself. But he turned and started down the line of doors. "Plus, we're not that much of a social fraternity or anything. We're registered with NC State as one, but we're really more of a cult."

Sophia looked up at him as if he was joking, but then her face went pale when she couldn't tell. "Is that why so few people apply to join?"

Chip smiled. "That's one of the reasons."

He came to the far door and pushed it open, revealing a whitewashed room with two angled sofas of different styles, and a four-chair table in the back with a chess set on top. As they entered the room Sophia's eyes were drawn to the massive television.

Surrounded by three smaller television sets and an epically-elaborate stereo system, the huge entertainment center, the only thing that looked cared for in the whole warehouse, was brimming with video game systems.

"Oh. My. God." She said, her eyes wide, her jaw gaping open. "You've, you've got everything." She bent down to look into the small glass case by the TV. "You've even got an Atari 2600. You really do have everything.

"Just about." Chip smiled with a mix of amusement and pride.

"Chip." Came Vincent's voice. The leader of the VGM looked down the hall to where Vincent stood by the elevator. "We need to go. It's almost time for us to be at Starcade."

Chip turned back to Sophia, smiling at her awe. She looked at Chip, her eyes wide with delight. "You can play with those later. For now, come on." He said, motioning for her to follow. "Oh," He said, pausing her steps. She turned back to him with a hint of worry on her face, but he smiled warmly. "Welcome to your first official day as a member of the Video Game Masters."

CHAPTER 2

Unfinished Business

"Here me now, Antiquity. Here me oh great conglomeration of spirits gone before. Make your will known."

—Carolinus, Flight of Dragons

A gentle, pale hand brushed the branches of the thickly green trees aside, stepping into the small clearing. Surrounded by the densely-packed trees, the cautious woman in the shimmering red dress cradled her silver pole arm along her left side, the flame-shaped blade resting carefully behind her, just above her slender shoulders.

A smokeless campfire populated the clearing, kept company only by a blanket tied by two ropes to a pair of trees opposite her. The blonde woman breathed out in annoyance and rubbed her eyes, making her short hair fall down around her neck. She looked around at the tight tree line that formed the campsite, searching the ground. "Trebor." She whispered to herself. "Where are you?"

With a sudden wave of cold, a black blade stretched across her neck.

"Right here, Cye." Came a voice in her ear.

The female stiffened as the katana's edge hovered near her milky skin. "Hey, little sister, what have you done?" Trebor whispered in her ear, holding her head by her pale hair.

The dark alternate looked up at the stars, a smile in his eyes. "You know, Vincent always wanted to be stronger than me." He leaned forward over the girl's shoulder, staring at her through the corner of her eyes. "But the last six months have been nothing but a learning experience for me. So while he's been back on earth, 'recovering' and 'resting'," Trebor said with spite. "I've been dug in, getting stronger by the day. So, I guess the question to you is," With a sudden yank, Trebor spun Cye around, glaring angrily into her eyes, the sword blade held between them. "What could you possibly do if I decided to deal with you like I'm gonna deal with him?"

"Knock it off!" Cye spat, knocking the sword away with her pole arm. But even as metal touched metal, Trebor let the blade spin around, catching Cye across the cheek, cutting her lip. She covered the slash of her skin, feeling the warm blood spill down the side of her jaw. "What was that for?" She yelled.

"A reminder." Trebor said warningly, stepping back as he slid the sword into its sheath over his shoulder. "I want it clear that whatever plea you're here to make, don't try to threaten me. Cause there's no one alive now that I'm afraid of." He said dangerously as he walked past her, towards the hammock.

Cye stood up straight, letting her breath escape. "Not even Ecnilitsep?"

Trebor paused. His head turned to the left as he stared back at Cye through the three thick strands of hair that fell over his left eye. "You've heard the name before, haven't you?" She asked.

"We all have." Trebor said, resuming his way to the hanging bed. He let his sheath fall into his hands, then tossed it against a tree. With a quick hope, he landed into the hammock's embrace and laid out. "It's part of the genetics that come with being an alternate; like a dog circling its bed before it lies down."

"Then you've felt the call too." Cye said, remaining at the entrance of the dense clearing. "Pihc can be resurrected, but we need to summon something called Ecnilitsep."

"We're doing no such thing." Trebor said lazily, closing his eyes.

"We have to." Cye demanded.

"No, we don't." Trebor said, lifting his head up just enough to look past the edge of the hammock. "Pihc's dead. And unless someone resurrects him, which is a costly and draining process no matter who you are or how much magic you know, he's staying dead. And that's fine with me."

Cye turned away from Trebor, leaning her naginata against a thin sapling. She cupped her hands under her elbows, staring off. "Ever since Pihc was killed," She said, taking her first casual steps into the clearing. Her voice trailed as she spoke. "Ever since Beth and I were separated..."

"Ah, the great Battle of the Four Armies." Trebor grinned. He looked over at Cye. "That's what they're calling it in Crossworld these days. The Battle of the Four Armies. The ninjas, the VGM, The Crossworld Castle Guard, and us."

"I've had this name, rolling around inside my head." Cye went on, ignoring Trebor. "It's like a song that I've only heard once, and can never find again." She turned to Trebor, a new intensity in her eyes. "Pihc's trusting us to summon Ecnilitsep. Now, I don't know what Ecnilitsep is or why Pihc left us that imperative, but every fiber of my being says we need to do it."

"One, there's that we again." Trebor said, holding up his arm, extending a single finger. "Two," he said raising a second finger. "That feeling of needing to summon Ecnilitsep will pass. Trust me. And three," His hand dropped as he looked up at Cye. "I do know what Ecnilitsep is. Or more accurately, who Ecnilitsep is."

Cye straightened up. "And?" she asked, still holding her sleeveless arms.

"Cye," Trebor sighed, lying back. "Ecnilitsep is not someone I ever want to see again."

"Why not?" The girl demanded.

"Because she's a damn monster, that's why." He said angrily, sitting up, causing the hammock to sway suddenly. Trebor grabbed the edges, trying to control the swing. He turned slowly to Cye, an annoyed look in his eyes. "If you're anything like me, you want to get back at Beth. For what exactly I don't know, nor do I care, but that's inside you. And also you probably want to get back at life in general. Again, like me. But where Ecnilitsep goes, there's nothing left, alive or otherwise."

"Trebor." Cye said sincerely. Her voice carried so sternly, the alternate looked across the campsite at her, staring at her through the waving heat trails from the fire. "Pihc is counting on us to summon Ecnilitsep. I'm going to do it." She walked the few steps over to her pole arm and picked it up. "Are you going to help me, or not?" She maintained as she turned back the way she had come.

"Ah, Starcade." Chip said, looking up at the backlit sign. Hanging over the single glass door at the far end of the brick shopping center, the sign buzzed slightly in the late dusk air. He glanced down the sidewalk towards the main street just a few doors down, as Sophia came up next to him, her head barely reaching his chest. "There are few places in this world more special than an arcade." He said with a smile.

He opened the door for Sophia, smiling as she stepped inside. He tried not to notice as Aria sauntered in next, instead looking at Vincent with a smile. The dark Vgm just gave him a cold look. Vincent passed through the door as Chip contorted his face mockingly behind his back.

Sophia stepped through the entrance, the rush of warm, perspiration-soaked air saturating her like a tide. Before her, the vast array of video games and other amusements choked the low-ceilinged room. In the small space with its red-carpeted floors and walls, the sounds of the game music and sounds were simultaneously muffled and reflected.

To the immediate left was a small tiled snack section, cordoned off by red metal pipes. A pair of soda machines and a snack vending machine sat quietly around four park-style benches. Meanwhile, the games lined the walls, with two pillars dividing the room in the center. The fighting games ran along the right side of the establishment, paired off with puzzle and strategy games along the left side. And at the very far end of the arcade, an open pair of glass doors led into the small indoor mini-mall that Starcade was a mere part of.

Opposite the mall entrance, up three steps, was a parlor area filled with ski ball, air hockey, and pool tables. Meanwhile, just off the stairs, the bored manager sat behind the prize redemption counter, his attention focused on a wireless laptop. The round man glanced next to the laptop at his veterans' hospital bill, then considered his current score on the on-line poker game.

"I love this place." Chip smiled at Vincent. He turned around to Sophia and Aria and grinned. "We'll start the meeting in ten-ish minutes, okay? Go enjoy." He turned from the others and moved into the populated arcade.

Tim sat with his back against one of the three pinball machines near the steps, rolling a clear ball along the length of his arm. He swept it up his right arm, letting it loop around before he touched his finger tips, letting the ball flow onto the back of his left hand. "The trick is control."

"Easy for you to say." Shane said, holding out his hand. Tim let the ball flow across his shoulders, and touched his finger tips to Shane's, letting the ball roll onto him. The street racer accepted the ball and kept it flowing around his body. "You played basketball for your middle school and high school. I spent that whole time toking up."

"And whose mistake was that?" Tim asked rhetorically.

"Hey, can I get a tongue ring?" Shane asked, spinning the ball over the edge of his left hand and balancing it on his knuckles.

“Do you ever want to be promoted past Intermediate?” Tim asked, accepting the ball Shane rolled into his hands.

“Yeah.” Shane nodded.

“Then I can’t say I’d recommend it.” Tim said, rolling the ball across his shoulders again.

Beth stood in front of the archaic Mortal Kombat Unlimited game, her character leaping across the screen, landing a deep jump kick. She followed up with a low blow to her opponent’s knees, then leapt forward with a flying punch. Her red ninja drove through the god she battled, knocking him to the ground.

But as she battled her way towards victory, a muscular hand snaked its way around her waist. Beth tensed up, then whirled around only to see the smiling Chip behind her. “Damn it!” She cursed, playfully slapping his chest. She turned back to the screen, then gaped at her defeat. She turned back to Chip, playfully angry. “I was finally going to beat him.”

“And if you’re that good, then you’ll beat him again.” Chip smiled, taking an elbow to the ribs.

“It’s all in the wrist.” Ben said, spinning the wooden ski ball on his fingertip. He looked at Emily and Eric, grinning. “I’m giving three to one that I can sink it in the hundred hole.”

“I don’t want to think about you sinking in any hole, Poulson.” Eric chided, standing with his arms crossed, his tan trench coat hanging at his knees.

Emily considered the ski-ball machine, then looked at Ben. She held up fifteen dollars. “**I’m in.**”

“Fifteen it is.” Ben said, reaching for the money.

“I’ll hold it.” Eric said, snatching it from Emily’s hand before Ben could get it.

Ben looked at the freckled red-head, then turned to the ski ball machine. He stood squarely before it and rolled his shoulders. He sighed out, then rolled his head around a few times, then started swinging his arms, loosening up. Emily looked at Eric, rolling her eyes, trying to keep from laughing.

But Ben finally settled himself, staring at the ski ball machine. He took a deep breath, then centered himself. Holding the ball like a bowling ball, his eyes locked on the hundred hole. He swayed his arm a few times, then let it build up force as it moved towards and away from the field.

Without any warning, Ben suddenly leapt forward at the ski ball machine, stepping up onto the field. Reaching out like a star basketball player, he popped the ball right into the small '100' marked cup, letting it fall simply inside.

Ben turned back to Emily and Eric, smiling pleasantly. "I win." He said.

"**Um,**" Emily said, glancing back at the ski ball machine. Ben's smile disappeared at her glance, then turned around as well. As he did, the numbers on the cups slowly faded away, revealing the '50' cup where the hundred had been just a few seconds ago.

"Ben, by now, you've got to learn not to make wagers with a sorcerer's apprentice." Emily said, her eyes flashing with a touch of ambient power as the magic left her voice. "Especially when Tim's my teacher. Now cough up my new dress." She said, holding out her hand.

"There are five ranks to the VGM." Michelle said, as she sat next to Jessica, the two looking across as Sophia. "Novice, Intermediate, Professional, Master, and Video Game Master, or Vgm." Michelle explained.

"I know." Sophia said. "But I thought the way to level up was determined by sparring with members of the group and beating video games."

"They are." Jessica added, her attention divided between the conversation and Dan and Jim's arm-wrestling match at the table next to them. "Leveling up in the VGM is done by in part by beating one hundred video games per level. So in order to go up from Novice to Intermediate, you have to beat one hundred video games. To go up from Intermediate to Professional, you have to beat another hundred for a total of two hundred."

"But you also have the time challenges." Michelle added in for the young girl whose wide eyes were darting between the two women. "You have to beat either a Mortal Kombat or Street Fighter fighting game with consecutively harder restraints."

"Like what?" Sophia asked.

"Well, to become a Vgm, you have to beat one of those games using only a light punch." Jessica said. "Not a light punch button, just the light punch."

Sophia's jaw dropped.

"Let me tell you about trying to beat Goro with only a jab." Jessica nodded. "Vincent's the only one who got around that for, well, yeah. And he still went through the testing after he became a Vgm."

"And the Vgms get the SkyFold glasses and the headsets?" Sophia asked.

"The Vgms get the SkyFold glasses. Everyone gets the headsets." Michelle explained. "But there's also the last qualifier to level up and that's you have to spar and beat a proportional number of members of the next stage in order to level up. That it, to go up from Intermediate to Professional, you have to spar and beat two professionals. To go up to master, you have to beat three masters in a sparring match. To go up to Vgm, you have to beat all the Vgms."

"Beat…you guys in a fight?" Sophia gawked.

Jessica nodded with a tight lipped smile. She looked over at Dan and Jim as the larger Jim worked away at the tautly controlled Dan. "He's winning, Dan." She sent over to the pair.

"No, he's not." Dan argued, trying hard not to show any exertion. "I've got him right where I want him."

"If your plan's to lose, yeah." Michelle chided before finishing her soda with one large chug.

Vincent stood before the fighting game, watching the demo screen flash with the fight. He watched every tiny move, taking in the whole computerized battle. "Vincent!" Came a shout. The dark Vgm turned back to Chip as the leader of the VGM tickled Beth, barely exerting himself as she struggled against him. "Go collect Aria from the back, will you? We're going to start the meeting." He said before he began to tickle Beth again.

Vincent nodded. He started towards the back of the arcade, nodding to Ben and Eric as they came in through the mall entrance. Emily followed right behind, counting a large wad of five dollar bills. He headed through the dark red arcade, bounding up the steps in a single leap. Past the ski ball and other games, at the farthest pool table, an angel was bent over.

Aria Geinosis leaned over the table with her cue in hand, aiming the tip against the white ball. Dressed in black jeans and a white tank-top, the ravishing beauty let her jet-black hair fall down over her shoulders as she stared at the ball.

With a fast thrust of her fingers, she snapped the ball into motion and sent it flying across the green table to clack against the other balls, sending the orange 5-ball into the corner pocket. She stood up, smiling at her performance.

"Aria." Came a dark voice. The woman turned with a smoky-eyed smile as Vincent came up behind her. "We're about to start."

"Whatever you say, Vincent." She said in a sultry voice while giving him a deep stare. But the Vgm ignored her and turned back. She watched him walk, then left the pool cue on the table, following after him.

The squat, wide steel doors parted broadly, opening up the familiar stench of death. The darkness fled from the intense light from the silver hallway just beyond the doors, revealing the circular, dark red room. The symbols inlaid into the bricks climbed up into the sky, disappearing into the darkness high above, while the single stone altar with the sloped surface filled the center of the space.

The silhouette of Cye cast into the room, followed by the long, dark shadow of Trebor. She stepped into the dim, ominous room with held breath. "This is where I was born." She whispered with a pale voice. "This place."

"Hmm." Trebor scoffed, stepping inside from the light to move around the circular space. "I was born about ten miles outside of Durham North Carolina."

"Pihc didn't alternate you here?" Cye asked, mildly surprised.

"He did." Trebor said, touching one of the stones. "But I wasn't born when I was alternated; I was born when Vincent and I separated. In my opinion, you were born in the fish market at Crossworld Castle."

He looked around at the symbols within the bricks, touching them hesitantly with his gloved fingertips. "I always wondered what these said." He looked up at the runes spiraling out of sight up the cylindrical wall. "I know those red-cloaked monks that appear whenever Pihc's going to enact some major spell were created for this place, to help channel the magic. I guess these runes are the same."

"That's not what I heard." Cye said in a soft, reverent voice, walking hesitantly inside the room, her echoed tone as fearful as her motions. "Brenard told me that they tell a story, and if you read the symbols in different directions, it tells different sides of the same story." She looked around at the room, then turned to Trebor. She placed her naginata against the altar and hugged her bare arms in close. "You know, the fact that we're bonded to this castle is kind of weird. I mean, if we ever have a knee-jerk reaction, we teleport back here. With just a thought, we can teleport back here. If we get killed, if that's even possible, we teleport back…"

"Unless you're killed with your own weapon." Trebor interrupted, annoyed. "I know how it works, and you're stalling." He said matter-of-factly.

Cye took a deep breath, but didn't release it. She almost spoke, but then turned away. With a deep sigh, she turned and stepped up to the altar, carefully placing her hands on the smooth, bowed surface. The low hum of ambient power resonated through her. She turned around to Trebor, her hands held behind her, still on the altar. "Are we really going to do this?"

"It's your show, little sister." Trebor said uninterestedly, staring at the emblems as if walking through a museum. "You're the one intent on obeying that genetic imperative that Pihc gave you. I, for one, am perfectly happy living out my life the way I have the last six months."

"You mean you've given up on revenge?" Cye goaded with mild disgust. "You no longer want Vincent?"

Trebor stopped and smiled. He turned his head just barely to see Cye over his shoulder. "Oh no." He whispered, turning slowly to face her directly. "Vincent's day is coming. He hasn't seen the last of me."

"But what about Pihc?" Cye asked regally. "Have you no loyalty to the one that gave you life? That gave you power?"

Trebor smiled. "That raped Vincent's soul, leaving me as the unwanted child of that crime? Um, gee, let me think, No."

"I don't believe you." Cye maintained with false confidence.

"Believe what you want." Trebor tossed back to her, looking back at the emblems. "You asked me to help. I'll help. So just get on with it already."

"But you know what I'm going to do, right?" Cye asked. Trebor said nothing. With his back to her, he continued to stare at the symbols on the bricks. "You know how to call Ecnilitsep, just like I do, right?"

Trebor sighed. "Yes. I know how to summon Ecnilitsep. Yes, I will help when the time comes. Yes, yes, yes. Just get on with it already." He retorted without taking his eyes from the runes. "Before I come to my senses." He grumbled under his breath.

"I think it should come as no surprise to any of you," Said Jessica Cameron as she leaned back against a coke machine, swishing a can of soda in her right hand. "That despite common belief, Jim did not beat his opponent today at an unsanctioned appearance at a fighting tournament, with any type of fighting skill." She went on, smiling at the fighter in question. "It was, in fact, that horrible body odor of his." Most of the gathered crowd nodded and laughed in agreement. The acrobat just smiled, laughing as well. "Still, Jim also was able to defeat Ben, who was the last professional he had to fight, in a sparring match after the two of them skipped class,"

"Which was so very hard to bring myself to do." Jim mocked in agony.

"Shut up." Jessica shot with playful harshness. "This is my speech." She jerked her head back to the crowd of the VGM. The group waited with amused anticipation, from Sophia laughing uncomfortably to Beth sitting on Chip's lap. "As I was saying," Jessica said, struggling to remember her thoughts as well as to keep from giving up to hysterical laughter. "He managed to kick Ben's ass, who was his final opponent in the quest for power. So, let it be written," She looked over at Michelle. "Are you writing this?" Michelle gave her a smile along with the finger. "That Jim Ayers has passed all the requirements and tonight is being promoted, if you can call it that, to the third rank within the Video Game Masters, that of 'professional'." She announced with some drama.

"A radical step up from 'intermediate'." Ben called from the other side of the small section of the empty arcade as the VGM applauded with varying degrees of enthusiasm.

"Oh, shut up." Jessica said with a snide look. "As a 'professional', he's now on our dental plan." She said proudly.

"We have a dental plan?" Eric exclaimed, looking up suddenly from next to Jim. "Kick ass. My wisdom teeth are coming in."

"Really?" Said Chip from the opposite end of the parlor. "Open wide." He said as he reached for the golden handle of his ever-present katana. "We'll take care of that problem real fast." Eric removed his wire-frame glasses and opened his mouth wide towards Chip. "You think I'm joking, don't you, Comstock?" Chip laughed, drawing the golden katana just a bit, the hint of its steel blade shimmering in the low light of the empty arcade.

"Chip, put that thing away." Dan called to the Vgm from across Tim and Emily as he covered Michelle's eyes. "There are ladies in here."

"Where?" Jim said, looking around suddenly.

Michelle snapped her fist at Jim's stomach, smacking him right below the chest. She started to laugh, the rest of the crowd joining in. The jovial air filled the group of friends, radiating out into the arcade all around, seeping into every space.

Except in the far corner.

Almost opposite the rest of the group, Vincent sat between the spheres of light from two hanging lamps. His dark hair and black clothing made him nearly invisible, as if he was masked in shadow, giving his intimidating appearance a surreal quality.

Michelle sighed, and turned away from the corner. "He's no fun." She mumbled to herself as the others laughed. Dan looked over, barely hearing her. "Vincent." The girl short explained, spreading her arms across the back of the bench, looking away.

"Yeah." Dan nodded, a somber tone in his voice. "Vincent's kind of a fast way to ruin any fun."

Cye stood before the altar, a pillar of soft, white light radiating up into the darkness above. Standing behind the red-dressed girl, Trebor watched as the light rose up into the heavens. Around Cye, whisks of white power shot above like fireflies on a summer evening, casting instant shadows that were gone as quickly as they appeared.

Cye kept her eyes closed and her hands on the surface of the altar. Slowly, her arms began to flex, her hair shaking as her body struggled with the power she poured into the altar. "**I've almost...**" She whispered. The power of the beam of light fluctuated and shifted. "**I've almost...**" She said again.

Around Cye, a darkness appeared. Her eyes snapped open to see Trebor's arms come around hers. Laying his gloved hands onto the altar next to hers, the light from the pillar suddenly intensified, distilling into raw power. The beam began to shift into a red, the color of rusted blood staining the dark room.

And then the light was gone.

Cye gasped in at the sudden darkness, her brow covered in sweat. She leaned on the altar for a moment, then turned around, the single act winding her. She looked up at Trebor, watching as he headed for the door. "Why didn't you do that to begin with?" She asked.

"I said I'd help, not that I'd do it for you." He tossed back at her. "I didn't want any part of this."

Cye swallowed hard, touching her throat. "I'm thirsty." She whispered.

"Which is odd, since you don't need to eat or drink." Trebor countered with a mocking tone, lingering in the doorway, looking around as if checking for intruders.

Cye gave him a harsh look, then stood up from the altar. "How long do we have to wait before this Ecnilitsep thing shows up?"

"Usually no more than a day or two." Trebor shrugged, turning to come back in. "Come on. We should get..."

The altar erupted in light.

Trebor and Cye whirled around at the blinding fury, their weapons drawn and ready. With a surge of wind and power, bolts of energy struck against the brick walls of the alternation chamber. The runes etched into the bricks flared to life, the red letters seeming to groan and chant with limitless power all their own.

And in a flash, the light was gone.

The two alternates gasped for a second, but it was Trebor opened his eyes first, looking back to the altar. His jaw dropped. Cye looked over at him, then to the altar itself. Her eyes widened in horror.

The woman was over seven feet tall. With ashen gray skin and white hair, her steel and blue body armor completed the look of a warrior. The towering form of strength rolled her hands into tight fists, as if adjusting to the new world. She pushed her shoulders back, the powerful muscles of her body flexing with coordinated strength.

With an executioner's fluidity, she turned around from where she stood atop the sloped altar; her piercing red eyes flashing with power as the whip of white hair snapped behind her head. Her gaze narrowed on Trebor and Cye, her look disapproving.

"*Tell me all that has happened.*" She demanded immediately.

Ecnilitsep

CHAPTER 3

Ecnilitsep

"End of passion play,
Crumbling away,
I'm your source of self-destruction.
Veins that pump with fear,
Sucking darkest clear,
Leading on your deaths' construction."

—Metallica, <u>Master of Puppets</u>

"So that's it." Trebor said, his head barely reaching Ecnilitsep's armored chest as he explained. "It's been six months since the VGM defeated Pihc here, and us at Crossworld Castle."

The giant woman took a moment to absorb the story, then focused her intense, glowing eyes on Trebor. "*Six months and you just now summon me?*" She charged angrily. "*You have been lax in your duties, alternates.*" She turned around to the altar, not even glancing at them as she spoke. "*Remove yourselves from my sight. Make yourselves in some way useful. Find me a recent map of this shattered nation.*" She shook her head, anger brimming over in her words. "*Just get out and do not return.*" She stretched out her strong arms towards the altar, making its surface glow instantly with an ambient light. "*I shall resurrect Pihc and your two fallen comrades.*"

Cye looked at Trebor, but he motioned with his head out the door. The two slipped quietly out of the alternation chamber and stepped into the silver hallway. Cye turned to him as he shut the massive doors to the room. "I, I didn't think she'd be that mad." She whispered quietly.

"Eeh." Trebor cast aside, considering the doors for a moment. Cye watched him think then turned to head off into the castle, but Trebor caught her arm. He held her still for a moment, then quietly pulled her farther away from the alternation room.

Once they were out of sight of the doors, Trebor pulled Cye close. "Ecnilitsep's got good ears, so keep it quiet." He whispered into her ear, pushing her blonde hair out of the way.

"Is she really going to resurrect Brenard and Yadiloh too?" Cye asked hopefully.

"It looks that way." Trebor said, looking around at the silver walls of the castle as he considered. He stared at the dark stars just beyond the window. "You realize she's going to resume our war against earth, right?"

"Yeah." Cye nodded.

"And you're okay with that?" Trebor asked, looking surprised.

Cye looked at Trebor; her head pulled back a bit. "Yes." She answered.

"You're okay with us solidifying reality to the point of stagnation, to the point of rendering it magically inert?" He asked, appalled.

Cye stared back at him, just as surprised at him. "Yes." She repeated.

He chuckled, not taking his appalled eyes off her. "You're more cutthroat than I imagined." He almost laughed. He turned away and started down the hallway in the opposite direction. "Even for someone like Ecnilitsep, resurrection takes a long time. As such, I'm going to go find something interesting to do."

"What about the map?" Ecnilitsep called. "She said…"

"I'll get the map, Cye." Trebor rolled, shaking his head even though he never slowed for an instant. "But she's going to be working magic for most of the night. I suggest you find something to do as well." He called as he disappeared into the darkness of the massive castle, leaving her alone.

Ecnilitsep stood before the pillar of white light, her arms spread wide. Her armor reflected the power of her will, intensifying the light. And while the blinding power drove out the shadows, it only strengthened the tempered fury within the woman's glowing red eyes.

The glowing pillar of intensity ebbed and grew, driving back the air like the fury of a tempest contained within the single act. Driving up from the altar, the blinding power drove up into the infinite darkness of tower, disappearing into the endlessness above.

Ecnilitsep turned her hands to face the light, her eyes flaring with energy. She aimed her palms at the light, her white hair whipping against the powerful wind. Bright blue orbs of light appeared in her palms as she focused on the pillar of fury. Around her arms, reality began to wash away. Space, time, and existence all began to push back like the tide against the pull of the moon. All the while, the surging force of her will grew, while the blinding power of her glowing eyes escalated.

A flap of fabric jutted out from the light.

Ecnilitsep smiled darkly as a pointed boot protruded out from the impenetrable wall of blinding light. A whip of fabric in the wind and the black-dressed cowboy stepped out from the pillar.

Yadiloh rose up, his head held high as he looked around the room. His pale skin and black cowboy hat added to his inhuman appearance, while his intelligent eyes patiently took in everything. But when he looked upon Ecnilitsep, he stiffened. Unconsciously, his hand moved towards the battle-worn revolver at his waist.

"*Do not be insolent with me.*" The woman demanded instantly, the power in her voice not fading even as the tempest of wind died down. "*You failed me in your death. Were your weak skills not desired, I would have left you to suffer in eternal limbo for all time. Or worse, sent you to the Oblivion where you deserve.*" Yadiloh showed no sign of response save for the flexing of his jaw.

The giant woman turned back to the pillar. "*You and your alternate kind have displeased me. Go forth and find your two siblings and make some use of yourselves. Leave me to clean up your wretched failure.*"

Yadiloh looked from Ecnilitsep to the steel doors. When he looked back at the woman, she was glaring down at him. "*I gave you an order.*" She commanded. The cowboy considered her for a moment, his eyes flashing a deep crimson. But then he turned from her, adjusting his hat as he moved patiently and calmly towards the door. Ecnilitsep watched him leave, then turned back to the pillar of light, agitated.

Cye pushed through the silver and blue doors, letting them spread before her like wings. As they parted, a spacious room opened up before her. Simple, but ornate furniture waited for her in the gorgeous but modest space. Vine-like silver metal wrapped around the royal blue bodies of the desk, bed, and other spaces in the room, while the deep blue walls were decorated by silver emblems and textures like the tears of the rain flowing down the walls.

But the girl passed through the room quietly, her silent feet carrying her like a dream over the pristine, blue marble floor. She laid her naginata against the far post of the draped bed and parted the soft, sheer curtains. She looked down at the smooth silver sheets and smiled. She stretched out her hand and placed it on the mattress, watching as the soft bed sank invitingly. With a smile of anticipation, Cye moved forward, spreading herself out across the bed. The warm, smooth mattress enfolded itself around the red-dressed girl. Cye breathed out with delight, closing her eyes in sleepy contentment.

Before the figure had even stepped out of the light, the powerfully chiseled form became visible. The red eyes led the body's way to existence, breaking free of the barrier of light.

Brenard dropped down from the pillar, his short black hair unbothered by the wind that surged about him. Contrasting his stone-gray skin, his black chitin and sandals completed his statuesque Greek form. He stood tall, his right hand resting on the handle of the gladius that hung at his side. He considered the room, then turned his head emotionlessly.

"*Brenard.*" Said Ecnilitsep as he turned to face her. "*I have yet to resurrect Pihc.*" The giant woman said, leaning on the altar as she breathed.

"You look exhausted." The alternate said. "Who else waits?" He asked, looking at the far door.

"*Your comrades, Cye and Trebor, took six months in alerting me to your failure.*" Ecnilitsep chided, her anger renewing. "*While Yadiloh failed me in death.*"

The gladiator squared his shoulders and locked his eyes on Ecnilitsep. "Yadiloh has never failed anyone." He defended.

"*Even you,*" Ecnilitsep charged as she stood up, towering over Brenard. "*My once champion, have failed me. There is not one of your group of misfits of whom I approve.*"

"Then by all means, my liege." Brenard said with a bowed head. "Resume your quest to resurrect Pihc from limbo. I shall go and address your grievances to the others." He turned from her and began towards the door.

"*I didn't dismiss you, alternate.*" The woman warned harshly, not turning from where she stared.

Brenard stopped, barely turning to look over his shoulder. "I was merely anticipating your desire." He said defiantly. "You were going to order me out, correct?"

Ecnilitsep turned to stare down at the soldier, but then turned back to the pillar of light. "*I do not have time for this. Get out of my sight.*" She spat at him; her back turned as he bowed deeply with overly elaborate motions, then disappeared out the doors.

It looked like any other wall, only bigger.

In the wide space of the ballroom, Trebor stood against the far wall, his hand skating over the silverish-steel surface. Smooth and pristine, the metal showed no flaw or blemish, nor any sign to give away that it was actually a giant door.

"When we touched you," Trebor said to no one, feeling the castle wall. "We both saw memories that I don't think either of us had; memories I was sure we must have lost in the alternation. And then you opened."

Trebor stepped back from the wall, staring up at it. He shook his head, not taking his eyes off the puzzle. He glanced up at the pommel of the katana he wore over his back, then back to the wall. "Somehow I doubt I could cut you open."

In a flash, Trebor whirled around, his sword drawn, his eyes ready. But standing in the far doorway of the ballroom was a familiar cowboy. "Yadiloh." Trebor called, a smile coming to his face. He slipped the katana back into its sheath, then started towards the alternate. "Glad to see you're back."

The two alternates clasped hands. Trebor nodded, then turned back to the wall. "I can't figure this out. It opened when it was me and Vincent, but now it won't."

Yadiloh looked back out the door, then to Trebor. "What? You want to go see Cye?" The cowboy nodded. "I don't know, buddy." He said, glancing over Yadiloh's shoulder, looking out the door. "She's asleep, which means one of us would have to die." Yadiloh nodded, heeding the caution.

Trebor suddenly smiled. "I've got it." He said, snapping his fingers. "I know what we need to do." He grinned. "Come on." He said, leading the way out.

The silver doorway parted.

Brenard stepped inside, closing the doors silently. Before him, in the sweeping starlight that flowed in from the floor-length windows like the surf, the royal silver room lay before him, the vine-like furniture resting quietly in the darkness. Brenard moved like a shadow across the room, coming up to the four-post bed. He pushed back the sheer curtains, to look down at Cye as she lay, hugging up against a pillow.

The alternate moved quietly, sitting down on the side of the bed. He reached out with his gray hand, stroking her neck-length blonde hair. "I knew it was you." She said, smiling without opening her eyes.

"I knew you knew, little sister." Brenard said with a proud smile. He started to move, sitting up. "I will leave you to sleep."

But as he started to rise, Cye caught his hand. He stopped, looking down at her. She looked up at the alternate, her sleep-filled eyes smiling at him. "Would you mind staying for a bit?" She asked, already lying back against the pillow. The gladiator said nothing. He lowered back down to the bed, staying still as he watched over her.

And then the room grew cold.

At the edges of the wall, frost began to spread like a malignant plague. Mist rose from the ground as the cold spread through the air and up the endless walls. Yet even as the frost grew, the inlaid emblems of the bricks that spun around the alternation chamber flared to life. Murderous red power summoned up from the runes. Rising up like a fury, the runes that lined the walls lit up, rising up into the darkness like the pillar of power, disappearing in to infinity. The shadows of the darkness spread back, a dark host of robed figures appearing behind where the walls should have been. Cloaked and cowled, the figures began to chant and pulse, like the flowing blood bringing life back to the departed.

Standing at the pillar, Ecnilitsep stood strong. Reality flowed back from her, encasing her inside a dark space that reality built up against. It flowed and rippled against her and around her, but it could not approach her. All the while, she focused her dark red eyes on the pillar.

The blue magic at her hands flared to life. Like two suns erupting in a brilliant explosion, flaring out one final gasp of desperate life, the light from her magic, from her soul, fractured the very core of existence.

And from within the pillar of light, a pair of dark red eyes ignited.

The runes and the pillar and Ecnilitsep's might collided. The world was filled with light and power, and then transposed as existence strained under the pulse. But the magic held. And the world returned.

Pihc stood atop the altar.

The ashen-skinned figure rose up to his full height, coming above even Ecnilitsep. He looked down at his mighty right hand, then to his left. Dressed in his black gi-like outfit with the long flowing coat that reached to his knees, he stood powerful and renewed. At his side, his long black katana waited.

The giant dropped down from the altar, still standing over Ecnilitsep. He put both his hands on the pommel of his sword, then bent down low in respect. "*Ecnilitsep.*" He said deeply, his powerful voice rumbling the room as he remained low to the armored woman. "*My lord and master.*"

The warrior woman breathed for a moment, struggling to show as little exhaustion as she could. She finally breathed out, pushing renegade strands of her white hair away from her face. She considered the room that had returned to its former state, dark and inert, then looked over the renewed Pihc, only to turn away disapprovingly. "*Come.*" She called in a slightly breathless voice, heading out of the alternation chamber. "*We have work to do.*"

Trebor twisted his body as powerfully as he could, then threw himself back around, whirling the metal discus out away from the balcony. The disc went flying into the night sky, coasting through the crisp air over the rocky landscape. "Now!" He shouted.

Yadiloh, just behind him, turned around quickly, drawing out his pistol. Without a breath, he leveled the gun, pulling the trigger. In the far distance, the disc exploded.

"Not bad, tex." Trebor said, pushing his black waist-length hair back over his shoulder. "That's ten for ten."

"Not bad?" Came a voice. The two turned as Cye led Brenard down the stairs into the main foyer. "That looked pretty impressive to me." Yadiloh tipped his hat to Cye, which she returned with a smile, but then Brenard moved over to the cowboy. He put his hand on Yadiloh's shoulder, smiling as he nodded. Yadiloh nodded as well, patting Brenard's arm.

Cye watched as Trebor sat down on the bottom step of the wide staircase, picking up the rolled-up paper that waited there. He watched as Brenard and Yadiloh walked over to the balcony, this time Brenard picking up one of the spare discs. Trebor just shook his head, pushing the three strands of black hair back from his left eye, even though they immediately fell back into place. "Penny for your thoughts."

He looked over his shoulder as Cye sat down next to him. He considered her for a moment, then gave her a smile. "What the hell am I going to do with a penny?"

"Oh shut up." Cye chided, playfully nudging Trebor in the side. "It's an expression."

"I know." The alternate said, looking away. He considered the three giant passageways and two massive stairwells that convened in the giant foyer. Complete with ornate silver decorations and pristine marble floors, the immaculate styling seemed counter to the ragtag alternates. "Just thinking. All this hubbub with Ecnilitsep has got me thinking about existence." As he spoke, Yadiloh's hand cannon erupted and another discus could be heard exploding.

"Existence?" Cye asked, watching as Brenard loaded up another disc. "What about it?"

Trebor looked over at Cye again. "Do you even know what we are?" He posed. She just stared at him. "We're paradoxes." He said, looking back at the large room. "We are creatures of magic, born of a broken rule of existence, which is a worrisome little fact if you realize the implications of what we're trying to do in this whole war and everything."

"What broken rule are we existing through?" Asked Cye.

"Two objects can not occupy the same space at the same time." He said, unrolling the paper just a bit to look at the edges of the map he held. "Are Ecnilitsep and Pihc ever going to get in here?" He grumbled.

"Maybe we should go to them?" Cye asked.

"No, this is where Pihc likes to have his meetings." Trebor said. "Which is fine with me. It's a nice room. But I imagine right about now, he's regaling Ecnilitsep with the exact same tale of how the VGM beat us." He looked up at Cye. "She's an incredibly thorough woman, if she can be called that."

"What is she?" Cye asked.

"Don't know." Trebor admitted, looking back again. "She's like us. Not an alternate, but a creature of magic. She maintains, and I have no idea if this is true, that she was born out of a 'need of the universe'." He said doing a fair imitation of her husky voice. "She'll say stuff like 'I wasn't born through some mundane creation or biological reproduction, I am of pure magic'." He laughed at himself. "What a bitch."

"But if we're paradoxes, how can we exist?" Cye pestered.

"During your birth, the alternation, when you were first created, there was a flash of light, like a surge of power. That power is the magic holding back the forces of Order and Law. For a brief second, the One was now Two. The exact same One, but in two different places. Until there were differences, a different perception from being in two different places, you were the same person in everyway."

"Oh." Cye accepted.

Another discus was destroyed.

"You know that neat shadowy-thing that Chip Masters and Jessica Cameron can do? They call it a Flash Forward?" Trebor asked. "Same thing. It's when they break-up the different parts of themselves. That initial 'flash' is two or more different things occupying the same place at the same time. It's against the laws of physics, and thus it's a paradox."

"But if Ecnilitsep was born of magic, and she wants to destroy magic, doesn't that mean that she'll end up erasing her own existence?"

"You see my point. As for her, well, she's dumb." Trebor shrugged, leaning back on the stairs. But as soon as he did, footsteps echoed towards them. "Though I imagine that she'd argue something like 'Order and Law should be served' or some similar bull. She doesn't seem to connect the idea that she'll end up in the Oblivion." He turned away, standing up. "Clearly, she's never been there."

Brenard and Yadiloh both turned from the balcony as Trebor and Cye stood. They all turned to the grand entranceway as Ecnilitsep strode into the large foyer. Behind her, Pihc walked with strength, the two moving in military unison.

The warrior woman came to stand before the long hallway that led out of the castle, her armor gleaming in the sourceless, ambient light. She looked over the five before her, her head held high. "*I will not burden myself to care about what has happened prior.*" She began, her glowing red gaze locked on the five. "*The Video Game Masters defeated you.*" She summed up. "*You, my greatest creation.*" She said, her head turned back to Pihc. "*And your subordinates.*" She added with some disgust towards the alternates.

"*The war against the Oblivion has taken its toll and our resources are suffering.*" She explained, her arms crossed over her chest as she paced into the center of the five. "*I can not allow any more time or effort to be wasted on this backwater world. Other domains require the attention and power that you, Pihc, command.*"

The woman stood up tall, squaring her shoulders. Her eyes flashed with power as her strength looked renewed. "*I refuse to waste any more time than is necessary on this task. I want it resolved immediately. Therefore, we shall immediately go to attend to the VGM. Directly. We shall strike at their power base, their leaders, and take them down in a single blow. And we shall attend to this now.*"

"Wait." Trebor chimed in, raising his hand, the act turning all the others in the room towards him. "Now? As in right now?"

"*Yes.*" Ecnilitsep answered bitterly. "*Now.*"

"Like now-now?" He asked in mild disbelief he shared with the other alternates. "Not later-now, but now-now?"

The woman turned to him, her glowing eyes flaring with a deeper power. She walked down the line of alternates, coming to stand directly before the long-haired Trebor. She bent over, lowering her head to stare directly into his startled eyes; her proximity making him lean back. "*Now.*" She rasped angrily.

CHAPTER 4

Cure for Passiveness

"Anyone who opposes me will be destroyed."

—M. Bison, Street Fighter II

"Magic is real."

In the small clearing illuminated by the soft starlight that filtered through the trees like smoky strokes of a painter's brush, Chip stood with Sophia and Shane. Crowded around an electric lantern, the Vgm spoke clearly, gauging the expressions of the two newest members before him. "All those old stories that you heard as a kid about witches and wizards and stuff like that, well, there was a bit more truth to them than you probably realized."

"You mean like Baba Yaga and stuff?" Shane asked, a bewildered look on his face.

"Well," Chip started defensively. "I mean, I don't know about Baba Yaga, specifically, but you know." He made sure both of the newest members were still following his words and went on. "In order to understand magic being real, you have to understand that magic is pretty simple. Basically, it's just shaping reality with your will, over the fabric of existence that is..." Chip stopped. "Okay," He resumed. "Think about it like this." He reached into his black jacket, pulling out a white sheet of notebook paper.

"Where did you..." Sophia started, but Shane put his hand on her shoulder, shaking his head.

"Reality, existence, etc, is like this sheet of paper." Chip said, holding it flat. "Now, magic is folding it." He said, bringing the ends of the paper together. "Just like origami is knowing how to turn a sheet of paper into a beautiful work of art, so is magic with molding reality into, well, it depends on the magic. We, the VGM, the Video Game Masters, are a magical organization."

Shane and Sophia stood before him for a moment, neither saying a word.

"Okay." Shane suddenly shrugged, glancing around the forest again. "That's cool. So are we going to get to learn some or what?"

"Oh, absolutely." Chip nodded.

"But, but why hide magic?" Sophia asked. "And if we're a magical group, then why do we also have the video games and the martial arts and stuff?"

"The video games are because, well, for starters they're a lot of fun, but because the VGM's magic is derived from imitating powers that you see in video games." Chip said.

Sophia stared at Chip for a minute. "Okay." Shane said from next to her. "Now I've heard everything."

"Yeah." The girl added. "I was following you up to that point. How's that work?"

"That's a long theory, but let me address your other question." Chip said, looking back at Sophia. "You asked about the martial arts and all that. Well, in order to understand why the martial arts and the secrets and how our magic got developed, let's go back to the paper." Chip held up the sheet of paper horizontally this time. "You see, there are some…people that want the paper, want reality, to be pulled so tight that it can't be folded. At all." He glanced over the paper at Shane and Sophia, a seriousness in his expression. "And these people figure heavily into the history of the VGM."

"Alright, Jim." Jessica said, as she stood with Michelle, the three in a clearing of trees pulled around an electric lantern. "The upper level VGM members know how to use the Flash-Forward. And the Vgms have decided that since you're out of your damn mind with your acrobatics, you would benefit from knowing how to do it even though you're not a master or a Vgm."

"Sweeeeet." Jim grinned.

"What you have to do is focus." Jessica said, turning to Michelle. The small girl stepped back a few paces, then took a deep breath. "The Flash Forward is breaking up the different parts of who you are into a cohesive movement, a single magical act."

"Right." Jim nodded as Jessica focused on Michelle. "Because that makes total sense."

"When you use magic to separate yourself like that," Jessica went on. "Separating the mental and the physical and so forth, each part takes on all properties of your physical self for a brief second. When you're 'flashed', you're strength and speed and everything is kind of like magnified by the shadows you have following you."

Michelle rolled her eyes and sighed. "Jim, just breathe." She said, interrupting Jessica. "You breathe. Close your eyes and breathe. You reach out to the world around you. And you reach inside your own skin and you feel every little thing that makes you up."

"You mean like organs and stuff?" He asked, his eyes closed.

"Whatever it takes." She nodded. "But you feel. Now, when you're ready, and not before, when you're ready, think about the motion. Think about where you are and where you want to be, but nothing else. Just think about the start and the finish and nothing in between. Like this."

Jim opened his eyes just as Michelle rushed at Jessica. But as she did, a burst of light appeared. And following just a second behind Michelle was a red imitation of her. Perfect in every detail, the red form mimicked Michelle's every move down to the tiniest motion, following just a second displaced. But then, just behind it, another shadow appeared.

Five shadows in all followed Michelle as she moved in a blinding rush at Jessica. But the Vgm was ready. She held out her hands low, joining them together as she caught Michelle's foot. At the same time as Michelle leapt forward, Jessica threw her hands up, hoisting Michelle up. With the power of the shadows, Michelle vaulted up into the sky, reaching up past the treetops. She hung in the sky for just a second longer than seemed possible, then dropped back down, landing silently as the shadows flowing back inside her.

She stood from the landing, looking at Jim. "What do you think?" She asked, slightly out of breath.

"So," He said, grinning massive. "So, like were your shadows red because you're on your period or something?"

Jessica sighed, her face in her hand, as Michelle calmly drew out her silver whip. "Okay, Jim." The short girl said with an exhausted tone. "Start running now."

"Like this?" Beth asked, holding up the large red stop sign. Struggling to keep the wooden post stable as she held it over her head, the girl swayed slowly like a reed in the wind.

"Perfect." Dan said, turning back to the Vincent and Ben on the other side of the clearing. "You guys ready?"

Beth looked at Ben and Vincent. The Vgm nodded. "Good to go." Ben said. He rolled his shoulders, then picked up his sniper rifle, cocking it and planting the butt against his shoulder. He looked back at Vincent. "Ready to go, buddy."

Vincent stepped back from Ben a few paces, then closed his eyes. Almost immediately, a slight white glow began to generate around his body. He held it for a moment longer as the glow turned blue, then slowly red. "Get ready." Dan called to Beth, watching the glow.

As soon as the red glow was maintained, Vincent held his hand just beneath Ben. A tightly-contained wind tunnel erupted up from the ground, sending leaves and debris scattering away. But Ben leapt up freely into the tunnel, being thrown up into the sky above the tree tops. Keeping his balance, he locked his eyes through his scope on the stop sign. Barely taking time to breathe, he lined up for a single shot.

Pop.

Beth looked up as the stop sign stuttered a bit, seeing the clean hole through the 'O'.

The wind tunnel began to fade and Ben lowered. Halfway down, however, the tunnel disappeared. Ben started to drop. But as he did, Vincent pulled out his silver stop watch. He hit the stop watch function and a wave of distortion spread out from him. He rushed over to Ben as the college sniper hung twenty feet in the air, all while the stop watch ticked away.

"Vincent?" Beth called, staring at the motionless form of Dan. "What's going on?"

"It's the Time Stopper. It's a spell attached to my pocket watch." Vincent called.

"Why can I move, but Ben and Dan can't?" Beth called.

"You're out of the affected area." Vincent sent back. He stood under Ben, then hit the stop watch function again, stopping the count down. Ben began to fall again, but Vincent caught him, stopping his fall just short of the ground.

Ben looked around at the world, then at Vincent. He smiled, fluttering his eyes. "Oh!" He shouted in a southern accent. "My hero!" He said, before hugging Vincent around the neck.

Vincent sighed. "And you wonder why so many of us think you're gay." Dan tossed in, getting a middle finger from Ben.

"Why did we have to come all the way out here to train?" Emily groaned as she stood in the nighttime wind, hugging her jacket around her arms. She looked around at the rolling hills of the endless farms that spread away from the forest behind her, then back at Eric and Aria as they stood with Tim. "I mean, we go play video games at the arcade, we play them at the warehouse, and then we exercise at the warehouse. Why do we have to come out here, to the god-damned beef educational unit, as well? If anyone at NC State finds out we're out here goofing off on the university's land, they're gonna be pissed. We could get arrested. For what? Training?"

"We need to train in places other than the warehouse." Tim explained as he wrote on a clipboard, staring up intermittently at the sky. "It helps in being spontaneous. And spontaneity is what magic's all about."

"Besides," Eric grinned as he watched Tim write. "This is fun!"

"Whatever." Emily said, rolling her eyes.

Aria came over to Emily, sauntering up to her in a scandalously sheer dress. "We're supposed to be working on magic." The woman said, coming up close to Emily. "So maybe we should consider a different type of…"

"No, no." Tim said, suddenly coming between Emily and Aria. The cheerleader looked at Tim, then Aria, confused. The Vgm turned to Emily and smiled. "Why don't you just work on some video game moves if you don't want to help me teach Eric some more traditional magic."

"Tim, you've been on this warpath for months about traditional magic." Emily argued. "You're trying to get the VGM to be a recognized magic style and still trying to get all of us in the VGM to study more traditional magic."

"Well, yeah. I thought you liked spell casting?" Tim struggled out.

"Yeah." Eric chimed in supportively.

"I do, but only compared to video game magic." Emily argued back. "I don't like video games, Tim."

"That's what it's about." Tim suddenly realized, sighing. "Emily, look, you need to…"

"I need to what?" The girl charged, standing her ground.

"Get over it." Came a shout.

The four turned as Chip came strolling up the hill with a distinct lack of sympathy in his eyes. He walked with an annoyed gait, coming over to the group. "I know you don't really care for this whole situation, Emily, but if you're going to be a part of the VGM, then you're going to need to train." He looked over at Tim. "Aren't you supposed to be doing something?"

"Yep." Tim nodded respectfully, before looking intently back at the sky.

"With all due respect, Chip," The girl said, crossing her arms as she fearlessly glared at the leader. "The only reason I stayed with the VGM was because of the little spook story you told me about how every magic community on earth would come after me, and that the VGM was my only hope of protection. I'm not here by choice; I'm here by coercion."

"Hey, whatever it takes." He shrugged as he turned away. "But I assure you that you're going to regret not having trained the next time you have a run in with Pihc."

"Pihc's dead, Chip." Emily yelled after him, not giving an inch. But as Chip kept walking away, she blinked and glanced at Tim and Aria. "He is." She said. She looked after Chip. "He killed Pihc. He did." Her arms lowered uncertainly. "You did kill him, right?" she called.

"Yeah, but Trebor and Cye are still out there. Or maybe you think they'll just go their merry little way?" Chip called from the base of the hill, heading back into the tree line.

"Um?" Came a sound. The others turned to see Eric, standing confused. "Who's Pihc?" He asked.

Dan stared up at the tree for a moment, taking a quick sip of his Dr Pepper. He screwed the lid on, then threw his foot forward, slamming into the base of the tree with a hard kick. With a resounding snap, Ben fell out of the tree, landing abruptly on the ground. He blinked twice, then looked up at Dan. "We need to work on your control, Hardin."

"Don't worry. I won't let anyone know that you scream like a little girl." Dan said as he helped Ben to his feet.

"Oh, I think they already know." Ben accepted as he pulled tree fibers out of his neon orange hair. The two strolled towards the middle of the clearing where Beth and Vincent packed up the small arsenal of guns into their cases. But as the four came together, a loud rushing sound flew by them. In a flash, Jim shot through the space between them, all of them turning to watch him.

"For a guy his size, he can really move." Ben said, leaning forward to stare after Jim as he unslung his sniper rifle.

"He's running from a girl." Dan said. "I'd recognize that panicked, hysterical look on his face any day." As he spoke, a flash of dark rushed by as Michelle tore after him.

Ben stepped into the path, looking back in the direction they had come, then after them. "What in the name of god is going on?"

"Jim decided he needed to crack on Mich." Came Jessica's voice. The four turned as the Vgm stepped into the clearing, an amused smile on her face. "Chip's calling for us to pack up and call it a night."

"Done and done." Ben said, shoving his sniper rifle into Beth's hands, nearly knocking her over in the process. "Here, make yourself useful."

"We're still waiting for you to." Vincent chided coldly, turning from Ben back to Jessica. He was about to speak, but as he did, Jim came stumbling back into the clearing, panting radically. The large acrobat bent over, gasping for breath for a few moments, then reached into his cargo pocket and pulled out a hip flask. He popped the top and took a healthy swig, biting on the taste.

"You know, Jessica." He said, as he wiped his mouth with the back of his hand. "Between you using Michelle like that to get us to run laps around the forest that one time, to the constant kick-boxing routine you make us all do every day of the week to…" His voice trialed off as he thought. He suddenly turned to her with an exhausted look. "Has anyone ever told you that you're a slave-driving dyke?" He asked with a half a smile.

Dan immediately put his hand on Vincent's chest, keeping him from moving. But Jessica just rolled her eyes at Jim. She extended her fist, the knuckles aimed between Jim's eyes. "Ayers, I don't really have the energy to hit you right now so just get a running start."

"Guys, Chip's waiting." Beth reminded the group, holding Ben's rifle as if it was a color guard prop.

"Yeah, yeah. Chip, schmip." Dan said, leaving the group behind to head out of the forest. "By the way, Jessica, you're bleeding from the neck."

She reached up to her neck, touching the blood and looking at her fingertips. "Hmm." She said with thought. "I guess that would explain why Michelle's been staring at me like I was a Golden Corral buffet." She shook off the blood and glanced at Vincent and Jim. "You guys ready?" They nodded. "What about you, Gay Station 2?" She asked to Ben.

"Guys! I'm not gay." He shouted to the group in general.

"Have you seen the shirt you're wearing?" Jim chimed in from across Ben, already following the others out. "Cause its saying something totally different."

The gathered VGM stood just inside the street barrier that lined the grassy fields of the farmland. With his back to the four cars of the VGM parked along the side of the road, Chip stood before the group, a simultaneously pleased and annoyed look on his face as he spoke. "Okay." He called to the group. "This went better than I would have expected given our break in activity due to midterms and the college being full of suck." That elicited some moans of agreement from the crowd before him.

"We managed to completely wig out the newbie." He went on, glancing to Sophia on his left who stared at the others in utter astonishment. "We also proved our theory that video game magic does, in fact, beat pro wrestling, but I fear for the sanity of those involved in the testing."

"As I think you should." Ben offered with a tight-lipped smile as he glanced at Jim.

"Okay, guys. Good job with the training. We've been out here in the October cold long enough. Load up and let's go home." He pronounced with a thumb back to the cars.

"So what are we going to do with the rest of the night?" Shane asked, as he led Jim, Ben, and Dan back to his tiny roadster.

"Sleep." Dan said, rubbing his neck. "I'm exhausted."

"Wuss." Ben grinned. "I've got a mind for some alcohol. I say we go hit up an ABC store and get us some brass monkey or something."

"None of us are 21." Shane said, coming up to the small car parked in front of the others. "How are we going to buy it?"

"Fake IDs." Dan said nonchalantly. Shane stumbled up at the words, his head turning in mild shock as Dan moved to slide into the backseat.

"Most of the upper-ranking VGM members have them, just like we've got fake security IDs for most of the big-wig places in and around Raleigh." Ben added, checking the clips on one of his pistols. He slid the spent clip into his left cargo pocket, then reached into his right, pulling out a fresh clip. He slammed the clip into the butt of the gun with evident delight.

"Do I want to know how we've got that kind of stuff?" Shane asked, concerned.

"Well, you'll learn how, if you ever get promoted past Intermediate." Dan said casually as he pulled a Dr Pepper out from his denim jacket.

"You're a 'Master', right?" Shane asked, getting a nod from Dan. "And you're a 'Professional'?" Shane now asked Ben.

Ben nodded, but looked back at Shane's car. "Now, Shane. You know you're my boy. And it's not that I think you're car isn't fast, it's just, well, are you aware that you've got a racing stripe that's bright yellow? And worse, the rest of it's red?"

"Yeah." Shane nodded, knowingly. "I painted it that way."

"Did you mean to paint the door 'bondo'?" Jim asked with a grin, unable to resist.

"So this is supposed to be a kind of regular thing for the VGM?" Eric said leaning forward from the backseat of Tim's car, looking up at Beth and the driver. "We only came out once or twice before we took that month-long hiatus. Are we going to start coming out here again?"

"Yeah. The last month's just been tough for mundane reasons like registering for next semester and stuff. But we're going to try and train out here at least once a week or so." Tim nodded, yawning. "I mean, hopefully the sessions will be a bit more organized. I know this time Chip just wanted to take Shane and Sophia and give them a quick tour of the VGM's video game magic. But I mean in the future we're supposed to do organized stuff like capture-the-flag games and so on. It's almost meant to be more playing than training."

"That's what Emily was complaining about." Beth said. "Too much training."

"Well, Emily's gotten a raw deal with all of this." Tim grumbled. "I sympathize, but she needs to get over it."

"So can you tell me more about Pihc and his guys?" Eric asked, leaning forward.

"Do you ever do anything besides ask questions?" Tim looked at him from the window, smiling. "When we get to the warehouse, I'll show you some of the files we've got on them."

"Why are you so curious?" Beth asked.

"This is wild." Eric grinned like a fool. "The whole idea of aliens and demons and stuff is cool."

"I guess." She said, looking away. Tim glanced over at her as she looked through her reflection in the glass.

"I love wasting my evenings." Emily grumbled, leaning on the driver's window as they sped along the highway.

"Oh, quite your bitching." Michelle charged at her from the passenger's seat of her car. "This was fun. Or it would have been if you hadn't spent the whole time moping."

"I wasn't moping." Emily protested. "I just don't like this stuff."

"Well, tough." Michelle argued. "It's your life now, like it or not."

"I don't." The cheerleader fought back, settling in to drive in silence.

From the backseat, Sophia watched the two girls go at it, apprehension awash on her face.

"You need to get a real car, Vincent." Chip said as he shifted in the backseat of the tiny cherry-red grocery getter that Vincent drove. Coasting through the downtown streets, Vincent's compact car cornered the turns and made its way through the heart of Raleigh.

"My car's fine the way it is." Vincent said, looking in the rearview mirror at the cramped Chip as he sat in the back of the two-door. Jessica laughed at the sight, then looked forward, just in time to see a spinning silver disc come flying at them.

The whirling buzz saw tore through the car, ripping cleanly through the entire front, stopping the vehicle cold. The spinning silvery blade tore up through the metal and into the windshield, then whisked away, flying up into the night, leaving the smoking husk of the car half divided.

The songs of crickets could be heard in the far-off distance as the silent car hissed away its life. Through the window, Vincent glanced out into the night, holding his head. He wiped away a speck of blood, then looked out. He banged against the door with his shoulder, but the mashed frame would budge. Drawing back he slammed his elbow against the glass, painting it opaque as it resisted the blow. A second impact and the glass bulged out, fragments falling away. A third eruption and the glass spewed out like stardust, leaving Vincent holding his elbow as he growled angrily in pain.

He focused away the pain, then with his gloved hand smacked at the remaining fragments of glass that bowed out, ultimately knocking out the rest of the window. He grabbed the top edge of the driver's side door and pulled himself free. He dropped onto the pavement, then reached inside to help Jessica as she crawled out through the window.

Vincent took her hand and wrapped an arm around her shoulders, helping guide her through the glass. The kick boxer landed on her feet and stumbled. Blood was gushing from her hairline, running along her right eye. She grabbed her head and winced in pain.

Vincent leaned over her, holding her head. "It's not bad." She whispered, trying to fight the pain.

Vincent searched through her raven hair, finding the large gash that bled freely. He put his hand on her head, focusing. "***Cure.***" He said, the magical tone in his voice echoing as the small swirl of light cascaded around Jessica. Almost immediately, her breathing began to ease up.

She stood up; flexing her shoulders, then winced again in pain. "What the hell was that?" She asked, looking at the demolished front of Vincent's car.

"Cye." Chip said, as he pulled himself out of the car. "You guys okay?" He asked, rolling his left shoulder as he looked around at the empty late-night city.

"Fine." Jessica said, for the first time looking at Vincent. He said nothing as he searched through Jessica's black hair for any more injury.

Chip turned around and around, scrutinizing the area, then pulled out the small combat headset in his jacket pocket. He switched it on and slid it over his head. "All Vgms, on-line." He called.

"Jessica, on-line." Jessica said, still working out the pain in her shoulders.

"Vincent, on-line." Vincent said, watching the perimeter. He waited for a moment, also glancing at their surroundings. "There's no one around."

"There never is in this part of town at night." Chip retorted, watching every alley and building top. "Is anyone there?" He called into the mouthpiece of the headphone. "Ben? Dan? Beth? Hello?" He yanked the headset off his head. "It's not working."

"Of course it's not working." Vincent said stoically, looking around. "It's Pihc."

"Don't jump to conclusions, Vincent." Jessica cautioned. "It was just Cye. That doesn't mean anything."

Vincent and Chip both stared at her.

"You're right, what was I thinking." She accepted.

"We're ten minutes away from the warehouse on foot." Chip said, looking at the wreckage of the car. "We either drop into the sewers, or we try and make a run for it."

"Given that I'm the only one here not in long pants," Jessica whimpered with a smile. "I feel bad about vetoing the sewers. I know the system, but still."

"We don't do either." Vincent said, looking around at the building tops. "We go and find Cye."

"As much as I'm spoiling for a fight," Chip smiled. "Taking on an alternate, and probably more than one, is a really bad idea without backup."

"If we go and get backup, they're going to be gone." Vincent answered coldly.

Chip sighed, looking at the wreckage. "You think your insurance will cover this?"

"Attacks by the henchmen of interdimensional demons? I doubt it." Jessica chimed in.

"It's the least of my worries." Vincent answered emotionlessly, still watching the outlines of the buildings.

"You do realize this is a trap, right?" Chip said to Vincent. "Cye just attacking the car and then not following up. She and Trebor and probably Pihc if you're right. They've set a trap."

"Of course." Vincent nodded. He looked at Chip. "But when has that ever stopped us?"

"He's got me there." Chip agreed. He looked around the brick area of warehouses and factories, trying to get his bearings. "So where are they?"

"There." Vincent said, pointing at a wide, city block-sized warehouse.

"How do you know?" Jessica asked.

"Because I can smell Trebor." The dark Vgm answered.

"Besides, it's the scariest place in the vicinity and that's Pihc's MO." Chip added sarcastically. He looked at Jessica and Vincent, then sighed. "Okay, kids. Let's go." He turned towards the warehouse and headed on.

"That is the absolute last time we let Dan do any shopping." Tim said to himself, closing the refrigerator door. "He's worse than Vincent and Chip, put together." He turned away with a jar of peanut butter and a handful of celery sticks. Unscrewing the lid, he started out of the spacious, industrial kitchen, scooping the crunchy peanut butter out with the celery stalks.

He came out into the training hall of the warehouse, looking up as Dan slide Jim's name off the section of plastic name plates in the second line of names under the heading 'Intermediate'. With the plastic tag down, Dan then shifted a bit, placing an iron tag underneath the title 'Professional'. "Wood for the novices, titanium for the Vgms, huh?" Dan said, leaning back a bit on the ladder to look at the five columns of names that hung between the stairwell and kitchen.

"And you're sitting pretty in steel with the masters." Tim said, enjoying another celery stick.

"Take a risk," Read Sophia as she stood at the base of the ladder, reading the shoddy metal banner above the five groupings of names. "Try your luck, test your might. That's the VGM's motto, isn't it?" She asked to Tim.

"Yeah." Tim nodded. He then shook his head. "Dumbest goddamn motto I've ever heard of." He mumbled under his breath.

"Um, I have a question." She continued. "Who's Jared Kresge?" She asked, steadying the ladder as Dan came down. Tim came around as Dan hopped off to look at the collection of black and white pictures that lined under the name plagues. Included was a photo of a smiling high school senior wearing a ninja outfit, holding a thumbs up.

"He's an exchange student." Tim mused, moving to look at the other pictures. Amongst them was a black and white photo of the most people, including a middle-school aged Vincent. Tim couldn't help but smile nostalgically.

As Dan came around to join them, Ben, Shane, and Jim came strolling out of the garage. Shane carried a bag of tools, while Jim carried a large piece of unidentifiable equipment. "Uh, guys. What's that?" Tim asked, pointing at the device.

"Not really sure." Shane said without stopping, glancing down at the device in Jim's hands as the three paused before the elevator. "We wanted to figure out what it is and how it works." The elevator chimed and Ben parted the doors.

"Okay." Tim said as the three climbed inside. "Where'd you get it?"

"A cop car parked across the street." Jim said as he followed Shane inside. Ben shut the door, leaving Tim at a loss. The Vgm looked at Dan.

"I don't know what worries me more," Dan offered. "What happens when Chip and the others aren't here, or…"

"Or how long they've been gone." Tim nodded. "I know. I'm starting to get worried too."

"Should we go look for them?" Sophia offered.

Tim looked at Dan, getting the same uncertain look. "Yeah, but that takes effort. I mean, we could go and look for them. Or we could go upstairs and play Final Fantasy. You got to see where I'm going on this one." The Vgm explained.

With a fast kick, the doors to the warehouse slammed opened. Chip stood in the light of the city street, his eyes scanning the darkness for any sign of movement. He stayed dramatically still, occupying as much of the space in the light as he could, while to either side, Jessica and Vincent silently snuck around the corners of the darkness, disappearing into either side of the warehouse.

Jessica folded herself around the side of the door, sliding her SkyFold sunglasses into her leather jacket pocket. She reached up to her headset and switched it on, glancing back at Chip. "Chip." She whispered. "Nod twice if you can hear me."

Chip stared forward as if challenging the darkness.

Jessica turned back around, as flash of shimmering red disappeared behind the edges of a doorway directly ahead. Jessica glanced back at Chip, but he was gone. "Damn it." The woman cursed. She turned back to the doorway and sighed, heading in.

Vincent walked without a sound between the boxes of the warehouse. With his hands held open and ready, he moved like a shadow, his eyes searching every space. Yet as he walked, he seemed unaware of the shadow that crept up behind him.

In a flash of motion, Trebor wrapped his arms around Vincent's neck, catching him from behind. "You've gotten sloppy, Vincent." The alternate grinned as he choked the Vgm with a rock-hard grip. "Life been nice and easy for you?"

In the blink of an eye, Vincent rammed his right fist directly over his shoulder, driving it into Trebor's face. Blood exploded from the blow as the alternate's grip was knocked free. He slammed up against the crates of the warehouse, his eyes wide with shock as Vincent's left fist came around in a hard punch.

The blow knocked Trebor down to the floor, his eyes wide with disbelief. He glanced up; holding his jaw clumsily, then yanked it to the side to reset it. "Holy crap." He breathed. He looked up in shock just in time to see the tread of Vincent's boot coming at his blood-covered face.

Chip walked with a long stride, his arms held out away from his body. He paned his head around slowly, the cadence of his movement keeping still and unbothered.

A flicker of motion.

Chip's head turned to follow the movement, seeing only the corner made out of the stacked boxes. He looked around, considering the massive maze-like array of wooden and steel crates. He took a deep breath, then burst forward. Leaping up against the side of the crates, he pushed off with a second thrust, landing on top of a large stack. Kneeling down in the high altitude, he looked down into the next haphazard aisle.

Nothing.

Crouching on the crate, he stayed low, his eyes hidden behind his dark sunglasses as he scanned the wide darkness of the warehouse. He turned his head slowly, carefully taking in every detail. He took slow, light breaths as he looked, considering every possible space.

Yadiloh

Standing in a clearing in almost the exact center of the giant warehouse, the cowboy stood warily, watching, waiting. Chip smiled as he reached for the golden katana at his waist. He pressed with his thumb against the hand guard, the blade sliding silently out. He gripped the handle slowly, not taking his eyes off his prey. Drawing out the katana with a familiar motion, Chip lifted up carefully onto the balls of his feet, shifting his balance delicately forward to the edge of the crates. But then he hesitated.

He glanced away from Yadiloh, then back to the cowboy. "If Yadiloh's there," Chip wondered. "Where's Brenard?" He asked, as the alternate stood directly behind him, silently drawing out his left gladius.

Trebor swung at Vincent with a fast hook meant to take his head off. But the Vgm ducked under the blow and came up with a powerful body-blow to the alternate's midsection. Sliding both his hands past Trebor's arms, Vincent grabbed him and yanked him down while throwing his right knee forward, catching Trebor in the chest.

But the alternate grabbed Vincent's knee as it recoiled. With a powerful flip of his body, Trebor lifted Vincent up and fell back against the hard cement floor. But before they landed, Vincent twisted his body, landing on his shoulders. Trebor rolled away from the sloppy landing while Vincent flipped up to his feet. He rushed at his twin, but Trebor moved too fast.

Sliding out of the way, Trebor sent Vincent skidding past, kicking him in the back of the knee to buckle his stability. Vincent nearly fell but by the time he recovered, Trebor came around with a hard elbow to the back of Vincent's head. The blow knocked Vincent's glasses off, sending him crashing to the ground. Trebor leapt down at Vincent, but the Vgm threw up both his legs, catching Trebor at the chest. With a fast kick, he threw Trebor back.

Jessica walked quietly, keeping the triangular blade of her steel kitar held close to her face. She glanced at the reflection in the blade, checking behind her as she searched. She entered a large opening, the space surrounded by boxes on all sides.

A loud explosion made Jessica jump, but she looked up at the air conditioning unit that had shocked to life. Relieved, she breathed out.

A step.

Jessica threw herself to the side just as Cye's naginata pierced the space where she had been a second ago. Jessica landed hard on her shoulder and rolled back up to her feet as Cye rushed at her. The girl's pole arm came dangerously close, but Jessica slipped just past its reach, then dove in. She swung with her left hand, barely missing as Cye stepped by the jab. But Jessica immediately came around with her right, the kitar's blade driving for Cye.

The female alternate came down with the blade of her naginata, aiming straight for Jessica's shoulder. The kick boxer parried it with her kitar's forearm guard, then caught Cye in the stomach with a shin kick. Cye shrugged off the blow and swung at Jessica with the blunt end of her staff, but as she did, Jessica phased out of sight, reappearing immediately behind Cye. The alternate swung around, redirecting the kitar that would have impaled her. But as she did, Jessica propelled herself at Cye like a top, her spinning body catching Cye across the face with her knee, knocking the alternate back.

Trebor threw a fast jab at Vincent's face, but the Vgm parried and riposted with a jab of his own. The blow opened up Trebor's nose and blood flooded out, but Vincent kept on. He came in with a hard cross, then caught Trebor in the knee with a shin kick.

Trebor twisted his knee to minimize the blow, then swung at Vincent with his left arm. Vincent slipped his own left arm inside the punch and caught Trebor around the shoulder. With a fast whirl that put him behind Trebor, Vincent slid his other arm up under Trebor's right arm, capturing him in a full-nelson hold. But even as Vincent momentarily immobilized the alternate, he leapt forward around Trebor's left side, swinging his body out around his foe's. Trebor's body bent violently at the waist, a loud crack echoing through the storage bay.

Brenard swung over his shoulder at Chip, but the Vgm managed to block it with an upward motion of his katana. Whipping around instantly, Chip slashed the curved blade of his sword down low, catching Yadiloh in the back of the leg. The slash took out a handful of tendons, dropping the gunfighter to the ground.

Chip came back around, parrying Brenard's second gladius as he lunged for Chip's midsection. The Vgm side-stepped the thrust as Brenard over-extended himself, spinning around to slice at the back of Brenard's head with all his strength. But the alternate shoved his other sword over his neck, narrowly stopping the katana slash. The blow still landed with enough power to send Brenard stumbling on top of Yadiloh.

Chip followed through with a fast kick right at the gladiator. But as he threw the hard side-kick, immediately following behind him was a green shadowy image of himself, perfect in everyway. The shadow followed just a split-second behind him, before another shadow appeared. The six shadows followed as Chip launched into a barrage of strikes against the alternate, moving faster than the eye could see. His katana sliced away at Brenard as he tried in vain to block the blows.

But as the attack launched, Yadiloh rose up, aiming his pistol. Chip glanced back at him, all but two of the shadows disappearing. The two that remained became vague purple colors as Chip dashed at Yadiloh, the shadows following less closely. The first shadow stayed in position as if it was running from Brenard to Yadiloh, while the second shadow continued its assault on Brenard. Meanwhile, Chip tore into Yadiloh before he could shoot, slicing at him with everything he had.

Vincent parried the punch with his hand, throwing it into a quick arm-bar. Pulling Trebor around to keep him off balance, Vincent ducked down and pushed into the alternate, tackling him between his legs. Standing up with Trebor spread across his shoulders, Vincent threw himself at the wall to his left, slamming Trebor's face into the steel surface. Throwing himself at the wall a second time, Vincent didn't even look when Trebor's head exploded like a popped pimple.

Vincent dropped Trebor's body, reaching down for the black katana. As he picked up the weapon, the blade flashed, a series of elaborate letters appearing on its surface. But Vincent ignored the reaction. He stepped over to Trebor's headless body, drawing the sword up over his head. "Now, together," He whispered as he glared down at his near-twin. "To the Oblivion, once again."

"Vincent!"

The sound of Jessica's voice jerked Vincent's head up, his eyes wide with fear. He turned away, forgetting immediately about Trebor. He looked off in the distance, in the direction that Jessica had called, then back to his foe. But the body of Trebor faded away, as did the katana in his hands. Vincent hissed like a vicious jungle cat, then turned away and burst towards the sound of the scream.

Jessica parried the naginata's blade and came in with a fast left shin kick. But Cye let the kick come and looped the rear end of the pole arm under Jessica's leg. With a fast yank up, Cye moved to throw Jessica's balance off. But the Vgm let her leg get pulled up by the silver naginata only to slam it back down onto Cye's shoulders.

Cye bit down on the pain of the kick, then shot in, tackling Jessica to the ground. Drawing back, the alternate slammed her fist into Jessica's face, knocking her head against the concrete flooring. Jessica gasped for breath as blood poured out of her mouth and nose. She looked up just as Cye drew back her fist a second time.

From out of nowhere, Vincent's feet punched into Cye's back, sending her flying off of Jessica. The female alternate slammed into a crate, coming up to her feet instantly. But as she did, Vincent looped around, catching Cye's arm. Twisting her back over his side, Vincent threw her to the ground, keeping a hold on her arm. Holding it straight and pulling against his knee, the Vgm threatened to snap her elbow like a twig as he drew back on his fist.

But Cye held up her hand, her face twisted with fear. "Vincent!" She screamed in a meek voice. "Don't!" Inside Vincent's mind, the image of Beth superimposed over Cye, loosening his hold. Cye winked up at him as she faded from sight.

The dark Vgm stood up, barely breathing hard. He looked over at Jessica as she got to her feet. "You okay?" He asked.

She smiled as she wiped the blood from her nose. "Never better." She grimaced as she reset her nose back in alignment. She breathed hard for a minute, then smiled at Vincent. "Thanks for coming to my rescue." She half laughed. "My knight in shining armor."

"I'm no knight." Vincent growled angrily. "Trebor and Cye both got a way."

Jessica's face suddenly became earnest. "That means Yadiloh and Brenard are…"

Vincent's head whipped back towards the center of the warehouse. "Chip!"

Chip was thrown back against the crate, blood pouring from his mouth. He looked up, his face filled with rage as Brenard rushed at him. Swinging with both gladius swords, the gladiator was barely able to get near Chip. As soon as he swung, Chip flashed incorporeal and swirled around the Brenard, appearing behind him.

The Vgm slammed a fast kick into Brenard's back, knocking him face first into the crate. He turned around immediately, catching Yadiloh's extended arm at the elbow. With a fast yank over his shoulder, Chip threw the gunfighter to the ground. Tossing his sword into the air so that he could hold it like a javelin, Chip jammed his katana blade into Yadiloh's chest, driving it down through his body and into the cement floor.

As soon as Chip regained his footing, Brenard attacked him from behind. Wrapping his thick arms around the Vgm's waist, Brenard bent his body powerfully back, arcing Chip over him and slamming the Vgm down onto the cement flooring. The suplex dazed Chip, leaving him stunned. Brenard stood up, summoning his twin gladius to him. But as he turned around, all he saw was Vincent's boot.

The kick knocked Brenard into the air, giving Jessica time to zoom in as she screamed. "***Flying Kick!***" She shouted as she shot like a bullet through the air, to knock Brenard to the ground. Vincent pulled Chip to his feet, then shoved him against a crate and burst towards Brenard. The alternate saw the motion, and shot down underneath Vincent's intended attack, shooting his legs. Catching his left leg between his arms, Brenard stood up into Vincent. But as he did, Vincent scissored his right leg around Brenard's neck, changing the balance of the two fighters and landing on his back. Vincent grabbed hold of Brenard's body and held him still while he clinched his legs together.

But as he cemented the hold, Brenard disappeared like the morning mist.

Vincent scrambled up to his feet, his hands ready as he looked anxiously around the darkness.

Jessica came over from the edge of the space, approaching Chip's empty katana as it stayed imbedded into the ground. She glanced over at Chip as the still-dazed Vgm tried to get his bearings. "You okay?" She called.

He stared at her for a minute, then shook his head. "What the hell was that all about?" He finally asked, rubbing the back of his neck, wincing with pain as he tried to move his head. "That wasn't the usual welcoming party we've gotten in the past. They were here with a purpose."

"And by purpose, you mean a plan." Jessica said, moving back towards the two other Vgms, keeping their backs together. "You okay?" She asked again.

"Yeah, peachy." He groaned. "How 'bout you, tall, dark, and deadly? You okay?" He sent over to Vincent.

"I'm fine." Vincent grumbled, still looking around. He searched the shadows and dim light of the warehouse, his head slowly turning. His dark eyes scanned the seemingly endless space, concern washing through him. "Did you guys just feel that?" He asked quietly.

"Feel what?" Chip asked.

"Yeah." Jessica nodded, looking around as well. "It's like the air suddenly got heavy." She turned her head, looking out into the crates of the giant warehouse, for the first time looking into the distance. "Oh no." She breathed fearfully.

"What?" Chip asked, glancing between the two of them. "What is it? Pihc? What?"

Jessica's face drained of all color as she stared into the far distance of the darkness. "Worse." She breathed in slow horror.

CHAPTER 5

Terror Given Form

"Did you think you could destroy that which does not perish?"

—The Undertaker, WWF Raw is War

At first it felt like a throbbing in the air. Like the pulsing of a subsonic heart, beating intensely and purposefully, but with no audible sound. Then, in the distance, encloaked in shadows, a figure appeared. Impossibly large, the form of an armored woman stalked towards them, the solid impact of her footsteps echoing far ahead of her presence.

"I think we're screwed." Jessica whispered.

"You think?" Chip whispered as well.

With an earth-shaking step, Ecnilitsep stepped into the clearing.

As if the light itself was afraid of her, the gray-skinned woman in her form-fitting armor remained cloaked in darkness. She towered over her foes, a look of almost-amusement on her pale-gray face. At her waist, the long curved blade of a scimitar waited patiently, but her strong body made no move towards the weapon.

She stood before the three, appraising them. With a condescendingly harsh gaze, she stared down at the Vgms, looking disapprovingly from one to the next. "*These?*" She said after a moment, her magically-charged voice echoing off the crates. "*These are the general-warriors that defeated you?*"

"*Yes.*"

They turned as Pihc appeared behind them. Vincent immediately whipped out his bowie knife, but Chip grabbed his shoulder. The dark Vgm glared back at him, but Chip's hard eyes kept him under control.

Ecnilitsep considered them for a moment, then squared her powerful shoulders. "*I am Ecnilitsep.*" She said powerfully, her booming voice drawing their shaken attention back to her. "*I have come here for one reason.*" She said, clearly. "*I wish for a resolution; an even and equitable end to these foolish hostilities between your forces and my own.*"

Chip looked back at Ecnilitsep, moving in wide steps to Ecnilitsep's right, as Jessica and Vincent did to the other direction. He glanced from her to Pihc, considering each. "There are a lot of directions I thought you were going to go with that one. That wasn't one of them." He said after a moment, never fixing his eyes on either. "Go on."

"*You will receive this offer only once, Chip Masters.*" She cautioned, her voice devoid of emotion as she considered the trio of fighters with slow, deliberate looks. "*After that, there will be no more chances.*"

"Fair enough." Chip said, still holding his golden katana ready, his eyes still darting patiently between the two. "What kind of resolution did you have in mind?"

"*You will cease any actions to undermine the workings of myself or anyone under my command, and you will allow us to go about our ordained duty and responsibility. In return,*" She said finally, crossing her arms over her strong chest. "*You will not be killed painfully.*"

It took Chip a moment to realize the offer had ended. When it finally did register, he snickered. "You have got to be kidding me." He said as Ecnilitsep's controlled faced tightened slightly with anger.

"*You would do wise to reconsider what I have said.*" Ecnilitsep said, very clearly. "*I will not extend my mercy again.*"

Chip glanced back at Pihc, then at Ecnilitsep again. "Oh don't worry." He quickly said, still smiling. "The response will still be the same."

Chip never saw the blow coming.

Ecnilitsep punched Chip so hard, he was sent flying against the far crates, crashing through the barrier they had formed. Ecnilitsep turned around as Vincent rushed forward her, his bowie knife drawn back. But as he raced at her, Pihc intercepted, catching the dark Vgm in the chest with a fast kick. The blow knocked Vincent off his feet and sent him crashing to the ground.

But Jessica dashed around Pihc's defensive stance and slid in at Ecnilitsep. The woman warrior swung with her fist for Jessica's head, but the female Vgm dodged around, bent down low, then came up with a powerful back flip. "***Flash Kick!***" She shouted, catching Ecnilitsep underneath the chin. The blow knocked Ecnilitsep back through the wall of crates while Jessica landed solidly on her feet. But as soon as she touched the ground, she leapt to the side as Pihc slammed his fist down where she had been.

The blow cracked the pavement as Pihc stood. Jessica rolled up to her feet, holding her fists ready. Pihc rushed at her, clearing the distance in the blink of an eye. But as he did, Jessica threw her hands forward, sending out a tightly-contained whirlwind of force. The air tunnel collided with Pihc, knocking him back against the pavement. He dug in his feet to keep from sliding, but it was to no avail.

In a flash of darkness, Vincent threw himself into the wind tunnel, letting himself be thrown at Pihc. Tackling the giant around the waist, Vincent knocked him to the ground, pinning his shoulders. Drawing back on his knife, Vincent plunged the blade down where Pihc's face had been a second ago. But the dark giant dodged his head out of the way, then shoved Vincent's chest with both hands. The powerful force threw Vincent from his body and sent him colliding with the crates next to Jessica.

"***Firaga!***" Jessica shouted as she threw her hands out, an explosion of fire igniting the wooden crates, forming a barrier between Pihc and the two of them. But the giant strode through the fire, stalking towards Jessica. The kick boxer rushed in at him, but Pihc casually knocked her aside. He stalked towards the Vincent, punching at the rising Vgm. But as he struck, Vincent slipped under the punch, connecting with a hard cross to the giant's rock-hard midsection. Pihc brought his knee up to catch Vincent in the chin, but he blocked it with both hands, then kicked Pihc in the knee with his left leg, making the gray-skinned giant stumble back.

Vincent pressed forward at Pihc with a false punch, which he blocked. Bending at the elbow, Vincent slammed into his chest with a hard elbow. Before the strike could land, though, Pihc twisted Vincent's arm with his maintained grip on the Vgm's forearm. Vincent went with the pull, however, and spun around, trying to connect with a fast roundhouse. Pihc ducked under the high attack, sweeping Vincent's legs out from underneath him at the same time, flipping the fighter over.

Vincent hit the ground hard, rolling to his feet. As he did, Pihc swung at him with a furious punch, but he ducked underneath that, and slammed into the giant with a hard shin kick to his massive back. The blow did little to Pihc's massive frame, but his balance was disrupted. Vincent leapt up and spun around in mid-air, connecting with a hard kick to the temple of Pihc's head. The blow sent the giant to the ground, skidding across the hard pavement.

Ecnilitsep stood up powerfully, an angry look on her face. She flexed her strong hands, then moved toward the crates she had been knocked through. But as she did, a reflection of light flashed over her eyes. She turned her head to the right to see Chip standing ready, his katana held before him. "I couldn't help but notice that you brought a scimitar to the party." Chip said, motioning with his eyes to the curved sword at Ecnilitsep's waist. "Since I'm the only one of the Vgm's with a sword, I don't see any reason for us to bother them. I'm sure Vincent and Jessica can keep Pihc entertained."

"*I am not here to dally with the likes of you.*" Ecnilitsep said as she stepped unfearfully towards Chip. "*Reality is my domain to protect. And I will not tolerate a danger such as you.*"

"Just answer me this one question, then." Chip asked. "What's so dangerous about magic? Why do you want to destroy it so badly?"

"*Magic summons the Shadows.*" Ecnilitsep said stalwartly as she drew out her scimitar with some reverence, its black blade flashing in the low light. "*And they can not be allowed within existence.*"

"The Shadows?" Chip breathed. "What are they?"

"*The Oblivion incarnate.*" Ecnilitsep answered, just before she lunged at Chip. The curved tip of her sword came in close at him, but he knocked it away with his katana. Sliding in underneath the blade of her sword, Chip slashed in a horizontal slash meant for her waist. But she stepped back from the slice, hacking down at Chip. The Vgm let her swing, then swung in with a fast barrage of alternate slices that drove her back several steps.

Ecnilitsep returned the barrage with a fast lunge, followed up by a quick slice meant to take Chip's head off. But the Vgm blocked the slice, riposting with a fast slash of his own. But the distance of the slice fell short and Chip's blade crossed inches in front of Ecnilitsep's neck.

"Almost got you." Chip goaded.

"*Almost.*" Ecnilitsep returned humorlessly. She swung at Chip with her sword, but he connected with a hard kick to her stomach. Ecnilitsep grabbed his leg, twisting her arms over to send Chip onto his face. He landed on the pavement, but his eyes opened wide as lightning erupted from them. A surge of electricity shot up his body, shocking Ecnilitsep free from her hold. She stumbled back as Chip came up to his feet, refingering the hold on his katana and readying himself.

Pihc caught Vincent across the side of his mouth with a hard fist, knocking the dark Vgm to the ground. He came back with the same arm, catching Jessica in the chest and sending her crashing to the cement floor. He turned back to Vincent, just in time to see the dark Vgm take a hopping skip forward.

The standing high kick caught Pihc in the center of the jaw and knocked him off his feet. The blow connected solidly and Pihc collapsed onto the boxes, sending him crashing over the side of the make-shift wall. Ecnilitsep and Chip both turned from their locked swords as Pihc landed hard. But the giant rushed up to his feet as Vincent came in after him.

Chip took the confusion to lunge forward and slash Ecnilitsep's unarmed hands. The slash severed two of her fingers, dropping the scimitar from her grip. He followed up with a fast slash with his golden sword. Ecnilitsep side-stepped the sword, slapping Chip's hands with her own, then she spun around, elbowing him at the base of the neck. Chip dropped to one knee, his vision blurring.

As Ecnilitsep came up to her full height, she picked her leg straight up, then slammed it back down on where Chip had been kneeling. But as the leg lowered, Chip whirled around and threw his hands forward. "***Hydoken!***" He shouted a blue ball of fire erupted from his hands, slamming into Ecnilitsep, throwing her off balance.

Chip was up in an instant, thrusting at Ecnilitsep. She parried the sword blade with her forearm guard on her armor, at the same time reaching down to the ground with her injured hand. The severed fingers jumped back to the stumps they had come from, while she gripped down on her scimitar. She held it forward, aiming the tip towards Chip. He just smiled.

Jessica caught Ecnilitsep in the center of her back with a leaping knee.

Ecnilitsep was thrust forward as Chip lunged to impale her. The female giant barely managed to parry the thrust, but Chip spun around as she parried, chopping powerfully at her neck. Ecnilitsep pulled her head away from the swing, letting Chip's own over-exertion throw him just a bit. She returned the attack with a hard right hook that knocked Chip off his feet.

Jessica jumped in at Ecnilitsep, swinging with her kitar, but Ecnilitsep dodged the hard punch, returning hard with a back fist to Jessica. It caught the smaller woman in the chest, knocking her against a pile of crates. Ecnilitsep moved forward to impale Jessica, but Vincent jumped between the two. Without enough time to parry the sword slice completely, Vincent grabbed the blade, guiding it into his stomach. The black scimitar slid effortlessly through Vincent's body, pinning him to the crate next to Jessica.

"NO!" Screamed Jessica as she watched Vincent get impaled. Ecnilitsep drove the scimitar deeper into Vincent, but he lifted his head up, grabbing the blade of the sword, holding it in place. With a hard cross, Vincent punched Ecnilitsep right in the face. Ecnilitsep turned with the punch, then came back instantly, slamming her fist into Vincent's head so hard, it cracked the crate he was pinned against. With the same hand, Ecnilitsep smacked Jessica, knocking her to the ground, then grabbed the handle of her scimitar and ripped out of Vincent. Chip was waiting.

Ecnilitsep swung around expectantly as Chip blocked the swing, stopping it cold. With their blades connected, Chip lunged forward, driving his katana into Ecnilitsep's chest through a weak point in her armor just below her shoulder. He drove the blade halfway to the hilt, then yanked it out and spun around, using the added motion to give power to his swing as he sliced at Ecnilitsep's throat. All he met with was the black blade of Pihc's katana.

Chip jumped back as Pihc riposted, creating a distance between him and Ecnilitsep and the Vgms. Vincent stood now, the slice through his black shirt showing no sign of the injury, while Jessica stood ready, moving cautiously to the side of the fight.

"*They are stronger than you led me to believe.*" Ecnilitsep grudgingly admitted with a whisper, standing up fully, the slice across her neck sealing up. She looked over at Chip, then to Jessica. "*Even the demon has become a force to be reckoned with.*" She asked rhetorically.

"You know, Pihc." Chip called out as he kept moving in a circle around the two giants. "I remember you being tougher. Apparently hanging out with this chick's made you soft."

"*Step forward,*" Pihc said, leveling his large black katana at Chip. "*And I will show you how soft I have become.*"

"Gladly." Chip seethed, moving towards the giant.

But as he took another step, an explosion of sound erupted through the warehouse.

A gunshot ripped through the cement at their feet, sending up a smoky array of debris. Both Pihc and Chip backed away as they turned. All eyes looked to the top of a pile of crates, to see a black-dressed biker standing aggressively, a silver revolver in his hand, aimed directly at Pihc's head. Staring down the barrel at the giant, the biker narrowed his eyes. "I didn't have to miss." He warned. He glanced at Ecnilitsep, then to the Vgms. "I don't know what's going on here," He warned. "But if your skin ain't red, brown, pink, or yellow, I strongly recommend you get the fuck out while you still can."

Jon
Chase

CHAPTER 6

New Reunions

"Why Johnny Ringo, you look like someone just walked over your grave."

—Doc Holliday, Tombstone

For a moment, no one moved.

Jessica glanced away from Ecnilitsep and Pihc, to the newcomer, then jerked her eyes back to her prey. "Do we know him?" She whispered across to Vincent.

"He's got a trench coat." Chip said across the two giants. "He can't be all bad."

"*He doesn't appear to be a member of their group.*" Ecnilitsep whispered.

"*I've not seen him before.*" Pihc offered.

"*Very well.*" The woman said, slowly standing up. She glared at Chip, then to Vincent and Jessica. "*I've seen enough.*"

The four's attention all turned back to the giants as they faded from sight, disappearing like smoke in the wind. Chip breathed out, then looked over at Jessica and Vincent. He chewed on a thought for a moment, then glanced over at the gunman. "Do we know you?" He called, his sword held ready.

"You might." The man said, jumping down off the crates. "Sorry for interrupting the private party." He said as he walked towards them, sliding his gun in the cowboy-like holster on his hip. "I was out walking my bike and I heard a rumble going on. Now, can you all disappear or were they just two of those 'super people' types?"

"Super people types?" Jessica asked.

"He's joking." Vincent whispered to her, his hard eyes never leaving the biker.

The man looked behind him, awkwardly considering the giant, dark space the fight had been raging through. "I might be mistaken, but I think you guys might be the people I've been looking for." He said, walking calmly into their midst.

"Really?" Chip asked, a hesitant look on his face. "And how's that?"

"Well, you see," The biker said, reaching into his pocket, pulling out the folded up piece of computer paper. "My name's Jon. And I'm looking for a guy that I haven't seen since I was five." He flipped open the paper and held it out specifically for Chip to see. "Cause, well, you see, he's my brother."

Chip's face went pale.

He was staring at an image of himself.

Eric strolled into the small white room, staring at the large mirror that covered most of the far wall. Lining the room occupied with a few couches and loveseats were bookshelves that held a modest collection of ancient books. He considered his reflection for a moment, for the first time noticing Beth sitting on the couch in the right corner, a large, old-looking book spread over her lap. "Hey." He said, sitting down on the loveseat in the corner across from her. "What's up?"

"Not much." She responded ghostly, sounding disinterested.

"What're you reading?" Eric asked, trying to peek over the edge of the book.

"It's a book on alternates. Well, I think it is." Beth said, turning a page as if to get reoriented. "I can't really read it, but Tim told me he found it from his order's library and that it talks about alternates so I thought I'd give it a try."

"If you can't read it, then why are you flipping through it?" The red-headed beanpole asked.

"Blind hope, I guess." Beth said, her voice carrying a strange edge of cold. "Thinking maybe if I stare at the pages long enough, then maybe the words will start to make sense or something." She shut the book hard. "I don't know. Don't mind me. I'm just being stupid."

"You're not being stupid," Eric tried, sitting down on the footstool in front of her. "It's just, I don't get it. I mean, like what's an alternate?" He asked.

Beth's eyes rose up, looking across at him from beneath her pale hair that draped down around her shoulders. "Are you trying to be funny or are you seriously asking?"

The slender guy held up his hands. "Hey, I didn't mean anything. I swear. I just, I don't have a clue what you're talking about."

Beth stared at him for a moment more, then her ghost-like expression came over her and she looked back down at the tattered red cover of the leather-bound book. "An alternate is what remains when a person has their soul torn in two. It's a by-product of when the darker regions of the soul are awakened."

"Okay." Eric nodded, rolling the idea around in his head. "You mean like a psychotherapy type of thing?"

"No." She said crossly, looking up at Eric as she clung to the book in her lap, her finger held curling over the hard edge as if for fear the book would disappear. "When Pihc captured me, he awakened all the dormant stuff in my mind, in my soul. All the little things that crawl around in the back of your mind or haunt your dreams, stuff like that. Things that are too deep for you to ever know about, much less understand. By doing that, he made me powerful; it made me Cye. But then we fell apart and Cye and I split. And now Cye's an alternate."

"Okay." Eric nodded. "So, like what does that make you?" He asked, disbelief barely edging across his face.

"I don't know." She said, looking back at the book. "I don't know what I am anymore."

"Isn't Vincent the same way?" Eric asked. "He's an alternate, right?"

"Yeah." Beth nodded, opening the book slowly. "But I wouldn't ask him about it."

"Why not?" Eric grinned.

"Because he once punched a guy in the face for even saying Trebor's name." Beth said, looking up at the new member. Eric swallowed. He glanced over his shoulder at the room full of books, then turned back to Beth. "Why did you join the VGM?" She asked, considering him as if for the first time. Eric moved to speak, but he didn't get the chance.

"All Vgms, on-line!" Echoed through the warehouse.

Beth looked up at Eric and breathed in. She pushed the book aside and the two rushed out.

Ben was the first one to come rushing out from the stairwell, stumbling into the main training room. Jessica and Vincent stood before the stairs, both showing the effects of their ordeal. Next to them, Emily stood with her arms wrapped around herself, dressed in a leotard and dancing shoes. "Hey, Emily." Ben said, sneaking up next to her, wrapping his arm around her should. "You look cold."

She smiled politely to him, before taking his wrist and twisting it sharply as she stepped back. "I told you to stop that." She said with an annoyed glare as she torqued the wrist lock.

"Hey, Emily." Michelle said from out of nowhere on the other side of the cheerleader, draping her arm across the taller girl's shoulder. "You look cold." Emily grabbed for her wrist too, but Michelle danced elusively away, laughing.

"Okay guys." Jessica called to the gathered VGM as the last of the group poured out from the stairwell. "We've got bad news."

"Are you going to let me go?" Ben asked the girl who twisted his hand.

"Oh no." Emily said sarcastically. "I've just been waiting so long just to hold your hand, I don't want to let go now." She said, adding an extra turn, torquing his wrist even more, forcing him down to his knee.

"I'd like to start by asking why not one of you was out looking for us when we've been missing for almost an hour?" Jessica demanded.

"Are you kidding?" Dan tossed in from next to Tim. "Our little team of misfits is the most lethargic organization ever."

"We study magic." Jim added. "What's the purpose of magic except to impress girls and to avoid hard work?"

"They've got a point." Vincent accepted.

"Well, fine." Jessica tossed aside. "Oh, and yeah, Chip's fine. Thanks for asking."

"We assumed he was too much of an asshole to actually be killable." Ben said, wincing as Emily torqued the hold even more. "God, would you stop?"

"Well, he's off with some guy who saved our lives when Pihc and some new woman attacked us." Jessica said to the group, crossing her arms as she spoke.

Silence

"Yo wait." Jim said, the first to break the stunned looks. "Wait, start over." He said in shock. "You guys got your asses kicked by a woman?"

Michelle turned to Jim, staring up at him in awe. "You want to die. That's it. I just figured it out. You want to die."

"Pihc's back?" Emily exclaimed, her eyes wide as she, like the rest of the group, ignored Michelle and Jim.

As she spoke, Ben slipped carefully out the submission hold and bounced away, grinning in delight. The sniper yanked away, holding his hand. "Yeah. Got free, baby!" Before he could say anything else, Emily punched him.

"Pihc's back and he's got company." Jessica resumed, speaking more seriously now. "As of this moment, the entire group is on alert."

"Which means…" Tim said from the center of the crowd of teens, moving his hands as he tried to illicit more information. "I'm a Vgm and I don't even know what you're talking about."

"It means we'll still go to classes and hold training like normal, but keep your headsets with you and be ready to drop everything." Jessica explained. "Pihc's back and this time, it looks like he may be gunning straight for us."

"Um, speaking of Pihc and everything," Sophia posed from next to Tim, raising her hand. "Where did you say Chip was?"

"I never thought I'd see you again, Jon." Chip said, as he watched the biker lay his black duster across the seat of his huge motorcycle. "It's been, what, twenty years? Twenty-one? What the hell possessed you to come looking for me?" He demanded, his arms crossed over his chest. His stare shot right through Jon, who casually disregarded it.

"Just to find you, believe it or not." Jon answered honestly, leaning against his bike, crossing his arms the same way. "I'd always wondered what happened to you, you know. And dad died last year." The biker looked up at Chip. "I don't suppose you care."

"Only enough to know where the grave is, so I can go desecrate it." Chip said with a cold look.

Jon nodded. "Can't say I blame you. The thought definitely occurred to me. Repeatedly." He looked Chip up and down, while the Vgm simply stared back. "Speaking of 'blame', how the hell did THAT happen?" He asked with half a smile. "I've seen some weird stuff in my life, especially tonight, but never anything like that."

"Like what?" Chip said, acting oblivious.

"Don't 'what' me." Jon said, standing up from his bike. "Your arm." He thumped Chip's right shoulder to be clear. He held up his own left arm, wiggling his gloved fingers at Chip. "In case you don't remember, that wasn't always there."

Chip just sighed. After a moment, he looked up at Jon, his serious gaze renewed. "What do you want?"

"Answer my question, Simon, and I'll tell you." The cowboy said, clearly.

"That's not my name, Jon." Chip said simply. "My name is Chip Masters."

"No matter what you say," Jon said, staring intently at Chip. "A name ain't a jacket you can just take off."

"Hhmp." Was all Chip said. He looked away, shaking his head slightly. He moved to lean back against the wall of the alley, but in a flash, he grabbed his katana, unsheathing the sword in an instant. With a quick, controlled motion, he stopped the blade just short of Jon's neck. "Tell me why you're here." He demanded.

"You tell me about your arm." Jon countered calmly with a simple motion of the revolver that was aimed at Chip's chest. Chip looked down at the silver gun, then back up at Jon. The biker winked, a slight smile growing on his face. "I might survive at slash to the throat. However, I doubt you'll look too favorably on having no chest cavity."

Chip's face slowly curled into a smile as he lowered the gun, but he quickly lost his restraint and began to laugh. "Oh, get over yourself." He balked, holding the blade of the lowered sword in his left hand as Jon lowered the gun. "You would have died before you could have gotten your finger on the hammer."

"Yeah, whatever." Jon disregarded with a light tone in his voice and a dismissive movement of his head. Chip smiled, almost laughing. He looked at Jon who wore the identical smile.

The Vgm looked down at his sword, seeing his reflection in the mirrored blade. The slight indent halfway up the blade sent an old memory racing through his mind, but he stuffed it away, determined to not think about it. He looked back up at Jon, who was simply standing before him, waiting. Chip finally sighed. "An angel gave it to me." He finally relented with a displeased look on his face. "While I was in San Francisco."

"I see." Jon said, with a nod of his head. Chip still couldn't tell if it was belief or not that he saw on Jon's face. The Vgm stood up straight, looking Jon straight in the eye as if for the first time. "What?" Jon asked after a moment.

"Why don't you join us?" Chip asked out of the blue, as he put his sword away. "Join the VGM."

"The what?" Jon laughed, his face turning into one big grin. "What the hell does that stand for?"

"Video Game Masters." Chip said, smiling still. "It used to be a kind of video game club. Now, well, now it's kind of something else."

Jon looked Chip up and down again, trying to decide if he was serious. "I don't know. I don't really like video games."

"You'll learn.' Chip said, stepping back, turning to head down the dark street. "First, though, you'll have to get through initiation."

Jon watched Chip walk for a moment, then he grabbed his bike by the handles and kicked the kickstand up. "Well how hard can that be?" He tossed out as he started to guide the bike forward.

"*They are not what I expected at all.*" Ecnilitsep admitted as she stood before Pihc. In the large ballroom filled with silver and blue decorations, Pihc remained still while Ecnilitsep paced in a wide circle, her eyes flowing as quickly as her thoughts. "*When you told me of Chip Masters, and of the defeat over the Video Game Masters, I had no idea that it was such a fortuitous event to have blackmailed the demon into revealing their location.*" She looked up at Pihc, her hard eyes burning intensely. "*Had you not known their strategy, they would have succeeded in killing you and undermining my plans.*"

"*Since I first encountered Masters, I have learned to never underestimate him.*" Pihc maintained with a stalwart strength.

"*Yes, back when he aligned himself with the Shadow Dragon.*" Ecnilitsep cursed. "*Even so young, he was a thorn in our side. I should have gone to greater lengths to slay him after I was done with him. I was a fool for believing I could let one such as him live. And on this, of all worlds. I was a fool to trust such an imperative task to anyone other than myself.*"

She stopped pacing and looked up, turning her eyes to Pihc. "*The VGM must be defeated, and this world rid of all threat of magic.*"

"*We will have much to contend with.*" Pihc said as he thought. "*The governments of this world are not as impotent as one might first think. The last six months have seen a laboriously slow, but steady return of magic. The magical communities have no doubt grown in strength.*"

"*The VGM was formed after Chip left Kageryu's service.*" Ecnilitsep remembered as she continued to pace. "*Then they launched the offensive against you years ago, from Crossworld. Perhaps we should finally attend to the domains of this plain as well.*"

"*The nation that once existed is fragmented and destroyed.*" Pihc cautioned, turning to stay facing the woman. "*Besides, we control this castle. That alone will keep them from interfering.*"

"*The VGM very nearly defeated you years ago. They succeeded in defeating you six months ago. I am not prepared to take risks on anything that is not completely under my control.*" She violently maintained.

"*Sometimes, Ecnilitsep.*" Said Pihc, looking across at the tall woman, his arms crossed over his chest as he stood before her. "*You must allow chance in order to succeed. Taking a gamble, taking a risk on an unknown quantity can yield remarkable results.*" He held out his hands as if revealing his example. "*Consider the demon. An unknown quantity. But she may well have saved myself, Yadiloh, and Brenard from defeat years ago.*"

Ecnilitsep stood still for a long moment, considering Pihc's words. But ultimately, she turned away from him. "*Never the less,*" She commanded, directing herself off into the distance out of the ballroom. "*We have work to do. I want the VGM destroyed and I want the earth under total domination.*" She stopped just outside the doorway, looked out the window of the beautiful hall, seeing the dark starry night outside. She lingered there for a moment, then turned with a fast jerk towards Pihc. "*Go and gather all the 'Shees you have available, even the ones that have escaped or run wild.*" She suddenly commanded. "*Send the alternates if needs be. But I want you to report to me as to what resources you have personally confirmed that we have to work with here, in this dimension.*"

"*Yes, master.*" Pihc said, bowing his head slightly.

Ecnilitsep turned away, walking with renewed vigor. "*The earth shall be witness to devastation the likes of which it has never fathomed.*" She pronounced, storming into the darkness, leaving Pihc staring after her. In the back of his mind, something kicked. A flash of thought, but the gray-skinned giant drove it away in a heart beat. He forced his strong face to remain emotionless as he began to walk, following Ecnilitsep into the darkness.

Chip pushed through the garage door into the warehouse to find the gathered VGM around Vincent and Jessica, all eyes immediately turning to him. He smiled, his arms held wide about to speak. But as he did, the group turned back to the two speaking Vgms as they continued.

Chip held out his hands in disappointment at the lack of uproar, only to have Beth step in, embracing him, her head burying against his chest. "That's a little better." He said, hugging the girl back.

"So, we at least know that Pihc is back and he's got some type of plan." Jessica surmised, turning to Chip as he tried to walk with the younger girl attached to his body.

Dan raised his hand. "Um, was there any doubt? About the plan part, I mean." Jessica looked down, trying to come up with a witty remark. A few ideas came to her, but none seemed good enough.

"Okay." Chip said, stepping forward, finally detaching himself from Beth's arms. He stepped into the center of the circle of teenagers, joining Vincent and Jessica. "First things first. We are not mentioning this to the other magical communities." He immediately turned to Tim, a sympathetic look on his face. "Sorry, but I don't want to deal with them period, much less explain why we have an interdimensional demon gunning for us. Second of all, we need to prepare to leave for Crossworld Castle to confront Pihc. Oh yeah, and this is Jon Chase." He said with a motion to the goon-like biker by the garage door.

"Hi." The biker said from just outside the door.

"Yo." Jim said casually, not even bothered.

The VGM blinked at the biker for a moment, then turned back to the conversation. "That's all." Chip pronounced. "Go back to goofing off or whatever it is you all do." He said with a dismissive wave. He turned back around to Jon, but Jessica, Tim, and Vincent stood between the Vgm and his brother.

"So what's the deal?" Tim asked, standing directly in front of Chip, his arms held out in scholarly confusion. "Who is this guy?"

"This is the guy that stepped up while we were facing Ecnilitsep and Pihc." Jessica explained, sparing a glance outside the circle at the biker who considered the warehouse with indifference.

"So let me guess. He's joining." Tim surmised, looking at Chip. "You know, in theory, we're supposed to vote on these things."

"And we should also talk about fairness." Jessica added to Tim's argument. "Sophia had been pestering us for almost a month before we let her join. It wasn't until she finally pinned you down in an argument about consoles versus arcade games that you were willing to let her join. Now this guy shows up and within an hour you're willing to bring him here? You know the others will call you on that."

"It's called rank." Chip cast over to Jessica as he turned back to Tim. "There's a reason you try to get more of it. As for Jon, he's in, but he's novice. He's not getting any special treatment. Well, beyond getting in. And I still want him going through some type of initiation testing."

"Say no more." Vincent said, breaking away from the group.

"Oh Jesus." Jessica groaned, turning around as Vincent left. "Go easy on him." She turned back to Chip, trying to keep all the troubling issues in order in her head. "Look, I don't mind letting him in, but we should still do a background check on him like everyone else. Okay?" She asked, rubbing her face as she thought.

"I'll do it." Chip said honestly. "He's my call, I'll take the responsibility."

"Hey, that's fine with me." Tim said with a shrug of his shoulders. "But that still leaves what to do about Pihc."

"He didn't do some type of massive hunt like he did last time." Chip thought quickly. "My guess is that this time, him and this Ecnilitsep chick are after us alone."

"Ecnilitsep?" Tim asked, looking at Chip. "I just heard you say it and I still don't know how it's pronounced."

"Eck-nil-et-sep." Chip said slowly. "It took me a second to get it too."

"Moving on," Jessica tossed in loudly. "That does open us up to a world of hurt. Like it probably means we have to worry about Trebor sneaking in here sometime tonight."

"No, but it probably does mean we're going to be looking at an assault in the next week." Chip considered. "But we can deal with that in a minute. "I want to watch this." He moved back, moving Tim with him, Jessica moving back the other way. She only took a few steps before she bumped into Dan. She turned back, suddenly realizing the whole VGM was still in the room, watching the preeminent fight.

"So what you're saying," Jon said, his voice carrying over the silence that had settled on the group. "Is that in order to be fully accepted as a beginner in this little club is I have only one test?"

"Correct." Vincent said. "And the title is 'novice'."

"That's not fair." Sophia whined to Dan as she stood with Michelle and Ben.

"Welcome to life, midget." Ben responded casually.

"And what's the test?" Jon asked.

"I had to do…" Sophia kept complaining.

"You have to fight me." Vincent said clearly.

"Never mind." The girl whispered meekly, backing away from the others.

"All you have to do is last twenty seconds." Vincent clarified, stepping back from the biker, rolling his knee-length black trench coat off his arms.

Jon looked the fighter up and down for a moment, then shrugged. "So, do I get to start at a higher level when I beat you?" He asked, taking off his cowboy hat. He whipped his air-messed dusty blonde hair behind his eyes as he followed Vincent out into the center of the apartment-sized wrestling mat, all while Vincent rolled up the sleeves of his black, form-fitting shirt.

The biker held up his fists by his jaw, while Vincent kept his hands in front of his face and body. The two stood before each other, neither moving for a second. "Ready when ever you are." Jon said impatiently, after he and Vincent had stood still for a few breaths. Jon never saw it coming.

Vincent moved in low, slamming a hard fist into Jon's stomach, then he came up with a fast upper cut. Jon narrowly dodged the rising punch, but was taken down to his knees by a fast chop from Vincent's left hand. As Jon landed, he went into a roll, coming up back to his feet. Vincent was on him.

The Vgm threw a fast shin kick to Jon's head, which was blocked. But he suddenly turned the leg over, wrapping it loosely around Jon's head. Before the biker could do anything, Vincent jumped up with his other foot, closing the space between his legs, catching Jon's head in between. Jon collapsed from the impact, dropping straight to his knees. But in the process, Vincent's head which was dangling between Jon's knees, landed first.

The force of the drop, combined with Vincent and Jon's weight, bent Vincent's neck hard to the right and his eyes went wide. "Holy shit!" Jon screamed, as Vincent fell from his arms. "Jesus Christ, I…" He tried to move carefully, but he grabbed at Vincent's head, holding it delicately. "Vincent! Vincent!" He called to the bent head. He looked up at the crowd. Sophia and Shane's eyes were wide. Nobody else had moved. Jon's eyes narrowed. The biker looked up at the crowd that didn't look bothered at all. His fearsome eyes slowly became filled with worry. "I'm going to assume I missed something." He whispered guardedly.

There was a loud crack.

Jon startled back from Vincent's head as the neck threw the head violently to the left, realigning the vertebrae. Vincent's eyes opened, anger burning in them. "Holy shit." Jon said again, his voice disappearing. He never saw the punch coming.

Vincent caught him across the chin with a right hook, knocking him down onto the mat. The Vgm rolled up onto his feet as Jon crawled away from him, terrified. "Calm down, Vincent." Chip called, stepping onto the mat behind him. Both fighters turned to Chip, Vincent in annoyance and Jon in horror. "He won." The lead Vgm said, patting Vincent on the back. The dark Vgm glanced between Chip and Jon, then backed away, fury raging across him.

"Great." Jim groaned as he stood with Shane and Emily. "Now he's going to be training harder and harder for the next damn week."

"And making us trainer harder too." Shane agreed with a glum look.

Chip turned to Jon, looking impressed. Jon was still on the mat, his eyes wide. He looked to Chip, to Vincent, to Chip, Vincent, the mat, Vincent, Chip. "Can you all do that?"

"Nope. He's the only one." Chip said, grabbing Jon's hand and pulling him to his feet. "Oh and welcome to the Video Game Masters."

Ecnilitsep stood alone.

In the grand courtyard that spread out almost beyond sight, she stood with her arms crossed, the massive starry sky spread over her, while she stared down in thought. Her dark armor shimmered in the night sky as she stood amongst a circle of massive stones, formed into a tight, incomplete ring in a wide field that stretched out into the horizon.

The woman turned back around, seeing the stone steps that rose up into the distance behind her, to the far wall that formed the barrier of the massive room. Certain she was alone, Ecnilitsep followed the wall that melded into the ceiling, dramatically covered in a painted mural that was the image of the sky high above. The stars twinkled and shimmered, like inanimate astrological predictions caught in time.

Looking down from the artificial sky on the ceiling, the woman turned her attention to the stones that surrounded her. Holding her hands out, Ecnilitsep slowly let the energy inside of her build. "***Darkness,***" She said, her deep voice rumbling in the giant room. "***Part, that my generals may join me in this domain.***" The words echoed and rebounded, not only through the room, but through all of existence.

From Ecnilitsep's outstretched hands came tiny rivulets of energy. Like a host of miniscule snakes, the lines of energy flowed out from her, tangling around the stones in the courtyard. The red lines activated the red emblems embedded magically in the stones and the ancient signs came to life with old and powerful magic.

Time and space slowly melded into nothingness, and darkness filled the room. The only hint of light came from the burning red symbols embedded deep in the ancient pillars. The dark crimson light cast shadows over Ecnilitsep, draping her in a murderous red.

And then, through the darkness, came footsteps. Ecnilitsep released her magic, smiling as the last of the tiny lines of power flowed from her hands and the dark emblems faded from the great pillars. The light slowly began to return and as it did, three figures came into view.

The trio stood before Ecnilitsep, bowing their heads to her in well-rehearsed unison. Dressed in armor befitting their command, the warriors stood before Ecnilitsep as if to be appraised by their dark lord.

The one on the far left was a middle-aged man, his face chiseled and scarred by countless battles. From across his brow, underneath the slight hints of gray hair, to his right cheek, he proudly displayed a deep scar. He wore deep green armor that was well maintained, even as it showed the wear of long and numerous battles. Sleeping on his back, a great double-bladed axe hung snugly from its leather holster.

In the center was a younger woman. Dressed in deep purple armor with heavy blue highlights, her armor shimmered from her perfect form while an ornate and ready saber waited at her waist. The dark-haired woman, seeming untouched by the wear of battle, held her head high, a confident smile on her lips.

On the far right, the third general stood in heavy ornate robes, a long staff in his hand. Dressed in crimson and gold, the wiry man stared at Ecnilitsep with eyes that conveyed the arcane and long-wished-forgotten secrets that rested within his grasp.

Ecnilitsep looked over her three generals, pleased by their presence. "*I trust that the war with the Shadows is at a satisfactory standstill, Livic*?" She said to the general in green armor.

"It is, my lord." Reported the older man. He turned to the younger general to his right. "Eminaf and I have been able to drive back both Htead's forces and the Dragons' armies, keeping them centered against each other and against the Shadows."

"*Excellent.*" The giant woman smiled. "*And you, Yerrbmot? What of the state of my army?*" She asked to the final general.

"The war costs us dearly, I fear." Answered the scholarly wizard in a less-than-optimistic tone. "The army stands weakened, but it stands ready." He took a moment to breath, then looked up at the gray-skinned giant. "We currently out-number Htead's forces by three to one, while we stand even with the dragons. But mostly, only 'Shees remain. If we are to require more advanced breeds, time and energy must be allowed for their creation."

"*Very well.*" Ecnilitsep said. "*We shall concern ourselves with renewing our forces at a later time. For now, we have other, more pressing matters.*" She eyed her generals, then looked back over her shoulder. She stretched out her long, muscular arm, pointing into the distance at the giant mural that stretched across the massive indoor space, aiming at a tiny blue dot on the farthest outskirts of the mural. "*This place, this planet, shall be your new battle ground.*"

"And who are our foes to be?" Asked Livic. "The dragons? The Shadows?"

"*We are here to exterminate all life upon this planet.*" Ecnilitsep said with a calculating voice. The generals shared worried glances, but said nothing. Ecnilitsep turned to them, their attention jerking back to her. "*Do I detect dissent?*" She asked in a cold tone.

"No, it's just..." Eminaf spoke, her voice hiding her apprehension.

"That is the world that..." Yerrbmot started. "That planet's proximity to the land that was once the Nation of Argentum makes the news of any battles there...very ill tidings."

"*Such as?*" Ecnilitsep asked obtusely, staring back at the wizard.

Yerrbmot looked at the other two generals, then up at her. "The awakening of the Oblivion."

Ecnilitsep stepped forward, lowering her eyes to Yerrbmot. "*Artemis sleeps and will sleep for eternity. Her prophecy,*" Ecnilitsep spat out, her disgust with the very concept evident. "*Can never, and will never, be fulfilled.*"

"We live to serve you, Ecnilitsep." Livic said quickly, turning her attention from Yerrbmot.

"*Then to service you shall go.*" She said quickly, giving Yerrbmot one last harsh look before stepping away from them. "*We have a new war to fight, one which will be waged in against a radically new foe. A war that must be won quickly and efficiently.*" She turned from the three generals, and stormed out of the circle of stones. "*We have more weapons to gather. This war must be won at any cost.*"

The echo of her words disappeared as she made her way to the winding steps, leaving the three generals alone in the clearing. They glanced at each other, but Eminaf was the first to smile. She looked at Livic, making him shake his head as he smiled. "Come on, boys." The woman general said, looking up after Ecnilitsep. "We're going to war. So let's have some fun." She said, leading them after their commander.

Livic

CHAPTER 7

S'ram

"Cry 'Havok!' and let slip the dogs of war!"

—Mark Anthony, Julius Caesar

Ecnilitsep stood within the mouth of the long walk that led into the depths of the monumental Greek-like castle. Creating a seemingly endless path that extended beyond where the castle should have ended, the rows of pristine white pillars sat quietly, while the marble and stone form appeared untouched by the harsh ocean environment that surrounded the rocks of its foundation. Above her, the slate ceiling's mural depicted the summoning of existence, and the creation of all that was. She looked forward into the fortress before her and stared it down.

"This domain is forbidden." Yerrbmot cautiously observed from behind Ecnilitsep as he stood quietly, keeping a careful hand on his staff. He nervously glanced around the rocks and pillars, watching the tiniest movement of the seaside shadows as they listened quietly underneath the bright, sunless sky.

"*Your fear tires me.*" The giant said as she strode forward into her first step. Placing her armored boot forward, she began to walk down the line of quiet pillars, her hard eyes staying cautiously aware.

"This," The wizard said as followed closely right behind her, glancing back over his shoulder, desperate to keep his sight on the distant shore just within the haze of sight. "This is the domain of…"

"*Who would you rather fear?*" She asked, turning her head calmly over her shoulder to the wizard. "*Them? Or me?*" Without another word, she turned on into the palace and resumed walking.

"I am anxious to get started." Eminaf said, as she stood out on the balcony, looking out over the land before the castle. In the far distance, at the edge of the horizon, the slightest glimpse of the three massive towers of Crossworld castle rose up, standing out against the natural features of the harsh desert. "I've always wanted to see that castle closer." The female general said aimlessly as she stared at the fortress. "I've only heard strong things about their captain."

"Kamen is a formidable foe." Livic said, turning away from the open air, uninterested. "What I want to know is where our wayward leader disappeared to." He said with annoyance, turning back to the ornate room of silver and blue behind him. "The longer we wait, the longer we are away from the battle against the Shadows and Htead."

"Didn't all this used to be farmland?" Eminaf said to herself, looking out in the distance at Crossworld castle. "It looks like a desert." She turned away, looking over at Livic. "I believe she and Yerrbmot went off, maybe to help Pihc find his lost 'Shees." The general looked back. "I remember Cye, or whatever that little girl's name is, said that she had something to 'attend' to."

"Oh yes." Livic nodded, remembering.

Eminaf stared forward as the two stood alone in the giant room. She considered the beautiful pictures that stood out on the walls, then turned to Livic. "I've got an idea." She said, a mischievous smile spreading across her face. "Why don't we go stir up some fun with Pihc's lackeys?"

It was a stone room, the walls and ceiling cut and designed exactly the same. Regular partitions jutted out from the wall, forming smooth eddies out of the very marble surface. Meanwhile, the floor was as smooth as glass, casting its pale white form across the darkness of the room.

In the torch light, Ecnilitsep held her hands together near her bowed head, her index fingers raised straight up. Her eyes closed, she concentrated. A few steps behind her, Yerrbmot sat on the floor, facing away from the giant woman. Resting cross-legged, he allowed his staff to lean against his gold and crimson shoulder. His head was bent over, as if asleep.

A crash echoed against the darkness.

Yerrbmot's head shot up, his eyes harsh and sharp. He searched the darkness, then glanced over his shoulder Ecnilitsep. "I fear we may have lingered too long." He cautioned. "We are no longer alone."

But Ecnilitsep did not respond. She stayed before the dead end, her attention focused beyond his words. Yerrbmot stood up, his power beginning to surge inside his veins. As he readied himself for what might lie just within the darkness that extended past his sight, Ecnilitsep looked up, sweat dotting her brow. "*It's done.*" She said with accomplishment, standing slowly. "*The seals have been washed away.*"

A heavy rumbling took over the sound of the distant waves. Yerrbmot stepped back against the wall, half-hidden by the eddies as Ecnilitsep held her arms wide as the wall itself began to part. Yerrbmot stared in awe, his eyes wide. "*S'ram awakens.*" Ecnilitsep commanded in elation. Light shot out from the wall, blinding the darkness and driving away all hint of shadow. Ecnilitsep stood proud and tall, her eyes filled with confidence.

The sound of a gun cocking echoed across the brilliant light.

Ecnilitsep barely had enough time to gasp before the shot exploded against her armor, erupting out through her back.

From out of the doorway appeared a dark form. Capped in a wide-brimmed hat, the monstrous beast stormed out towards Yerrbmot, its glowing red eyes locked on the wizard. With a powerful thrust of its muscled hand, it grabbed him around the neck, lifting him off the ground. It pulled him close, the dark red fire of his eyes illuminating the horror on the wizard's face. "*How long?*" Its inhuman voice seethed murderously.

"I, I…" The wizard stuttered, trying desperately to breathe.

The black-dressed giant tossed Yerrbmot down to the ground, crashing him into the smooth marble. The wizard at his feet, the giant lifted his head up and, seeing the marble ceiling of the giant maze around him, smiled.

Holding up his right hand, he aimed a large revolver at the sky. With a single motion, the weapon issued a deafening explosion, shattering the ceiling and all the layers to the sky above. Light spilled into the domain as debris continued to fall, the walls of the temple crumbling under threat of a cave-in. The massive gunman's face turned down to Yerrbmot, then looked towards Ecnilitsep. It fired three more shots into her unconscious body, then turned to the hole in the ceiling. Squatting down powerfully, the beast threw itself up at the sky, disappearing into the light.

Yerrbmot crawled uncertainly towards gaping hole up to the sky, but he heard one last shot. Suddenly rocks and marble came falling back down the hole. The wizard dove away just as the palace came collapsing down onto itself, sealing the domain into endless darkness.

"Move them closer." Brenard said, standing in front of the giant spider-like 'Shee. The twisted monster, like a nightmare from a fevered night of torture, hissed and roared at him, but he showed no sign of fear. The beast's twisted head that looked like a dragon's head before it was dunked in corrosive acid ripped open its massive mouth at Brenard's head, but it snapped it's thick, spiny teeth shut as Trebor grabbed its hind leg. The pole-like leg that ended in a single, pinpoint threatened to break under Trebor's strength as he pulled it back.

Behind the alternate, lines and lines of the 'Shees stood in motionless attention. Roaring and hissing like rabid dogs, the denizens of the darkness snapped at each other as well as the alternates. "They're not very happy." Cye observed sympathetically from the front of the army, looking at the monsters.

"They don't want to be roped in again." Trebor complained, yanking the 'Shee back into place. The one directly behind him snapped at his long black hair, making him whirl around. He tore out his katana, glaring up at the monster. "Do that again." He said to the monster, making it stumble back a step. "Do it again, mother-fucker. Do it again."

"Well, Brenard." Came a harsh voice.

At the front of the army, the gray-skinned alternate straightened up at the familiar voice, his eyes taking on a hard red glow as his expression turned grim. Yadiloh and Trebor looked to each other in vain hope. Innocently, Cye was the first to turn to the voice.

Standing just outside the main entrance to the castle was the armored Livic. With his shock of graying hair and condescending grin, he stood with his arms crossed, looking down on the four alternates from the stairs. He glanced out at the grasslands that extended from the rocky foundation of the castle and spread down to the fields below the mountain, then almost laughed. "How pastoral." He said, with a nod to the 'Shees. "How fittingly low for one such as you."

"Livic." Breathed Brenard with anger. Behind him, Yadiloh and Trebor both moved subtly to flank the gladiator as he moved to the foot of the stairs before the general. But as Livic stepped towards Brenard, the purple-armored Eminaf came out of the doorway as well, her hand resting casually on her saber.

"Well, well." Trebor said with one eyebrow raised as he broke away from Brenard and Yadiloh to move to the left of the generals. "Look what the rat dragged in."

"I see you keep the same company, centurion." The war-weathered Livic said, walking boldly towards the group. "You still associate with the scum of humanity."

"Come say that to my face and I'll smack you around like a red-headed step-child." Trebor retorted, moving towards the general, his hand on the handle of the black katana. Brenard and Yadiloh looked to each other, than to Trebor, neither understanding the insult. Livic, however, turned to stand toe to toe with Trebor, eyeing the alternate. Still, he said nothing. "Come on." Trebor goaded, almost whispering. "Come on. Hit me. Take that axe out and give me an excuse to kick your ass in front of your girlfriend."

"You couldn't stand a hit from him, alternate." Eminaf chimed in from the stairs, speaking up for the first time as Livic stared down into Trebor's dark eyes. "It would be a short fight."

"That's right, dick head." The vibrant fighter called over Livic's shoulder at the woman. "There'd only be two hits." He turned his eyes back to Livic, stepping dangerously close. "Me hitting you; you hitting the floor."

"Who are these guys, Brenard?" Cye whispered quietly, watching Yadiloh and Brenard stare down Eminaf.

"I suppose the best way to explain it would be, they are Ecnilitsep's versions of us." The gladiator said with a quiet tone while the generals focused on Trebor. "They are two of her three generals."

"Generals?" Cye whispered, confused. Slowly, she accepted that. "Okay, but why do they hate us? I thought we were all on the same side?" Yadiloh looked back to the pale girl, shaking his head slightly.

"I'm not certain why Eminaf hates us. And I don't know why Livic hates all of us." Brenard's voice grew cold and hard. "But I do know why he hates me."

"Why?" Cye asked.

"For the same reason I hate him." He growled, his eyes flaring with power. "Old sins."

"Ecnilitsep." Came Yerrbmot's voice in the darkness. With a sudden strike, the top of his staff lit up, filling the small stone hallway with light. The bearded wizard looked up, then around in the chaos from the explosion. "Where are you?"

The rubble not far from him shifted and the gray-skinned giant sat up. Her chest plate was torn open by the blast, the bloody wound exposed to the air. She tried to gasp, but her exposed lungs flared and writhed as they threatened to fall free of her chest.

"Stay still." Yerrbmot said, laying down his staff to look over the woman's wound. He considered it for a moment, then looked up at her pained face. "The wound will not heal properly." He said, looking back at the gaping hole in her chest. "It would seem his gun has the same properties as your scimitar. The wound is..."

"*Heal...*" Ecnilitsep breathed, panting hard against the pain.

"I can't." Yerrbmot said emphatically, looking up into Ecnilitsep's eyes. "The wound is..."

In a flash, the woman grabbed Yerrbmot's throat, yanking his face within inches of her own. "*Heal me...*" She seethed with a sick gurgle. "*Or I shall feed you to the Oblivion myself.*" She shoved Yerrbmot back from her, still trying to breathe. She rubbed her face, struggling to stay conscious.

"What, what are we going to do about S'ram?" He asked, putting his hands over the injury. He began to focus as a golden glow appeared within his palms. "**We can not allow him to go rampaging across the countryside. He will destroy all in his path. And you know Pihc will ultimately go after him.**"

"*Livic.*" Ecnilitsep whispered with a strained voice. "*Livic and...and...and Trebor.*"

"**Trebor?**" Yerrbmot stumbled, looking up at Ecnilitsep. "**Of all the alternates, why that murderous...**"

"*Brenard and Yadiloh...*" She whispered, then shook her head, her voice a death rattle. "*Cye...too weak.*"

"**What about Eminaf?**" Yerrbmot asked, glancing down as the golden glow from his hands encouraged the tissue to fold back over itself, sealing up again. "**She, she knows this territory. She knows Crossworld and Tech-Noir and Teemlayln. She would be...**"

"*Trebor and Livic.*" Ecnilitsep fought to say. "*As much power...as can be mustered.*"

"**Alright.**" Yerrbmot said, turning his attention back to the wound. With a deep breath, the glow of his hands turned blue. The blood and skin began to churn and twist, resisting the magic. "**I will contact Livic and give him his orders.**" He looked up at the giant. "**But you must lay back, master.**" He tried to give her a sympathetic look. "**This will take some time.**"

The woman simmered angrily, but nodded.

The light sprinkled down like rain drops from the canopy of leaves. The tall forest extended on into endlessness, while the thick underbrush teemed with life. And on the breeze, the warm, comforting scent of summer crested at the edge of the warm wind.

S'ram stood in wide-mouthed wonderment, standing there in the warm sky of the forest. His black cowboy clothes and massive frame stood out against the woodland realm, while his thick, toothy grin only widened. He stalked into the forest, looking up and down at the trees. With a fast swing of his arm, he slammed one of the mighty trunks down to the ground, splintering the ancient tree. He looked down at the devastation he had caused and grinned. Like a child, he marveled at the world, delighted in the possibilities it offered.

As the beast stalked through the forest, he never saw the movement behind him. Blended into the bark, a trio of ninjas sat quietly, kneeling on the sides of the trees as if squatting on the ground. They watched him as he carved a path of destruction through the forest, tearing free whole trees while desecrating any life he could find.

"What do we do?" Asked the nearest ninja, looking across as the female ninja on another tree. "He's rampaging through our forest, unchecked. We need to stop him, but, but how?"

"I know." Said the leader. She sat quietly, watching the giant's continued tour of destruction. "Where is our leader when you need him?" She cursed with an annoyed tone.

Emily dropped down in the roomy chair in the TV room, a book and a glass of water in hand. She flipped on the TV out of habit, checking to make sure that the pirated cable channels didn't have anything good on. Satisfied that all the good shows were on later, she leaned back to enjoy the book and tuned out the rest of the world.

As she settled in, trying to find her place in the book, a deeply tanned college-aged stranger casually strolled into the room. Dressed in his blue jeans and a green t-shirt, he smiled at her as he walked by, and she waved back to him. She went back to her book, staring down at the droll pages while taking a sip from her water.

Emily spewed out a mouthful of the water and whirled around in her seat. "JARED!!!" She screamed, immediately jumping out of her chair, wrapping her arms around his neck. Jared smiled hugely as she attached herself to her friend, nearly knocking him over. "Oh my god!" She exclaimed. "What are you doing here? Where have you been?"

"Stop!" Jared yelled breathlessly, before Emily could go on. "You're choking me." He exclaimed, laughing at the same time. She pulled away just a bit, smiling still, pulling fallen strands of hair out of her face to see Jared better. "Let me get some air first." He said, prying her free of his neck. He smiled back at her, and then was forced to endure another bear hug.

"*You seem to be welcome here, Jared.*"

Emily turned as a large man stepped into the VGM's television room. "Kageryu." Emily said, struggling with the pronunciation of the man's name. She stood from where she had tackled Jared, shaking the large man's hand as he extended it. Dressed in a casual business suit, the dark-skinned ninja smiled warmly to her, bowing respectfully. "What are you doing here?" She asked politely, returning the bow awkwardly.

"*I'm here on a matter of great importance.*" The ninja said, noting to Jared. "*And I thought I would bring one of my brightest pupils this time to help the VGM.*" Emily looked over to Jared, laughing as he blushed slightly.

"*All formalities aside.*" Kageryu continued, his face expressing the seriousness of the time. "*It would seem that sinister plans are now at work, plans which are much more ambitious and diabolical than any of us ever could have suspected. I must see Chip Masters immediately.*"

"I'm afraid he's not here." Emily said, shifting uneasily under Kageryu's friendly gaze. "He, Tim, and Jessica went out to survey the VGM's stockpiles. I think he'll be back soon, though. Vincent's here. Somewhere." She offered.

"Probably training." Jared grinned, getting a nod from Emily.

"*Very well.*" Kageryu said, taking a more casual pose. He looked around the room, taking note of the television, as if for the first time. He turned back to Emily. "*Would you mind if we waited?*"

Livic knelt down to the ground, smelling the wet grass. He sat up in the warm summery wind of the open plains and sighed. His eyes never leaving the horizon, he called back at Trebor. "This doesn't look good, alternate."

"Yeah yeah yeah." Trebor disregarded as he squatted down on a fallen tree's splintered trunk. "I want to know what I did to Ecnilitsep to make her so mad at me that she saddled me with you."

"Would you have preferred Eminaf?" The older general asked callously, still looking around at the terrain.

"Actually, yes." Trebor answered as he jumped down next to Livic, both considering the grass. "That way I could have knifed her without having to worry about you or Yerrbmot interfering."

"You underestimate her, Trebor." Livic warned, standing up and stepping back from Trebor. "She's never been defeated. Even that monolith, Brenard, can not make such a claim."

"Yeah yeah." Trebor said, his eyes closed as he skimmed his hand over the ground. "I'm getting something, but it feels like Pihc. I think it may be from our assault six months ago."

"Make no mistake. It's S'ram." Livic assured him, looking up at the sunless sky as the canopy of leaves began to take on hints of orange. "It'll be dusk soon."

"What is S'ram? I've never heard of him." Trebor asked, still considering the ground with growing concern.

"What he is, sadly, is unimportant at the moment." The general said with some clarity. "All you and I must concern ourselves with is where's he heading."

"Well, that's pretty easy to answer." Trebor almost laughed. "Those are the Barrier Mountains." He said, pointing at the impenetrable rock face that lined the far northern edge of the world. "Over that way," He said, pointing to the south, "Is some more, slightly less impenetrable mountains and then it just drops back down into the sea again." He turned and pointed down the fields of green grass. But in the distance, the grass began to fade, turning into a harsh, unforgiving desert. "There's only one real way he can go."

Livic ignored Trebor though, staring off into the distance. As the light of the day was just beginning to fade at the edges, the firelight of population could be seen in the distance against the sky. "It would make sense that he'd go for the nearest population." The general whispered with worry.

In the depths of Crossworld Castle, the cells flickered and coursed with the pulse of the many torches. In the deep prison, hidden far away from the rest of the castle, the steel door was opened by the blonde captain of the guard as she shoved a scruffy man into the cell, sealing the door behind him.

"You'll have to wait here until your trial before the Queen." Kamen said clearly, the lights causing her red and golden form-fitting armor to glint like jewels. "Do you understand?"

"Yeah, yeah." Sighed the man, looking around the small chamber as the long-haired soldier turned to leave. "I just wish we could get it over with."

Kamen paused and turned back to him, confused. "What's the running sentence for theft in this city anyway?"

"Usually several months of labor, though it can vary." The woman answered. "Anything else?"

"No, that's about it." The man said. He started looking around at the brick walls and their intersection with the door. "Do I get fed?"

"Twice a day." Kamen answered, taken back by the question.

"Okay." The man said, with a bit of sigh. "I've been in some prisons where they expected you to either catch a rat or eat your cell mate."

Kamen nodded. "I've heard of such places." She said, a spark of sympathy for this prisoner appearing. But then it faded instantly. "And since you were a guest of such places, then you shall no doubt be comfortable within this domain." With that, she disappeared as quickly as she had arrived.

"Yeah, I'm a big shot criminal for this burg, aren't I?" The man said to himself, still looking around the cell, appraising its stability. "I'm more embarrassed than anything else about getting caught." He looked around to see if the captain was still around, then laughed. He fell down on the small cot in the corner of the room and sighed. "Geez. How was I supposed to know the queen's one of the only mystics in this whole place?" He sat up; glancing in the direction Kamen had disappeared. "You realize I'll probably be out of here before tomorrow morning?" He said with a grin to no one. Then he looked around again. "Of course, when I think I'm up a creek, I start talking to myself. So I should probably stop."

The man turned away from the door, taking a moment to appraise the place. The single bed seemed fairly soft, with a thick blanket and pillow provided. He knelt down by the small spring of fresh water that billowed out and disappeared down a small drain. He took a sip of the water that spilt down from above the basin, then turned around to the entrance. He took hold of the metal bars and shook them a bit. They didn't give in the slightest. "Damn." He grumbled. As he stared at the bars themselves, he looked across the way. In the cell across from him, a small girl sat staring off into space, as if meditating.

"Sorry." The man offered, almost immediately. The girl didn't look up at him. "Hey, what are you in here for, kid?" She didn't respond or even seem to notice.

"Talkative type, huh?" The man said, leaning back from the door, holding onto it as he leaned back. "I'm Cassius." He suddenly slinked back to the bars, almost as if he was trying to squeeze himself through them. "And if I can, you know, get out of here, I'll take you with me." She didn't respond. "You see,"

Cassius said, prompting her with his hands. "That's supposed to be the part where you offer me some information, like where the guards keep the keys or their rotation schedule or something like that. Anything? At all?"

The girl looked up for the first time, her unnaturally pale eyes registering on Cassius. He stumbled awkwardly back a step from the bars, surprised by the empty look in her eyes. "I am not allowed to leave this place." She said in a low monotone.

"What are you? A Jim'dar or something?" Cassius asked with a laugh. "Well, don't worry kid." He said, more to himself, once again looking at the door. "There isn't a prison that can't be gotten out of. And I guarantee you this; I'll get out of this one." He pressed himself against the bars, but they didn't give at all. "Eventually." He added, under his breath.

Vincent stood alone at the farthest pool table at the rear of Starcade, staring down at nothing. With his hands spread wide as he leaned against the smooth wooden surface, he simmered away from the others while thoughts raced through his mind. He glanced up at the arcade, as the VGM and other patrons moved from one section of the compact world to the next. He watched the VGM's more experienced members gathering around Kageryu and Jared over in the snack area.

Vincent reached around behind his back, producing his familiar bowie knife. He took the fingerless glove off of his left hand, laying it over the 5-ball. He placed the ungloved hand on the counter of the pool table and spread his fingers wide. As he did this, a shadow spread out over the table. He looked up as Jessica paused across from him, watching silently. Vincent hesitated for a moment, glancing from his hand to her, then back to his hand. His hesitation evaporated.

As if cutting carrots for a soup, Vincent sliced his bowie knife down onto the wooden edge, cutting off lengths from each finger. With quick, repeated cuts, he diced up his fingers completely all the way to the knuckle. With each slice, blood squirted out from the severed fingers as the bits of flesh and bone scattered in the tiny area around Vincent. The effects and music of the video games in the distance did little to muffle the sounds of the crunching bone or severed flesh. He didn't shout or bite down. He didn't even flinch.

Before he was even done slicing, the tiny capillaries and arteries reached out to one another. Like a myriad collection of tiny ropes that danced in a desperate flurry of motion to find a mate, they wrapped and coursed around one another, pulling the fragments of Vincent's hand back together. The finger pieces were drug across the velvet surface of the pool table, reattaching themselves instantly to Vincent's stub of a hand, fidgeting and flexing as the nerves reconnected and the blood-flow was restored.

Vincent held up his hand, examining it as he flexed. It moved with the same fluidity, the same well-trained precision that it always had. He looked across at Jessica, who stood stunned. She stared at the hand, then her eyes slipped beyond to Vincent's face. She looked down at the pool table, where only blood remained. No skin fragments or pieces of bone. Everything except the blood had been recollected.

"If death is the opposite of life," Vincent said quietly, staring absently at his hand as his voice just barley carried under the noise of the video games and pinball machines in the distance. "Then I will not die tomorrow," He turned morosely back to the bar. "For I have not been alive for many years."

"Why did you do that?" Jessica asked sadly, looking down at the gashes in the pool table to confirm the obvious.

"To help me know I'm alive." Vincent said, stepping back from the table.

"Alive?" She asked, trying to keep him talking. "What do you mean?"

"I mean, pain." He said as he wiped the edge of his knife off with a white handkerchief, his usually strong and callous voice unnaturally soft. "All my life, I've been defined by the pain of my existence. At every turn, there was torment and fury." Vincent picked up his knife again, staring at the ray of light that glinted off the razor blade. "As my life has gone on, I've gotten stronger. Thus, my tolerance to pain has increased. And in order to keep on living, the pain I felt had to increase as well. It's almost like life is trying to tell me that the more I became who I have to be, the more I deserve to die."

Jessica slipped around the edge of the pool table, coming to stand just steps from the dark Vgm. She stared at him with a shocked wonderment, her eyes tearing up. "But...why?"

"Because god hates me." He humorlessly chuckled. "He proved that to me himself by abandoning me in Pihc's castle. And now Pihc's taken away the very last thing I have to prove I'm really here." Vincent took the knife and placed it against his heart. He looked at Jessica over the rims of the SkyFold glasses, gazing at Jessica's eyes.

With little effort, Vincent silently slid the knife into his chest, all the way to the hilt. His lips curled up at the pain, but he said nothing. In a moment, he pulled the knife out. He closed his eyes and leaned weakly against the pool table. "I can't die." He said slowly, almost as if he would cry. "And death was the last thing I had. It was the last thing I could rely on. And now it's gone."

Vincent returned the knife to the sheath in the small of his back, then looked up to Jessica again. "If it wasn't so sad, it would be funny. Since I can't die, living's lost all it's meaning to me." Vincent chuckled humorlessly. "I guess it's not a big loss." He turned away from her. "I never really liked living that much anyway."

Jessica swallowed her words and kept silent. Standing at Vincent's back, she breathed out, biting on her lip. She looked down at him, seeing a silver chain dangling from his trench coat pocket. "Is that Joe's watch?" She asked, getting a nod but nothing more. "The one with the Timestopper spell guilded to it?" She pressed.

"Yes." Vincent said, idly. "Jared found it in Joe's hut, back in Crossworld. It's the last touch of Joe's life." He mumbled to himself, then turned to Jessica. "I miss them." He said clearly to her, his honesty and candor surprising her. "I can barely remember the original VGM, thanks to Trebor. But I still miss them so much." He continued.

Jessica watched Vincent's anger and hopelessness deteriorate into utter sadness and the depths of loneliness. She reached down and took his free hand. He turned to her, as if her touch had shocked him. She picked his hand up and kissed his fingers gently. "I know you miss them." She said, softly. "I know." She rubbed his hand against her cheek, then let go of it. Vincent withdrew it, a surprised look on his face. Jessica smiled at him weakly, then looked away, as if she was afraid he would yell at her.

From the far side of the arcade, Aria watched the two, jealousy burning in her gaze.

"*So Ecnilitsep has manifested here.*" Kageryu summarized, sitting across from Chip in the snack section of the arcade. Dressed now in casual, trendy clothes, the ninja watched as a middle school boy walked past him, his dollar intent for the soda machine in his hand. "*And on top of that,*" Kageryu said, trying to ignore the boy. "*She was driven back by the appearance of your brother and his gilded pistol?*"

"Well, that and the beating we gave her and Pihc." Chip explained with a confident grin, opposite the ninja.

"*This is still troubling news, Masters.*" Kageryu said with a sigh. He looked over his shoulder again as the boy tried to get the machine to take his dollar. After the sixth try, the ninja hit the machine with his fist, making the whole thing shake. "*Make your selection.*" The wide-shouldered man said without taking his attention off Chip. He listened as the startled boy hit the button, collect the soda, then nervously rush off.

Chip watched out of the corner of his eye as the kid disappeared into the arcade, then half-laughed. "Do you take pleasure in scaring small children?"

"*Well, I am a dragon, after all.*" Kageryu retorted, allowing a small smile. "*It's either that or eat virgins, and they give me terrible indigestion.*"

"I don't know." Chip said, glancing towards the back of the arcade where Beth struggled against Ben at a fighting game. "I rather like them, personally."

"*Virginity is no longer a treasure to be guarded, but a weapon to be used by the morally-cowardice to bludgeon into submission those who would lead a life of greater fun.*" Kageryu said, half-laughing at Chip's confused look. But all too soon, he cast off the jovial look, seriousness taking its toll. "*But Ecnilitsep's moving against you is a tiding of ill-times, times that have been forewarned, but could never be fore-prepared.*" He said as he stood, towering over the vending machines and coming within inches of the low arcade ceiling. "*I have spoken with Jared and I will leave him here with you. He shall act as my envoy to the VGM. And I shall return when I know more.*"

"Care to explain any of that, or is this another 'I'm a ninja so I must be cryptic' thing?" Chip asked, mimicking Kageryu's tone as he stayed seated.

Kageryu paused, then glanced at Chip. "*You do a good impression of me.*"

"I'm a man of many talents." He grinned, looking up at the ninja. "We'll be here if you need us." He said with a sincere look.

"*It's not me you should concern yourself with.*" Kageryu cautioned. "*Ecnilitsep came and did not succeed. She will come again. And she will come in force.*" He nodded to Chip, then headed out, leaving the Vgm sitting with a worried look.

S'ram

CHAPTER 8

Alliances and Betrayals

"You're always hiding behind your so called goddess,
So what you don't think that we can see your face,
Resurrected back before the final fallen,
I'll never rest until I can make my own way,
I'm not afraid of fading,
I stand alone!"

—Godsmack, I Stand Alone

"I hate these meetings." Chip grumbled as he followed Jessica and Vincent into the pizza parlor. Barely glancing at the uniformed delivery guys who gawked at their audacity from the front counter, the three Vgms moved through the parlor towards the back freezers.

Chip came up to the drink freezer and pulled open the door to expose a small hallway with another door in the back of the freezer. He hit a small button hidden as a thermometer next to the door, then stepped back, keeping the door open with his shoulder. "Ever since the incident in May," He went on. "The magical communities in this nation have gone haywire. And it's bad enough that they never liked us, but then Tim's got to go as soon as he makes it to Vgm and make it his mission in life to get the VGM recognized."

"It's not just the US communities that have gone nuts." Jessica shivered in the cold of the fake freezer, her hands in her pockets as she stood with the two.

"Everywhere has gotten..." She stopped and looked back at two of the delivery guys staring just beneath the bottom of her black leather jacket. She snapped her fingers just below her waist, getting their attention. "Up here guys." She called, pointing at her eyes. They quickly scrambled off.

"Yeah, it's gotten bad everywhere, but these meetings have got to..." Chip stopped and looked at Vincent. He tilted his head, then stood up on his toes to get a better look down at Vincent's chest. "How'd your shirt get cut?"

The dark Vgm looked down at his shirt for a second, then looked back into the freezer. "Long story." He grumbled.

"We seem to be in for a long..." But as Chip spoke, the freezer groaned with motion. The trio bent over to look into the freezer as the door in the rear wall opened inward. "Ladies first." Chip smiled to Jessica. She gave him a sarcastic look, then bent over to step into the metal hallway, then through the small door.

Inside was a dark brick room with another steel door directly across from the entrance. Jessica moved out of the way as Chip stepped inside. He smiled politely to the older, thick muscleman waiting just inside the room. Once Vincent stepped inside, the man touched the steel door in front of them, causing it to open up, revealing an old freight elevator.

"Shall we?" Chip said to Vincent and Jessica, motioning for them to go on first. The three Vgms loaded up inside and Jessica hit the descend button.

"Hold the elevator! Hold the elevator!" Cried a voice, echoing strangely through the freezer.

Jessica looked at Chip and Vincent. The three stood up straight, looking peaceable while Jessica banged on the close button.

Skating around the large guard, a leather-clad young man slid into the small room as the elevator doors were closing. He lunged forward with the handle of his ancient katana, barely getting the weapon between the doors as they closed.

"Damn it." Chip grumbled as the doors opened. Stepping inside, panting as he moved, was a young blonde man, dressed in black leather and carrying an ancient katana in his hands. He looked at the three, slowly realizing who he was amongst. "Hello, Charles. I didn't see you." Chip said with an artificially polite grin.

"Of course you didn't." The witch said, glaring at Chip.

"Hello, Mancuso." Vincent said coldly, staring from the corner of the elevator at Charles. The witch stiffened, but didn't back away. The room shook into motion and a low hum overtook the ambient light from above.

"So, Charles." Chip said as he settled in for the slow ride. "Eaten any babies today?"

"No, I've been too busy drilling your mom." Charles recounted, turning his icy glare at Chip. "There's been a lot of talk around the coven, Chip."

"See, I told you that whole hooked-on-phonics thing would help you guys out." The Vgm grinned.

Charles scoffed, then looked away. He glanced at Jessica and Vincent, then turned back to Chip. "My friends at the coven," Charles started.

"You have friends?" Jessica grinned with a heartwarming smile. "Oh, that's so cute."

"My friends told me this joke, saying it would wipe away any awkward moments, like when you find yourself in an elevator full of people you hate."

"Or hate you, I imagine." Vincent added with a deadly gaze.

Charles shook his head from Vincent, turning to Jessica. He looked her up and down as if she was a steak, then looked back at Chip. "So this girl," He offered with a confident smile. "She calls 911 and says 'help, I've been reaped'. The person at the 911 place says 'what happened?'. 'This guy broke into my house and sexually assaulted me' the woman says. 'Don't you mean raped?' The 911 guy says. 'No', she says. 'He used a sickle'."

The three Vgms stared in disgust. "You're a sick fuck." Jessica said, staring at Charles.

"Sick?" Charles laughed as the elevator rumbled ever downward. "Sick is wanting to put your limp penis inside a baby just so you can hear its bones crack as you get erect."

Vincent's head lifted up, his hard eyes hidden behind his SkyFold sunglasses. "Didn't you tell me out in Salt Lake City that you wanted to do that?" He asked, getting an appalled look from Jessica.

"Wanted to?" Charles asked with a growing grin.

"How the hell did an evil little troll like you get to be the leader of the Enforcers?" Chip asked, his eyes never coming off Charles.

"Promotion by necessity." Jessica explained before Charles could answer, getting a glare from the witch. "Charles was one of the few who survived Pihc's assault in May. When it was all said and done, he came out of hiding and was given a promotion purely because there was no one else around."

"At least I stayed and fought, rather than run away." Charles smiled, glancing at Vincent. "You went into hiding with the mages."

"Well, you can hardly blame him." Chip interjected. "He could have thrown in with you guys, but then he'd have to deal with you begging him to let you go down on him."

Charles stepped forward grabbing the katana at his waist. But before he even could pull on the handle, the elevator came to a stop. Chip looked past the smaller man at the doors that parted. "You're lucky." Charles whispered threateningly.

"You're impulsiveness always seems to get interrupted, no matter what." Chip said with a smile, not moving as the doors spread light across his dark sunglasses. "One must wonder what would happen if you weren't interrupted?"

Charles stepped back from the three Vgms and stormed out of the elevator.

"Remind me again why we don't kill him?" Vincent asked.

"For one reason," Chip said, stepping out after Jessica, the three magical misfits staying cloistered together. "All fingers would immediately point to you. Your history with him is well-known and well-documented. The second, I hate to say, is out of fear of someone worse. Hard to believe as that is. But in this community," He said turning around, to the grand ballroom, filled with people of all varieties. "Anything's possible."

The room was a converted basement, with the paneling and drywall cracked and broken in places. But a crystal chandelier hung from the ceiling, and fine stained wood tables lined the walls, filled with foods and delicacies of all types.

Filling the room was a local diversity of magical types. Pagan teenagers and ancient professors shared conversations with conspiracy theorists and hardcore internet junkies. At the far end, a podium sat empty while the conversations choked the room with a low, roaring din.

"Can you at least explain to me, again, why we don't tell everyone that we stopped Pihc?" Jessica asked, keeping her voice low as she stayed with the two other Vgms, none of them moving to interact with the larger group.

"Because," Chip sighed. "We tell them, even a little bit and it will ultimately get out that we got to where Pihc was hiding. And people will try to get there as well and the next thing you know, Crossworld Castle has a damn McDonalds. That's why."

"Fair enough." Vincent said callously, turning away. "But I still say we reconsider our stance on Charles' continued existence."

"I second." Jessica complained. "Most guys try to pretend they're not staring at my breasts. He doesn't even bother to pretend. Except when he's staring farther south."

Chip looked about the room, noting the different people. "They got a good crowd this time." He admitted under his breath. He looked back at Jessica and Vincent and motioned into the room. "Come on, kids. Just because it was Tim's turn to stay behind doesn't mean we shouldn't mingle." He said less-than-enthusiastically as he led the way into the crowd.

The two huge gates, the sizes of buildings in their own rights, went flying off their hinges. The massive metal forms slammed into the buildings directly before them, crumpling down on top of the medieval bazaar. The gates crashed into the buildings, crushing them against their neighbors, while dragging a long path of destruction deep into the inner grounds of the giant castle.

As the smoke settled, the massive figure of S'ram stood in the wake of the destruction. His eyes glowing, the smoke from his silver gun wafted into the air. A giant grin on his face, he stalked into the castle grounds, watching as the soldiers rushed at him.

Swarming down off the gates and out from the town, the red and gold-dressed soldiers rushed at the giant, their weapons glinting in the nighttime glow. But as they neared, S'ram welcomed them, beckoning for them to bring the fight.

The first solder swung with a double-bladed axe, but the giant moved like a flash of light out of the way, grabbing the man's head from behind. With a fast shove, he threw the man into a brick wall. Steel and flesh bent equally as the man's entire body was flattened with the impact. Another solider jumped off the battlements, dropping to impale S'ram from above. But as he leapt, the giant turned his massive gun up to the man, blasting him back up into the sky, sending the remaining pieces of his body showering down beyond sight.

S'ram turned as more guards came, but their weapons never made contact as the giant moved with inhuman agility. He swatted aside attempts to strike him down, devastating each of the soldiers with singular blows. He whirled around to catch one man in the face with a fast strike, then came around with a hard punch, nearly taking another soldier's head off.

The instant battle was stopped almost immediately. The soldiers backed away, their dwindling numbers moving back from the giant, unsure what to do. And as they backed off, S'ram turned his head. Grinning, the giant refocused his attention to the massive, three-tiered castle before him.

As the giant grinned, his head turned back to the castle. As smoke billowed around him and the fallen soldiers were drug away by their comrades, S'ram sniffed hungrily the air. Like a child smelling flowers, he took deep chestfuls of breath, then smiled devilishly. "*I smell a goddess.*" He breathed with cruel delight. He took a solid hold of his gun, then locked his eyes on the closest of the three towers before him. "*Let's see what color she bleeds.*"

The red-haired girl grabbed up her sword by its hilt, rushing towards the door. Still draping her mail shirt over her evening dress, she struggled with getting her head through metal hole. But shoving her eyes finally through, she yanked her head all the way out, only to have her face jerked back by her caught ponytail. She reached back and freed her hair, then shook the annoyance away. With a running start, she raced down the steps.

But just as she started to build speed, a hand flew out at her shoulders, stopping her short. Niya moved to duck under the arm, but the queen turned out from the corner and stepped in her path, her eyes turned down at her daughter. "Niya, you are not going down there." She said emphatically, fighting against the drape of cloth connecting her dress to her wristlet.

"We're under attack!" The girl screamed, the flickering from the castles' torches mimicked in her eyes. "They need me."

"The castle guard will handle it." January barked. "You and I will be needed for the healing after the battle is…"

"I can fight!" Niya yelled, forcing her way past her mother. She shot down the steps, her mail shirt and long blue dress flapping behind her. "Don't worry, I can do it!" She called back.

"Hey Chip!" The Vgm turned around as a dreadlocked figure came up, slapping Chip's hand, then moving in to embrace him. "How you been, man?" He asked in a heavy, Trinidadian accent.

"I've been better." Chip smiled, moving subtly to the wall of the large, square room. "Look, Ester, do you know what this whole meeting's about? Because I hate to sound like I'm not a team player, but I'm not a team player. We're here just long enough to make an appearance and for me to steal some of the cheese snacks, then me and the other Vgms are going to sneak out."

"Not a night to go disappearing, Chip." The black man said back, checking the space around them. "It's something of an emergency meeting. Bad mojo everywhere. Fortune tellers and other types, they all be saying the bad's about to get worse."

"Come on, Ester." Chip groaned. "Magic's on the rise for the first time in centuries." He looked at the crowd of people, all pooling together into clichés. "What could you guys possibly have to worry about?"

"You may not know, Chip, but things have been getting freaky something fierce." The older man said, looking out at the crowd also. But then he whipped his dreadlocks back at Chip, slapping his shoulder. "But hey. It ain't all bad. I heard you finally recruited some new people."

"Yeah." Chip suddenly nodded, trying to sound jovial. "Word gets around fast."

"And I heard they're all white." The white-haired man said, his smile disappearing in the blink of an eye. "That's what, thirteen or something and all white? That's a bit suspicious."

"Oh, not this again." Chip groaned, rolling his eyes. "Look, I choose who's best for the position. Not for any..."

"I'm just saying Chip;" Ester interrupted with raised hands. "It looks bad for the Video Game Masters to be the honky brigade." He turned and walked off, leaving Chip staring.

The massive doors of the main keep were thrown wide. Standing against the backdrop of the carnage and destruction that rained in from outside, S'ram stretched to his full height. His heavy duster swayed around his legs as he vaulted up onto the long wooden pew-like seats of the giant room. He stared at the torch-lit chamber, smiling, taking in the cathedral-like establishment. "*I smell goddess.*" He grinned, his eyes searching.

"Get him!" Screamed a soldier from the far side of the keep, rushing at S'ram. The giant laughed as the three men closed, then jumped off the pew and sailed through the air, skidding to the ground behind them. They quickly turned, but the one on the far right turned to a boot to his face.

S'ram stepped down with the kick, standing on the man's head, crushing it like a grape out onto the stone ground. The middle guard rushed at S'ram with a spear, but the giant bent down low, coming into the man's jaw with a hard upper cut that knocked the man off his feet and crashing down onto the pew S'ram had just stood atop. Slamming into the heavy wooden pew, the seat fell over, knocking over the few behind it, the final one landing on the doors, knocking them shut.

The last guard turned to S'ram, his eyes wide with fear. S'ram smiled devilishly, lowering down like a tiger. "*That's right.*" The beast seethed in delight as the man shook in terror, but focused his spearhead on the giant. "*It's your turn now.*" The giant delighted as he stalked towards the tiny creature before him.

"The Video Game Master's magic is heretical and foolish!" Charles Mancuso yelled to the gathered circle of mystics as he jammed his finger at Chip, coming just inches from the Vgm's nose.

"That's ridiculous." Chip disputed, looking away from Charles only to plead his case. He stepped into the large circle of witches and witch-burners. "The VGM's magic is benign. It barely even qualifies as magic. It's chi-based. We copy video game powers, for Christ's sake. We are not a threat or a concern. If anything, we're like the annoying cousin people only call at Christmas."

"If that's true," Said an ancient-looking man dressed in brown pants and a green knitted sweater. "Then what does the VGM hope to accomplish with their magics?"

"Our concern, our only goal, has always been the destruction of Pihc." Chip said to the group. "We have never had, nor will we ever have, any other goal."

There was some grumbling throughout the room. People talked and whispered, as if they wouldn't be noticed, while the crowd itself ebbed and moved like a physical membrane around the conversation. "Chip Masters," Said a round woman from the far end of the room, all heads turning to her, the cacophony of whispers dimming slightly. "As one of the six governing mystics of Raleigh, I must ask then, why it is that this council had such trouble governing the VGM before its disappearance years ago."

"Here it comes." Jessica whispered to Vincent as the two stood cautiously with their backs to the wall.

"Well," Chip sighed without remorse. "That's because we're not under the jurisdiction of you guys." He said nonchalantly, getting a series of enraged cries from the crowd.

"Then explain why you're here?" Asked the skinny, bearded man next to the woman.

"It's out of the spirit of cooperation." The head of the VGM said, turning so he could look towards the whole crowd. "The VGM and the traditional magical organizations need not be enemies. We all want the same thing, and that's to live in a safe, free world. Am I right?" No response.

"Tough crowd." Jessica mumbled to herself, looking around. Vincent nodded.

"The VGM will, as always, stand at the fore front in the battle against Pihc and his agents." Chip continued. "And we will, as always, stand to save lives and to help those in need."

"Then what happened that made the VGM hide from Pihc when he attacked in the spring?" Came Charles' voice from over Chip's shoulder. The

Enforcer swung around into Chip's gaze, standing up on his toes, so he could stare into the reflection off Chip's opaque black glasses, lingering just inches from his face. "We had to defend the earth without your help. Where were you hiding then? Where was the VGM then, huh?"

"Elders of the magical traditions," Chip said with a tired, but respectful voice, looking casually past Charles. "I understand that this council, and these organizations, have need for an enforcement agency. And I understand that this Council imported Mancuso from Salt Lake City due to his record for handling incidents out there,"

He then turned his covered eyes back on Charles, leveling at the witch a gaze that would have stopped a charging bull dead in its tracks. "But if this man does not immediately shut the hell up," He said, sending Charles' frightened reflection back at the witch along with his heart-stopping stare. "I will be forced to put a painful end to his annoying life, right now."

Silence dropped over the room. The mystics all stared in shocked awe. Even Charles was too scared to speak.

Chip stepped forward with a cat's fluidity, making the enforcer stumble back, falling over himself to get away from the Vgm. Chip stood over Charles, glaring down at him, then looked up at the crowd and to the magical elders. "You need to keep this pooch of yours on a tighter leash," He warned, his patience clearly spent. "Otherwise, we're going to have to housebreak him."

Without another word, Chip turned from the crowd, storming towards the only door in the stone room. Jessica and Vincent rushed through the stunned crowd as well, hurrying to catch up with Chip. "That went well." Jessica whispered sarcastically, not looking back as they slipped into the elevator.

"Better than last time." Chip admitted as the door closed behind him.

Standing just before the wide platform at the far end of the cathedral, S'ram grabbed a soldier's arm and hoisted him into the air, letting the man's dangling body flail. Surrounded by the mangled, destroyed bodies of other soldiers, the giant grinned with delight as he stared into the horror on the man's face.

But as the beast considered the desperate solider, Niya lunged at him from behind. Stabbing the giant beast in the leg, she jumped back as S'ram collapsed down to one knee. The soldier in his arms landed roughly, but was able to pull himself away.

S'ram turned around as the girl stood ready, her sword held fearfully in her hand. She backed away as S'ram smiled. "*Truly you are a sad creature, to throw away your life so recklessly.*" The monster smiled, standing up on his once-hurt leg.

The girl stepped back, unable to turn and run. But as she stepped, a form stepped between her and S'ram. Kamen held up her shield, the golden emblem of Crossworld Castle flashing S'ram in the eyes. "Niya, get him out of here!" Kamen barked, shoving the red-haired girl. The girl, her wits snapping back to her, rushed around the pews, running at the wounded solider. Ducking up under his arm and lifting him awkwardly to his feet, she pulled him to the far door on the left-most side of the keep.

Amidst the destruction of the keep, Kamen stood ready. Her sword held knowledgably in her right hand; she kept her body guarded behind her shield. Left alone to face the monster, she showed no fear as she stood her ground. "*You are a fool to stand before me, little girl.*" The giant smiled.

"I will do more than stand." She shouted just before charging at the monster. S'ram slammed his fist at her, but she ducked around it, bringing the blade of her sword up across his arm, slicing open his heavy duster and the flesh underneath. Bringing the sword back down, she slammed the blade into the meat of his leg, laying bear the flesh down to the bone. S'ram roared in agony and threw his hand back, slamming his fist against Kamen's shield. The blow sent her skidding against the ground, but she kept her footing.

But as the captain of the guard readied to charge, she watched as S'ram stood up, already healed. As he turned to her, he lowered the barrel of his pistol, his eye lined up through the sights. "*Now you die.*" He smiled.

The blast slammed into Kamen's shield, igniting the air around her. The blazing fury engulfed around her even as she threw herself against the force with all her might. But she was overwhelmed instantly and sent flying against the far wall. Blood erupted from her mouth as she fell to the ground, the air disappearing from her lungs. Smoke rose from the shield that fell from her left arm as she gasped painfully, her golden armor fractured.

And as she breathed, struggling to gather her strength and wits, S'ram stalked slowly towards her. The giant stepped up next to her, smiling. He reached down towards her, but as he did, she lunged up suddenly, grabbing his wrist. With a fast shove, she yanked him down to the ground, then grappled his head, trying to constrict his neck. But the giant stood up straight without any effort, throwing the female soldier from him.

Kamen landed hard, slapping her body against the stone floor. She gasped, rolling onto her side as she fought for clarity. She kept her left arm held close inside, feeling her forearm where she could visibly see the break in her bone.

She looked up as S'ram stalked towards her again, smiling with each step. "*There's no one to save you now.*" He whispered, reaching down to the back of her head.

Like a bullet, Kamen's sword slammed itself in between S'ram's shoulder blades. Knocking the beast off balance, he grabbed onto the pews near him, knocking them over as he tried to keep standing. Both he and Kamen looked back at the far podium of the cathedral to see Trebor standing ready. "Alright, S'ram." Trebor called, his black-bladed katana held ready. "We can do this the easy way or we can do this the hard way, and either way sucks for you."

"*We will do it,*" The giant said, holding up his giant hand cannon. "*My way.*"

Trebor didn't flinch as S'ram moved to fire the gun, nor did he flinch when Livic dropped down from the ceiling, hacking his massive axe blade deep into S'ram's neck. The metal of his armor reshaped, his boots transforming into spikes that dug themselves into S'ram's waist. The giant roared, but Livic drew back with his right hand, his green armor's forearm guard becoming a long sword blade extending out from his hand. With a fast shove, he drove the blade through S'ram's back, puncturing his chest and sending Kamen's broadsword skittering across the stone floor of the cathedral.

S'ram threw himself to the ground, bucking Livic off of him. But as he stood, Trebor launched up into the air, spearing the giant in the chest with his katana. The blow drove down into the hilt, making S'ram roar. But the giant slammed his open hand into the alternate's throat, stopping him cold. He stood on his weak legs, lifting Trebor off his feet, only to have Kamen's sword came down on his elbow, severing the beast's arm with one clean swing.

S'ram's arm dropped next to Trebor as the giant swung at Kamen with his other arm. But Livic came in with a fast kick to the giant's knee, knocking him to one leg. S'ram swung back around to strike at the general, but Trebor threw himself over the giant, stabbing him in the other knee with his katana. The stab brought the monster down.

S'ram looked up just as Kamen stood before him. Standing tall, she stared level into his eyes, holding her broadsword flat as she lined up the razor tip with his eye. S'ram barely had time to scream before she impaled his face.

The giant fell over, her sword shoved through his head.

Kamen released a gasp, holding her left arm as she fell to her knee. Her lungs burned as she panted, struggling to resist the pain that racked her body. After a moment passed, she looked to her left at Trebor, then to the general at her right. "When did you two start cooperating?" She finally asked, blood trickling out of her mouth and down from the back of her hair.

Trebor panted as well, looking at the general. "We're under new management." He finally said to the female soldier as he pulled his katana out of S'ram's knee. He looked at Kamen and smiled. "Be seeing you." He winked.

"Not when you end up like him." She said, as he and Livic gathered around the giant body. "With my sword puncturing your head." She said, struggling up to her feet before them.

"I assure you, next time we meet," He smiled as the two and the body began to fade away. "One of us will definitely do some puncturing."

And they were gone.

"Well, that sucked." Chip said, as he undid the fourth lock on the main door to the warehouse. The lock slid open with a satisfying metal-on-metal tone. Chip opened the door and moved to go in, but Vincent stopped him, allowing Jessica to enter first. The Vgm looked at Vincent, then shrugged as Vincent followed her in. Chip went in last, locking the door behind him. "I mean, Ecnilitsep and Pihc are apparently on some type of a warpath against us," He continued. "The VGM's still not up to par with what they need to be, and now the magic-type people are starting to think they have some right to breathe down our necks more than usual. What could make this night possibly suck more?" Chip flipped the light switch to the main light.

As he did, eleven men in black clothing with machine guns stood up suddenly, leveling the guns at the three Vgms.

"You had to open your damn mouth." Said Jessica, giving Chip a death stare.

"Down on the ground and spread 'em!" Shouted the evident leader of the group as he and his men charged at the three from the center of the giant room. Vincent looked to Chip, and then motioned with his eyes back towards the black-clad men.

"Don't do it, Vincent." Chip whispered with a closed mouth, moving his hands to surrender. But it was too late. Vincent had already leapt into motion.

Dropping down and sliding along the matted ground, Vincent cleared the distance to the men in a heartbeat. He collided with the leader, slamming both his feet into the man's right knee. The man's leg bent violently the wrong way as he fell to the ground. Behind him, three more of the men converged on Vincent. The Vgm stayed on the ground, spinning on shoulder like a top, letting his legs connect with two of the men's knees, taking both down.

"Damn it." Chip cursed as he dashed at the nearest solider, ignoring the man's rehearsed warnings. He dodged around the swipe with the machine gun stock, landing a hard kick to the man's stomach. He spun around again, roundhousing the guy's face, shattering his combat goggles and knocking his helmet clean off.

Jessica charged into one guy, pummeling him with a few boxing shots to the abdomen, then finishing him off with a hard right elbow across his face. But as she did, another soldier came up from behind and slammed the butt of his machine gun into her neck. Jessica collapsed.

"Ops!" Yelled the team's second-in-command as he pulled the leader back away from the fighting. "We have resistance. Request permission to open fire!"

Vincent's eyes flashed as he saw Jessica fall. He launched up from the soldier he was mounted on top of, leaving him unconscious on the ground. His eyes locked on the soldier who struck her from behind, his gun trained on her pained form.

"Negative." Came the voice over the intercom from inside the operations bay. "You do not have permission to fire."

Chip's head turned at the sound of the voice over the intercom. But as he tried to place it, another man swung at him. The Vgm ducked under the soldier as he slid back around. He parried the gun's stock away from one hand, then knocked it into the air. He slammed a hard shin kick into the guy's stomach, then spun in the air, connecting with both feet in a fast spin kick. He landed, still spinning. He caught the gun as it fell and threw it stock-first at the nearest solider.

Vincent caught the guy in the back, nearly breaking him in half with the impact. The man landed on the ground and tried to get his gun between him and Vincent, but the Vgm grabbed the gun barrel and slammed his fist into the man's face, driving his head back into his helmet.

"Request permission to fire." Screamed the second-in-command, moving his machine gun between the three targets as they took the operatives apart. "Five of our men are down. The other five are…"

"Negative. You do not have permission to…"

"Vincent, NO!" Screamed Chip, as more of the soldiers rushed against the dark warrior. The men converged onto him as Vincent roared against them, ripping free his bowie knife. They backed away, their guns trained. But as he did, Jessica looked up, still holding her head. She stared up at Vincent as the startled soldiers turned their guns to between the two of them. Vincent moved towards Jessica, reaching out to grab her away.

But before he could reach her, he was stopped instantly by the fast barrage of machine gun fire.

All motion stopped.

Vincent eyes went wide in petrified shock as his hands dropped.

Blood splashed over Jessica.

"God damn it!" Screamed the intercom into the ear of the second-in-command. "Who fired?" The voice demanded nearly hysterical. "Who was hit? Where was the hit?"

"In the head sir and chest, sir. Repeatedly." Came the leader, almost proud, as his men turned their attention on Chip. The Vgm put up no fight as he stared at his two down friends. "Direct shots, sir." The second-in-command continued. "All rounds hit. Subject is dead."

"Which one was hit?" Called the intercom again, the voice turning Chip's head. "Which one was hit?"

Shane

CHAPTER 9

The 4th Vgm

"Roads? Where we're going, we don't need 'roads'."

—'Doc' Emmett Brown, Back to the Future

"What the fuck is going on?" Whispered Ben, as he and Tim ducked down behind the sweatshirt rack. Crouching amongst the clothing displays in the rear of the convenience store, the two glanced back at the bored mid-week counter guy as he flipped through a magazine behind the register.

Tim turned back to the double-glass doors they had snuck through, looking across the narrow indoor mini-mall, into the back of Starcade. "Tim, what's going on? Who were those guys?" Ben pestered as he knelt next to Tim.

"I can't be sure, but I think they were cops or CIA or something." Tim gasped, still out of breath from the bent-over running he and Ben had done. "They were asking about me and the other Vgms." Ben thought about that for a moment, but couldn't place any significance to it. "It figures they'd show up not an hour after Chip and the others disappear."

"If all this government stuff is going down, then why the hell'd you drag me into this?" Ben suddenly shouted back.

"Keep it down, Poulson." Tim hissed aggressively, peeking through the door. He watched for a bit longer, his mind racing. "Okay, okay, get back inside and get two or three people, not the whole group, and have them meet me in the front of the store, through the front door."

"What's going through that clunker of a brain of yours, Tim?" Ben asked, more worried than interested. "It's not going to get any of us..."

"Just make certain you get Shane at least. He's the only one with a real car." Tim said, as he got up. But as he did, he turned back to Ben. "Don't get overzealous and try to get the whole VGM. Just a few people." He turned to move, then turned back. "And tell Jon to buy us some time."

"Jon?" Ben said, turning back to Tim from the door. "Why him? He hasn't even been..."

"**Now wait a second,**" Tim said, the magical power resonating within his voice. "**You're telling me** you're going to trust Jon and do what I said, right?"

"Whatever." Ben said, turning towards the door, the magic only partially taking effect. He started to move, then turned back. "We've had this conversation about your magic, Tim." He said wagging his finger at the larger college student. "Either cast it fully so I don't notice it, or don't do it at all. This halfway stuff only makes me mad."

"Just go!" Tim shoved, pointing into the arcade. Ben gave him an annoyed look, then ducked off, leaving Tim to center his thoughts and move deeper into the convenience store.

"We're looking for Chip." Said the blonde man, his fake smile spreading across his face. "I'm from the university."

"Uh-huh." Emily said nervously, looking around the front of the arcade, checking to see where the other members of the VGM were scattered. "He's not going to be back tonight, I'm afraid."

The man smiled a toothy, shark-like grin at her. "I guess I must've just missed him then."

Emily stared back at him, the corners of her mouth turned up, not even fully forming a polite smile. "I guess."

"Is everything alright, Peters?" Came a voice behind her. She and the man turned as Jon strode confidently up behind her, his black riding glasses reflecting brightly into the man's eyes.

"These guys are looking for Chip." Emily squeaked to Jon, motioning to the man over her shoulder. Jon turned to the man, appraising him quickly.

"Chip isn't here, as you can clearly see." Jon said, subtly moving Emily behind him so there was no one between him and the blonde guy. "But I'll be sure to tell him you came by." Jon turned just a bit to usher Emily a few steps farther back.

The man considered Jon for a moment, then looked down at his waist, to the handle of the gun protruding from his duster. "Do you have a permit for that?" The blonde man said, a strange hint of legal authority coming through in his voice as he glanced again more dramatically at the gun.

"Do you have a warrant to ask for a permit?" He retorted immediately, staring down at the man. "Because if you don't, then I suggest you leave it be. And while I'm at it, I suggest you get out of here." The man was about to speak up, but Jon stepped forward, coming just inches from his face. "While you still can."

Vincent? Tim called telepathically. **Vincent?** When the telepathy didn't connect, he reached into his breast pocket, feeling for his headset. He almost pulled it out, but left it there. He looked out from his hiding place between the freezer and one of the clothes racks in the gaudy college supply store, hoping he was adequately concealed.

A ring of the front door bell and a handful of college freshmen came wandering in, already beginning their pitch to convince the clerk to let them buy some beer. The crouching Vgm sighed, flicking his blonde hair away from his glasses.

The door chimed again, this time with two of the men from Starcade entering. They were dressed like co-eds, making them stick out like a sore thumb. Tim moved quietly to the back wall and leaned against the cooler. He closed his eyes and focused his mind. "Legend of Zelda 3, Legend of Zelda 3." He whispered, thinking back to the game. He clasped his hands together, then pushed them apart. A small burst of smoke appeared around him, but when he opened his eyes, he could see a giant black spot on the ground where he should have been standing. He stepped invisibly to one side then the other, the black spot moving with him. "***Yeah, like that isn't noticeable.***" He thought. He crouched down, one of the agents moving towards his corner.

Tim checked the spot, then looked at the reflection of it in every surface. He cursed. "***Oh well.***" He finally sighed. "***I like real magic anyway.***" He held his hands against his chest and whispered as quietly and as quickly as he could as his hands went through a rapid series of motions. "**Light and sight, drift away. Disappear now, to reappear another day.**"

The agent turned the corner, his trained eyes surveying the area quickly. He saw nothing. As the man turned away, Tim let out a light sigh and stood still.

The door chimed again, and in walked Shane. He looked around the store quickly, trying not to look too conspicuous about it. Tim picked up a can, making sure no one else was watching and moved it in a wide arc from one side of the aisle to the other. Shane caught the motion and nodded. He looked around and quickly grabbed a random soda as he watched the two impersonators mill around the convenience store. "Did you see the game yesterday?" Shane shouted at the clerk behind the counter, interrupting the two freshmen in their continuing efforts towards beer. "Man, that was a hell of a score, wasn't it?"

Shane's voice filled the store, covering any ambient sound. Tim lifted himself from his haunches and snuck across the tile floor, keeping as low as he could.

"It was 6 to 28, Virginia." Said the clerk, looking at Shane as if he had a third eye. "We lost."

"Yeah, I know." Shane continued. "Hell of a game, though." Shane took his change and moved to leave. He opened the door, but turned back to the clerk. "Hey, do you know where Cream and Bean is?"

With the door propped open by Shane, Tim took a quick look back at the agents, then rushed quietly through the doorway, staying low as Shane turned outside as well. The street racer stopped and pretended to count his change. "You here?" He whispered out of the corner of his mouth.

"**Yeah.**" Tim nodded, peeking over the edge of the window to see inside at the two agents. "**Let's go.**"

"Right." Shane nodded, breathing out anxiously.

"Any idea where Tim and the others disappeared to?" Michelle asked, looking around the arcade.

"Nope." Jon answered, his hat pulled down over his eyes. "And is this all you people do? Hang out at an arcade?"

"More or less." Emily said, keeping a subtle eye on the growing number of official-looking men that filled the arcade, scaring off the other patrons.

"Man. Maybe I should have gone to college." The cowboy half laughed.

"There's more to it than that." Beth argued as she finished a bag of chips.

"Do they really think they're being subtle?" Michelle asked to the world at large as she sat with the three others around the red-toped table in the snack area. "They stick out like virgins at a strip club." Beth and Emily both turned to her in confusion.

"They're just waiting until they think they've got enough men in here to hold the place, then they'll make their move and arrest us." Jon explained nonchalantly.

"But why wouldn't they come in with guns?" Michelle retorted. "You know, do it the usual way."

"Would the usual way work?" The biker asked. "These guys, whether they're FBI or CIA or whatever, undoubtedly know a thing or two about you guys. I'd be worrying about why they want to arrest you?"

"Um, if they're going to spring at us, shouldn't we, I don't know, run?" Beth asked, looking around at the men.

"Where would you recommend?" Michelle returned harshly.

"Chip and Vincent always said if anything happened, we should disperse, then return to the warehouse." Emily answered in Beth's place. She looked at Michelle and Beth, then to Jon. "We've got all those 'contingency plans' and stuff that we're supposed to follow in case of this or that."

Jon shrugged. "Going back there sounds like a plan to me. But you do know that the moment we try to leave, we're going to be tailed and more than likely have to fight."

Emily looked at Beth, then to Michelle. She got ready to say something, but then just sighed.

"I..." Beth started, but she couldn't think of anything to say. With a worried breath, she balled up her bag of chips and tossed it into the trash.

"I'm ready when you are." Michelle said without much concern.

"Okay." Emily said, standing up. "Now!"

The four exploded towards the front door, all of them barreling past the agent who was walking inside. As they rushed out, three men came running after them. Michelle didn't bat an eye as she launched herself at the nearest one. The man moved to tackle the young girl, but she spun underneath his lunge, then kicked the back of his knee. Coming down with a hard hit to the back of his head, Michelle knocked his face into the ground, then backed away.

Another man grabbed Michelle around the arms, catching her in a bear-hug as he lifted her up off the ground. But as soon as he had her in the hold, Emily rushed up to them, throwing her right leg up high, kicking over Michelle's head and caught him right in the face. The blow knocked the agent back, but he didn't have time to recover before Jon followed up with a bone-crushing punch that knocked him out.

The third man whipped out his gun, aiming it for Jon's head. Jon mimicked the move simultaneously, leveling his revolver at the man's face. "Freeze!" They both shouted.

"***Good idea.***" Michelle declared. She threw her hands forward at the agent, a ball of ice rocketing from her palms. The ball collided with the man, instantly encasing him a hard layer of solid ice. His motionless body remained still as Jon backed away.

"Come on!" Emily barked, already running towards the back streets into the rural neighborhood behind the corner shopping center.

"We can't run all the way back to the warehouse!" Beth called, beginning to fall behind.

"Says you." Jon said, rushing past her.

Emily made it to the waist-high picket fence enclosing the first yard, putting her hand on the white teeth and swinging her legs over. Right behind her, Jon barely noticed the fence as he hopped over it in a single bound.

Michelle rushed up to the fence, but stopped and looked back as Beth stumbled after them. "Come on." She yelled. "They're going to..."

"I can't!" Beth shouted, limping as she walked. "I can't run!"

"Not that tendonitis crap again." Michelle cursed under her breath. "If you can't run, then how are we going to get out of here?" She yelled.

Beth stopped, then looked back as more men poured out of the tiny mall. She looked down at the street she stood in. "How well do you know the layout of the city?" She called to Michelle. The girl looked puzzled, but Beth turned and rushed further back down the street.

Michelle suddenly rolled her eyes. "Damn it!" She groaned as Beth stopped at a manhole cover. She grabbed the heavy disc with her bare hands, turning back to Michelle. "Not the sewers."

"***Come on.***" Beth yelled as she hoisted the disc effortlessly over her head. Michelle groaned, then rushed for the opening. She coiled her hair around her arm and started to climb down into the cement hole. Beth turned back around as the men saw her, the sight of her holding the heavy metal disc stunning them almost to motionlessness. She glanced down as Michelle disappeared into the darkness, then climbed down herself, replacing the cover as she did.

"Jesus." Shane said, sliding behind the wheel as he handed the newly-purchased bottle of Dr Pepper to Dan in the backseat. "This is some scary stuff. Those guys looked serious."

"They are." Tim said, checking behind them as he sat down in the passenger's seat of the small, souped-up race car. He wiped sweat from his face as he tried to focus.

"Good. Great. Let's go, please." Ben called, from the car's narrow backseat.

"Hear, hear." Agreed Dan, squishing Sophia who was sitting in the middle.

"'Nuff said." Shane said, turning the ignition key. The engine kicked and groaned, then sputtered to a halt. Tim looked over at Shane with a less-than-confident look. The driver smiled weakly, then tried the key again.

And again.

And again.

On the fifth try, the engine jumped and groaned, but after it cranked, it purred. Shane pulled out of the rear parking lot and into small side street that led to the wide NC State campus. And waiting for him were four giant all-terrain vehicles.

"Oh, shit." Shane swallowed nervously, as several men walked towards the back of his car. They were merely silhouettes against the giant lights of the huge jeeps, but the guns in their hands were obvious. "Any suggestions, oh fearless leader?"

"I'm not fearless." Tim wavered, looking back through the rear window over the cowering Sophia. "And yes. Floor it!"

"You got it!" Shane grinned, throwing the car into drive and slamming his foot on the gas.

The tiny vehicle seemed to levitate off the ground. Then the smoking wheels grabbed the pavement and rocketed the tiny car forward, leaving the pursuers in a small cloud of pavement dust.

Shane didn't bother with a road. He jumped the car up onto the sidewalk and nimbly dodged around mailboxes and small trees. He came to the end of the residential street and pulled the emergency brake, skidding the car into the lane he wanted and then released it, taking off once again.

"You're gonna kill us!" Screamed Sophia, as she bounced off her seatmates.

"Or die trying!" Tim yelled back with a terrified grin as Shane dodged out of the way of the furiously fast inanimate objects that were flying by.

"You drive like a fucking maniac!" Ben screamed from the backseat, holding on to the handle over the door.

"This?" Said Dan from the other side of Sophia, calmly sipping his Dr Pepper. "This is nothing. You should see the way Vincent drives."

"I've seen Vincent drive." Ben shouted back. "I was with him when he first learned to drive. This is worse."

"Either way," Came Tim from the front. "They'd be crazy to follow us."

"Well, apparently they're crazy." Yelled Sophia, risking her neck to look up out the rear window. "'Cause they're right there."

In the rearview mirror, four pairs of evil-looking headlights appeared, all four barreling after the tiny car as it sped into the night.

"Do what you do, Shane." Tim said calmly. Shane nodded, smiled, and shifted the car into fourth gear. The engine roared, as if some demon under the hood had come to life, and the car shot into the night.

Jim looked up from the pool game, staring at the crowd of adults in the arcade trying to pass off as college students. "Where the fuck is everybody? And what's with all the cops?"

"Good question." Jared said, looking around. He moved away from the table and leaned on his pool cue. He listened for a moment, concentrating.

"Using your super-ultra-ninja-magic-powers?" Jim asked as he considered his next shot.

"Yeah, so shut up." Jared waved back at him. He listened for a moment more, hearing underneath the sound of the arcade machines, then turned back to Jim and the pool game. "They're federal agents. They're here to arrest the VGM." He said, considering a shot.

"Oh." Jim shrugged, just before he hit the six-ball into the corner pocket. "So where is the VGM?"

"Scattered, apparently." Jared said, still listening, ignoring the federal agents as they turned, one by one, to look up at the two of them. "We're the only ones left here."

"Nice of Tim and the others to let us know." Jim nodded. He stood up and looked over at Jared. "I'm good."

"That's only because you're losing." Jared said, putting his pool cue down. He squared his shoulders, then looked over at the arcade manager. He waved casually good-bye to the man, getting a barely-aware wave back as the round man didn't even look up from his on-line poker game. Jared and Jim turned to face the crowd of federal agents. Jared smiled, then slashed his hand towards the floor, a flash of smoke and light appearing. In the second it took to clear, Jared was gone.

The agents turned and looked at Jim, wide-eyed.

"Fucking ninja." The round acrobat grumbled. He put his hands in his pockets, then smiled at the agents. "***See ya!***" He said, just before blinking out of existence, reappearing just behind the agents. They all whirled around to follow him, the two nearest diving for Jim. As they did, Jim threw himself around, spinning into a tight ball. Rolling through the air like a bullet, he slammed into the wall by the front door, cracking the carpet-padded paneling and collapsing onto the floor.

"That's gonna cost you, Ayers!" The manager shouted from the other side of the arcade, still focused on his computer screen.

Jim's eyes rolled in his head as he struggled up to his feet, then rushed out the door. "After him!" They shouted as Jim slammed the door behind him. The arcade emptied, all of the federal agents rushing after the disappearing VGM.

Against the rear wall, where the small collection of pinball machines sat, Aria looked up, pulling her walkman's headset off of her ears and looked after the departing crowd. She thought for a minute, then turned around a few times, watching as the empty arcade seemed to settle. She shrugged to the arcade's manager as she slipped her headset back on, then went back to her game.

Jim raced along the wall of the mini-mall, skidding to a halt at the curb. He looked around, quickly trying to figure out where to go in the crowded street.

"Ayers! Up here!" Came a shout. Jim looked up to see Jared on the edge of the second story of the mini-mall. Jim looked back as the federal agents barreled out the door, then smiled. Bending down, he threw himself up, leaping impossibly high to grab the edge of the wall.

Jared grabbed Jim's hands, falling back to pull Jim up. "Jesus, you weigh a lot."

Jim fell down onto the roof, panting. "More of me to love, baby."

"I thought Mario could jump higher than that." Jared groaned, looking at the ledge. He got to his feet and took off over the mall's pebbled roof.

"Funny, so did I." Jim grumbled, following.

"***God, it stinks.***" Michelle grumbled, the soft glow emanating from her, spreading out through the circular tube that was the sewer line. The long-haired girl carried her knee-length dark hair in the crook of her arm as she covered her nose and mouth with her other hand.

"Chip always said the VGM needed to know the sewer system." Beth said, moving just a few feet ahead of Michelle. "He said 'if you know the sewers, you know the city'."

"***That's only because he spent three months of his life living in sewers.***" Michelle protested. Beth's splashing footsteps stopped, causing Michelle to look back at her. "***What?***" She said. "***You didn't know that?***" Beth shook her head. Michelle shrugged, walking on. "***I guess Mr. Masters hasn't told you everything, has he?***" She walked ahead of Beth, glancing back as the pale girl stood still, her mind frozen as she tried to process what Michelle had said.

"***He's more like Vincent then you give him credit for.***" She warned, turning on down the sewers.

"Chip is nothing like Vincent." Beth protested.

"***They talk the same, they train the same, they even dress the same.***" Michelle said, turning to stare down Beth.

"They do not!" Beth yelled.

"***Oh, I'm sorry.***" Michelle yelled back, her voice drowning out the echo of Beth's shout. "***Chip wears a karate outfit; Vincent looks like a bad sci-fi movie reject. Is it that big of a difference for you, Beth?***" She mocked.

"Stop it!" Beth screamed, tears coming down her cheeks. "I'm sick and tired of you trying to push me around, trying to pick on me. I'm not as strong as you, Mich. Is that what you want? Vincent chose you over me when he moved out to Salt Lake, is that what you want? Is that what you WANT?!"

Michelle stared at Beth for a moment, then just turned away. She began to walk again down the sewer. "Answer me." Beth demanded. But Michelle kept walking. "Michelle, you've got to answer me." Michelle didn't even slow as she turned the bend, leaving Beth in the darkness. "Michelle?" The girl said, her voice shaking as the darkness encroached on her as Michelle disappeared. The darkness enveloped Beth, seeming to devour her completely. "Please, don't leave me too." She whispered in the darkness.

"Run!" Emily screamed, but Jon ignored her. Whirling in mid-stride, he came around with his fist, catching the remaining agent in the face, knocking him to the ground. Immediately dropping down with his right knee into the man's gut, Jon bent the man's body with pain, knocking the wind out of him.

The biker came up as another agent appeared, swinging an extendable baton. Jon caught the man's arm and flipped him over his shoulder. The man landed on the soft grass and kicked back up, catching Jon in the chest, knocking him back. Both came around ready, but Emily dove into the man's knee, knocking him to the ground. Jon swung the handle of his pistol at the agent's head, knocking him out cold.

"Come on!" Emily shouted, already starting back into her run.

"I've got me some fighting to do!" Jon yelled back, ready for more of the agents.

Emily stopped cold and whirled around. "**Now wait a second,**" She called, her voice charging with power. "**Are you telling me** you're going to remember that I outrank you in the VGM? I say we run, we run!"

Jon turned back to her, growling. "Fine." He seethed, reluctantly following her.

Jared leapt off the top of the building, barreling through the night, soaring across the narrow street onto the next building. As he landed, Jim got a running start and vaulted over the distance. He curled his shoulders under his hips, sending his legs flipping over his body so that he landed the acrobatic leap squarely, landing inches behind Jared. The ninja looked back at the acrobat and started to smile. Jim laughed and they both sped off into the night. "What about Aria?" Jared asked as they ran.

"She'll be fine." Jim grinned.

"We are in pursuit of suspects' vehicle." Called the lead driver of the four massive SUVs bearing down on Shane's tiny roadster. "Subjects' vehicle is heading north-bound on Glenwood Avenue, driving erratically." There was a slight pause as he spoke, then he swerved the steering wheel to the right. "Vehicle is now headed south-bound on Glenwood, traveling at approximately...vehicle is now headed on west Peace Street, heading towards, vehicle has changed direction, heading through a residential section."

"Who are these guys?" Roared the Federal Marshall sitting in the passenger seat.

"They're the Video Game Masters." Came a voice over the radio from the base of operations. "Now hurry and apprehend them before they cause too much trouble."

"Is there any chance they're a danger to my men?" Asked the Marshall.

"Probably not." Said the operation's manager, blatantly lying.

Shane's car spun in controlled a circle on the second floor of a parking deck, causing two of the all-terrain vehicles to scream to a halt, almost tipping over. As they settled back onto all four wheels, Shane's tiny vehicle grabbed the ground, then propelled itself into the night, zooming by the third vehicle like a bolt of lightning.

The giant SUV barreled after Shane, its gigantic wheels roaring along the pavement as Shane's car dashed down the street. The tiny car swerved into a high-end shopping center's parking lot and spun around. As the monster powered into the turn, Shane pushed the gas, aiming straight for the monster.

"You're crazy!" Ben yelled, hanging onto the handlebar over Tim's door. Opposite him, on the other side of the car, Dan held on with one hand, sipping on his Dr Pepper as Sophia clung to his same handle bar as if it was all that protected her from death.

"Never play chicken with someone braver than you." Tim said as the car shot forward. The tiny car barreled at the still turning vehicle. The giant vehicle slammed on its brakes, hoping to block Shane's car in. But in the last second before impact, Shane sent his car diving to the right, then back to the left, coming within just inches of the great beast. But Shane's nimble car squeezed through the gated opening of the shopping center and shot out onto the road.

"I think I lost 'em." Shane mumbled, grinning widely. A single set of headlights appeared. "Well, make that three of them, at least."

Shane sent his car into a fast spin, but amazingly, so did the SUV. It hung onto Shane, speeding right behind him. "That last one's hanging on." Sophia said. "Tim, what are we gonna do?" She asked. "That's the police, isn't it?"

"Actually, it looks like Federal Marshals." Ben added, looking over the rear seat. "I wonder why they haven't started shooting yet?"

"My money's on them being CIA." Stated Dan, still calmly sipping his Dr Pepper, as if oblivious to the danger.

"Whoever!" Sophia yelled. "They're government. Our government. They've got guys at our warehouse, probably. They've probably got people at our parents' houses. Where are we supposed to run?"

"She's got a point." Dan mused, first to Ben then to Tim. "What ARE we going to do?"

"Mexico?" Ben posed, looking around Sophia at Dan. "I could go for some tequila."

"Me too, actually." Dan admitted, frowning at the nearly-empty bottle of Dr Pepper. Sophia looked at both of them, almost certain they weren't joking.

"One thing I'm sure of, though. I'm not getting arrested tonight." Ben said, now obviously serious. "We've got enough contraband in this car to get us shot on sight."

"I told you not to bring that god-damn arsenal with you." Shane yelled with a quick glance back before sending the car diving to the right. The great beast of his pursuit hung diligently in his rear view mirror.

"We'll lose these bozos, then met up with Chip and the rest of the guys." Tim said, grimacing as another turn nearly caused the SUV to flip. "Right now, we just need to get rid of this guy."

"Say no more." Announced Ben. "Shane, get us to a straight away. I need at least twenty seconds of straight."

"Got it." Nodded the driver, checking his rear-view mirror.

"Dan, you and Sophia, hold my legs." Ben said, lying across the laps of the other two passengers. "Tim, I'm going to need you to scoot forward." Tim looked back, not understanding what Ben was going to do. He pulled the seat up as far as it would go, but Ben looked at the Vgm. "No, Tim. Farther."

"But then I…" Suddenly Tim got it. He pulled the switch and leaned the seat forward, giving Ben access to the passenger door.

"Straight-away in ten seconds." Shane yelled back to Ben. Ben reached into his jacket, producing a boxy, matte-black handgun.

"That's a military jeep, Ben." Dan pointed out, with another drink of his Dr Pepper before he took hold of Ben's legs. "It's probably bullet proof." Ben looked at Dan and winked. Dan handed Ben the soda. The sniper took a gulp then tossed it back.

"Now, Ben!" Shane yelled. The car skidded again, then straightened out on the empty nighttime road.

"Get me close. At least twenty feet." Ben yelled, opening the door as he pushed on Tim's seat, flattening the uncomfortable leader against the front dashboard. The force of the speed made keeping the door open difficult, but Ben immediately leaned out, with Dan and Sophia clinging onto his legs for dear life. Ben bent over, hanging just a few inches from the flying pavement, his head dangling just inches from the pavement.

Behind the tiny car, the great jeep loomed closely; its blaring lights like the eyes of a great demon. Ben held out his hands, steadying the solitary gun. He closed one eye, using the open one to line up the sights. He pulled the trigger once.

The gas tank beneath the car exploded out one side of its armed hull, sending the giant vehicle veering off course and slamming into a telephone pole. The speed and force of the impact knocked the pole down and sent the vehicle into the air, rolling violently.

The pole fell over, bringing down the power and phone lines for blocks, leaving the pavement behind their get away car like a tangled mass of electrified spaghetti. Shane slowed the car to the local speed limit while Ben pulled himself back in. Continuing on calmly, the car disappeared into the night.

Aria stepped out of the arcade as the owner shut the door behind her. She looked down either side of the empty street, then turned back and waved to the owner as he switched off the last of the lights. She stepped away from the late-night strip mall and turned to her left.

She made the short stroll down to the main street that passed by the university, coming to the intersection near the massive library. She looked up at it, then held out her hand, sighing. "Taxi!" She called.

"All clear." Said Ben, as he walked back into the main training hall of the giant warehouse. There, Tim and the rest of the VGM stood, awaiting his return. "No bugs, no taps, no tracers, no nothing. I checked it with every trick and tool I've got. Nothing."

"Well, I'm not going to subscribe to Chip and Vincent's usual paranoia." Tim said, drawing up everyone's attention as they gathered around in the center of the training hall. "If everything checked out, I'm going to assume that means it's clean." Tim looked at the assorted members who remained. None of them looked too hopeful. "So what have we got?"

"Well, this blood was sprayed with ammonia," Dan answered professionally as he motioned with his head back to the small spot on the training mat. "So I can't tell whose it is. To make matters worse, the burns on the floor were made by spent shells." He went on, pointing just past the blood stains. "Ben maintains they're probably machine gun shells given their dispersal and the number and whatnot, but your guess is as good as mine. I couldn't find any shells though, so I guess it's academic." He completed, rocking back on his heels.

"So whoever did this cleaned up after themselves." Said Ben, standing next to Tim. "I think it was probably what's-his-name, Charles Man-sucks-so."

"Mancuso?" Michelle said, laughing. "It's not his style." She lowered down into a crouch, looking across at the burns on the mat. "Charles would have knifed everyone. He wouldn't use a gun, nor would he let one of his men. No magician in his right mind would." She said, getting a snide look from Ben.

"She's right." Tim agreed, scratching underneath his chin. "Besides, he would have left the bodies." Tim turned to Aria, giving her a considerate look. "Is there anything you can do?"

"Nothing that would give us any answers." She admitted, staying away from the group. "My powers are pretty weak without Jessica." Aria turned to the blood. "I can't even say if that's their blood or not. I just can't get any type of reading."

"It's okay." Tim said, trying to sound comforting. "There's not much of an impression, psychically, anyway. I can't get anything about Vincent."

"Which would be about par for the course." Beth added from next to Tim. "Alternates disrupt magic and psychic impressions like that."

"Either way, if it's not Charles or anyone else, that just leaves those government guys that were looking for Chip and the others." Said Emily, sounding withdrawn. "If it was Pihc," She continued, her voice shaking just a bit. "They're bodies would still be here."

"And so would Pihc." Dan added, morosely.

"Wow." Was all Jared could say, also in shock over the evening. He looked down at the bloodstains, putting his hands over them. "This blood isn't too stale. This couldn't have happened more than an hour or two ago." Jared looked up, and looked around. "Where's that Jon guy?"

"Good question." Ben said, also looking around. "That fucker keeps disappearing. Maybe it was him."

"It wasn't Jon." Emily defended, giving Ben a harsh look. "He and I were the first ones here. He left on his bike to tail the guys chasing us."

"Okay, I have to give him credit for thinking to do that." Jared said, standing up. "I didn't even think to try that."

"Yeah." Jim said, grinning at the ninja. "And you're supposed to be the secret agent of the group."

"Whatever." Jared countered with an awkward smile. "I'm just a yutz."

"Okay, guys." Tim called, quieting everyone. "So, where do we stand?"

"Well, we know this much." Ben summarized casually. "Chip, Jessica, and Vincent have undoubtedly been arrested, probably after leaving the magic community meeting. Despite the blood here, odds are at least two of them are alive. The amount of blood spilled isn't enough to be more than one person."

"Which means whoever's left is probably being held at some government installation." Said Tim, standing up, slowly joining the group on the mat. Ben nodded, looking to Tim, as if waiting for some type of sign. The rest of the VGM turned to the only Vgm still around. Tim took off his glasses and wiped his face with both hands, as if trying to pull his face off. "I could really use some good news right now." He almost laughed.

"*'Good news' only comes after there is 'bad news' for it to counteract.*"

Everyone pivoted towards the front door at the sound of the familiar voice. Ben leveled his gun on the door as Michelle drew out her silver whip, and Dan unsheathed his stout kukri.

Out of the shadows stepped Kageryu. Dressed in a black business suit with his hair slicked back, he seemed like a new person. Tim stared past the Celestial Dragon for a moment, then exclaimed. "How the hell did you get through there?" His voice grated, as if he had just survived a heart attack. "It was locked five different…"

"Tim," Whispered Jared from behind him. "He's ninja. It's what we do."

"*The bad news mounts even as we speak.*" Kageryu continued with the VGM's undivided attention. "*Ecnilitsep is about to launch an all-out offensive against the Earth. Beyond that, Chip and your two strongest warriors have been captured, betrayed by your own nation. With them out of the way, there seems to be no real hope of fighting off Ecnilitsep, Pihc, or their waiting army.*"

"Yeah, that about sums it up." Said Ben, lowering his guns.

"Nicely." Michelle agreed.

"Wait a second." Sophia chimed in, her voice weak. "Their waiting army?"

"*And the bad news continues.*" Kageryu went on, ignoring Sophia as the worried looks from the VGM grew more concerned. "*In addition to waging this war on her own, Ecnilitsep has awakened an ancient evil, one that has been restrained and held far away from the living for many years.*" The gathered warriors listened with silent concern. "*But that is where the 'good news' comes in.*" Kageryu stood aside, making a motion with his hand.

Through the dark doorway, a figure walked in. Dressed in a dark business suit, he carried an air of an ancient danger. He looked around the giant warehouse and seemed unimpressed. He ignored the VGM.

Behind him, a pair of identical twins followed. Dressed in suits as well, they both wore reading glasses and carried ornate broadswords in their hands. The one on the left, with brown hair, held his sword by the sheath near the crossbar as he looked at the VGM, smiling genuinely. The one on the right, with black hair, took off his sunglasses and simply stared at the gathered group, appraising them seriously.

Finally, from behind them all came a last figure. Dressed in black and red form-fitting armor, he walked in with quiet power that was immediately evident. On his back, a great sword rested while his short black hair seemed ruffled by wind.

"Oh my god." Jared said, the first to speak as he gaped at the sight of the five men. He suddenly remembered himself and bowed respectfully, getting confused glances from Jim and Shane.

"*Allow me to introduce my…'brothers'.*" Kageryu said with a smile. With each name, he gestured with his hand. To the first one, he smiled. "*Leviathan.*" To the twins, to the brown-haired one and the black-haired one respectively, "*Bahamut and Tiamat.*" To the last, in the armor. "*And Oroboris.*"

"Oh my god." Michelle said with awe, now grasping who it was that stood before the VGM. She bowed respectfully as well.

"I get the impression we should be doing something respectful-like." Ben whispered to Jim. The acrobat nodded, but neither made any move.

Oroboris stepped forward, greeting the VGM with a polite gaze. "*We're here to help against Ecnilitsep's coming assault.*" He said, his voice resonating with the same power that lay within Kageryu's words.

There was still no response from the VGM.

"*I think we scared 'em.*" Mumbled Bahamut, to his twin, a slight accent hidden in his voice.

"*I think you may be right.*" Agreed Tiamat, with the same accent. "*It must be our reputations.*"

"*That or your breath.*" Grinned Leviathan, from in front of the twins.

"*Or your manners.*" Kageryu said sternly, silencing them all.

After a moment or two of silence, Tim finally found the initiative to speak. "Are you…five…really the…" Tim tried to say more but found it hard. All five heads nodded in unison. "Oh boy." He shuddered, bending over and trying to put his head between his knees.

"*We are not here to help you, per say, against Ecnilitsep.*" Cautioned Oroboris, looking at the rest of the VGM. "*But we will face her armies which even now are poised to begin their assault.*" The man turned to Kageryu. "*It would seem Ecnilitsep has chosen Earth as the final battle for reality.*" He grinned. "*Strangely, I think we all knew it would it would ultimately be this way.*"

"So, I take it you won't be helping us to free Chip and the others?" Dan asked, not sounding hopeful.

"*Not directly, no.*" Kageryu answered, hesitantly.

"Well, that's not very helpful." Ben said, a bit annoyed with their indifference to the situation. "But let's get back to that bit about the assault and the armies and all."

"Whoa. One thing at a time." Tim said, finally standing up straight. He blinked a few times, glancing from the five men to the VGM. Oroboris snapped his fingers, getting Tim's attention, then pointed at the VGM. "Right." Tim nodded, turning to the group. He stared at them for a moment, gathering his thoughts, then spoke. "I am not prepared, nor willing, to deal with interdimensional invasions until the staff of this organization has been fully recovered. As such, we need to rescue Chip, Jessica, and Vincent."

"Easier said than done." Sophia offered up. "We don't know where to find them."

"That may not be true." Emily chimed in, her arms crossed over her chest. "We do have one wild card." She looked at Tim, then to the others. "Jon's tailing them."

"Yeah, but can we trust him?" Ben asked.

"I don't see why not." Michelle shrugged.

Tim laughed uncomfortably, then smiled. He glanced from the VGM back at the five men, as if unsure who to address first. All five men immediately pointed at the group. "Right." Tim said, turning back to the VGM. He readied to speak, but nothing came out of his mouth.

"Tim? Are you alright?" Emily asked, tilting her head down a bit as if that would give her a better view of him.

"Yeah. I'm alright. I'm fine. Jon." He breathed out again. "I think we can trust Jon." He turned to Emily and Michelle. "You guys were with him last, yes?" They nodded. "See if you can get a hold of him. I know Chip gave him a headset. Try it. If he's got a phone, call it. Emily, I've taught you some location spells. Now's a good time to give them a try." He turned to Ben and Dan. "You guys. I want to be ready to move the moment we get in touch with Jon. Go make it happen." Finally, he turned to the others. "Okay, guys. It's the Vgm thing to always have alternatives and back-up plans or what have you." He said, his arms tucked tightly under his chest as he spoke. "So, so go get me some." He said nervously.

The group disbanded, breaking up into fragments as they scattered into the rest of the warehouse. Once Tim was alone with the five men, he turned back to them. "Can I just ask one question?" He asked to Kageryu. "How bad is this going to get? I mean, really."

The tall ninja smiled. "*Even I do not know all things, Tim. But I do know this. It will get darker before it gets lighter. For that's the way of all things.*"

"That's not very useful." Tim half-chuckled humorlessly.

Kageryu grinned in response. "*I said it would be good news. You'll have to get your useful news someplace else.*"

Eric

CHAPTER 10

Locked Up and Breaking Out

"Help I'm stepping into the twilight zone
Place is a madhouse feels like being cloned
My beacon's been moved under moon and star
Where am I to go now that I've gone too far?"

—Earrings Golden, When the Bullet Hits the Bone

"Vincent?" Jessica said, her voice so soft and caring.

The young boy opened his eyes, not sure of what to expect. In front of him, leaning on the side of the bed was a girl as nervous and scared as he. She reached out for him, touching his chest, letting her warm fingers drip down to his abdomen. The small ridges above his waist bumped her fingers up and down, making Jessica smile. "Vincent, please tell me...if I shouldn't." She asked, slowly slipping off her own white shirt, revealing a thin wrap of silk beneath it. Vincent's breathing became hard, but he said nothing. Outside, he could hear the rain pelting against the window. The room was dark from the clouds, despite the early afternoon.

Vincent's mind skated along the edges of his consciousness as he sat. Staring down at his own shadow as it lingered on the edge of the steel table in front of him, the dark Vgm remained motionless beneath the solitary bulb that shed a meager light onto him. His dark brown hair hung over his eyes, while his shoulders slumped forward. Between his knees, his hands were bound by multiple handcuffs, while at either side, guards waited anxiously, watching for even the smallest movement.

There was a groan of metal and Vincent looked up through his hair as the door behind the opposite chair opened, the light of the outside world pouring in. A form stood in the doorway, a light trench coat hanging down near the slender figure's legs. Vincent's lips twitched up, fury spreading across his face.

"Hello." Eric Comstock said as he sat down in the metal chair across from Vincent. The dark Vgm immediately struggled against his handcuffs as he stared a hole through the man across the table. Eric fought to look unafraid as he opened the file he carried. At the top, it read 'Pierce, Vincent'.

Vincent tried to stand, but the two guards in the corners of the room stepped forward, simultaneously slamming their nightsticks into the back of his knees, dropping him to his chair. Vincent struggled against them, but the shackles that strained against his rage managed to hold.

"You're looking pretty lively, Vincent." Eric tried to speak calmly as he leaned forward on the table. He looked up at Vincent, trying to convey some sense of sympathy. Vincent glared back at Eric. "You look incredibly lively," The college-looking agent continued. "Really, very lively for a guy who just had fifteen-odd slugs unloaded into his chest cavity."

"Hello." Eric said, as he stepped into the chair across from Jessica. She looked up at him, a hateful glare on her face. "I see you're about as happy as Vincent is right now."

She half smiled with heavily-lidded eyes. "Oh, I imagine so. In fact, I'm probably thinking of the same innumerable ways of causing you pain that he's been considering."

"You know, I just came from his room." Eric half-laughed as he adjusted his tie. "He's not feeling very talkative right now."

"Or cooperative, I'll bet." Jessica finished, her voice full of spite. "Wonder why, Comstock?" She asked sarcastically.

"Kids these days." Eric tried, looking down at the file.

"Vincent Pierce." Eric said, as he opened up the inch-thick file on the metal desk. Opposite him, Chip Masters just rolled his eyes. "Quite a file. We've been keeping tabs on him ever since he joined the first Video Game Masters all those years ago." Eric thumbed through the file. "He's become quite a celebrity around the office. All the stuff he got into during the year or so that he was in

Salt Lake is nearly half of this file. Including his little run in with Sam Mancuso, Charles Mancuso's brother. He ever tell you about that?"

Chip yawned.

Eric slid the file off the top of the stack. "Jessica Cameron." He said, eyeing Chip over the metal rims of his glasses. He opened the manila folder, shifting through the pages. "She's an illegal alien if I ever saw one. Her social security number's totally wrong. Her bank and tuition grant records, her accounts, all blatantly forged." Eric held up an x-ray to the single, hanging light over the table. "Even her dental records. Jeez. Thorough, but forged." Chip looked away in boredom.

"And then there's Chip Masters." Eric said, pushing Jessica's file over Vincent's.

The simple folder sat empty.

Eric's eyes rolled up as he looked at Chip. The Vgm grinned comically, raising one eyebrow. "I like my privacy." He said, his face taking on a dangerous expression.

"Uh-huh." Eric nodded. "I don't doubt that, Chip." He said, reaching under the table into his briefcase. He sat back up, tossing a fourth file onto the table. "Or should I say 'Simon Chase'?"

Thicker than both Jessica and Vincent's collective files, Eric opened it, thumbing through the familiar pages. "Born in Claremont Valley, California. The first documented case in that county of," He looked up at Chip. "Conjoined twins." When Chip had no reaction, he turned back to the file. "Hitchhiked to San Francisco when you were…" Eric's words stumbled over the number, tripping him up. "…when you were six."

"Five, actually." Chip chided, with a bit of a sarcastic smile. "I didn't like my drapes."

"Yeah, apparently." Eric said, staring at the file. He slid the files to the side of the desk, folding his hands and leaning over the table. "Chip, you may or not believe it, I'm trying to help you."

"Okay. I don't believe it." Chip riposted quickly, his smile still in place.

"Look," Eric tried over. "The VGM is in a lot of danger, and not just from Pihc. The US government is seriously interested in the actions and movements of any known cults or mystic organizations. You think we don't know about the local covens and orders?"

Chip laughed. "I bet you boys pat yourselves on the back for info that elementary kids can get off the internet." He leaned over the table, his hands in tight cuffs. "Eric, believe it or not, I'm actually willing to play ball with you.

But you've got to understand, there's shit in this world that you simply aren't prepared for. Stuff that would make you lose your mind in an instant." He sat back, dropping his hands into his lap.

"You think we don't know about all of that stuff already?" Eric laughed, leaning back in his seat. "We've got satellite photos of stuff all over the world. From the tiny little plots of land next to interstate onramps, the ones with trees that nobody ever thinks about, all the way up to the whole Pacific Ocean. That's some scary stuff in and of itself."

"I'll bet." Was all Chip said. Before Eric could say anything more, however, Chip interrupted him. "Look, Eric. I don't want to be a pain in the ass. But I want out. How can I get out?"

The FBI agent sat back, considering Chip. "You'll have to cooperate with us."

"Yeah, but I don't like cooperating with people who shoot my friends. Or people who lie and infiltrate my team." Chip explained, suddenly leaning forward, his hands free of his cuffs.

Eric's eyes went wide as the two guards in the corners of the room sprang into action. But Chip just winked at Eric, then grinned. The guards grabbed his shoulders, but couldn't even get them to budge.

"Is that magic supposed to impress me?" Eric asked with a breathless voice.

"This?" Chip said, looking down at his arms which the two guards couldn't move. "This is just a little Aikido parlor trick I picked up back in the day. ***This,***" He said, his voice taking on a flash of magical power. "***This is something different.***"

The light in the room exploded as Chip's body erupted with electricity. The two guards were thrown from him as he shocked them off their feet. Chip immediately stood up, knocking the chair back and slamming the table up against Eric, knocking him out of his chair. Chip glared down at Eric as the two guards got to their feet, drawing their guns. Chip just smiled at Eric, who stared petrified in fear. "***You should have known not to burn us.***" Chip said calmly, just before he burst into motion.

Jon sat on his bike at the gas station, holding the handset of the payphone next to him. He glanced down the abandoned street, at the large six-story building standing out in the middle of nowhere. He listened to the ringing, turning back to the phone.

"Larry's House of Sodomy. What can we do you for?" Came Ben's voice.

"Ben, its Jon." The biker said, checking over his shoulder. "I trailed our wayward kids and they're in it deep. Can you trace those stupid little headset things?" He asked, looking down at the headset in his hand.

"Why don't you just tell us where you are?"

"Well, because this phone's bugged and the dude in the gas station I'm at is undoubtedly with the pimps who kidnapped our kids." The biker retorted. "I'm switching on the headset. Try to follow it here, okay?"

"I'm not sure if we can..." Ben began, but Jon hung up.

Jessica looked up as her interrogation room door opened, surprised to see Chip coming inside. The one guard at the rear rushed at Chip, but the Vgm kicked his lower leg, then grabbed the man's head. With a fast slam, he drove the guard's face into the metal table. He then yanked the man's head back in the other direction, throwing him against the wall, not even looking as he slid down the metal surface. Jessica looked down at the guard, then up at Chip. "What took you so long?"

"Oh, you know me." The Vgm said, moving around behind the chair to where her hands were cuffed. "I like to small talk with the people who betray us."

Chip and Jessica stepped out of the interrogation room, sliding along the wall. Looking like any corporate office, a wide maze of federal cubicles spread out around them. With half the lights off, the place looked like a graveyard, occupied by a few ambitious workers who were too focused on their computers and notes to notice the two criminals. "Where do you think Vincent's being held?" Jessica whispered, marveling at the few people who worked away the night.

"He's probably being held in...hey!" Chip suddenly exclaimed. He reached over the side of a cubicle, grabbing up his golden katana. "It's Hatsumi." He leaned over the side, looking into the cardboard box. "It's all our stuff."

"Chip, quiet." Jessica cautioned. "We are in an office with lots of heavily armed people that are trigger happy."

"Good point." Chip said, pulling out Vincent's silver pocket watch. He took Jessica's hand as he hit the stop-watch function.

"Okay." Tim said as he leaned back in the passenger seat of his own car, not evening glancing over at Ben as the sniper drove. "Here's the deal. I'll be taking

Ben, Jared, Dan, and Jim in with me." He said into the microphone of his headset.

"The hell you will." Came Michelle's voice from Shane's car. Tim looked up to the car in front of them, at the dark haired girl with her mane done up in a tight bun, ready for action. She stared back through the rear window at Tim, a furious glare on her face. "You're not leaving me out of this one." She said over her own headset.

"This battle won't be won with numbers, Mich." Came Jared's voice. Tim looked in the rearview mirror over Sophia's head to see into Emily's car in the back, carrying Jared next to her, with Beth in the back.

"Then he can leave your ass." Michelle retorted angrily, the static over the headsets swooping in on them in bursts.

"Michelle." Came Dan's voice from next to her. "Just calm down. This isn't a fight. We're just going in to get the others out. Save your…"

"Why don't you save it, Mormon-boy?" Michelle bit to her friend. She turned and glared back at Tim. "You're not leaving me behind again." She demanded.

Tim looked over at Ben. He shrugged. "I'm afraid of her, so defy her at your own risk, big-big-Tim."

Tim looked forward. "I wonder what Chip would do?" He mumbled. He then sat up and looked at Ben, getting the same disgusted look he had on own his own face. "Jesus, did I really say that?"

Chip and Jessica stepped inside the small, soundproofed room as the time-stopper ended. An abrupt shift in time reverberated at the edges of their perception as Chip shut the door behind himself. The two turned back to Vincent as the dark Vgm slumped over the table, blood on the metal in front of him. Jessica stopped, watching as the blood dripped from the front of his face. "What happened?" She breathed.

"Vincent, wake up." Chip said, slapping Vincent on the back of the head. The Vgm looked up, his eyes refocusing. "Did you hit your face into the table so it would look like you needed medical help?"

Vincent looked down at the blood on the table, then up at Chip. "Maybe." He said uncertainly.

Jessica dropped down behind the chair, looking at the handcuffs that held Vincent down. But the network of metal links dizzied her, making her step back in shock. "I've never seen anyone this locked up before." She stepped back and looked to Chip. "We need to hurry." She said. "Eric and the guards will wake up soon. Where are your guards?"

"I think they went for help." Vincent said defiantly. He looked up at Chip. "But she's right. We don't have time for this.

"Alright." Chip said, drawing out his katana as Jessica moved away from the chair. He held the blade to Vincent's elbow, then drew back the powerful sword. "Ready?" He asked carefully. Vincent just nodded.

The entire front of the building exploded.

A fiery wave of destruction slammed into the far wall of the main entrance. The metal door beside the entrance whirled open as three federal agents rushed through the doors, their weapons drawn. They positioned themselves beside the metal door, taking aim with their weapons, searching for those who had done the damage.

Through the fiery wall of destruction stepped a single figure. Dressed in all black, the cowboy leveled his gun at the first of the guards. The man struggled to see through the fiery destruction, unsure if he really was really seeing what was before him. His hesitation was the last thing he knew.

A gray-skinned gladiator dropped down behind the other two, his twin short swords impaling two of the guards at the base of their necks before they even knew they weren't alone. The third whirled around, his gun trained on Brenard, but as he leveled his weapon, a spinning buzz of silver whisked by as his own blood erupted over his face. He turned from his amputated hand to see Cye catch her naginata as it returned to her hand, then jam the flame-shaped blade forward, impaling him through the chest.

Yadiloh joined the others, then they turned as Pihc stepped out of the fires. Carrying his black katana in hand, he moved through the once-impenetrable doors, stalking into the federal building.

The floor came alive. The handful of after-hour agents in the offices leapt to their feet, drawing their guns. The red warning lights came alive along the walls, while the population funneled towards the doors, following the meticulously ordained emergency scenarios.

An FBI agent turned the corner, running with his gun ready. But as he turned, he skidded to a halt when he saw a stone statue of a monk standing near the corner. He looked it up and down once, then discarded all thought of it and raced on ahead.

As soon as the man rushed by, the statue disappeared in a flash of smoke, leaving Chip standing where it had been. He looked at the closest cubicles as Vincent appeared out of thin air, while Jessica dropped down from the ceiling. "Any idea what that loud explosion was?" Chip asked.

Jessica looked at Vincent, then back to their leader. "Was that rhetorical or did you really not think it was an explosion?"

The Vgm rolled his eyes, then looked away. "If all the feds are going that way, I say we go the other way and get the hell out of here."

"But what caused the explosion?" Vincent asked.

"Gas main?" Chip offered, turning to go. "I don't know and I don't care."

"Even if it's Pihc?" Vincent asked. "Do you really think it coincidence that this place gets attacked in the middle of the night when we're being held here?"

"Vincent, you're not suggesting we try and take on Pihc and whoever he may have brought along to the party alone are you?" Chip asked, speaking over the cacophony of war preparation taking place on the other side of the office. "I know you're suicidal, but that's just stupid." He turned away, rushing away from the sound of gunfire. "Come on."

Vincent fumed. "I don't like running."

"Think of it as choosing a more appropriate battle site." Jessica humored, subtly pushing Vincent ahead of her. He went with the push, but as she moved to follow him, a rock-hard forearm wrapped around her throat. Vincent and Chip both whirled around as Brenard yanked Jessica off her feet and threw her to the ground.

The gladiator held up his hands to fight, but Vincent tackled him from behind, wrestling the thick warrior to the ground. As soon as the two landed, Brenard rolled to his back, grabbing Vincent's right arm. While the Vgm rained down blows with his left hand, Brenard bent Vincent's arm against the elbow, sweeping him to the ground. Pinning Vincent, the gladiator reached to his waist for his sword.

A sharp pain ripped through Brenard's chest as Chip's golden katana punctured the gladiator's sternum. Chip shoved Brenard's body off Vincent, then pulled him and Jessica to their feet. "We're not staying." He said immediately, already pulling Vincent towards the stairwell.

"They're here. We're here. Why not?" Vincent implored angrily.

"We're no match for them." Chip bit harshly through clenched teeth. "Pihc and the alternates versus the three of us? And that's assuming Ecnilitsep isn't with them." He said, motioning at the devastation that was moving towards them. "We didn't stand a chance at the warehouse; we don't stand a chance here. Now come on!"

Two FBI agents turned down a hallway, assault rifles held ready. But all they found waiting was darkness. The red flashes of the emergency lights sprayed over them like their own fear, but they kept the guns ready, their bullet-proof vests standing out against their suits and business attire.

The two men moved further down the hallway, carefully watching for the slightest movement. They stalked on quiet feet, not noticing the gray-skinned cowboy moving in behind them.

"Any word from Trebor yet?" Cye asked as she came over to Pihc, stepping over the fallen remains of the cubicles.

"*I have been told he is still attending to Ecnilitsep's bidding.*" Pihc said, moving away from her, continuing to survey the devastation. He pushed a piece of rubble back, looking down at an unconscious red-haired agent in a light tan trench coat. The giant turned away, disinterested.

"Well, the agents are giving us more trouble than we expected." Cye went on. "Yadiloh and Brenard are up on the fourth floor, routing them out. But even though they're using guns, which they refuse to accept can't hit us, they're troublesome to kill. They're very resourceful it seems."

"*Not all humans are weak.*" Pihc allowed, pushing more rubble aside. "*But only the VGM concerns us.*"

The stairwell was lit by the red emergency lights. Down the long winding metal steps, the VGM raced, trying to move quietly through the concrete domain. Chip led with Jessica behind him and Vincent bringing of up the rear. They raced down the steps in rapid, metal-rattling unison. Finally, the steps ended at a final metal door. Chip paused at the door, holding his hand against the metal as feeling its temperature.

"We might be in the basement." Jessica offered.

"This is North Carolina." Vincent answered. "The red soil's too thick. Nowhere's got a basement." He glanced down at Chip. "What's wrong?"

"Something's happening on the other side." Chip said. He put his ear to the metal door, listening.

"Well, it is an exit and the building IS under attack." Jessica pointed out.

"Quiet." Chip called, still not opening the door. Vincent moved to stand behind him, also feeling the door as Chip listened. "I hear voices."

"And?" Jessica asked.

"One of them's Ecnilitsep." Chip whispered slowly. "But I can't place the others."

"All Vgms, on-line!"

The three jumped at the voice, but Jessica was the first to pull out her headset. She held it on her head, pulling the microphone to her mouth. "Jessica, on-line." She said quietly.

"Jessica?!" Came Tim's voice, the loud burst of sound filling the quiet stairwell. "Where the hell are you? That doesn't matter! Get your ass out here. We're at the bottom of the parking deck and we're getting our ass kicked by Pihc's sister and her personal henchmen."

"Pihc's sister?" She said, looking at Chip and Vincent.

Their faces turned grim simultaneously. "Ecnilitsep." They breathed.

Jared sliced at Eminaf with his katana but the female general moved around him, slashing at his leg with her saber. The ninja leapt awkwardly over the blow just before it could land, but ended up on his back. She moved over him, drawing back her sword to impale him through his jaw. As she dropped into position, Jim tackled her around the waist, practically breaking her in half.

Livic swung at Tim with his double-bladed axe, but the mage stepped back, trying fearfully to deal with the general. As the older man moved in, Tim threw his hands forward, shouting "***Blizzaga!***" An explosion of ice erupted under Livic's feet, knocking him back and giving Tim time to retreat.

Ecnilitsep moved towards Ben but the sniper dove out of the way, unloading with a fast barrage of shots from his two pistols, the bullets skating around the giant woman. He landed against a car in the parking deck just as the fire door burst open. Chip dashed up to the car, landing next to Ben. "Where the hell have you guys been?" The sniper asked as he frantically changed clips.

"We had some legal trouble." Chip explained as Jessica and Vincent joined him. He looked over the hood of the car as Dan parried a slice from Ecnilitsep, barely avoiding having his head taken off by her riposte. "Listen, Pihc and his boys are upstairs." He flinched as Dan was thrown into the side of a car.

"Good, cause Pihc 2.0's down here and she's a lot fucking worse." Ben bitched, checking his temple, for the first time realizing it was bleeding. "That bitch made me bleed. I'm gonna light her fucking ass up."

"Ben." Chip said, holding him down at his shoulder. He sat up and looked over to his immediate left. "Vincent, you, Jim, and Dan, take care of Ecnilitsep's team." Chip said, barking out the orders over the roar of the fight. "Ben, grab Tim and Jared and you guys clear us a path out of here. Jessica and I will take on Ecnilitsep."

"What about the others?" Ben asked. "We've got Jon and the girls waiting at a gas station about a quarter of a mile down the road."

"Have them be ready to gun it at a moment's notice. I want them to be ready to drive down here and pick us up when we've got an escape window." Chip said. "But we've got to move because Pihc's going to be coming down any…"

The door burst open as Yadiloh came through, his pistol leveled.

"Second now?" Ben said, looking at Chip. "Is that what you were going to say?"

"Chip, I invoke my clause in the VGM contract to call for our free-for-all Hail Mary plan." Jessica yelled from the car she was hiding behind, pulling out her kitar. "Each of us, one-on-one until we outnumber them. Now!"

"I'm with her." Vincent said, following Jessica.

Chip sat for a moment, then looked at Ben. "Sounds good to me."

"I'm strangely comfortable with the idea." Ben agreed sagely just before the two burst into action.

Vincent leapt over the car as Dan got his bearings with a shake of his head. He looked up as Vincent coasted over him, bursting into motion himself to follow the Vgm. The two launched over the side of another car, landing just as Brenard and Cye came into view. Neither slowed for a moment.

Dan immediately tackled Cye around her knees, taking her to the ground. As she tried to use her pole arm to break her fall, Dan slid around underneath her, wrapping one arm around her neck and the other around her leg. Pulling in with all his might, he bent her body backwards, as if trying to touch her foot and her forehead together.

Vincent landed, snapping a hard kick into Brenard's groin, then slamming him with a vicious right across the face. Brenard took the blow, then tried to tackle Vincent around the waist. The Vgm sprawled out, driving both his elbows into Brenard's back. As the alternate tried to roll up, Vincent whipped out his bowie knife, driving it in the base of Brenard's neck.

Ben fired off two more shots with his pistols at Livic, the bullets barely missing the general. When the guns clicked empty, Ben threw out his hands as a swarm of missiles went flying out from his back and curving towards his foe.

The magical weapons collided with Livic, but did little more than slow him down.

As Ben stood from the spell, Tim reached into one of the cargo pockets on the sniper's shorts, pulling out a hand-sized sub-machine gun. Cocking the weapon, he braced himself, unleashing the gun on the chaos around him. "I wanna go home!" The mage screamed angrily. The gun clicked empty. Tim looked at it as if not understanding.

"Would you try to not waste bullets?" Ben yelled, grabbing the gun from Tim. "These things cost money." He whirled around as Livic jumped at him, but just before the general could connect with his swords, he was shot out of the air. Tim and Ben both turned as Jon strolled up, calmly loading more bullets into his gun. "What the fuck are you doing here?" The sniper yelled.

"When you guys have a fight, you really have it out." Jon said, slamming the chamber of his gun down. He looked down at Livic's body as the gaping wound in his chest slowly began to close. "Who's this guy?"

"Don't know." Tim said. "He's with Ecnilitsep."

"The big chick?" Jon asked, motioning to the other end of the underground parking deck. "The one that's kicking Jessica's ass?"

Tim and Ben both turned as Jessica went sailing into the concrete wall. Flipping in midair, she slammed against the wall with her feet, throwing herself back at the giant with all her might. "That'd be her." Ben nodded calmly.

Jessica threw a hard kick at Ecnilitsep's chest, but the giant woman knocked the kick casually out of the way, barely noticing Chip's slash at her as she nimbly slid out of the way of the blade. She came around, catching Chip in the side with a hard punch, then came back to connect with a hard elbow to Jessica's body.

The blow knocked Jessica off balance and sent her stumbling to the ground. She landed hard but sat up into a crouch, panting hard. She stood, shaking the confusion from her head as she gasped for air. But as she stood, Dan and Vincent rushed by her, yanking her from where she stood, just as debris from an exploding car crashed where she had been standing.

The two pulled her to the edge of the sub-level parking deck, kneeling by the cement barrier. "We need to get out of here." Dan said to Jessica and Vincent as they stopped to get their breaths. "The police will be here any second."

"I wouldn't worry about that." Jessica winced as she struggled to get her right arm behind her back. She pulled her arm back around, her metal kitar in her hand. "The police are the least of our worries."

"Then what's the most of our worries?" Asked Dan. As the words escaped his lips, the metal door that the Vgms had emerged from exploded out, colliding with the car directly in front of it. Behind the smashed wall, a giant form stood with a massive gun held in its inhuman hand. S'ram stood ready to fight.

Dan turned back to Jessica, pointing a steady finger at her. "Not a word, Cameron."

"What the fuck is that thing?" Ben gaped.

A few feet from the sniper, Eminaf stared in horror. "S'ram." She whispered in fear.

Ben looked at the female general, glanced back at Jim who stood next to him, then looked over at her again. "You're pretty hot for any enemy." He said. Eminaf returned Ben's gaze with confusion. She stared at him for just a moment, not having time to move before he shot her in the head.

Vincent and Jon both rushed at S'ram but the giant beast punched Vincent's chest, sending him off his feet and crashing into a car. The entire metal form skidded a few inches back as its front side completely crumpled against the landing. Jon slowed, looking up at the massive form. He blinked once, then leveled his pistol. S'ram aimed his pistol down at Jon, the two guns passing each other. "I'll shoot." Jon warned.

"*I'll live.*" S'ram grinned.

Jon stared into the eyes of the monster before him, his gaze narrowing. "Why do you look so much like me?" He asked. S'ram just grinned.

"*S'ram!*"

Both Jon and S'ram turned as Pihc roared at the giant. Standing with his katana drawn out, his dark eyes burned murderously. S'ram casually knocked Jon away without a thought, turning to face off against Pihc.

The giant form stared at Pihc, as if staring at a leaner twin. "*Pihc.*" It seethed hatefully. "*And where have you been hiding?*"

"*Brenard! Yadiloh! Cye!*" Pihc roared. He turned his blazing eyes at S'ram. "*Destroy him.*" He shouted as he turned his black katana to face the giant gunman.

"*Generals.*" Ecnilitsep yelled from the far side of the battle. "*Stop them!*" Her command whipped Pihc's head to her, his face blank with shock.

"Hey, Chip?" Came Jim's voice over the headset. "This looks like an internal struggle. I say we get the fuck out while the getting's good."

"Sounds like a plan." Chip nodded, looking around at the VGM as Pihc's alternates rushed at S'ram, and the generals rushed at the alternates. "All Vgms, on-line!" He shouted. "Retreat!" He called before the others could respond.

"What?!" Vincent yelled across the battle. "There's no way we're..."

"Retreat." Tim said, grabbing Vincent's arms and yanking him to the side. Before they could hit the ground, Tim called out "***Exit!***"

Brenard shot in at S'ram, moving to slice the giant's knees to ribbons. But as he moved, the huge beast kicked him aside. The alternate hit the ground and rolled up, only to be hacked from behind by Livic's massive axe. Cye and Yadiloh turned to the green-armored general, while Pihc faced off against his twin. The giant leveled his pistol at Pihc, but the dark warrior sliced at his arm, keeping him from getting a bead.

Chip watched as Jim and Jared leapt up through the cement gratings to the next level, while at the same time Dan and Ben snuck off like shadows. Jessica faded from view like Tim and Vincent had done, leaving him and Jon. Chip looked over at his brother, then at Ecnilitsep. She watched as Pihc engaged S'ram. And he watched a smile spread across her face.

"Dude." Jon whispered as he crouched down next to Chip, hiding behind the wheel of the car in the destroyed parking lot. "What's the deal with her and them?"

"I don't know." Chip said, getting up to his feet to move. "But I think it's going to turn out very badly for us." He moved back from the car, moving away from the war that raged. "Come on. Let's get out of here."

CHAPTER 11

Outcasts

"My, my. Look at all the men gathering around us. I wonder what they do when they're not so busy?"

—Rally Vincent, Riding Bean

There was a bright flash of light, and then the world went white. Eric squinted his eyes, but could only make out gray shapes against the featureless world. He reached up to his throbbing head, feeling the warm wetness of blood.

"Special Agent Comstock?" Came a voice, tiny and distant as if coming through an ancient telephone. All around him, the world buzzed painfully.

"Yeah." He said, his eyes slowly focusing into view. Washed out color began to manifest and within a few seconds, he could see the gray-haired man sitting low in the make-shift benches across from him. Dressed in a grey suit without the jacket, the man looked at Eric's head, concern across his face.

"You look like crap, Eric." The man called over the rush of air, his voice sounding more normal.

Eric blinked a few times, then recognition hit. "Director?" He said in shock.

"Glad to see you remember who signs your paychecks." The graying man said with a sarcastic smile.

Eric looked around the olive-drab helicopter that he was strapped into. He looked out the large bay window next to him, seeing trees stream by. "Where are we? What happened?"

"We're flying into Fort Bragg. We left RDU just a little while ago." The FBI director explained in a semi-shout. "All they had available was this Coast Guard Chopper. As for what happened, you were pulled unconscious out of the FBI's regional office by fire fighters just a few minutes before the whole building collapsed."

"Collapsed?" Eric called, his head raging. "What happened?"

"Pihc." The director said simply. "We have visual confirmation of him now, on US soil no less." He looked over his shoulder at the two pilots behind him, then undid his seatbelt. He shifted his weight carefully in the jerking chopper and sat down next to Eric. "Your case just got bumped to top priority, Comstock." He looked down at Eric with some remorse. "I wish I could say congratulations, but, well..."

"What about Masters?" Eric asked, fighting against the seatbelts to turn to the director. "What about the VGM? If it's Pihc then we need to..."

"The VGM has other problems than Pihc right now." The director said, calming Eric down. "I need your debriefing now, before we get to Bragg. You and I have got to get the FBI's house in order."

"Now? Us?" Eric gawked. "Sir, I'm the laughing stock of the FBI. I'm like Moulder off of the X-Files, only less respected."

"You're an FBI undercover agent." The director said with some pride. "And you're the bureau's only expert on these aliens. And you are escorting me to a meeting with the Joint Chiefs."

Eric's eyes went wide. "I'm what?"

"We came by Raleigh specifically to pick you up." The director explained. "We are meeting with the Joint Chiefs because the VGM case and the alien ordeal have been turned over to the military. By executive order."

"What?!" Eric screamed.

"This has gotten political." The director carried on, unbothered by Eric's volume. "I don't know why, but the military suddenly got very interested in what's going on. I've gotten rumors that the Army suspects Pihc and his men of beginning a troop build-up within the borders of the United States."

"That's impossible." Eric yelled.

"So is stopping time for half a week." The director replied, stalling Eric's protests. "Eric, decisions are about to made that are going to determine the US's policy regarding extraterrestrial contact. And if there is actually troop build up, then the military..." The director looked away. "I know you think highly of the VGM. From everything I've read, from your reports and others, I have to admit they seem like good guys. But we have got to decide how we are going to present this whole thing to the military."

"What are they prepared to do?" Eric yelled. But as he did, he felt a shift in the weight. The helicopter was beginning its descent.

"If they think the VGM is in any way connected, for ill or for good, with Pihc and the other aliens, they may consider them a threat to national security." The director said over the whipping wind. "I'll let you do the math."

The small military helicopter dropped down out of the thick clouds, aiming its bloated metal belly at the single landing pad in the middle of a field. The wheels popped out like tiny legs and the giant beast dropped to the ground, landing squat on the tarmac. The glass door on the side was flung open gracelessly, exposing to the two FBI members to a team of armed men waiting patiently at the edge of the landing pad.

The Director of the FBI got out of the helicopter first, leaving Eric by the door. He started across the gray tarmac. In his hand, he held out his badge and ID. From the front of the military entourage stepped the commanding officer. "Sir." Said the sergeant, as the Director took the last two steps. "By order of the Commander and Chief, we are to take into custody any material you have on the Video Game Masters cult and escort you to a meeting with the Joint-Chiefs."

"Understood, Sergeant." Said the Director, without a hint of reservation. "Let me get my bag and my agent and I will accompany you."

The Director walked back through the gale of wind to the chopper and grabbed a brown satchel from behind the pilot's seat. "Sir, we can't lead them to the VGM." Eric implored quietly, leaning in so that only the director could hear him.

"I know." The director said, scratching his chin, trying to think quickly. "You know the plan, though. Just let me do the talking and we'll all make it through this." He said, standing up. "Now come on. These are not men you want to keep waiting."

Eric hopped out behind the director and followed him to the waiting team of army men. As they all turned towards the far end of the giant concrete landing pad, the helicopter immediately flared to life, the wind carrying it up into the sky and past the clouds again. Eric watched it lift off, his heat sinking as he watched it escape.

He turned when he felt the director's hand on his shoulder and followed the man. The two were led by the military team to a small dugout-sized building at the far end of the tarmac. Rolling up like a garage door, a dark stairway greeted the two. The director glanced at Eric then started down the steps.

The two were led along a string of uncomfortably narrow underground hallways with too few lights, ultimately being delivered to a single metal door. When the military officer opened it, Eric was awed by the vast array of highly decorated military commanders and government officials sitting at a blue lit table in a wide situation room.

Eric paused at the door, stunned to see faces he had only previously seen on television but the director subtly grabbed his elbow and moved him to the far end of the table. As soon as he and the director sat, the door was sealed and a man at the head of the table in an army uniform stood. "Gentlemen, this meeting is officially marked classified. No information is to leave this room without proper clearance. Understood?" Everyone around the table nodded.

"Should I even be in here?" Eric asked, leaning into the director as he glanced at the numerous pieces of high-tech gadgetry that littered the borders of the room. The director raised a cautionary hand.

"Ever since the temporal disturbance that occurred in May, the US government has been carefully monitoring any and all paranormal activity in the US." The man started, still at the head of the table in the dimly-lit room. "We have specifically been concerned with the 'Video Game Masters', a semi-magical cult based out of Raleigh North Carolina. As you all know, it is the general consensus that this organization has had dealings with the entity responsible for the time-displacement."

The man looked up, looking directly at the FBI director and Eric. "The FBI, in conjunction with the Homeland Security department, was given the task of infiltrating the organization and garnering as much data as they could on this group, to access their threat potential to the security of the nation. Their under-cover agent, after an unsuccessful attempt to bring their leaders into custody, has been brought here to speak about the cult from direct contact."

Eric blinked in confusion but the director spoke up. "Through months of direct contact, Special Agent Eric Comstock, with the bureau's Cults and Mystics division, has identified that the VGM is not a threat to security, but actually in opposition to the real threat. That threat being the extraterrestrials outlined in file 86-B. Special Agent Comstock will give you a brief overview of the ETs as we now have visual confirmation of them."

"Visual?" Asked a general in the middle of the other side of the long table. "They've actually manifested recently?"

The director looked at Eric. The young agent swallowed and stood up. "Um, twice, actually." He stumbled out nervously before the gathering of military and political men. "The first time was a few days ago, in an isolated and direct confrontation with the VG…I mean Video Game Masters. The confrontation took place in a general warehouse in Raleigh North Carolina. The second confrontation took place," Eric looked at his watch. "Roughly two hours ago, at the FBI offices in Greensboro North Carolina."

Eric stopped and looked down at his hands, thinking quickly. "Okay." He said nervously. "The VGM, that's the Video Game Masters, seems to be the only organization that has taken an active stance against the aliens to date. All the other mystical groups seem unable, unwilling, or unaware of the threat posed by the aliens. And to date, the VGM has not openly admitted their actual contact with the aliens." He managed to get out coherently.

"How is it that the VGM are fighting these aliens? Effectively, I mean?" Asked a general that Eric didn't recognize in a uniform he could only assume was naval. "What makes them so effective versus other groups?"

"Well, they combat the aliens largely with unarmed techniques and archaic weaponry." Eric thought that would be met with laughter, but no one cracked a smile. "The aliens seem to be somewhat impervious or otherwise unaffected to most projectile weapons, including almost all guns."

"Can we see the pictures please?" Asked an older man with sadistic eyes. He glanced back almost demonstratively at the man who sat at the head of the table. "If we're suddenly so concerned about the aliens rather than the domestic threat."

Eric blinked, then looked at the director. But as he did, the lights in the room dimmed and a digital projector shot an image onto the wall. Eric turned to the picture and nodded.

"This is Trebor." He started, breathing out with a ragged burst. "Trebor appears to have some type of relationship with one of the VGM's highest ranking members, a man named Vincent Pierce. Their relationship is magical in origin, but very few amongst the VGM are willing to speculate or even discuss their history. The two seem nearly identical in physical capability and in appearance, save for hairstyle and their general attire. But where Vincent seems cold and emotionless, Trebor is described to be very cruel and sadistic." A new picture appeared.

"This is Cye." Eric continued. "Up until recently, this was the only female member of the group. She, like Trebor, has a relationship with a member of the VGM, but it's a lower ranking member, one Elizabeth Phillips or Beth as she's called. Cye seems to be a fairly new addition to the aliens' team as the VGM has only encountered her once or twice. Almost nothing is known about her." Another picture.

"This is Yadiloh. Not much is known about him. He is the only member of the aliens who uses a firearm. It seems to be an old-style revolver, but its rounds are of a type that FBI Forensics has not yet been able to identify. It is confirmed that both he and Trebor were present during the time displacement in May."

One of the generals spoke up. "Why the gray skin? Is it paint?"

"That's unknown." Eric said, feeling inadequate about the answer. "Trebor and Cye are the only two with skin that isn't gray. It's been speculated that it's due to the age of the aliens, since Trebor and Cye both seem to be less than ten years old. Another is the apparent lack of a human equivalent."

"What do you mean, 'human equivalent'?" Asked a general two seats up from the director.

"Well, both Cye and Trebor have human counter-parts in the VGM, Beth Phillips and Vincent Pierce, respectively." Eric tried to explain, while struggling to keep his knees from giving out. "And they're referred to as 'alternates', though it's never been fully explained, not to me at least, what that means. But no one knows who or if Yadiloh or the others have counter-parts or not." Without another question, the next picture appeared.

"This is Brenard. Like Yadiloh, there's almost no information on him aside that he's said to speak with a strong Latin accent. This is in keeping with his attire, but no speculations have been afforded. Like Yadiloh, he has the same gray skin that you had pointed out. There's been some speculation that Yadiloh and Brenard may both be very old, since at least their attire, is very ancient. If their attire is indicative of their age, then that would mean that Yadiloh was over a hundred and thirty odd years old and Brenard is several thousand years old." Eric chuckled at the idea. No one else did. He swallowed his laughter.

Another flash. This time, all eyes locked on the figure.

"This is Ecnilitsep." Eric said, with some reservation in his voice. "She is a complete enigma. The VGM have made no speculations concerning her, except that she seems to be the dominant personality. All data we have on her has come from second-hand accounts by the VGM's first and only encounter from a few days ago, and then what little we saw tonight. We don't know who she is or what she is or where she comes from. All we do know is that she seems to be the one in charge."

"Now does she have a counter-part or whatever?" Asked a man dressed in a suit with a White House emblem on his chest.

"Not that we know of." Eric said, certainly. "There's no suspicion that she has a counter-part."

"But she has the same gray skin as them?" Pressed the man.

"In her case, that seems to be her natural pigment, rather than a magical affliction like with the others." The interrogator nodded and Eric continued. There was one last flash.

"This is Pihc." Eric said, swallowing hard. "Pihc is the leader of the group, except for maybe Ecnilitsep as his commander. He is very ruthless, intelligent and very powerful. His origins and history are almost impossible to pinpoint, but it is known that he and the VGM's leader, Chip Masters, have had dealings before. Some speculations have been made regarding his clothing style being vaguely similar to that of Chip Masters, the leader of the VGM." Another flash.

This time, a collage of three images appeared. Two were of men, one in form-fitting armor, carrying a massive, ornate axe, while the other looked like a biker mixed with a cowboy. The third image was of a woman dressed in accentuating armor, swiping a saber at her off-image foe. "These three are unknown quantities." Eric said. "We do not know who they are or where they came from. Indeed, we've never even seen them before tonight."

"It's a god-damned invasion." Breathed a general at the far end of the table. Eric wanted to say something, but he sat back down as the picture faded and the lights rose slightly.

"Okay." Said a gray-haired general, getting the whole table to turn to him. "We have evidence of spatial anomalies in two separate locations in the US. One near San Francisco California, the other up near Redmond Washington. They match the same type of disturbances that were measured when these aliens were supposed to appear a few days ago and tonight. This clearly indicates a troop movement onto US soil. My question is, what are the chances a direct assault on the aliens will be successful?"

All eyes turned to Eric.

"Well, uh, it's, uh, it's very doubtful." He finally managed to get out, regretting the look he saw in the old man's hopeless eyes. "Even if they had a base of operations and we could pin-point it, Pihc's forces seem nearly invulnerable to any type of attack save for magical."

"So this 'Pihc' character was behind the time-anomaly in May?" Asked a Navy general.

"That's the prevailing theory, sir." Eric said, his voice shaking a bit.

"And they now seem determined to get the VGM and only the VGM?" The general said.

Eric looked at the director, then back to the older man. "Uh, I guess."

"Well, then." The man said, closing up his folder. "I see only one solution."

"Agreed." Came a few voices around the table.

Eric looked at the faces, taken back by the solemn resolve he saw. "What solution is that?" He asked.

The general turned in his chair to look at the young agent. "Son, if the aliens are here for the VGM, then if the VGM is no longer with us, then they may very well leave of their own accord."

Eric's face went cold.

"It is the decision of this meeting," The general said. "That the Video game Masters are in fact, by their relationship to these aliens, be it antagonistic or whatever, but they are a clear and present danger to the United States of America."

"But," Eric started. "Only the president can…" he stumbled out, his voice a whisper.

"Calm down." The director said to Eric quietly. "Remember the plan."

"Contact the SWAT team that's standing-by." The general said, pointing to one of the aides around the room. "Tell them they have clearance."

"Well that was harrowing." Michelle said as she slammed the door of Tim's car, looking over the hood of the Jim who stood up across from her. "I mean, my god, we spent twenty minutes sitting in that gas station parking lot. We could have gotten ticketed for loitering or something."

"Oh shove it." Tim groaned, getting out of the driver's seat. "We needed people to be available for a fast getaway. Like it wasn't needed."

"Tim," Michelle stopped and turned around to him, staring up at the Vgm who towered over a foot above her. "Do you simply not remember that I can do more than four times as many push-ups as you in one go? Did you know I've fought Brenard or Trebor or any of Pihc's alternates more times than you are years old?"

"Here it comes." Ben grumbled, covering his ears as he kept walking.

"I can fight!" The long-haired girl screamed. "I've been…"

"Hush." Chip said, rubbing the back of his head. "I don't want to hear it. I really, really don't want to hear it."

"Well, this hasn't exactly been our night." Jessica pointed out as she led the group towards the double doors into the training room of the warehouse.

"First we get busted up by the council, next we get arrested, then Pihc and Ecnilitsep show up." She opened the door and the whole team filed in. "I mean, what else could possibly happen tonight?"

As Jared flipped on the lights, the windows of the warehouse flared to life. Lining the walls on either side of the long training hall were armed SWAT officers, their guns trained on the VGM.

"You are under arrest." Called the nearest of the dark blue-clad man as the whole cascade of men burst towards them.

Emily's hands started to go up, but Chip grabbed her right arm, yanking it down. "Don't you dare." He glared. He glanced over his shoulder as SWAT officers swarmed out of the woodwork from within the garage. With a fast kick, Tim slammed the double doors shut as Dan grabbed up a metal barbell from the corner and shoved it through the handles. Chip threw himself through the group, slamming his shoulder against the near wall. He held up his hands shouting "***Wall!***"

At the sound of his voice, a barrier formed nigh-invisibly in front of him, stopping the approaching SWAT officers. Groups of armed men rushed in towards the side of the group. Jessica and Vincent both held up their hands, shouting out as well, forming a continuous barrier all around the VGM.

"***How the fuck do these people know where we are?***" Chip exclaimed as the closest SWAT officer blasted the wall with a burst from his machine gun. "***I mean, Jesus Christ, an inter-dimensional demon can't find us on a good day, but these bastards know our exact god-damned location?***"

"Drop the shields. You are under arrest." Called a man as he reached for a grenade dangling from his tactical vest.

"***Okay.***" Chip said, his mind racing. "***Ben, Jon, we're going to need cover fire. Dan, Mich, Jim. You guys clear us a path to the stairwell.***" He looked back for nods, getting them. "***Everyone stay close. We make for the third floor, for the exit in the library.***"

"What about Aria?" Beth yelled over the continuing gunfire.

"***I'll get her.***" Vincent called, straining against the hail of bullets striking against his invisible barrier.

"We're going to the library?" Sophia chimed up. "What exit's up…"

"Don't worry." Emily said, grabbing her wrist. "Just stick close."

"***Feel free to take out anybody else you might run into along the way.***" Jessica yelled as well, dropping down to her knee as the magic field buckled under the force of the gunfire.

"Does that include nobody?" Shane asked weakly.

"***I'm almost done here!***" Jessica yelled, the magical barrier in front of her beginning to turn prismatic, its form fading.

"On the count of now." Tim yelled.

"***Now!***" Vincent shouted.

The three Vgms dropped their hands, while Tim threw his forward. "***Flash!***" He yelled as a blinding light exploded out at the SWAT. As the men reeled back from the intense light, the group burst into motion.

Ben threw out his arms, a pair of machine gun pistols dropping into his waiting hands.

"Drop your weapons and…" Came the call of the lead officer even as he tried to see through his blindness but it was too late. Ben straightened out his arms and began to fire. A burst of fire from each of Ben's hands and a pair of officers dropped.

"***Ben, keep the death toll to a minimum.***" Chip yelled back as he rushed towards the stairwell. "***We don't want a massacre on our hands.***"

"I think that ship has sailed." Jon said from beside Ben, drawing out his revolver. The officers along the far wall blasted randomly with their guns, but the bursts of fire mostly shot off target. As the machine guns rattled away, the bullets reflected off a blue energy ball that appeared around Ben, encompassing Jon as well.

The sniper threw himself to the ground, diving to the right as more SWAT officers unloaded their clips. His gun rattled like steel bearings inside a lead pipe as he aimed and shot, more officers' falling. Behind him, an officer ran towards him, his machine gun ready. Ben turned towards the officer and threw himself forward, rolling over the ground in a fast series of tumbles. He came up in a crouch just in front of the SWAT officer. With a fast punch, Ben cracked the guy just above the knee, then sent himself driving into the man with a low slide, knocking him off the ground.

Ben came up as Jon rushed behind him, reloading rounds into his pistol. "Next time you do that force field thing, don't jump away without warning me first!" The cowboy yelled, flinching as a bullet rang close. "Come on!" He called, leading Ben towards the stairwell.

Ranging ahead of the rest of the VGM, Dan and Michelle kept low. Dan tackled the first SWAT officer he came to, taking the larger man down to the ground. Michelle swept past both of them. She engaged the next officer, catching the man in the side with a fast punch when he tried to connect with a wide swing of his machine gun stock. She came back around with a kick to his other side, then a hard smack to the man's helmet, then tore her silver whip from her belt, lashing the man across the head. Its metal teeth tore through his helmet, cutting deeply across his head.

Jim leapt high into the air over both. As he went up, his body suddenly angled back down. "***Rising Tackle!***" He shouted, just before his fist burst into flames and drug him down ahead of the fighting. He slammed into the ground just in front of the other SWAT officers, then flipped over at them, his heel flashing with bone-smashing power as he shouted "***Jaguar Kick!***"

"The SWAT team has already moved on the VGM's warehouse." The director called over the roar of the helicopter as the propellers began to pick up speed. "We're going to need to have a plan for the military boys by the time we land."

"We've got an immediate solution. It's after that that's the problem. We've just got to figure out how to get them away from the military completely." Eric called as the helicopter began to lift, making him grab for a handhold. "I, I just don't know how we can get them entirely out of their jurisdiction."

The director stared off into space for a moment, then looked at Eric. "How many men do you trust at the bureau?"

The door to the garden burst open, startling Aria. She looked up, as Vincent rushed in. "I heard shooting but I thought it was Ben." She said, taking the headphones of her CD player off, standing up from the indoor rose bush. "What's going…" She started, but before she could say anything more, he grabbed her up in his arms and rushed back towards the door. Two SWAT officers were coming through.

Vincent slammed his foot into the door, knocking the metal edge into the closer officer. The other whipped around, but Vincent was already spinning in a tight circle. His left heel caught the man's gun at the barrel, knocking it away, then his right foot came around, catching the man on across the face. The blow spun his helmet around, knocking him to the ground.

By the time he landed, Vincent was already rushing through the doorway, carrying Aria in his arms.

Chip rushed into the stairwell ahead of the others, jumping forward. As he did, he suddenly flipped around, his body inverting upside down as he landed on the bottoms of the stairs above. Rushing up along the stairs while everyone else followed in a normal fashion, he came bounding up to the second floor landing where two SWAT members were waiting.

Chip got as close as he could before they recovered from seeing him running on the ceiling, then jumped back down, his body flipping again. As he landed, he spun around like a top, shouting "***Tatsu-maki-sempu-kyaku!***" The blow landed on the first SWAT officer, but then Chip disappeared, reappearing right behind the guy. He grabbed the guy's gun arm and slammed it against the wall. Throwing his head down, he kicked backwards, catching the guy in the mouth. Gathering himself in a crouch, Chip leapt up, fist first, catching the man in the jaw as he shouted "***Sho-ryu-ken!***"

Chip landed first, then the guard landed, unconscious.

"Come on." Jessica said as she rushed past Chip, leading the VGM. From the back of the procession, Tim watched the others. He waited for Vincent to come rushing by, Aria in his arms, then he waved Ben and Jon on through. The last one at the base of the stairs, he held out his hands. "**Spirits of fire, ignite this well, give us protection and send 'em to hell!**" He said, pushing his hands towards the stairwell. The steps turned red-hot as the banisters caught fire. The SWAT officers that came running up behind skidded to a halt. They readied their guns, but Tim was already disappearing in the distance.

As he barreled up after Vincent, Tim's cell began to ring. He whipped it out, not even getting the chance to speak. "Chip?" Came Eric Comstock's voice over the cell phone as soon as it picked up.

"Sorry." Answered Tim as he ran. "It's me, Pierce. Aren't you the guy that ratted us out?"

"Listen, I know the VGM might not trust me right now, but I don't have time to explain." Eric called as Tim ran. "Tell Chip to gather the VGM and meet me at Crossroads Plaza as soon as he can. And hurry."

"Riiight." Tim nodded sarcastically, slamming the phone shut. He came into the third floor, unbothered by the din of battle that preceded the group. Tim rushed around the side of the door, paying no heed to the several unconscious SWAT officers that lay about. "Chip!" Tim called.

"***I'm busy!***" Chip yelled, punching the light switch in the library. The plastic broke and Chip pulled the fragments out, hitting a small red button next to the actual device. Across the room, the center bookshelf popped open a few inches. "***Go!***" He shouted to Sophia and the others. "***Follow the stairs.***"

Jim rushed at the stairs, then stopped. He looked at Chip. "Shouldn't this just open up into the space over the parking lot?" He asked. "I mean, that's the wall and so..."

"***Jim, thinking's not your strong suit, so just run.***" Chip yelled angrily, turning back to Tim. He took a deep breath, then sighed it out. "We're kind of in the middle of an emergency, Tim." He said, the magic releasing from his voice. "What is it?"

"Eric called me on my cell." The other Vgm said, holding the door shut as Chip started to fasten the long procession of heavy gauge locks along the door. "He said for us to meet him at Crossroads Plaza, ASAP."

"Riiight." Chip nodded, getting the final lock.

"That's just what I said." Tim admitted as the two rushed towards the far book shelf. "But he did sound sincere. And I think he said he could explain everything." The mage offered.

Chip watched as the last of the VGM rushed into the stairwell behind the wall. "Come on." He said, sliding into the dark passage. "I hate to admit it, but I would like to know why the FBI was after us before and now it's SWAT."

"Want to give Eric the benefit of the doubt?" Tim asked as he pulled the bookshelf shut. He listened as it sealed shut with a gasp of air, then turned into the darkness.

Chip held out his hand, a white candle appearing in his grasp, giving light to the impossibly narrow brick stairwell. "***Not really.***" He mumbled.

"What have you got in mind?" The director asked, as Eric closed the phone.

"Well, if we can get them to Fayetteville airport, then maybe we can smuggle them out of the country." Eric started.

"The military will track the flights if there's a last-minute party of a dozen plus." The older man said as waited at the large airport's passenger pick-up.

"What if we broke them up into three or four groups?" Eric asked, fighting to get the phone inside his jacket pocket. "One goes to Fayetteville, one goes to Greensboro, one goes to RDU."

"RDU's risky." The director said, thinking as a car pulled up to the curb. "Hell, what am I saying, this whole plan's risky." He moved around the valet as the college-aged youth stood up.

"We'll make it happen." Eric said with a weak confidence, getting into the passenger-side door. "We've got to."

"Let's just hope this little plan fools Pihc and his guys as much as it fools the military." The director said as the car roared to life.

The metal tool rack rolled away from the wall a fraction of an inch, letting Jim and Michelle peer into the garage. Light cast a thin line over their eyes as they looked out at two SWAT officers standing in front of the garage door. "How many do you think there are?" Jim asked.

Michelle thought for a moment, then reached out with her mind. "***Scan.***" She said, with a flick of her fingers. But when nothing happened, she sighed. "They're too far." She whispered, her voice returning to normal.

"I've got an idea." Emily said, peeking her head around beneath Jim's head.

"What are you going to do?" The acrobat asked. "We need line of sight to use any of the teleportation moves."

"***I'm not going to teleport.***" She said, her eyes filling with power. She formed a triangle with her fingers, then closed her eyes. A green bolt of electricity shot away from her hands, hitting both SWAT officers. They both froze.

"Good job." Jessica said, pushing through the door. She rounded it quickly, ready for any others, but saw none. She rushed over to the two SWAT guys and grabbed their cuffs off their harnesses, handcuffing them before they could move.

"What are you doing?" Jon asked, coming up next to her.

"Restraining them so they don't get away and give away our location." She answered.

Jon looked at the second officer she handcuffed, then punched him in the face, sending him sprawling to the ground. "They could still shout." He said as he punched the other officer.

"Load up into the cars!" Chip called, the last one to rush through the doors. "We're making a break for it."

"What about my bike?" Jon started.

"Can it carry five people?" Jim asked, getting in with Shane.

"If they hold on real tight." He handed back. He glanced between the bike and the others, then grumbled as he rushed over to get into Emily's car.

"Tim, give us some cover." Chip yelled, getting behind Tim's steering wheel. The tall Vgm moved to the garage bay doors and put his hands together. He closed his eyes and began to chant. "Let's hope that boy's got enough power to buy us an escape, or this is going to be a short drive." Chip mumbled from the front seat.

Chip watched as Tim held out his hands, a strange shaking of power reverberating over the doors of the garage as it rolled up, revealing the Raleigh nighttime. He turned back to the cars as they rumbled to life, nearly falling over himself as he tried to open the passenger side door. He fell down into the seat and looked over at Chip, swallowing hard. Sweat poured off his face, his skin pale. "We've got sixty seconds before they'll notice. Go."

"Done and done." Chip said, shifting the car into gear. He looked down at the pedals. "Which one's the gas?" He asked just before the car shot into motion.

Out of the late night darkness, the three cars pulled up the center of the Crossroads Plaza parking lot. The giant shopping center was empty at the late hour, devoid of even the occasional late-night driver in the sparsely lit parking lot. The solitary street lamps lit up the dark night sky, encloaking the shopping center in a veil of the half-lit sky against the impending storm.

Emily stepped out of her car, shivering a bit as thunder rocked the sky above. "This was where it all started." She said to Michelle as the VGM unloaded. "This is where Jared and I first ran into Trebor." She shivered, but not from the cold. "In all that time, I've never come back here." Michelle had nothing to say.

"All Vgms, on-line!" Called Chip, as he stepped out of Tim's blue four-door.

"Jessica, on-line!"

"Vincent, on-line."

Chip was about to speak but stopped and looked across the car's roof over at Tim. The mage glanced at him, lost. Chip motioned to him with his hand. "Oh come on. I'm right here, for crying out loud. I was fucking next to you the whole way from downtown." Tim implored. Chip gave him a serious look. Tim sighed and looked away. With no enthusiasm he mumbled, "Tim, on-line."

"Thank you." Chip said, with a tight-lipped and sarcastic grin. He turned back to the group, standing before them. "Alright." He said, cordially, getting everyone's attention immediately. "Everyone, I've got good news and I've got bad news."

"As long as there's some news." Michelle commented. "I'm getting a bit tired about getting dragged around this city without any type of explanation."

"What's the good news?" Sophia asked, meekly, her hands held together in front of her like a schoolgirl.

"Why don't we start with the bad news." Chip said, with a slight look of regret. He took a deep breath, then looked everyone in the eye. "As we were driving over here, I was on the phone with our contact, our own beloved Eric Comstock. Yes, the very same guy who got Vincent, Jessica, and me arrested earlier tonight. He says we're about to be deported."

Silence.

"Hmm." Ben said after a moment, finally shrugging. "Stranger things have happened."

"You're telling me." Dan agreed with Ben, downing more Dr Pepper. As he finished, Michelle stole the bottle from him and finished off the contents. She handed it back to Dan, burping slightly as she did.

"Deported?!" Screamed Jim. Everyone looked at him, surprised to see a giant grin on his face. "Woo-hoo!" He screamed as he began to jump around, doing his patented victory dance. "Suck it, you losers." Everyone continued looking at him, some hoping he'd explain, others hoping he wouldn't. "Sorry." He said, after realizing everyone was looking at him. "I just won a two hundred dollar bet."

"Collecting on it's gonna be a bitch, I imagine." Said Michelle, with a sharp look.

"Only as much as you are." Jim said in response. Dan and Jared grabbed Michelle as she lunged for Jim's throat.

"How long are we going to be gone?" Sophia implored, not handling the news well. "And why are we being kicked out of the country?" She sniffed back a hysterical tear. "Can we at least tell our parents?"

"You can't tell your parents." Jessica said as comfortingly, putting one hand on Sophia's shoulder. The youngest VGM pulled her shoulder away violently.

"Don't they have a right to know?" Sophia nearly yelled, clutching her jacket like it was her last shred of sanity.

"If they knew, they would be in danger." Vincent answered, his cold voice freezing Sophia to the bone.

She started to argue but Tim put his hand on her shoulder where Jessica's had been. "**Sleep.**" He said quietly. Sophia immediately lost consciousness, falling into Tim's arms.

"Agent Comstock, the guy who's helping us, insists that his operation with the FBI has been taken over by the military under executive order." Chip said, his sharp tone getting everyone's attention once again. "The military isn't going to arrest us; they're supposed to neutralize us. Eric's going to use the FBI's resources to get out us out of the country."

"So if we're out of the country, what's going to happen with Ecnilitsep and Pihc?" Jessica asked, glancing at Chip. "They're probably going to follow us."

"Why don't we just cross over to Crossworld?" Asked Michelle. "Let's get the hell out of Dodge and take Ecnilitsep on at Crossworld Castle. We had a pretty good thing going against Pihc."

"No dice." Tim took up. "With Pihc here, the first thing he did was seal off all magical routes off of earth. The whole place is locked down."

"Which is why we couldn't side-step into the FBI compound when Jon told us where they were being held." Dan offered up, pulling another bottle of Dr Pepper out of his denim jacket.

"And that's why we have to play this by Eric's rules." Chip said to the VGM. "I don't like this any more than you guys do, but he's our only chance. We're not going to make it out of the city without his help. He'll arrive in a matter of moments and we'll split into three different groups, be taken to three different airports leaving for three different locations."

As Chip said this, three huge vans appeared at the edge of the huge shopping center. The gathered VGM turned confrontationally towards the arriving vehicles, their silence steeling them all. The great giant vehicles barreled towards the group, sweeping up to half-surround the VGM. As the vans stopped completely, the passenger door in the lead van flew open. Eric Comstock jumped out. He stood before the group, his eyes immediately falling on Sophia. "Oh boy." He whispered. He looked away from her, smiling weakly at Chip. "Is she okay? Is everybody ready?" He asked hurriedly. "We need to go now. The military's being held up at the warehouse, but the director can't cover for you guys for long."

"I think we're ready." Chip said, as he looked back at the group. "Three teams." He continued to the VGM, concisely. "Each team will go to a different location. When the smoke's cleared, we'll return."

"If the smoke clears." Eric corrected as the group began to load into the vans. "There's no guarantee that this will end in the immediate future."

"It'll end." Came Vincent, his arms crossed across his chest. Eric looked at him, realizing he was the only one who had heard.

"What do you mean?" Eric asked, as the rest of the VGM loaded quickly into the vans. "Do you think the military's going to be able to drive out Ecnilitsep and her forces? Do you think..."

"All I said," Vincent said clearly, his low voice only reaching Eric. "Is that it will end."

CHAPTER 12

Reorientation

"Wherever any one is against his will, that is to him a prison."

—Epictetus

Jared, Ben, and Shane sat in the back of the large van, marveling at the comfort laid out before them. The interior was warmly designed with three rows of seats, with a small two-seater between the two front seats and the massive couch at the rear. "This is nice." The ninja remarked as he played with a rear air conditioning vent. He looked as Shane took out a portable CD player, while Ben popped out a pair of portable video game systems. He handed one to Jared and the two linked their green and black screens and began to play against each other.

Beth looked back at the three boys in the back, then sat down more permanently in the window side of the middle seats. She looked at Chip, smiling weakly. "You're handling this well." Chip said, taking her hand. "When everything started to happen, I got worried that…" He didn't finish his sentence.

Beth stared at him for a moment, then smiled warmly. "You've been doing a lot to toughen me up in the last six months." She said. "Give me some credit. I'm a bit tougher than I was."

"Maybe a bit." Chip smiled, getting a playful slap to the shoulder.

"I just don't understand why we can't go to Crossworld." Beth asked, a more serious tone taking over her voice. "We could find a way." She went on, mostly under her breath.

"It's kind of funny." Chip said, holding the pale girl's hand. She glanced at him, confused. "That you're more comfortable traveling to another world than you are with leaving your own country. That just strikes me as odd."

"I guess…I just feel at home there." Beth tried. She looked away, leaning her head against the window, her breath fogging up the glass.

"Here are your vouchers." Said the FBI agent in the passenger seat. He held out a handful of coupons to Jon and Dan as they sat in the middle seats of the van. "Take these to any airport desk and get the first tickets available out of the US. Any airline, any destination. These vouchers will be accepted."

"What if all the flights are full?" Dan asked, looking over the glossy slips of paper.

"It's mid-October." The FBI agent explained. "The chance that every flight is full is next to none." As he spoke, the van began to slow and the lights of the small airport loomed into view. "Alright. Here you are." He announced.

"It's still not clear to me why the military wants to kill us." Michelle said towards Eric as she sat next to Tim in the middle seat.

"Because," Eric said, mulling over a fist full of hand-written notes while he tried to talk. "The government is convinced that if you guys are dead, then Ecnilitsep will leave of her own accord, without any type of confrontation."

"So why is the military trying to kill us and the FBI trying to save us?" Continued Michelle. "It doesn't make sense. Isn't the FBI going to get into trouble for helping us out on this?"

"Probably," Eric half-laughed, looking at the driver. The driver chuckled almost stoically, but stayed quiet. "But if and when it hits the fan, it'll be my problem. This is all technically my call." He turned from the road back to Michelle. "You guys just need to worry about what you're going to do when you get to wherever you're going."

Jon sat on the plane, looking out over the placid blue ocean. He bent his head down a bit, looking out at the sharp contrast between the clear sky and the smoky clouds that filled the space above the pristine ocean. "Hey, Dan." The cowboy said, looking over at the Mormon next to him. Dan looked up with a smile, taking his headphones off. "What's with that line?" He asked, pointing at the clouds. "Is that like some magical barrier around the earth or something?"

Dan looked out the window, then looked at Jon with apprehension. "Yeah. It's called the dew point."

Jon looked back out, then back at Dan. "Oh." He said, sounding disappointed.

"I'm worried."

Dan turned and looked back at Emily where she sat with her head back, her eyes staring up into space. In the empty airplane, the five sat spread out, each occupying their own row of seats in the first-class cabin, while the stewardesses up at the front settled in for the pan-oceanic flight. "What about?" Dan asked, just as the lights dimmed for the simulation of night.

"Too much." Emily said with a sigh. "Pihc. Ecnilitsep. Getting kicked out of the country. Where the other teams are going. Too much." She closed her eyes, massaging her temples.

"Don't worry." Dan encouraged, getting a weak smile in return. "I assure you, everything is under control."

"Come on!" Yelled Chip as Ben and Jared rushed passed him in full sprint. Shane and Beth came up behind him, the long-haired girl practically running to keep up. Chip turned the corner to the terminal, practically shoving the tickets into the face of the woman behind the boarding desk. "Here." He breathed. "Did we make it?"

"Just barely." The woman said, moderately impressed as she accepted the tickets and began to tear the stubs. "Pre-flight is almost complete. Hurry up and get on board." She said, pointing at the door that led to the plane.

"Dibs on the window!" Ben yelled, bursting ahead of Jared.

The woman watched the two college-aged boys run, then looked at Chip. "Family?" She asked sympathetically.

"Thankfully, no." He said, accepting the ticket stubs and leading Beth and Shane onto the plane.

Jessica sat alone in the airport terminal, her black leather jacket draped in front of her arms. She looked up at the florescent world in the silence of the tiny international airport. She glanced up at the televised monitors as the large red numbers of the digital display counted away the minutes to the arrival of the plane.

As she looked up, Tim sat down next to her. He handed her a hot dog and smiled weakly. "All they had." He grinned apologetically. She smiled at him, then pushed her jacket into her lap to accept the food. She pulled her black hair around over her left shoulder, then tilted her head, biting into the ketchup-covered hotdog. "You okay?" He asked, his mouth half-full.

She nodded. "Yeah." She got out, wiping a smudge of ketchup from the corner of her lips with her thumb. "I'm just tired." She swallowed the ambitious first bite. "The last couple of days finally caught up with me, I guess."

"Well, we've got about another hour." He said, shoving the rest of his hotdog into his mouth. "I say you try to get a nap or something." He said, his words barely coherent.

Jessica yawned and looked away, glancing around the small, one-terminal airport. "I'm amazed this place has international flights, especially at this hour."

"Well, you know." Tim yawned, spreading his arms on the seatbacks to either side as he got comfortable. "Everybody wants to go on vacation." He leaned his head against the wall behind them and closed his eyes. Jessica turned to say something, but saw that he had passed out. She half-laughed, then rubbed her eyes. Yawning herself, she leaned up against the wall as well, closing her eyes.

Michelle leaned over the metal sink in the bathroom, running her hands under the cold water. "God-damned FBI." She grumbled angrily. "If Tim can't use his fairy magic to get my whip past security, so help me, I'll…"

The door burst open. Michelle whirled around ready for a fight, but Sophia threw herself into a bathroom stall, tears running down her face. Michelle watched for a moment, then glanced at the door. "Maybe I should go get Jessica." She whispered to herself.

Her feet carried her over to the bathroom stall instead. She stopped a few feet away and leaned towards the stall, apprehensive about getting closer. She glanced around the bathroom, as if hoping to find help, but the girls were alone. She glanced at the door, then just sighed acceptingly. "Fine." She grumbled, slumping her shoulders. She knocked on the door, trying to push away some of her callousness. "Sophia?" She asked, pushing gently on the door. "Is, are, is everything alright?"

The stall door opened and Sophia looked out at Michelle, tears staining her face. "My mom wasn't home." She said, her lower lip trembling.

"You tried to call her?" Michelle said, shocked. Her eyes went wide, a mixture of fury and fear seeming to rush across her face. "You intentionally did what Chip and Jessica both told you expressly not to do?" Sophia, recoiling from Michelle, nodded. "Oh, honey." Michelle suddenly grinned, holding out her arms. "I'm so proud of you."

"It's not funny, Mich." Sophia yelled back, shoving Michelle's shoulder. "I'm scared." She burst out, more tears coming. "So scared. Jesus, we're getting kicked out of the country. I mean, we're getting kicked out! And Pihc or whatever his name is trying to kill us. And now we've been split up…" She turned away, shaking as her tears continued.

As she moved, Michelle caught her hand. The girl turned back, but Michelle slid like a cat between her arms, embracing Sophia. Holding her tight, she pulled Sophia's head down to her shoulder, cradling her protectively.

And Sophia lost it. Every ounce of control she had broke down and she collapsed into Michelle's arms. Michelle leaned back against the stall door, supporting Sophia as she cried, shaking in her friend's arms.

"So this is England." Emily said, as she and Aria stepped through the door of the smallest hotel room either of them had ever seen. Two single beds filled the great majority of the poorly-wallpapered room with great ease, while the bathroom in the far corner was little more than a sink with a stand-up shower.

"I guess I was expecting more." Emily went on, touring the tiny room. She threw her jacket onto the bed farthest from the door, then turned to look out the window. There was nothing but a brick wall to see. She turned back from the window, more depressed than ever. She sank down on the edge of her bed, feeling even more lost.

Aria sat down on opposite her, feeling the mattress' firmness. "It's not too bad. We have beds." She said slowly as she looked into Emily' eyes, captivating the girl's gaze with her own eyes. "And beds are all we really need tonight."

Jon strolled down the seedy looking street, his large frame drawing the attention of the many unsavory types around him. The single street lamp at the far curve of the street flickered on and off, making the night's shadows seem even darker.

The biker came to a small mobile home parked in front of a burned-out lot; a woman sitting on the stoop with a deck of cards in her hands. "Ya wan sumtin?" The woman asked in a strange accent.

"I'm just looking." Jon said casually, stepping back from her innocently. "I left my bike in the states. I was seeing what type of scene there was around here."

"Ah, yur a bikah." The woman nodded, grinning through several missing teeth.

Jon looked down at the woman, taken back. "Yeah. Sure." He said, stepping to move on. He turned from the woman, only to see four stout men standing a few yards in every direction. Forming a semi-circle around him and the mobile home, he had no space to move away.

Jon looked at the men, then smiled. He took a deep breath, then popped his neck. The men started to crack their knuckles. Jon grinned widely, then threw his hands at the man farthest from him. "***Sonic Boom!***" He shouted.

To both Jon and the men's utter astonishment, a fast swirl of sound erupted from his hands, slamming into the guy and sending him flying to the ground. Jon stepped back from his hands as the rest of the men stepped back as well. "Son of a bitch, it works." He grinned. He turned to another man, throwing his hands at him again. "Sonic Boom!"

His hands slapped against each other, nothing happening.

Jon looked down at his hands as the remaining goons gathered closer. "Apparently not all the time." He said, just before the first punch landed.

Jim and Dan sat down at the hotel bar, the large acrobat massaging his neck with his hands. A round man with white muttonchops walked up across from them, an angry look on his face. "What are you two doing in here?" He snarled at the two college boys.

"We'll take something in a glass bottle with a high alcohol content." Dan said, covering his mouth as he burped. "We've had a really bad day and we're jet-lagged."

"I don't care." The man said, leaning across the bar at the unbothered Dan. "You don't get nothing," He turned and glared at Jim. "Until I see some IDs."

"Here." Jim said, taking out his wallet. He held it open as the plastic holder flipped out, revealing a wide array of driver's licenses, student account cards, bus passes, video rental cards, and other IDs, all with different names and ages, but the same grinning face in a variety of posses. "Pick whichever one you think looks the most legitimate and go with that."

The bar tender scrutinized the IDs for a moment, then turned away. He slammed a large glass bottle down on the bar, then stamped two glasses next to the bottle. "I'll be expecting a tip." He said, pointing a knobby finger at them before shambling away.

"How 'bout a breath mint." Jim mumbled as Dan screwed the lid off the glass bottle. "What is it?"

"Smells like bourbon, mixed with suck." Dan said, grimacing at the smell. He looked at Jim. They shrugged and filled the glasses. The two picked up the twin shot glasses and chinked them together. But as the glasses moved away from one another, Emily rushed up, grabbing the shots from Dan and Jim's hands with inhuman fluidity. With two seamless motions, she threw one drink after the other into the back of her mouth, swallowing before her head could even finish tilting back.

"Whoa." Jim said, his eyes wide with amazement. "You okay?"

"Oh yeah." Emily said, as she carelessly pushed Dan into the next seat so she could sit down between the two. Dan took a quick look around the hotel's pub, to make sure she wasn't attracting any unwelcome attention. An unsavory-looking patron, one of the few who was vaguely coherent, looked up at Dan after watching Emily and gave him a drunken thumbs up. Dan returned the signal, uncertain, then turned back.

"What's wrong?" Jim asked, after downing a spare shot of the liquid.

"That girl…" Was all Emily could say, pointing aimlessly back the way she had come. With her other hand, however, she poured herself a third glass of alcohol.

"Aria?" Jim asked, his eyes following Emily's extended hand, lowering it for her as he turned back to the bar. Emily nodded absently. "What's wrong with her?" Jim looked at Dan to try and give him an idea but Dan didn't get it.

"'What's wrong with her'?" Emily repeated rhetorically, her eyes locking onto Jim's with a death-stare. "Jim, she's a lesbian." She exclaimed quietly.

"And?" Dan asked. Emily's gaze swung around to him like a pair of laser beams but he was able to ignore them. "So are about half of the VGM's female population." Dan said, taking a shot. "Michelle is. I think Jessica counts. I don't know about Sophia."

"Yeah and there were even some suspicions about you, too." Jim added. "I mean, you don't have a decent boyfriend and you won't date any of us."

"But then we all kind of decided that you just simply had good taste." Dan countered to Emily.

"Well, you know," Jim pointed out as Emily's head turned to keep track of the volleying conversation. "Technically, none of them are lesbians. Even Mich is 'bi-sexual.'" He clarified as he filled both glasses again. "And everybody and their mother knows that Jessica's got the hots for Vincent."

"Except Vincent." Dan pointed out.

"And, male or female, Aria's hit on just about everyone."

"Twice." Dan announced with a mix of pride and shame as he held up his hand, not letting Emily rest. He took another shot, then turned to the cheerleader, whose head was practically spinning. "Why does that bother you?"

"She…she…she hit on ME!" Emily stuttered, having trouble dealing with that concept.

"Hit on you or propositioned you?" Dan specified, pairing a shot with a gulp of Dr Pepper.

"What do you mean?" The girl stumbled in a shocked stupor.

"Well," Jim took over. "If she wanted a date, that's hitting on you. If she wanted…how can I put this delicately?" Jim thought for a moment. "Dan, you want to handle this?"

"You're doing just fine." Dan said, taking another shot, immediately followed by a swig of Dr Pepper.

"If she wanted to, how can I…oh screw it. If she wanted to fuck you, that's propositioning you." Jim finished.

"I…" Emily started, still stuttering. "I think it was that second one."

"Well, good." Jim said, rubbing her lightly on the shoulder with friendly support. "You shouldn't feel alone." He said with a harmless grin as he stood up, leaning forward to reach under the bar. He glanced down the bar to make sure the bartender was still engrossed in a football game, then pulled out a glass, sitting down quietly. "I think she's propositioned just about everyone in the VGM, at least once." He went on, making Emily's eyes bug out.

"Oh yeah." Dan said, swiveling the poor girl's head around. "You should hear some of the stuff she wanted to do with Chip."

"Chip nothing." Jim laughed, clinking Dan's glass with his own. "You should hear some of the shit she and Jessica did. Man, I don't know how Michelle knows, but she's got all sorts of shit on them."

"It's because she's in the room next to them." Dan pointed out. "The walls at the warehouse aren't the thickest things in the world, you know."

"You're next to Chip." Jim said, with a sly grin, speaking across Emily as if she wasn't there. "Anything you'd like to share?"

"Not really." Dan nodded. He poured another round of drinks. All three friends grabbed a drink, chinked them together and took the shot.

"But that doesn't make any sense." Emily thought aloud after a moment, her eyes still closed from the alcohcl. "I thought she and Jessica hate each other. Or, not hate, but, you know. Why would they, you know, spend the night together so often if they don't like each other?"

"No idea." Dan said, staring at the bottom of his empty shot glass, deciding that had to change.

"It's to keep her under control." Jim answered, in between gulps of Dan's Dr Pepper. The other two looked at him, expecting a follow-up explanation. "Aria Geinosis is a nymphomaniac." He explained with a grin. "She's a complete sex fiend. If Jessica didn't keep her, as she says it 'satisfied', then Aria'd end up sleeping with anything that moved."

"Wow." Emily mumbled, with a frown.

"Wow's right." Jim repeated, a thoughtful grin spreading across his face. "She's a veritable succubus." He said, his grin getting wider with each second as he considered that idea.

"I don't know 'veritable' it is." Dan mumbled as he considered his empty shot glass.

"No." Jon said, holding a bag of frozen peas against his swollen black eye. Sitting around the stoop of the mobile home with the woman and the four goons, they passed a brown bottle around, all of them suffering the effects of the fight. "I'm telling you, we pay the bill a check."

"See, 'ere, we pay the check wid a bill." Said the stringy little guy across the way from Jon.

"Yeah, but that doesn't make sense." Jon said, taking his turn at the bottle. He took a heavy swig, his head spasming from the swallow as he passed it on. "But then, you guys drive on the wrong side of the road, so who am I kidding."

"You da ones dat driv on de righ side." Said the round man to his left. "Don be tellin' me da leff side ain't de righ side."

Jon blinked for a moment, then shrugged. "Yeah, okay." He allowed as the others started to laugh.

Tim collapsed onto his double bed, covering as much of it as his six foot frame would stretch. As soon as his stretching had stopped, his snoring began. Jessica and Sophia were left at the door to the bedroom, staring in awe. "How does he do that?" Sophia asked, in amazement. "It takes me half an hour just to get into bed."

"I know." Jessica nodded, equally as amazement. "Vincent's the same way." Jessica realized what she had said and turned away quickly. Sophia followed her out of Tim's room, her dulled mind trying to work in spite of the early morning.

"I wonder where everybody is." The small girl thought aloud, sitting down on the giant couch in the living room. "I mean, I wonder where they went and all? I wonder if everyone's okay."

"They'll be fine." Jessica said slowly. But a door opened and she looked down the small hallway to the other bedroom in the Caribbean hotel's suite as Michelle stepped out from the room. Dressed in a skin-tight outfit that accentuated ever curve and motion of her body, the girl spread her arms, opening herself up for appraisal. The skirt was so short that it seemed to perpetually threaten to ride up beyond her hips, while the top dipped down in a sharp V to reach her navel.

Jessica just stared. "Where are you going?" Sophia managed to get out as Michelle headed for the door.

"We're in the Caribbean, aren't we?" She answered with a smile, grabbing up one of the four room keys on the kitchenette counter. "Just because we're here during a crisis doesn't mean I'm not going to enjoy myself." She stepped out the door, stopping just before she closed it. "Don't wait up." She said, just before disappearing.

Chip sat low in the corner of the tiny hotel room, staring aimlessly out through the head-sized window at the expansive Japanese city. The reclusive hotel was designed like a traditional Japanese inn, but was equipped with all the features of a regular hotel, minus the beds. Five futons were laid out on the floor, with pillows at the opposite end from the bundled heavy blankets.

"Why do girls take such long showers?" Shane remarked, as he unloaded the contents of his pockets into a small pile next to his mat.

"For real." Ben agreed, unloading his jacket. As he dropped various knick-knacks, he finally produced a pair of black guns.

Shane glanced down when he heard them fall on the ground, then did a double double-take. He looked at Ben, his eyes wide. "Jesus, Ben. Don't you go anywhere without guns?" He exclaimed as Ben picked up the pistols. "What the hell ARE those, anyway?"

"These?" Ben asked, innocently. "Oh, just a little plastic insurance." He said, sliding the clips out and producing rounds from his jacket pockets.

"Yeah, but..." Shane tried. "Aren't guns, like, illegal in Japan?"

"So is street-racing. And why were you so excited to come here again?" Ben shot back with a grin, loading the clips of his pistols. Shane was about to speak, but stopped. He just nodded in sheepish agreement.

"I think you both are crazy." Jared said, shaking his head as he sprawled on his own mat. He situated himself on the thick padding, but then looked up at their leader. During the exchange, Chip continued to lean against the wall of the hotel room. His golden katana was stretched across his body, from the floor to his right shoulder. Behind his opaque sunglasses, thoughts raced through his head. "What's wrong?" Jared asked in a whisper under Ban and Shane's continued conversation.

Chip started back from his wondering mind, glancing at the ninja. "I don't remember which van Vincent got into." Chip said, turning his gaze away.

"He's probably with Jessica." Jared offer, looking away as he searched for a comfortable position on his tiny mattress. "Don't worry."

"I can't." Chip admitted hesitantly, still thinking. "If he…if Vincent were to realize that he had an opportunity to go toe to toe with Pihc, or worse, with Ecnilitsep, do you really think he'd pass it up?" He asked, looking down at Jared intently. The casually-dressed ninja looked back up at Chip, unable to respond.

"I hope you're right, Jared." Chip said, worry filling his voice. "I hope he's with Jessica. I really do. But…" He turned away, his gaze once again turned out to the neon glow of the boundless city beyond the window. "I've been going over our leaving again and again. And I just…" His voice stopped. He took a deep breath, his thoughts coming out with a sigh. "I'm afraid Vincent may have done something very, very foolish."

CHAPTER 13

Existential Rape

"Like fountains of sorrow, the faces are crying,
I'm witnessing all of their pain.
Death is so final for only the living,
The spirit will always remain.
Bury me deep just to cover my sins,
My soul is redeemed as the journey begins."

—Ozzy Osbourne, Back on Earth

The small pool of blood on the concrete floor grew, forming a rich crimson circle. In the echoing darkness of the giant warehouse, still showing the chaotic devastation of the Vgms' fight with Pihc and Ecnilitsep, Vincent squeezed his forearm, letting more blood drain out of his flesh, finishing the intricate diagram, leaving clear the five-pointed star in the center, the ominous space of importance.

The Vgm stepped back from the blood, holding his head as a wave of dizziness passed over him. He swayed a bit, then fought through it, steeling his mind as he moved around the circle. He came to the first of the eight candles around the soupy design, drawing out a box of matches from within his trench coat. Striking a match, Vincent lit the first candle, then picked it up and carried it with him. He set all the candles ablaze before returning the first to its place.

Standing before the circle, Vincent paused. He took a deep breath and swallowed his thoughts. He stared at the symbol for a moment. "Tim, your books better be right." He mumbled. Moving into the center, Vincent passed delicately over the emblems drawn in his own blood, heedless of the police tape and crime scene warning signs left so long ago.

Sitting on his knees in the center of the large star, Vincent put his hands on his legs and bent his head over. He took another deep breath, encased in the light of the silver moon as it filtered through the sparse windows. "Angels and ministers of grace, defend us." He quoted quietly. He took another breath, then focused.

The blood on the mat bubbled and ebbed, flowing from the splotchy design into flawless lines. The flames of the candles flickered in the stale air, their smoke bending inward over the design. In the corners of the room, the shadows grew. Darkness encroached upon the circle. The room beyond the eight candles and the blood-drawn symbol began to slowly fade away. All that remained was the silver light and the eight candles.

In the darkness, Vincent lifted his eyes. Glowing a deep, murderous red, his eyes stared into the void beyond while his emotions pumped through his veins. "**Ecnilitsep**." He declared clearly, his hard voice echoing into the infinite darkness.

Pihc leaned back against the huge red altar in the dark room, his black katana laying on the bowed surface near his hands. He stood facing the two large doors that opened into the room of horrors, his eyes twisted in tempered fury.

The two doors opened majestically as Ecnilitsep walked commandingly into the room. Her head high, her armor seemed to gleam with her own self-satisfaction. Pihc stood from his place, the exhaustion momentarily forgotten by her arrival. "*S'ram.*" He accused, the tone of the single word carrying like a battering ram. "*How is he free?*"

Ecnilitsep lowered her arms, her powerful eyes never moving from her gaze at Pihc. "*I freed him.*" She said clearly, her almost-smile seeming to grow.

Pihc's eyes widened in horrified astonishment. "*What?!*" He yelled in terrified surprise, his voice a light rasp. Disbelief crossed his mind as he reeled from the news. His knees began to give a bit as he stumbled back to the altar. Ecnilitsep followed his stumbling steps with her own well-placed ones as he finally placed his hand on the central structure to the room. "*You…released…him?*"

"*I did.*" Ecnilitsep said, very clearly, coming towards him.

"*But why?*" Pihc yelled. "*You tempt disaster by thinking you can control that mindless beast!*"

"*I have no time to waste on this back-water world.*" Ecnilitsep said adamantly as she walked securely towards the back-pedaling Pihc. "*The Shadows and Htead both constantly vie for my attention, drawing my resources to more pressing matters. I can't waste any more time here.*" She placed her hand on the surface of the altar, following Pihc around as if maintaining a cadence of a dance. "*I have no intention of dealing with this planet any longer than is necessary. This place, Earth, of all places, was supposed to have been completely drained of magic ages ago. And yet, the magic clings stubbornly to this wretched place.*" She continued, her voice belying her confidence. All the time, Pihc reeled at each word, barely able to believe what he heard. "*That is why I plan on committing fully to its total destruction. No more peaceful protection, no more quiet solidification; it shall be destroyed once and for all. The Shadows can not take that which is not.*" She looked away from Pihc for the first time, her gaze like her thoughts turning distant. "*But to do that, I need more powerful warriors than you or your wretched minions. S'ram shall be one such instrument in realizing my plan to demolish the Earth, beginning with the VGM's home nation and moving from there. There are no weapons that can stand in our way, no armies mighty enough to face me or my forces.*"

"*But, destroy the Earth?*" Pihc tried, not believing the words. "*That's insanity and you know why. And even if so, what after the Earth is destroyed? What then?*" He stood now, reaching for his black katana. "*After Earth is destroyed, S'ram will rampage once more.*"

"*I doubt that.*" Ecnilitsep said, finishing her circle to stand in front of Pihc.

"*Then who will control him?*" Pihc pressed, his anger returning. "*Surely you don't think that you could fight your battles and control that monster at the same time?*"

"*The question is,*" Ecnilitsep said slowly and clearly, as she picked Pihc's katana up from the altar. "*Who will control the two of you?*"

Pihc's face drained of what little color it had as terror filled his mind. "*WHAT?!*" He finally roared as his fear was replaced with fury. "***I will have no part of this plan, Ecnilitsep.***"

"*Pihc, the time has come for you and S'ram to rejoin.*" She said clearly. She moved her hand along the surface of Pihc's great katana she held in her hands, noting the razor's edge.

"***Absolutely not!***" Pihc roared again.

"*Pihc.*" Ecnilitsep repeated in a calm voice, her powerful eyes reflected in the dark surface of the katana's blade. She motioned past Pihc with a glance towards the still-open doorway behind her. Pihc's eyes followed Ecnilitsep's, coming to terms with the dark figure that stood in the portal. Under the large hat, S'ram's eyes glowed the same dark red of Pihc's. "*You don't have a choice.*"

Pihc looked from S'ram to Ecnilitsep, then back to S'ram, not even batting an eye. With a fast leap, he vaulted over the altar, launching himself at S'ram. The larger creature rushed at Pihc, but the gray-skinned giant drove in with a hard punch to S'ram's stomach. The blow knocked the black-dressed beast against the wall, giving Pihc time to catch him across the face with the palm of his hand. Pihc moved to come around from the other side, but S'ram lifted up his revolver. A single motion of his finger and Pihc was sent flying with the force of the explosion.

The giant 'Shee bent its monstrous head down to Cye, its spiny, misshapen mouth parting a bit, as if it intended to bite. But the girl reached up unfearfully, touching the monster's thorny skin. The beast rubbed against her as if it was a cat.

"They can be quite docile."

Cye turned as Yerrbmot stepped out of the castle. The small alternate fingered her naginata as she cautiously considered the general, but then turned back to the 'Shee. "Brenard told me you know a lot about them." She said.

"I know a lot about everything." Yerrbmot gloated, stepping into the rocky domain that surrounded the castle. Covering the grounds out of sight, the rows and rows of the twisted spider-like monsters milled and shifted, but they did not move out of formation. "It was I who created the elder forms of the 'Shees. The Serishee, the Cherishee, all of them."

"You must be very proud." Cye smiled at him, then returned to the monster. She scratched under an outcropping over its eye, making the beast release a strange growl that seemed appreciative. "Trebor told me you created the robed figures that Pihc uses when he alternates someone."

"That's true." Yerrbmot boasted. "I created them to help him focus his magical power for such a monumental spell, as well as to…"

"I really hated those things." Cye interrupted without turning to him. She scratched the 'Shee for a moment longer, then turned to the wizard. "I suppose then you, indirectly, had a hand in my alternation, seeing as how you made them."

Yerrbmot smiled. "My dear child, if you are trying to intimidate me, I should caution you. Trebor said something very similarly to me once. And we dealt with him for it."

"That may be." Cye said, looking at Yerrbmot out of the corner of her eye. "But I'm not Trebor."

The wizard smiled with a hint of approval. "No, that you are not." He turned from her and started away from the castle. "Let me show you something." He started. "Have you ever seen the catacombs beneath the..." He didn't get far.

"Cye!" Came a call. The two turned as Brenard led the other alternates out of the castle, anger covering their faces. "Come with us." The gladiator said, stepping down the short flight of steps towards the girl. "We are going to take our issue with S'ram's appearance directly to Ecnilitsep."

"Ecnilitsep's actions are not yours to dispute, alternate." Yerrbmot called from the front of the 'Shees as he turned back towards him.

"Nobody asked you, you mealy-mouthed little bastard." Trebor cut in.

"Nor did our liege ask you." Came Eminaf's voice. The alternates turned as Livic and the female general stepped out, both carrying their weapons.

"Bitch, this ain't the time." Trebor warned coldly, glaring mostly at Eminaf. "I'm in a foul mood and I'm by far the most civil of us at the moment."

"For once, Trebor's right." Brenard cautioned, his eyes locked on Livic. "Our issue is with Ecnilitsep, not her lackeys."

"Lackeys?" Livic said, moving towards Brenard specifically. But as he did, the sound of a gun cocking echoed against all of them. Livic looked over at Yadiloh as the stone-faced cowboy stood with his hand on his still-holstered revolver, the hammer pulled back. "Be careful." Livic warned. "That might..."

A gun shot echoed through the rocky terrain.

Trebor turned and gawked at Yadiloh. "Did that thing really go off?"

"That wasn't Yadiloh's." Cye exclaimed, looking up to the castle in horror. "That was S'ram's!"

S'ram had his thick hands around Pihc's neck, squeezing as hard as he could. But on his back, Pihc scissored his legs around S'ram's arms and shoved against him, pushing the giant away from him. With a flip of his legs, he leapt up to his feet as S'ram dove for him. Pihc slipped around the tackle and threw S'ram into the stone wall, kicking him in the lower back.

As the giant monster landed against the wall, the door to the alternation chamber swung open. The alternates rushed in, shocked to find Pihc collapsed over the altar. "*Brenard!*" Pihc roared, holding his bleeding throat. "*We are…*"

Like a curtain closing, Ecnilitsep moved between Pihc and the alternates. The gray-skinned warrior stood over the four, her red eyes surging with power. "*You have a choice to make.*" She commanded as the three generals moved up behind the alternates, boxing them into the tiny space of the doorway. "*Your loyalty to me is called into question. Do you choose to stand by me, your god, or by he who shall soon cease to exist?*"

The four turned in unison as S'ram grabbed Pihc around the waist. Arcing back, he threw Pihc over his shoulder, suplexing him to the ground. S'ram stood up, smiling at Ecnilitsep. But when they both turned back around to the alternates, they found Brenard missing. The two whirled around to find the gladiator between them and Pihc. "I will not stand by and watch you do this." He said, drawing out his twin gladius swords. "I will not."

In a flash, Ecnilitsep's arm shot out, catching Brenard around the neck. Lifting him up one hand, she held him out, glaring into his eyes. "*You can't survive against me, Brenard.*" She said, holding him at arm's length as he struggled against her unyielding strength. "*I am invincible.*"

A gun's barrel leveled against the back of Ecnilitsep's head.

She turned her head just a bit, to see Yadiloh with his revolver at her head.

"No one is invincible." He hissed in a gravel voice just before pulling the trigger.

Ecnilitsep's head ceased to be.

Livic tackled Yadiloh to the ground, throwing him to the far side of the room. The general stood up from the tackle, just in time to catch both of Trebor's feet to the back as the alternate drop-kicked the older man against the stone wall.

Trebor leapt back as Eminaf slashed at him, but Cye's naginata swung in, catching the blade just short of Trebor's head. Cye skated in with a fast elbow to catch Eminaf across the face, then chopped in deep with the fiery blade of her pole arm, slicing her blade through Emianf's purple armor, nearly cutting the female general in half.

But a burst of power slammed against Cye, knocking her away. Yerrbmot moved up behind Eminaf, his golden staff glowing with power. He turned the weapon onto Trebor, but as the alternate prepared to move, Livic slid into his back with his forearm guards extended like blades. "How do you like getting stabbed in the back for a change, Trebor?"

"It's not that different from getting stabbed in the front!" Trebor roared just before jamming his katana over his shoulder into Livic's face.

Brenard grabbed Pihc's hand, helping the giant to his feet. "We've got to get out of here." The alternate cautioned. But as he tried to help Pihc balance, Ecnilitsep grabbed the alternate's head. With a casual throw, she tossed him into the standing Yadiloh, slamming both of them against the wall. She turned back to Pihc, catching him in the stomach.

Pihc came back up with a hard punch to Ecnilitsep's chest, then folded the punch in to sweep his elbow across her face. Knocking the giant against the altar, Pihc grabbed up his black katana, his eyes erupting with red power.

Catching Pihc from behind, S'ram slammed his leg against the small of Pihc's back. The kick threw Pihc onto Ecnilitsep, but she caught his fall and cradled his head in her arms. Squeezing with all her might, she threatened to crush his skull.

Trebor got a running start and leapt into the air, bringing his katana down in a fast arc just along the edge of the altar, slicing off the top part of Ecnilitsep's head, severing everything from her ears up. The top half of her head splattered against the ground, only to be stepped on by Trebor.

A huge hand grabbed Trebor around the neck. S'ram lifted the small fighter up into the air, holding him at arm's length. Trebor grabbed S'ram's arm, trying to free himself of the iron grip, but it was no good. Throwing Trebor up into the air, S'ram reversed the motion, slamming him back down to the ground. Trebor hit the floor with the force of a hurricane, his body exploding apart on impact.

"Trebor!" Cye screamed. S'ram turned just as the small girl threw her naginata in a fast arc. The spinning pole arm buzzed like a saw, sweeping through the air to within an inch from S'ram's face. But the giant ducked out of the way of the attack, turning back to Cye with his hand cannon. Cye barely had time to scream before S'ram flattened her against the far wall, a gaping hole where her chest had been.

Pihc's arm wrapped around S'ram's neck. With a flip over his waist, Pihc slammed the giant against the stone floor before driving his katana into his chest. Pinning the monstrous form to the ground, Pihc turned as Livic and Eminaf both rushed at him.

Livic hacked at Pihc's knees while Eminaf leapt up at him, pulling back on her saber to impale him. Pihc let them both get close, then slammed his left fist down onto Livic, driving the general into the stone floor. Eminaf landed her leaping stab at Pihc, but the giant let her impale him with her sword. He caught her body with his hand, then planted her down into the ground with a force of a car wreck.

Yerrbmot whipped his staff to the left, slamming Yadiloh into the far wall. "You can not survive, gun man." The wizard yelled confidently, but as he did, he felt a ripple of air. He tried to call out but a burning choked at him. He dabbed at his throat with the tips of his fingers, only to feel blood. He looked up, trying to shout, but his head fell away from his body, landing just a few seconds before his knees did.

Brenard rushed over to Yadiloh, helping the cowboy up. The gladiator yanked him to his feet but neither was prepared as Ecnilitsep slammed her fists into both of them, sending them flying against the far wall. The woman whirled to Pihc as he faced her. "*Come, Pihc.*" She seethed angrily as she drew out her scimitar. "*Let us finish this.*"

"*I will not let you…*"

But another sound echoed through the room. It was a gun cocking. Pihc and Ecnilitsep both turned as S'ram held up his gun from his pinned body. He aimed it right for Pihc. The giant didn't even have time to blink.

The explosion of force startled the recovering Trebor back to consciousness. He looked up just as Pihc fell over, his torso almost completely gone. "No!" He moved to scream, but the sound of Cye's voice drowned him out. Trebor stood on uncertain legs, watching as the generals and the alternates all stood at the same time.

The three glanced at the four, but Yadiloh moved first. Letting out three shots, the cowboy made the generals duck, then turned his gun to Ecnilitsep. He fired a shot, but she moved out of the way, coming towards the cowboy. But as she did, Cye's spinning naginata swept in front of her.

Brenard grabbed Yadiloh's arm and yanked him towards the door. "Retreat!" He called, moving towards the exit, Cye moving ahead of him. The generals all locked their eyes on the alternates, but Trebor skated in front of the door, his katana held ready.

"Trebor!" Came the sound of Brenard's voice. "Trebor!" He called. "Retreat!"

"Go!" The long-haired alternate yelled, standing between Livic and Eminaf and the doorway the alternates backed through. "I'll cover you."

"Not if you don't survive." Eminaf growled sadistically.

"Bitch, please." Trebor said with a smile, shaking his head. "I've been waiting for this." He lunged at Eminaf with his katana, but she quickly parried, riposting with a slice to Trebor's neck. He retreated, but she caught him twice in the legs to bring him down to his knees, then came down with a hack to his shoulder. But Trebor caught her saber with his hand, letting it drive into his skin. He smiled at her, then stepped forward, pushing from his knees as he punctured her armor with his katana.

In the hall, Cye turned to head back, but Brenard caught her arm. "We've got to help Trebor." Cye said. "He…"

"He can take care of himself." Brenard insisted, pushing her as Yadiloh staggered down the hall. "Come on!"

Trebor stepped back from Livic and Eminaf as Ecnilitsep released Pihc's katana from S'ram's chest. Trebor looked at the unconscious body of Pihc on the ground behind the altar, then looked to the generals. "Well, it's been fun kids." He said with a smile.

"Why do you stand by Pihc when you hate him?" Livic asked, pairing off with Eminaf as they looked for an opening in the alternate's defensive stance.

"Lesser of two evils." Trebor smiled with a wink just before he faded from sight.

Behind the altar, Pihc began to stir. The fragments of skin and fabric rolled and kicked their way back towards his body, sealing up the final injury. With a flash of anger, Pihc's eyes flared open, power surging from him. He sat up, his attention locked on Ecnilitsep and S'ram. The giant rose up from the ground, but Ecnilitsep turned to him with a pleased look. "*Your alternates have betrayed you.*" She said. "*They have abandoned you.*"

"*They know they will serve me better alive.*" Pihc said with grim eyes.

"*Not when you're gone.*" Ecnilitsep said confidently.

"*Especially when I'm gone.*" Pihc returned defiantly, just before he reached out for his katana. The black sword flew to his hands and he turned to S'ram. The giant held up his massive cannon, but Pihc moved too fast. Severing the beast's arm with a single swing, Pihc slammed into him with his shoulder, knocking S'ram against the wall and off his feet.

Turning from the slam, Pihc threw back his foot, catching Ecnilitsep in the stomach. Coming around with a fast chop, his slash aimed for her neck was barely parried by her scimitar. Pihc immediately reversed the slash down low, catching Livic across the neck. The hack sliced off his head and sent it flying past Yerrbmot. The wizard threw his hands forward, a ripple of existence flying at Pihc, but the giant lifted his hand against Yerrbmot, sending the ripple to him. The wizard frantically reversed the ripple yet again, but this time it collided with Eminaf as she leapt to where Pihc had been just a second ago. The female general shrieked in agony as her body twisted and contorted, her armor digging into her flesh, tearing its way into her skin.

Pihc threw a fast pair of kicks at Ecnilitsep, then swung in with his katana. She blocked the slash, lunging in with the tip of her sword blade. Pihc moved around the sword, catching her across the face with the pommel of his sword.

But as the giant moved onto Ecnilitsep, S'ram grabbed hold of his neck from behind. Pihc turned his katana over, driving it behind him, but S'ram roared in pain, still holding onto Pihc. He drew back with his right hand, flaring his fingers wide. Then with the power of a tidal wave, S'ram slammed his fingers at Pihc, driving his muscular hand through his cape-like jacket and into Pihc's back.

But rather than blood, light erupted from the gray giant. Pihc threw his head back, roaring in agony as the light punctured the darkness of the room. S'ram roared as well, but in joy. He pushed his hand deeper, the light growing larger as his whole hand reached inside Pihc. The giant shook and bucked, but he couldn't get free of S'ram. And before the two, Ecnilitsep watched with delight.

From the front of the castle, the four alternates watched as the light ruptured out from all the windows of the castle. Cye turned away, burying her face in Brenard's chest. "We have to get to earth." The gladiator whispered quietly, loss awash over his face. Yadiloh put his hand on Brenard's shoulder, nodding his head as he tried to swallow. He looked at Trebor, but even the long-haired alternate looked lost. The four gathered close before fading away.

The vivid body lay on the floor, unconscious. Smoke rose from its form as the light patched and frayed in different segments, its intensity varying and ebbing like a living skin.

Standing over the massive, incoherent form of pure light, Ecnilitsep stood with her three generals. "What will you do with him?" Livic asked in a hard voice, holding his neck in pain. "Do you believe you can control his mind?" The towering woman said nothing. She simply stared down at the form lying at her feet. "Ecnilitsep, are you sure?" The general pleaded. "The combined form of Pihc and S'ram was made by Htead, made to do what he could not; destroy you."

"*I know.*" Ecnilitsep answered confidently, barely sparing Livic a glance. "*But I shall make Htead's pawn into my own. I shall turn him into a weapon with which I will strike down my former master.*" She answered with a smile. She turned to the three, gathering their attention.

"*But now for earth, we have much planned.*" She announced, leaving the brilliant glow behind her. "*As I began with Pihc and S'ram, I will continue with him who shall replace them. We will assault the earth and devastate it. I want to leave it as a lifeless corpse that not even the Shadows would take note of.*"

"*Already we have begun to move the 'Shees on earth. My plan is to divide into two forces.*" She said, barely glancing at the body behind her. "*You three will drive two-thirds of the 'Shees across the northern portion of the VGM's home nation, while I take the rest and will move across the southern portion. We will converge at the VGM's home in the city of 'Raleigh' in the sub-country of Northern Carolina. There, we will crush them.*"

"Why not simply attack directly?" Livic asked. "Why the march?"

She glanced at the body once, then crossed her arms to turn back to Livic. "*So that they may feel the weight of their failure to defeat us. Before they die, they must know the cost of their impertinence and their dedication to undermining our efforts to protect existence.*"

"What of the alternates?" Eminaf asked, standing behind Livic and Yerrbmot. "Will we hunt them down as well?"

"*We will deal with them only if they present themselves. They have served me without too much disappointment. Let them rot out the rest of their eternities.*" Ecnilitsep said with disgust. But as she spoke, her head turned away. Listening, she looked back at the generals.

The three generals waited for a moment, then Livic motioned. "What is it?"

Ecnilitsep listened for a moment longer, then turned back to the generals, a cruel look across her face. "*For the past several hours, I have heard a voice, weak and willowy, like a breeze. I could not attend to it before, but it is growing in strength.*" She said, stepping back from the three. But as she did, her face turned up in a sick smile. "*Apparently at least one of the VGM has the will to face certain death on his feet,*" She said confidently. "*For I am being summoned.*"

CHAPTER 14

Anti-Salvation

"Sealed with a curse, sharp as a knife.
Doomed is your soul, and damned is your life."

—Jeffery, SCUD: The Disposable Assassin

"Gentlemen, we have a troop build-up." Said the white-haired general as he tipped his jungle camouflage army cap to the back of his head, looking more like a cowboy with each passing moment. "We have a definite invasion from these aliens. And you're telling me that the one thing that they wanted has just…up and disappeared?"

Standing on the other side of the glass map that monitored air traffic, the FBI director and Eric stood still. Both dressed in identical suits, they stared back with rehearsed precision. "Sir, the VGM is highly resourceful." The Director started.

"It's very likely that they anticipated your attack." Eric added with just a hint of emphasis on the ownership.

"Or that they merely were planning to evacuate at that time to begin with." The Director finished up bureaucratically without missing a beat.

"Boys," The general said, clearly getting frustrated as he turned away, looking out over the expansive mobile command center build up inside the ancient movie theater. "We've positioned this command center here in Nevada to be able to deal with the alien invasion that will be coming from California. We are also aware of a similar invasion coming from up north, from Washington."

The Director turned and looked at Eric. "An Invasion?"

"The aliens are getting ambitious." Eric said back.

"Damn it!" The general yelled, whirling around. "Those bastards killed six SWAT officers!" His voice echoed across the command center, getting the attention of many of the hands. Heads turned, but no one spoke up. "They evaded a multi-agency search for them. And you're telling me they've just disappeared."

Eric swallowed hard. He glanced over at the Director, but the older man stayed cool. He gave the general the weakest smile Eric had ever seen. "Apparently." The man said with infuriating calm.

Ecnilitsep was dwarfed by the size of the warehouse. The gray-skinned giant stood amongst the massive boxes like a child. In the perpetual darkness, she could see where the cleanup had undergone for her and the VGM's fight from days ago. Still, much of the debris remained to be attended to.

The giant woman stepped over a broken box, coming into a different wing of the huge steel building. She turned her head, the blowing of a late-autumn breeze catching her white hair. The light through the high windows from a distant street lamp glinted off her armor, while her sure hand rested on the handle of her scimitar as it waited patiently.

In the dark, her red eyes shone out. Even the dim light showed like brilliant fires, her presence given away by her gaze. She stepped farther into the darkness, cautiously moving without a sound, her attention spread out around her.

"***You've come.***"

Ecnilitsep turned, her dark eyes going narrow as she stared up into the darkness at the top of the destroyed crates, at the pair of silver eyes that glowed out from the shadows. "*Of course.*" The grey-skinned giant pronounced, standing up tall in her proud armor. "*I have no reason to fear you, or to fear fighting you.*"

"***Then you are a fool.***" Vincent proclaimed.

"*Vincent.*" Said Ecnilitsep, "*This is not game, boy. There is no one here who can save you now.*"

"***Believe me, Ecnilitsep.***" Came the voice from atop the crates. "***There will be no need for me to be saved.***"

Ecnilitsep whirled around, grabbing the charging Vincent by the elbow, spinning him into a group of crates. "*Clever trick, boy.*" She said as she thrust forward with her sword. Vincent dodged out of the way, parrying with his bowie knife. He dashed forward, swinging the blade of his knife in a wide arc. Ecnilitsep sidestepped it, making a slice at Vincent's waist. The blade nicked at his black trench coat, but did nothing more.

Vincent stopped short, spinning at Ecnilitsep, slamming the butt of his bowie knife into her temple. As she stumbled back a step, he drove forward with his knife, stabbing it into her forearm. Her hand went limp momentarily, her curved scimitar dropping to the wooden floor. With a quick kick, Vincent sent the large sword sliding away from the fight.

Vincent took a powerful step back for room to slam his foot into Ecnilitsep's chest, knocking her against a steel crate. He followed through across her face with a hard punch. He carried the momentum to spin around and catch her with a hard back fist, then spun again and landed a hard roundhouse kick.

Ecnilitsep was knocked along the crate, but Vincent kicked ahead of her spin with a forward kick. His heel slammed into the metal as Ecnilitsep stopped suddenly just before the kick could make contact. With her balance regained, she punched Vincent's knee, straining it audibly. Vincent danced away from the punch, only to have Ecnilitsep throw a fast kick at him.

The Vgm blocked the kick, using its force to fuel the momentum to drop and spin around, sweeping at Ecnilitsep's feet. She jumped over the attack, however and slammed both her feet down onto the ground where Vincent's leg had been just a second ago.

Vincent slid away, coming up in a defensive crouch, his hands at his side. Ecnilitsep charged at him, clearing the distance before he could move. She grabbed his head, kneeing him in the face. He fell back to the ground, blood covering his nose. Ecnilitsep tried to jump on top of him, but Vincent raised his legs up, their feet meeting perfectly. Vincent shoved against her considerable weight with all his might as she drove into him. Their combined strength sent her flying back up into the air. She let the shove carry her, letting her legs arc over her head just before she landed expertly. She threw her white notch top back over her head with a whip of her neck, then dashed in once again at Vincent.

The Vgm rolled up onto his haunches, only to roll out of the way in the knick of time as a crate as big as he was went flying over him. Ecnilitsep hoisted another crate into her hands, hurling it with frightening accuracy. The huge boxes collided with the wooden floor, sending up a shower of debris from the destroyed floor as well as the boxes and their diverse contents.

Vincent dove out of the way of a crate, taking refuge behind a larger box. He put his feet on the one behind it and pressed with all his might. The giant wooden cube began to slide across the floor. With all the strength he could muster, Vincent shoved against the box until it was sliding freely across the smooth floor, aiming it straight for Ecnilitsep. The giant foe saw the crate coming and leapt straight up; landing on the crate's top as it hit the pile she had been hurling at Vincent. She looked about quickly, trying to find Vincent, but he was nowhere to be seen.

Ecnilitsep whirled around just in time to see the giant blue ball of energy come flying right for her. The ball of power slammed into her and sent her flying from her feet. The giant woman crashed down from the heavy crates, her body surging with the mystical attack. She tried to roll with the impact, but the damage was too great. She landed hard and struggled to move, smoke rising from her armor and body. She spat out blood as she fought up to her feet. "*Damn.*" She whispered against the strain. She turned, watching as Vincent closed the distance to her. She yelled out at him, kicking a pile of crates. The huge pile shuttered backwards, nearly crushing Vincent as they fell.

As the boxes fell, Vincent threw up his hands, a ball of blue energy appearing around him. The boxes collided with the barrier, breaking around Vincent. But it gave Ecnilitsep the time to launch into a charge. By the time Vincent dispelled the video game power, Ecnilitsep was right on top of him.

Ecnilitsep threw a hard kick at Vincent, but he dodged beside it, grabbing Ecnilitsep's leg, pushing it up, throwing her onto the ground. But before Vincent could get his hands free of Ecnilitsep's leg, she wrapped her other leg around his arms and spun around on her back. Taking Vincent along with her spin, she used her legs to throw him into another crate.

Vincent turned his body, landing sideways on the crate itself and immediately shoving back to leap off the crate. Ecnilitsep was barely standing just as Vincent launched back into her, firing both his feet into her chest. The attack collided with Ecnilitsep hard, but she remained standing. As Vincent fell, though, he threw his hands onto the floor and pushed off, spinning rapidly. As he spun, he yelled "***Spinning Bird Kick!***" The kicks knocked Ecnilitsep back, but Ecnilitsep grabbed his still-spinning legs. With a tremendous force, she spun him around, throwing him.

The crate exploded with the impact, the top falling as Vincent was thrown through the giant cube, landing on the far side. This time, it took Vincent a second to get up. As he pushed himself free, he turned around to see Ecnilitsep grab him around the neck. He pushed away from her, grabbing her forearm as he tried to free himself of her hold. The gray giant, however, turned around, throwing Vincent as hard as she could. Vincent went flying through the air, slamming through another crate.

The ground was littered with splintered wood, bent metal, and a snowy field of linen and packaging. The light from the outside world did little to illuminate the darkness in the wide storage warehouse, even as the two fighters stood ready before each other. Vincent stood up tall, wiping blood from his mouth. Before him, Ecnilitsep held her stance, her eyes narrowed at her foe.

"*Never has anyone given me such trouble.*" She spat out devilishly, blood still dripping from her mouth.

"***Shut up and fight.***" Vincent said angrily before exploding towards the woman. Ecnilitsep was barely able to move before Vincent closed the distance to her. She threw a fast punch for his head, but he dropped down too low, placing his hand onto the ground. Pushing off, he shot his body forward, tackling her in the stomach. The impact knocked them both over to the ground.

Vincent wrestled his way on top of the fight, planting his knees over one of Ecnilitsep's arms. With his hand drawn back as far as he could reach, he slammed his fist down onto her head, the sound of a skull giving in filling his ears. He drew back again, opening his hand to smash his palm down onto her head.

Ecnilitsep suddenly flipped over, dislodging Vincent off her arm. As she rolled, she took his arm and pinned him to the ground. He tried to fight free, but the goliath drew back her own hand, slamming her fist down onto Vincent's head. The blow drew blood as Vincent felt his head literally split open. But he didn't stop.

Slamming his fist into Ecnilitsep's head, he knocked her off of him. He tried to roll away, but the disorientation from the head wound undermined his motions. From behind, Ecnilitsep grabbed Vincent around his waist, lifting him into the air. Arching her back while he was held closely to her, Ecnilitsep flipped him over, suplexing him down onto the wooden floor.

Blood spilled everywhere as Vincent flopped lifelessly down onto ground. Ecnilitsep stood over the dead body, panting hard. She looked over the body for a moment, then stood. She picked up her foot, slamming it down onto Vincent's chest. He jumped from the impact, his ribs shattering from the blow. She lifted up again, preparing to slam it down onto his chest.

Vincent grabbed Ecnilitsep's foot by the ankle, throwing off her balance. While she struggled to stay up, he spun around on his shoulder, connecting with both of his feet to her standing leg, knocking her to the ground as he flipped up to his feet.

Ecnilitsep rolled up, only to have Vincent throw his leg over her head, slamming it down onto the base of her neck. She was knocked onto her hands and knees, barely able to stay up. Vincent jumped up over Ecnilitsep, landing elbow first into her back, driving her back down to the wooden floor. He came up, backing away from the gray woman.

As he stepped, this time it was Ecnilitsep who grabbed his ankle. "*You shouldn't retreat.*" She roared at him, yanking him towards her.

As she yanked however, Vincent went willingly with the pull, suddenly spinning towards her, feet first as he yelled "***Cannon Drill!***" Both feet collided with Ecnilitsep, knocking her back as Vincent slid to a stop. Ecnilitsep rolled back, coming to tower over the crouching Vincent. She moved in.

Vincent threw his hands forward, yelling "***Firaga!***" A huge explosion of fire erupted on Ecnilitsep, sending her flying away, landing hard on the wooden floor. Vincent took the opportunity and leapt into the air, launching himself as high as he could. He put his hands together again, letting the energy flow openly. The ball of blue incandescent energy erupted between his palms as he prepared to launch the attack. Ecnilitsep stood up as best she could, taking her fighting stance. Vincent charge the ball until his upward momentum slowed and he began to fall. With all his might, he threw his hands forward, releasing the powerful ball.

Ecnilitsep narrowed her eyes, timing the ball carefully. She let it fly at her with the speed of a missile, but when it was nearly on top of her, she threw out her hands with a wave of wind and power. An explosion rocked the warehouse as the fireball was sent back to its origin, straight at Vincent.

The blue ball rammed into him full force, knocking him straight across the huge warehouse. Vincent landed hard, the force of the impact driving him across the rough, littered floor.

The smoking crater of devastation trailed through the debris of the battle, ending with Vincent's final resting place. His body lay mangled in the wide fissure of the concrete floor. Struggling against unconsciousness, Vincent opened his mouth, but blood poured out like rich soup while his eyes filled with the blood than ran off from his face. He reached out, trying to stand, grasping for something to provide some sense of stability.

His hand touched the shin plating of Ecnilitsep's armor.

She reached down to hold Vincent's neck, dropping down onto him with her knee, pinning his chest to the ground with a soggy flop. "***Now, Vincent.***"

She whispered, a sadistic smile on her gray face as her eyes flared with magic. "***You die.***" She reached out, summoning her scimitar to her hand. The black-bladed weapon lifted up from the ground and flew to her grip. She angled the weapon's razor blade down against Vincent's back, just between his shoulder blades.

With slowly, dangerous precision, she began to slide the weapon into his body. Vincent's eyes opened wide as he felt the sword's presence puncture surgically through his trench coat and shirt, then into his skin. He opened his mouth to scream out, but the pain grabbed hold of him.

"***Die.***" She whispered as the sound of her sword splintering through her sternum, nailing him to the splintered concrete as her magic echoed in her ears. "***Die.***" She said again. As she whispered, the blade of her sword began to shimmer. In the dim light of the warehouse, a fine, green film appeared on the blade. Vincent's eyes went wide, the magic fading from his gaze as the seeping liquid slowly dripped into the wound. "***Die, by my hand.***" She seethed into his ear.

Trebor's head lifted up.

Hidden at the mouth of the cave, the four alternates stayed hidden away as the rays of the sun slowly crept over the distant horizon. Turning his head to look out into the distance, Trebor blinked his eyes, slowly standing.

At the mouth of the cave, Cye sat with her naginata across her shoulders, keeping careful watch over the endless desert. As Trebor moved unsettlingly towards the mouth of the cave, she turned to look at him. Moving away from the other two sleeping alternates, the long-haired fighter sat down next to Cye, a heavy weight hanging on him. "You okay?" She whispered.

"I…" He started slowly, pushing the three strands of black hair away from his eye. But he stared off, unable to locate his thoughts. "I don't know." He reached up, rubbing his chest. "I feel like I've got heartburn, but of my soul. It's, it's hard to explain."

Cye looked back out to the desert as the horizon turned pink at the edges. "What are we going to do, Trebor?"

"I don't know." He confessed with a deep breath. He squatted down next to her, looking around at the cave for a moment. A surly smile came to him, getting her attention. "Isn't this how you used to say it was supposed to be?" He asked.

Cye got a strange look in her eyes. "What?" She asked, confused.

"We were supposed to wake up in a cave somewhere, somewhere perfect and wonderful." Trebor smiled, almost laughing. He looked up at Cye and winked. "Good night, little sister." He said, turning back from her.

Cye watched him go, still confused. "Good night." She tossed back, looking back at the sun rise.

"We're supposed to deal with this whole nation using less than four hundred 'Shees." Eminaf complained as she stood amongst the gathering of twisted monsters. Surrounded by the trees of an expansive forest, she walked over where Livic and Yerrbmot waited. The wizard carved away at an apple, leaving the yellow skin on the ground, while Livic consulted a cheap tourist's map of the state. "And we're supposed to perform a forced march from here to the other side of the continent, destroying everything in our path, and be on the other side in less than a week."

"Well, we're going to have to teleport." Livic said, still considering the map. "If we travel in a straight line, we'll be attacked and rooted out for sure."

"What can these people do to us?" Eminaf scoffed.

Yerrbmot looked up, his mouth half full from the apple. "Technology isn't that weak, Eminaf. Our magic may make us superior in every way, but that does not completely alleviate the threat of their tools and devices."

"I say we spend no more than six hours in a given location." Livic plotted, looking at the two generals. "We arrive, destroy, set fire to absolutely everything, salt the ground, that sort of thing. And within six hours, we move on to the new location."

"But that's hardly destroying everything in our path." Eminaf said caustically, still pacing, the edges of the distant horizon just beginning to grow light.

"Eminaf, short of evaporating the atmosphere, transforming the molecular structure of oxygen, or causing a worldwide plague, we're not going to make all life on this planet extinct." Yerrbmot spoke up. "We do some damage, we set into motion some more damage, and we deal with it later."

"But Ecnilitsep has demanded that we..." The female general started.

"Eminaf, Ecnilitsep has commanded us to solidify reality." Livic argued. "But reality cannot exist at all where there is nothing. Static existence must still rely on something there to exist." He shook his head folding up the map. "We can not..."

"*Generals.*"

The three's heads all lifted up as the 'Shees all turned towards the sound of the disembodied voice. "Yes, my lord." Livic said to the nothingness in the field with them.

"*My business is done.*" Came Ecnilitsep's voice. "*The time has come for you to launch your offensive.*"

Eminaf turned to Livic, grinning with dark delight. "Finally."

Ben stopped in mid-stride. Shane stopped a few steps past him and turned back to his friend. Ben paused, looking back over his shoulder at the entrance to an alleyway back off the empty street. "What is it?" Shane asked, but Ben was already backpedaling.

The sniper stopped at the entrance to the alley, stepping into the center to plainly see the host of cars that sat waiting, kept company by a diverse collection of street toughs and geeks.

Shane came up next to him, a cautious look in his eye. "Looks like a street rally." The street racer said, scoping out the cars as the people prepared and appraised them. "We probably should go, since they don't usually like foreigners and this is decidedly illegal."

"Yeah, whatever." Ben said, heading into the alley. Shane winced, then followed.

Ben strolled up to the nearest car, bending down to check beneath the hood at the spotless engine. "You know much about these cars?" He said back to Shane. As he did, a Japanese teen came over, glaring at Ben. He started to rant in Japanese, accompanying his words with a host of quick, threatening gestures. Ben slowly stood up as the boy gathered a crowd with his yelling. Ben straightened his fashionable jacket, then quickly spat back a fast barrage of words that sent the boy stumbling back a step or two, eliciting laughs from the crowd.

Shane stared at the crowd, then looked over at Ben. "Did you just talk Japanese?" He asked.

"Yeah." Ben nodded, examining the engine again.

"I didn't know you knew it." Shane marveled, staring back at the crowd.

"I don't." Ben said, touching a piece of metal, jerking his hand away at the heat. "I got a dictionary while we were waiting at the airport before we left Carolina."

"And you've been reading it?" Shane gaped. "You learned the Japanese language in less than a day?"

Ben looked up at Shane, bewildered. "Not all of it." He defended.

"I'm worried about home." Sophia admitted, walking through the crowded shopping center. Shoulder to shoulder with Michelle, the girl walked with her head down, barely aware of the shopping bazaar that spread exotically before the two girls. "I mean, we don't know what's going on. We don't know what's happening to our parents. We don't know anything."

"I don't know." Michelle said, smiling at a teen boy who walked by her. She winked at the kid but kept walking. "There's not a lot we can do about things, so we might as well enjoy the situation we're in."

"But our home's under attack." Sophia argued. "What if Pihc and Ecnilitsep come after us here? What if they figured out where we are? There aren't enough of us to stop them, or even to…" She turned away, her voice on the edge of hysteria. "I don't know. Maybe you're right, Mich. Maybe I am over-reacting." She stopped and looked around. "Mich? Mich?"

She turned around to see Michelle leaning against a vendor's tent pole, nearly swallowing a teen boy's mouth. "Michelle!" Sophia yelled.

"Uh? Yeah? What?!" She exclaimed in a panic. When she saw it was Sophia, she smiled at the boy, kissed him one last time, then bolted off to join her friend.

His footsteps sounded like drops of rain on a sunny day.

His breath moved in and out like a breeze coasting over a rocky beach.

His will moved like the clouds, patient and unyielding.

Jared raced over the roof tops of the Japanese industrial district. Sprinting across the metal tops of the warehouses, the ninja leapt from roof to roof, making no sound, his body casting no shadow. Bounding like a snow rabbit at the dawn of spring, he raced across the shining sea of metal, grinning massively.

The rays of sunlight warmed the metal world he ran atop, the reflection of light off the morning air sparkling into an array of prisms out of the corner of his eye. And with childlike abandon, he raced on, leaving his worries behind as he ran like the wind.

"This whole thing is weird to me." Emily admitted as she walked. She looked over at Jim, sighing. "First Chip and the VGM and all of that. And now we've been smuggled out of our own country. This hasn't been a stellar year."

"What do you think about me?" Jim posed as he spun a marijuana pipe between his fingers. "I find out one of my best friends had his soul ripped apart by a demon and I get recruited into this whole VGM thing and have to move across the US."

"Yeah." Emily sighed, looking around the overcast day at the Piccadilly Circus. "I just hope Pihc and the others don't come looking for us."

"So do I." Jim smiled. "At least, not until we're ready to go looking for them."

Emily looked back over at Jim. "Ready? Jim, we can't be ready for Pihc. I was there at Crossworld six months ago. I was there when we all were 'ready' for Pihc. And we barely survived. And I do mean barely."

Jim slowed and looked at the girl, smiling a bit. "Don't you see what you're doing? You're giving him strength." He said, confusing her. "As long as you think he's stronger than you, he will be stronger than you."

"Is this some kind of magical, positive thinking pep talk?" She asked hesitantly.

"No." Jim said, shaking his head. "It's more like a general positive-thinking pep talk. You can't live in fear. You can't let Pihc rule your life, especially when he's not even here." He put his arm around Emily's shoulder, making her turn away in disgust as she was overwhelmed by his body odor. "You see, Emily, there's very little in this world you can control. And there's just a tiny little bit that you can control. You're currently pulling your lovely brown locks out over something you can't control. Pihc. Instead, why don't you focus on something you can control? You."

"Me?" She said, finally pulling free of Jim. She took a deep breath, then turned back to him. "Soap, Jim. Soap."

Jim looked at her, then lifted up his arm, revealing a small sweat stain. He sniffed his arm pit, then looked back at her, shrugging. "What?"

Beth leaned against Chip's shoulder as he sat with his arms wrapped around her, the two leaning against the wall of the neo-retro sushi bar. Chip focused on the television mounted up by the bar, while Beth considered the bountiful variety of sushi before her on the plastic plate. The aimless ramble of the news prattled on as she picked up a delicate piece and placed it in her mouth.

With a satisfied look, Beth glanced back at Chip, following his gaze from behind his sunglasses to the television screen. She glanced up at it, but was instantly lost by the language barrier. She looked up at Chip. "What's going on?" She asked, breaking the silence as she reached up, brushing Chip's dirty blonde hair with her finger tips. "You keep watching the news. Do you think they're going to say something about Pihc?"

"I don't know." Chip whispered, watching. "I'm afraid that Ecnilitsep may have more on her mind than just us." He shook his head. "There are just too many unanswered questions right now. I hate leaving those kinds of loose ends lying around."

"What loose ends?" Beth asked, turning in his lap to look at him.

"Well, for starters there's…" But Chip's words stopped with a knife's edge. Both he and Beth turned as the music from the news report stopped urgently.

Jon looked up at the electronics store as all the TVs suddenly came to life with the same image. He turned along with a handful of English natives to face the store, looking at the stack of televisions in the window.

An empty screen appeared, then filled with script, announcing a BBC special report. "I got a bad feeling about this." The biker whispered, rubbing the back of his neck.

The screen came to life with a woman sitting at a news desk, a grave look on her face. "We're sorry to interrupt your regular program, but an international state of emergency has been declared."

"International?" Came a voice behind Jon. "Did I hear her right?"

"Can't be."

"What kind of emergency?"

"Yeah." Jon agreed, his eyes glued to the set. "What kind of emergency could cause a…"

The screen changed and Jon's eyes went wide.

"The US under attack!" Jessica gawked, staring at the television screen in the Caribbean hotel room. She swallowed hard, then turned to the door of the living room suite. "Tim!" She shouted at the top of her lungs.

The tall mage stumbled into main room, holding his face as he tried to fight off the effects of his sleep. "Yeah? Yeah. I'm up, I'm up." He stumbled out. He squinted at Jessica as she stared intently at the television screen. "What is it?" He asked, putting his glasses on while blinking furiously.

She turned to him, her face pale with fear. "It's started." She breathed, looking back at the TV.

"I don't believe it." Dan said as Aria sat behind him on the bed, both watching in awed silence. "She did it." He said. "Ecnilitsep attacked the US, head-on." Before them on the small screen, footage was being shown of army troops falling over the horizon, disappearing amongst a wide mass of explosions. And then from the horizon, 'Shees came swarming.

"And won, apparently." Aria finished, watching in shock. "Is this really happening?" She asked without a voice, her eyes on the verge of erupting in tears. "This can't be really…happening." She breathed, her hand over her mouth.

"This is really happening." Dan said, his eyes sharpening with anger.

"What was originally suspected to be a media prank has been now confirmed and is without a doubt a crisis of truly epic proportions." Said the BBC reporter into the camera. "The American military was sent in to investigate a possible troop build up that they believed belonged to a terrorist cell. However, upon arriving, the American soldiers were sent running as they were confronted with, what appeared to be, some type of biological weapon."

"Biological weapon, my ass." Chip rumbled as he looked on with Beth in his arms, the two watching the English Channel in their hotel room. "Ecnilitsep's declaring war on the US."

"Why?" Beth whispered, hypnotized by the report.

"To get at us." He seethed, his anger simmering behind his eyes. "To destroy magic. I don't know. Pick a reason. There're plenty to choose from."

"And still," Came the voice of the field reporter, standing with the Nevada state border sign to her back. "While a second offensive has begun in upstate Washington, the state of California has been cut in half by the destruction of these battles. And now, the seemingly unstable army of unknown origin is poised to begin their march across the Nevada state line."

"She's going to take the US apart state by state." Chip breathed. "This can't be just for us." He whispered in disbelief. "It can't be."

"Chip." Beth whispered quietly, clinging to his neck. "We've got to stop this."

Chip said nothing. He simply stared at the screen.

CHAPTER 15

Raising the Stakes

"How we deal with death is at least as important as how we deal with life. Wouldn't you agree lieutenant?"

—Admiral James Kirk, Star Trek II: The Wrath of Khan

"This is where you were born, wasn't it?" Brenard asked, as he and Yadiloh surveyed the desert landscape that stretched out before them. Yadiloh crouched atop a collection of rocks on the edge of a massive canyon while Brenard stood on the ground a few steps back from him. Behind Brenard, Cye watched the two from a distance.

Yadiloh nodded, gazing out over the desert, as the moonless sky sat filled with waves of stars. He waived his hand over the desert, a nostalgic look in his glowing eyes. He looked down to the two others, getting a warm smile from Cye.

"It's hard to go home after all that has happened to us." Brenard said, agreeing with his friend. Yadiloh nodded, absently. "It's been what? 70 years since the last time you visited here?" Yadiloh said nothing, simply staring out over the valley.

"When was the last time you were 'home', Brenard?" Cye asked, walking up behind him.

"Home was burned long ago." Brenard lamented. He turned to Cye, reaching to his belt. A drew out his gladius swords, holding the blades flat in the moonlight. “Nero and Caesar.” He said, holding out the short swords for Cye to see. Above them, Yadiloh watched with interest.

“There’s writing on the blade.” Cye said, touching the cold iron edges. “What do they say?”

“Nero and Caesar.” Brenard said again, patiently. “It’s Latin, however.” Brenard lifted the swords back over his shoulders, the twins disappearing. “All guilded blades have a name; a name of something special and sacred that is held inside. For me, those names are reminders of home.”

Cye nodded with a smile, understanding. “What’s Yadiloh’s gun named?” She asked to the cowboy. Yadiloh looked down at his pistol, considering it with something close to a smile. “I didn’t mean to be rude.” Cye apologized after a moment. “I hope I didn’t…”

“Its name is Wyatt.” Brenard answered for Yadiloh. “Trebor is the only alternate with a weapon that has no name. At least, he doesn’t know its name.”

“What’s my naginata’s name?” Cye asked, making the black pole arm appear.

“See for yourself.” Brenard said, motioning to the long metal pole. Cye held up the handle, having trouble seeing in the dark night. Brenard opened his eyes wide, making them glow a bright red. The illumination made a single name, etched in the middle of the handle, appear before Cye.

“I’ve never noticed that before.” Cye remarked, reading the word. “Evan?” She read, looking up at Brenard. “That doesn’t make any sense.”

“It doesn’t always seem to.” Brenard explained. He closed his eyes tightly, opening them with no red glow. He looked out at the desert, a paternal look on his face. “But it does. Somewhere inside you, that name is important.” He looked up at Yadiloh, but the cowboy turned back to the desert.

“Curly fries?!” Trebor exclaimed. Staring up at the menu that stretched over the ordering window of the small gas station, his eyes grew wider as he read more and more of the menu.

“Grill’s closed.” Called the middle-aged man from behind the counter. He was reading a magazine, barely paying attention to the brightly lit store that sat around him. There was no one else in the store, nor was there anyone else up at that time of night.

“I could really, really go for some curly fries.” Trebor nodded, still staring at the menu. He looked back over at the attendant, not even getting a look from the man. “I’ve got a big order. It’d be worth it.” He gave a friendly grin.

"Sorry, kid." The man grumbled, still not looking up from the magazine. "Like I said, grill's closed." The man flipped a page in the magazine, but the spine of the magazine suddenly fell apart in his hands. "What the hell?" He said, watching as the magazine fell between his hands. He looked down, then up to see Trebor standing over him, holding the blade of his black katana right at the man's face.

"Okay, you Burger King reject." Trebor said, with an evil grin, inching the blade closer. "Let's try this one more time. I'd like two orders of curly fries, two sodas and as many hot dogs and hamburgers as you can fit on your grill."

"Got him." Exclaimed Chip in a whisper as he stared at his tiny laptop's screen. He suddenly realized his situation and looked around at the room. The others in the dark room didn't stir, not even Beth. Chip let out his held breath and punched a few buttons, reading carefully the display that lit his screen. "Oh my god." He mumbled, his jaw slowly dropping as his eyes raced across the screen. He fell back against the wall he had been leaning against, the laptop sliding off his lap. "Oh no."

"What's wrong?"

Chip looked up, seeing Jared sitting up on his haunches. The ninja stood up from his sleep mat, his eyes glowing ever so slightly with latent magic. "What are you doing?" He pressed.

"I've been trying to track down the rest of the VGM." Chip explained, staring into the soft glow of the laptop computer screen.

"Where'd you get the laptop?" Jared suddenly asked.

"The computer store down the street." Chip explained, scrolling down the screen he was staring at.

"We had the money for it?" Jared asked. Chip gave him a hard look. "Please don't answer that." Jared said, shaking his head.

"I've been tracing all the airline flight purchases about the time that the other teams would have arrived at their airports. North Carolina doesn't have that many airports and a lot of them aren't within driving distance, so it that was a pretty short list. And I've been following up on all the different international flights." Chip hit a few buttons. "But the thing that got me was that Ecnilitsep attacked almost a full day after Eric said there was a troop build up."

"So." Jared shrugged. "It takes time to bring an army through a spatial border I guess."

"Or, she was busy." Chip said, looking at Jared. "And that's what made me start looking around at the various hospitals and, well..." Chip's voice trailed off.

"So what do you think you found?" Jared asked.

Chip took a deep, hesitant breath. "I think...Vincent." He said, looking back at the laptop. He crossed his arms, thinking desperately. "Ever since we left the states, I've been going over in my mind who was with what team when we left." He looked up at Jared. "I can't for the life of me remember Vincent ever getting on any of the vans."

"And you think he'd..." Jared breathed.

"Stay behind to try to deal with it himself?" Chip asked with a half a laugh. He looked back at the computer with a worried face. "And, and I think...I think I found him."

He stood up suddenly and walked into the bathroom. "Chip," Jared cautioned, getting up as well.

"When you get my signal," Chip said, turning on the light, staring at his reflection in the mirror. "Get ready to move."

"What?!" Jared shouted, causing the others to stir. But as he moved, it was too late.

Chip shoved his hand into the mirror over the sink. But rather than break the glass, his hand passed into the liquid as if it was thick, soupy water. Rippling away, the reflective surface parted as Chip pushed farther into the mirror.

Jared stood in the bathroom doorway as Chip passed completely into the mirror, almost instantly disappearing out of sight. "What the fuck's going on?" Ben asked, squinting as he stepped into the light. He looked at the mirror, then threw up his hands. "Son of a bitch! What happened to 'oh, we can't possibly side-step, it's much too dangerous'." He turned away from the bathroom and shoved his way past Beth and Shane. "What a dick." He pronounced, throwing himself back on his mat.

"Where's he going?" Shane asked, groggily.

"I thought side-stepping was too dangerous with Pihc around?" Beth exclaimed, staring at the mirror.

"I don't know." The ninja said, swallowing. "I, I thought..."

"What do we do?" Beth asked. "I mean, without Chip..."

"We'll be okay." Jared quickly said, turning back to Shane and Beth. He put his hands on their shoulders, giving them both reassuring looks. "Chip knows what he's doing. He said that he'd contact us. Odds are, he'll be back by morning. But he said he'd give us a signal."

"What signal?" Beth begged.

"Beth." Jared said with a charismatic smile. "This is Chip we're talking about. What do you think the chances are that he clarified?" He asked rhetorically, getting a chuckle from Shane. "Now come on. Back to bed." He looked over his shoulder at the mirror. "Chip, he knows what he's doing." As Shane and Beth turned back into the dark hotel room, Jared slid into the bathroom and switched off the light. "He better." He breathed silently as he followed back to the beds.

"Momma?" Sophia whispered, clutching to the white telephone. Sitting on the couch as the Caribbean sun rose outside the balcony, she pulled her legs in close. "Momma? Are you there?"

"Sophia?" Came the woman's voice. There was a cough and the sound of a cigarette lighter. "Do you know what time it is?" The female voice suddenly barked.

"Momma, I wanted to call and say, say I'm alright." Sophia said, huddling in close to the phone.

"You're not pregnant, are you? Lord have mercy on me, I told you that the first thing you'd…"

"Momma, I'm not pregnant." The girl said, shivering in the warmth. "It's just, I'm, I'm on a field trip, with my class. But I, I'm home sick and I wanted to…"

"Field trip?" Her mother burst in. "Girl, do you think I'm stupid? Do you think I'm just some willy-nilly dummy? You think I don't know where you are? I watch TV. I know what you college kids do away from home. You're down at one of those Spring Break resorts, boozing it up and spreading your legs. Damn girl, I tried to raise you right. I made sure you went to…"

"Momma, please don't be mad." Sophia said, her eyes tearing up. "I just wanted to say I miss you and that I…"

"Well, homesick serves you right." Her mother cursed. "The lord'll strike you down, you get pregnant. And if you so much as kiss a boy before your wedding night, I swear, you won't have no place in this house ever again."

"Momma? I…" Sophia started. But the door to the master bedroom opened. Sophia's eyes jerked wide. "I gotta go." She said, putting the phone down.

Tim came stumbling out into the small foyer of the suite. His hair was stuck straight up, his eyes bleary and uneven as he struggled to slide his glasses on before he bumped into the kitchenette wall. He felt around for the coffee maker, hitting the button to start the automated process. Content with the vague smell of coffee, he turned around to Sophia. "Hey." He grumbled, swaying as he tried to stay awake. "Your mom home?"

Sophia took a deep breath, panic crossing over her. "How'd you…"

"Mage." Tim said groggily, pointing at himself. "I know these things. Besides, if I still had a mother, I'd call her too."

"What about your father?" Sophia asked, still buried against the far end of the couch in the wide room.

"My dad's part of the Center for Disease Control." Tim said, turning back to the coffee maker. He switched it off, pulling out the pot. He opened it up and poured the black sludge into his mouth, mindless of the heat. "Uhhhh." He said, putting the pot back and starting the machine once more. "The FBI will be monitoring his every step during all this."

"Does your dad know about, I mean, everything?" Sophia asked.

"No, but I imagine he suspects." Tim said, rubbing his eyes, his conscious mind slowly taking over. "With me being a mage and Vincent being weird beyond all rational thought, he's got to know something's up. He and Vincent have been kind of estranged ever since Vincent moved out to Salt Lake City with him. I wasn't too thrilled about dad living out there alone when Vincent moved back, but there wasn't a lot that I could…" Tim stopped. He stood up, listening.

He heard crying. He turned around to see Sophia on the couch, sniffing back her emotions. She looked up at Tim, tears streaming down her face. "Sophia?" Tim asked. But as he spoke, the door on the other end of the hall opened up and Michelle stepped out. Dressed in only a T-shirt, she glared at Tim, but then heard the crying as well. She turned around the corner, looking at Sophia.

The girl turned away, wiping her face, but the tears just broke out even harder. "What's wrong?" Michelle asked, moving towards her.

"I'm scared." Sophia blurted out, almost laughing. "I'm so scared; I don't know what to do with myself." Michelle sat down next to her, putting her arm around Sophia's shoulders. The girl leaned into Michelle, bawling.

Behind Tim, the bedroom door opened and Jessica stepped out. She looked at Tim, but the Vgm quickly turned to her, gently leading her back into the room, leaving the two girls alone.

"I'm scared I'm never going to see home again." Sophia confessed, shaking as she cried. "I'm scared I'm never going to see my mom again. I'm scared I'm, oh god I'm so scared."

"Hey, it's okay." Michelle said, stroking her hair. She moved a bit, lifting up Sophia's face to look in her eyes. "Believe me; I know what it's like." She said with a smile. "It was almost two years ago when Vincent moved to Salt Lake City. And not long after that, Dan and I were both dragged into this little world." Michelle laughed, looking away. "And I remember the first time I ever dealt with Trebor. God." She laughed, her own breath becoming ragged. "I was so scared. He hunted me like I was a rabbit. I was scared to go home. I was scared to be at school. I was scared to be anywhere. I couldn't feel safe. And I thought he was going to take everything away from me."

"How'd you get over it?" Sophia asked, sniffing at her tears.

Michelle thought about it for a moment, then looked at her and smiled. "I guess partly because I punched him." She said, getting a laugh from Sophia. She smiled and winked. "I punched him right in the nose. And I saw him bleed. And it's like it clicked in me, you know. I realized that he wasn't all that different from all the other guys I'd had trouble with all my life. I could beat them up; I could beat him up." She shrugged. "And partly, I never did. I'm still afraid of him. A lot. Probably more than I am of Pihc."

"Wow." Sophia whispered.

Michelle patted Sophia's shoulder, then leaned in close. "Come on. We'll go put on some slutty clothes and find some guys to buy us breakfast." Sophia tried hard to keep from laughing, but couldn't manage it.

The nighttime hours of the hospital echoed with an eerie calm. The doors of the empty rooms stayed patiently open, while the distant lights from the used wings scattered shadows into the dim section where the silent nurse's station sat, unattended in the early morning.

The mirrored closet door at the nurse's station inside the silent hospital rippled violently as a gloved hand slipped through the surface. The hand grabbed onto the doorframe and flexed powerfully as it pulled. Chip's head and shoulder punctured the reflective surface, his upper body coming through. But as his left hand came out, he was suddenly yanked back in up to his shoulders. He grabbed the doorframe and pulled as hard as he could. He struggled to pull himself out up to his waist, but then was yanked back again. Blood poured from a wound on his forehead and ran into his eyes.

Gritting his teeth, Chip closed his eyes and focused. His body suddenly erupted in an electrical charge, allowing him to yank himself free of the mirror. Vomiting out from the reflective surface, Chip threw himself towards the chair at the nurses' station, knocking it into the hall as he collapsed onto the floor. Panting desperately, he fought for air as his body ached with each movement.

Wiping the blood from his eyes, the Vgm took off his glasses and rested painfully on the tile floor. "Fuck." He finally said, replacing his glasses and using the desk to pull himself to his feet. "No, no." He grumbled to himself. "'We can't side-step with Pihc around. Not only is it dangerous just being in there, but we could lose our way. No one in their right mind would pull a stunt like that.'" He rubbed his face again, still trying to calm his breathing. "I'm going to get myself killed someday."

He stood up slowly, finally breathing out one last time. He touched his forehead, wincing at the pain as he felt the cut. "I can't believe Pihc's got this place locked down like this." He grumbled, still wiping blood from his face. He looked back at the mirror, seeing the cut across his brow, then grabbed a towel from a neatly-stacked pile. He held the white linen against the cut and looked around the empty station. He grabbed up a chart, scanning it quickly, flipping pages as he searched.

"Why am I not surprised?" Came a voice from the hall.

Chip whirled around, his hand at his golden katana. Down the hall a few paces near the entrance to another wing was a familiar face. A fit black-haired doctor just a year or two older than Chip stared back at him, shaking his head disapprovingly. "Well, well." Chip smiled as cordially as he could. "Orlando Townsend. Let me guess. It's Doctor Townsend now, right?"

"Glad to see you remember." Orlando said with a slightly aggressive tone. He looked Chip up and down, shaking his head. "You don't look that different. What happened to your head?"

"I got into a fight with a mirror." Chip smiled. "Sorry to sneak in, but you know how it is."

"Oh, I remember." Orlando nodded. "I haven't seen you in, what? Four years?"

"Not quite." Chip said cautiously, looking around the dark wing of the hospital. "How's life been treating you? If you're a doctor in Raleigh, I guess you must be doing well. You seem healthy."

"My Tae Kwon Do instructor's not the slave-driver you were." Orlando said. "But then, he's not the crackpot you were, either."

Chip sighed. "Look, Orlando, I don't have time for this." He said honestly. "I know you were never willing to believe in what the VGM…"

"Oh, I was willing." The doctor interrupted. "I just didn't. I wasn't like those kids you manipulated. How people like Joe or Quincy or Jessica could eat it up, I'll never know." Chip just let the accusation hang in the air.

After an awkward moment, the doctor scratched under his eye. "Well, I'm guessing you're not here about your head, are you?" He surmised. Chip just watched the doctor. Finally, Orlando just sighed. "Alright." He said, as he turned from Chip, heading away from the nurse's station. "Follow me."

"What do we do now?" Cye asked as she sat next to Brenard. "Now that Pihc is..." She didn't say any more.

"I don't know." Brenard admitted. Behind the two of them, Yadiloh threw stones into the giant canyon. "But without Pihc, I am not inclined to acquiesce to Ecnilitsep's plans."

"Me too." Cye nodded.

"Soup's on." Announced Trebor's voice from the rear of the group. Brenard and Cye turned to find Trebor carrying two bags of food.

"What in the world have you got?" Brenard challenged with an annoyed tone. But Cye stepped forward, elated by the aroma.

"Smells good." She grinned. Behind her, Yadiloh jumped off the tower of rocks, attracted by the scent of the food as well.

"Look's like you're out-voted, Greek-boy." Trebor chided, as he put the bags down, allowing the foot to topple out. "I got you a couple of hamburgers, though."

"I would rather not." Brenard said, turning away.

"Oh, come on." Cye pressed. "They're good." She said, holding one out to Brenard. The gladiator looked down to the silver-wrapped food, then at Cye. Hesitantly, he accepted one.

"I got you a hot dog, Tex." Trebor said, handing a loaded hot dog to Yadiloh. He took the thing, staring at it. One eyebrow went up as he stared intently. Finally, he decided it was food and tore the meat from the bun and toppings.

"That'll work too I guess." Trebor said, blinking as the cowboy devoured the solitary strip of meat. He laid the food down on the ground so everyone could reach, then leaned back against the rocks. In the middle of the desert, the hot winds skated over them, rustling the bags of food. Trebor looked down at his burger for a moment, then at the other three. "Look, I'm just talking." He said with a cautious look each of the others. "But I think we all are less than a little pleased about the recent change in events."

"Ecnilitsep's assaulting the United States." Brenard said clearly, looking up from his food at Trebor. "She's planning to utterly destroy it and then the rest of the world beyond." Yadiloh looked away, uncertain how to respond to such news. Cye simply withdrew into herself, focusing on her food.

"We need to stop her." Trebor said with cold decisiveness, looking the gladiator straight in the eyes. "She forced Pihc to rejoin with S'ram. I didn't even know Pihc was an alternate. But still, that's just something you don't do. You can't do. There's no love lost between me and Pihc, but still. With Pihc…" His voice trailed off.

"Trebor's right." Cye spoke up. "We've got to stop her."

Brenard stood now. "It's all fine and good to decide we should." He said. "But how do we go about doing it?" The others were silent.

As the door to the room opened, the familiar stench of death hit Chip like a wall. Orlando went in first, turning to Chip once he was in the room. Chip, hesitant to enter, took a deep breath, trying to prepare himself for what he was certain he was going to find. He still wasn't ready for the sight that awaited him.

On the bed in the center of the room was what remained of Vincent Pierce. Chip's jaw dropped as he took his first unstable steps into the room, his eyes locked on the monstrosity on the bed. The bloated and deformed body was completely discolored, covered in an assortment of unidentifiable protrusions, and misshapen almost beyond recognition.

"What the hell?" Chip tried to ask, but nothing more came out.

"This is Vincent Pierce." Orlando said, his voice gentler than it had been. He didn't look up from the bed. "If you're wondering what's wrong with him, a better question would be what ISN'T wrong." Chip looked over at the distant doctor as Orlando continued. "Every disease, every virus, anything and everything that can go wrong in a body is going wrong with him."

"How did…" Chip tried to ask, but nothing came out still.

"He seems to be inhumanly resistant to the injury and disease." Said the doctor, still amazed by the boy's tenacity. "As such, the assorted diseases aren't able to kill him. Not right away, at least." Chip closed his eyes tightly, reopening them to Vincent.

"But they will kill him." Chip more affirmed than asking. "Eventually?"

"Let's hope so." Orlando said. "Most people would have died from the sheer shock of that many viruses in them at once. The body would simply shut down. I have absolutely no idea how he's still alive. But imagine that you, as the leader of the Video Game Masters, might be able to shed some light on that little detail."

"He was given an accelerated healing." Chip answered, inattentively.

"Right." Orlando said, with a disbelieving nod.

"You don't believe me?" Chip asked, without caring much.

"Chip," Orlando said with a smile. "I never believed any of that shit about 'Crossworld' or 'Pihc' or whatever. I'm sure as hell not going to buy 'that' excuse."

"Even when the evidence is right in front of you?" Chip countered, his temper beginning to flare. He motioned to Vincent's body for emphasis, but Orlando was unphased.

"When I see this mystical being 'Pihc' and his army of twisted monsters, than I'll believe it. Until then," Orlando left it at that. He walked around from the foot of the bed to Vincent's right, checking some of the machines that were plugged into the Vgm. Chip simply stood still, in shock.

"You might get your wish, Orlando." He finally mumbled, low enough that the doctor didn't here him. "Can he hear me?" Chip asked a bit louder, waiving his hand, trying to see if he would get a response from Vincent.

"At the moment, no." Orlando said, with a bit of remorse. He stood up from the machines' once again looking over Vincent with an almost-paternal look of concern. "He's too drugged up. We're doing what we can to kill the pain, but even illegal painkillers aren't enough."

Chip sighed, a single word appearing in his head. "Euthanasia?" He asked slowly. Orlando glanced over at him, but didn't say much. Chip leaned down onto the edge of the bed, holding himself up on the footboard.

"I can't really make that call." Orlando finally said. "I'd personally want to give him a while longer, see if a miracle happens." Orlando sighed, with a dismissing waive, more for his own emotions than anything else. "I'm trying to get a hold of any of his immediate family. Last I heard, he had moved out west. Needless to say, I was surprised to find him here."

"How'd he get here?"

"He crawled." Orlando said, almost laughing. "Scared the devil out of some poor woman on her smoke-break. She nearly had a heart attack." Chip smiled at the thought also, then turned back to Orlando.

"Orlando, things are going to get very rough soon." Chip said, reaching out to put his hand on Vincent's.

“Don’t touch him.” Orlando warned, quickly. The harshness of the doctor’s voice froze Chip’s hand. He looked up at the doctor. “At least a few of the illness are contagious through touch. None are airborne, though.”

“Okay.” Chip said defensively, taking a step back from the bed. “As I was saying, it’s going to get rough. Can he stay here for a few days?”

“Yeah.” Orlando said, with a surprisingly sentimental nod. “I’ll keep him here until we track down either his brother or his father.”

“Thanks.” Chip said, genuinely. He turned to leave.

“Chip?” Said the Doctor, stopping Chip in his tracks. The Vgm turned his head to Orlando, who was still at the foot of the bed. Orlando tried to ask something, but his squeaking voice wouldn’t take. Finally, though, he forced it out. “What ever happened to Joe and the rest of them? I never saw them after Vincent told me that the VGM had…disbanded.”

“They met their fate.” Chip said with guarded honesty. “I’m afraid they…” Orlando waved his hand at Chip, trying to stop him.

“I miss them.” The doctor said after a moment, looking back at Vincent. “I missed meeting at Starcade.” He smiled, a bit teary eyed. “Needless to say, I was glad to see Vincent, even in this state.”

“Yeah, Vincent’s all any of us had for a long time.” Chip said, with a deep sigh as he turned and left.

Jon sat up in the space between the beds of the tiny, British hotel room. In the soft glow of the blue television screen, he looked up as Dan sat on the foot of the farther bed, watching the news. “What are you doing?” The biker asked, blinking the sleep from his eyes.

“Keeping track of what happens in the States.” Dan said, doodling on a notepad. “I’m trying to figure out who’s leading which force, and how much they’ve got with each of them.”

“Got with them?” Jon asked, rubbing his bleary eyes in the television-lit room.

“Yeah. Who’s leading how many ’Shees.” Dan said, jotting down some notes as figures were flashed onto the television screen. “The death toll is mounting fast.”

“What’s a ’Shee?” Jon asked, actively avoiding turning too close in the direction of the television’s light.

“They’re Pihc’s shock troopers, I guess.” Dan explained, glancing down at Jon. “They’re like big spiders, only scarier.”

"Like a tarantula?" Jon asked, putting his hands together and wiggling his fingers.

"Think less Arachnophobia and more Jurassic Park." Dan explained, continuing his note-taking.

Jon's eyes went wide, then he glanced again at the television, then at the clock on the tiny table between the beds. "So why are you taking the notes?" He asked.

"Just in case." Dan said, still monitoring the almost-silent television.

"This sucks."

Both Jon and Dan turned to the other sleeping bag on the floor as Jim leaned up on his elbows, looking at the two of them. "Why do four of us have to be in here?"

"Because we divided up the rooms by gender." Jon answered.

"Right. So explain to me why I'm on the floor?" Jim asked.

"Because I'm on the bed." Dan said.

"The one that's not being slept in?" Jim asked. "Explain that one."

"There's nothing to explain." Jon defended. "You need to learn how to play 'paper-rock-scissors' better."

"Yeah, but there's a perfectly good bed in the other room." Jim went on. "And more than that, there's a perfectly fine girl in that afore-mentioned other room."

"Damn it, Jim," Emily shouted, suddenly sitting up from the other bed. She snatched her key from the bedside table and threw it at him. "Then you go in there and sleep with her. You deal with her making all sorts of innuendos and overtures and whatever else that tramp wants to do."

"Done and done!" Jim grinned as he bounded towards the door, the key in hand.

Chip walked with his hands stuffed in his pockets down the empty halls of the hospital. Following his feet, he paced absentmindedly, unconsciously avoiding the occasional third-shift worker or the overnight guest.

The sound of a television caught his attention. The Vgm stopped and turned to see a small café built right into the hospital. Behind the counter, a bored college student focused on a set of books, while in the far corner, private computers sat in isolated booths.

Chip looked at the student behind the counter for a moment, then up at the 24-hour news station on the television set. He waited for a moment, then moved like a shadow over to the computers. Sitting down with his back to the wall, he looked the machine over for a moment. Finding the credit card slot, he pulled a wallet out of his black jacket. A diverse collection of credit cards came tumbling out, each with a different name, Chip chose one and slid it into the machine. The computer screen came to life, displaying a common desktop.

He looked up at the television for a moment, watching the news display the latest information concerning the continued assault on the US. He studied the figures and diagrams as they showed how the military was getting beaten back at every turn. He turned to the computer and switched on the internet, bringing up a map of the US. Chip compared the map on the computer to the map on the television, then turned fully to the computer. Working fast, Chip brought up a host of new windows, from the internet as well as from the computer's innermost workings. Focusing most of his attention on a simple black window with white letters, he occasionally glanced around the empty café, all while he continued to type away.

In no time, the screen was filled by the black window, its white letters and numbers arranged in a seemingly random pattern. He manipulated the symbols a bit more, then looked up at the television by the counter. He considered it for a moment, then leaned out from behind his screen. "Hey!" He called to the late-night college worker. The guy jumped at the sound of the voice, startled to anyone in the all-night cafe. "What channel's that on?" He asked, pointing at the screen.

"And that was the scene here in the Nevada Desert." Said the reporter, looking more than a bit scared. "The American forces have been laid completely to waste. There's barely anything left but rubble and death."

Around the corner shop in New York City, a small crowd of watchers paid close attention to the report. Each one struggled for a clear view, trying to keep abreast of the newest news about the 'terrorist attack'. Meanwhile, the real danger passed through the Midwest, undaunted. The televisions continued to show the shocking footage taken from far, far away of the destruction and the mayhem that had rocked the country and the world.

And then the television screen suddenly went blue.

The watchers looked around but all of the screens in the store front had turned blue. They looked to one another, a few errant questions flying, but no answers presented themselves. Desperate for more information, the crowd stayed at the store, waiting for the next development.

In London, the international news was interrupted as the screen suddenly went blue. At the television station, the anchors and the staff were all completely baffled as the signals went dead, replaced by the simple monochromatic sight.

A group of Cuban kids rushed across the early morning street, bringing a pair of cars screeching to a halt. The kids ignored the calls from the drivers and rushed to the local bar, peaking in the window as the bartender sat by the large front window, staring at the blue screen on his large television.

In Beijing, a host of college students all gathered in the university's student lounge around the provided public television, staring at the enigmatic blue screen that had appeared over the 24-hour news channel.

Around the world, the same occurred. Every television's screen, no matter where in the world, no matter what channel was on, became a solid blue.

And then, just as the viewers prepared to turn away, a single white cursor appeared. The cursor blinked quickly, like a hyperactive warning signal. It sat at the top of the screen for a brief moment, then burst into motion. Moving quickly along the screen, it left large white letters as it went. The cursor finished in the blink of an eye, leaving the message on the screen for the entire world to see. All around the world, English speaking or not, the same message was broadcast onto every television.

All Vgms, On-line.
Wikieup, Arizona.

CHAPTER 16

Here There be Dragons

"Yippie-ki-yay, mother-fucker."

—John McClane, Die Hard

"Sir!" Screamed the squad leader over the relay as his team of five jets crested above the crimson clouds high above the Montana wilderness. "I have four UFOs on my radar. Repeat, four UFOs on radar, coming in fast. Do you copy?"

Back at the base, the radar-operator was going crazy. His hands moved with an unnerving precision as he tried desperately to get information on the four signals which had just appeared out of nowhere in the middle of their airspace. Over his shoulder, his Commanding Officer was not in a much better position. "Roger." Said the Radar man into his head-mike as he stared at the screen, throwing switches and turning all manner of dials. "I have four targets moving at…approximately Mach 4." The man punched up a few displays, tracking their course. "They seem to be heading directly for the engagement sight."

"Satellite." The CO yelled across the room. "I need…"

"I have visual!" Came the panicked voice of one of the other pilots. All heads whirled to the speakers as the pilot rattled off what his eyes refused to believe. "Repeat, I have visual. There's five of them, not four. Five. I repeat, five targets. Five UFOs." His voice barely held against the near-hysteria that was washing over him.

"What type of aircraft are they?" Called the CO, grabbing the Radar man's microphone away from him. Yanking the headpiece off the subordinate, the commanding officer choked the enlisted man with the cord. "Can you identify the targets?" He yelled while beneath him the soldier's face turned blue. "Are they hostile? What type of aircraft are they?"

There was a long pause before any of the pilots responded. Finally, it was the squadron leader who spoke up. He squeaked out the words, his mind finding what he was saying impossible to believe. "They're dragons, sir!"

Rising through the cloudbank with his wings spread out, Bahamut roared through the darkening sky. The last light of the setting sun glinted off his brown armored body as he was followed by the serpentine blue form of Leviathan. The two kept rolling higher into the sky as Oroboris' black form reared up, his thick snake-like body keeping just ahead of the others. As they moved, Kageryu's black frame rose up as well, his wingless body flowing as if riding the crest of waves. And then, parallel with his twin Bahamut, Tiamat roared up, his black body reflecting brilliantly the sun's rays back into the sky.

"*Slaughtering 'Shees is not my idea of a good war campaign.*" Roared Bahamut, almost smiling as the clouds shot past beneath them. "*We have bigger foes to deal with.*"

"*We are not here to win a war; just to even the odds.*" Kageryu countered, his deep voice echoing through the thin air and gusting winds. "*If the Celestial Dragons and the creations of Ecnilitsep were to truly clash with all our might, then the eyes of the Shadows would be on us in an instant.*"

"*Say what you want.*" Tiamat growled as he coasted down a bit. "*I just want Livic.*"

"*Until we land, Yerrbmot is the one that should concern you.*" Oroboris cautioned. "*But whatever the consequences, we have our course set before us.*" He called from the lead. "*Let us deal with our immediate future now and concern ourselves with tomorrow when it comes.*"

With that, Oroboris bent his massive body and changed directions with a fast whip of his armored form. Diving at a sharp angle, the other four dragons followed him, maintaining their wedge-shaped formation. Below, the ground was approaching.

"Do you hear something?" Eminaf asked, looking around as she stood on a rock above the marching 'Shees.

Livic leapt up with her, looking around at the ebbing sea of monsters. But as he did, the whipping wind caught his attention. He looked up, just in time to see the clouds swirl together. The two generals jerked back in dismay as the five dragons dropped down out of the funneling cloudbank, angling towards the marching army. "Oh no." Whispered the aged general.

The dragons leveled off just yards above the ground, their targets coming into focus with magical clarity even over the great distance. "*There he is!*" Called Tiamat, from the rear, his eyes set on Livic.

"*You know the plan!*" Leviathan called from between Oroboris and Bahamut. "*One barrage and we engage the generals face to face.*"

"*One barrage is all we'll need.*" Bahamut called confidently, sweeping up next to Leviathan, both surging ahead to take the lead. The two dragons drew their massive heads back, their mouths swelling with power. As the five shot towards the army of monsters, energy collected before their gaping jaws.

"Yerrbmot!" Livic screamed, turning back to the wizard at the rear of the army. But the magical general was already working. Holding up his staff and hands, a bubble-like reverberation cast across the three generals like a delicate shell as the dragons moved in. The fluctuation of existence wavered, then moved out, leaving only a slight distortion to be seen.

"This won't hold against dragon's fire." Eminaf pointed out from behind Livic as her left forearm guard reformed into a shield the size of her torso. "Especially not those dragons' fire."

"It'll hold." Yerrbmot said confidently, even as he wiped sweat from his brow. He glanced at the top of his staff; the ornate endcap reforming like liquid into a golden sphere there surged with greater power, reinforcing the sphere of protection.

Leviathan swooped down low, coming in under the other four. With a fast snap of his head, the power that had gathered within his mouth burst free. A beam of white-hot incandescent fury erupted from the blue dragon's mouth. Like a slice of the sun, the beam ripped through the air, to collide with the ground. The sizzling beam of power instantly incinerated the ground, its ambient heat spreading out like a wave of light, devastating all within sight.

But as Leviathan maintained the blast, Bahamut swept down just beneath him, his armored brown body skimming just above the tree tops. With a hard whip of his long neck, he spat five flaming spheres of superheated energy. The giant balls of fire shot through the air, evaporating the morning mist they passed through while blasting towards the surrounding devastation of Leviathan's beam.

The five balls slammed into the world like a bomb. Exploding on impact, the flames of Bahamut's power erupted out in ring-shaped waves of devastation, driving the dragon's fire across the wilderness, spreading the destruction like a plague, incinerating the woodland trees indiscriminately next to the 'Shees.

High above the Nevada desert, clouds owned the sky. The stark orange sky layered out against the dark gray clouds, contrasting with the harsh, unforgiving stone world. But echoing out from the clouds came a deep, heavy sound.

Three jet fighters shot like demons through the sky, bearing the symbol of the United States Air Force. Streaking beneath the clouds, the fighters began to drop their bombs, covering the entire desert with a layer of fire and destruction. Hell raised high into the sky, nipping at the heels of the jets as the flames threatened to escape from the earthly prison and engulf the fiery sky and dark clouds above. All life was destroyed in the fire. And yet again, the fighters laid down their song of destruction, killing everything. Again and again.

After the fires had died down and the desert cooled enough to support life, the ground troops moved in. Tanks. Soldiers. Artillery. Everything the soldiers needed to obliterate all life in a small nation was focused here on this tiny desert of their own country.

One soldier walked along, his M-16 at ready. A slight motion caught his eye. He turned quickly, firing numerous shots. After the barrage was over, he looked closer. A charred bush had fallen. He took his position again, his eyes watching.

Here and there, soldiers fired. Some at half-dead desert creatures that twitched a bit. Some at a shadow that they thought was dangerous, only to find it was their own. A group of soldiers came to a large rock formation that still stood. Three were chosen and the soldiers moved over the rocks, checking it thoroughly for any signs of life. After the intense investigation, the soldiers backed away, calling it clear.

Then it exploded.

Out from beneath the rocks swarmed the 'Shees, the sight of the twisted monsters paralyzing the minds of the soldiers. On their spindly legs, they raced across the hot desert ground faster than the soldiers could retreat. Their spiky teeth made quick work of the soldiers, while their acid-covered tongues tore through the ranks of the military men.

A thunderous boom came from a cannon two hills back, the arrival of its shell scattering the 'Shees in clouds of dust and sand. The cannon turned its turret, training its sight on another pack of 'Shees. But as the men inside readied to fire, there was a jam. The driver looked up through peep hole just in time to see a black scimitar blade driving through at him.

Ecnilitsep withdrew her blood-tipped sword from the tank's visor. Whipping away the remains of the life she ended, the woman leapt off the tank, slashing down. The blade's damage carried through the tank itself, slicing the metal beast cleanly in two. Before the tank could fall apart, the friction ignited the fuel lines and ammo beds, turning the tank into a massive ball of flame.

Ecnilitsep was thrown back but she landed on her feet as the 'Shees swarmed past her. The platoon of army men fired their guns, but the bullets whizzed by, barely grazing the giant monsters. Ecnilitsep stayed back, proud of the destruction wrought by her beasts.

A sound turned her attention. She turned to see in the distance a single, armored figure tear through the rear flank of the army men. Slicing with a black-bladed katana, the massive form cut effortlessly through the soldiers with barely a notice. Ecnilitsep smiled and turned back to the scene of the carnage.

As the fires subsided, Eminaf and Livic stepped beyond Yerrbmot's shield as he leaned panting against his staff to remain standing. The two considered the fiery world of destruction that had once been an untamed wilderness. Standing at the edge of the only grass remaining, they marveled at the very surface of the land as it sizzled away.

"I…" Livic started to say, but his mind was left at a loss. But a rushing of air caught his attention. The three generals looked up as the first two dragons descended.

Leviathan and Tiamat were the first to land. The great blue snake of Leviathan flowed down along the ground, until its four tiny claws were hovering over the charred dirt. The great beast flipped forward, at the same time becoming the shape of a man nearly instantly. Dressed in blue and black armor, he drew forth a mighty and ornate pole arm, holding it ready.

Tiamat landed, the dragon's rear legs morphing into the strong legs of a human, the metamorphosis continuing over his entire body. Dressed in black armor, he wielded a sturdy broadsword, cautiously staying shoulder and shoulder with Leviathan.

"Two dragons?" Eminaf smiled, drawing out her saber. "That's it?"

"There are still three more up above." Yerrbmot gasped, still on the grass, struggling to catch his breath in the superheated air. "And we're without any 'Shees now."

"Trust me." Livic warned to the woman at his left, the forearm guards on his armor becoming small shields as he readied his thick axe. "Two will be quite enough."

"Want me to get him?" Eminaf asked as the two humanoid warriors approached carefully, motioning towards the black-armored dragon with her saber.

"There are plenty of dragons for you." Livic growled, slamming the blade of his double-bladed battle axe against his shield. "Tiamat's mine!"

Livic launched at the black-armored warrior, swinging his axe in a fast slice. Tiamat slipped around the slice, swinging with his sword for Livic's head. The general moved out of the way and slashed again at Tiamat. The two's weapons met as the dragon shoved into the general. "*It's been what? A few weeks?*" Tiamat said with a mocking smile. "*I missed you.*"

"You always do." Livic yelled, lunging forward with the head of his axe, jamming the central spike at Tiamat's head.

Yerrbmot watched as Livic and Eminaf engaged Leviathan and Tiamat. Still on the ground, he blotted the sweat with his sleeve, only to feel a cool wind rush down on him. He yanked his head back at the refreshing wind to see Oroboris swoop down from the clouds, his body the size of a small plane. With a thrust of his head, the black dragon sent down a fast blast of fire. Yerrbmot rejected the fire with a panicked wave of his hand, but the blow knocked him off the ground and sent him rolling across the grass to land amongst the smoking heaps that had once been 'Shees.

The wizard came up, searching the sky. Oroboris and Kageryu spiraled around each other with Bahamut gliding nearby. "Perhaps we should even the odds." Yerrbmot called defiantly to the dragons, his eyes bursting into blue flame. He held out his hands, a pair of fireballs bursting into existence. From the right hand, a flaming bird erupted with a crystal shriek from out of the blue fireball. From his left hand, an orange firebird rocketed into the sky from the red ball of flame.

"**Twin Phoenixes!**" Yerrbmot called. "**Slay them if you can!**"

"*I'll get the guardian spirits.*" Bahamut called as he angled towards the flaming birds. "*You guys get the wizard.*"

Eminaf rushed at Leviathan, swinging her slender sword in a fast arch. He parried the stab with his pole arm, then swung the free end to take Eminaf's feet out from underneath her. The female general leapt over the sweep and aimed a fast hack at Leviathan's neck. Her blade got within inches, but Leviathan knocked her blade back with his forearm guard, spinning his pole arm into a more offensive position.

Leviathan lunged nimbly forward, slicing his large blade at the general. She bent at the waist, delicately shifting under and around the staff. As she came back up, Leviathan spun around to impale her with the other end of the staff.

Bahamut rushed around the orange firebird's talons, his long brown tail barely escaping capture. Swooping around the bird's grasp, he whipped his head around, blasting the bird's head with a shot of blue fire. The blast incinerated the firebird's body instantly, but it left Bahamut open as the blue firebird tore through him.

Knocking Bahamut through the chest, the firebird passed right through the brown dragon, rocketing up into the sky. The brown dragon roared in pain, then turned his furious gaze up into the sky, his eyes locking on the bird. He pulled his wings close to his body as the dragon's whole form streamlined and became smooth.

Rupturing through the sound barrier without a precursor of motion, Bahamut shot almost straight up at the elusive beast. The blue-flamed firebird turned to face his quarry just in time to get an incinerating blast through the body. The beam ripped through his form and shot off into space. Bahamut swept in a wide arc as the bird's body evaporated, turning his attention back to the ground.

Oroboris swooped in close to the ground, sending Yerrbmot a fast blast of fire. The wizard deflected the blow with a wave of his hands, then returned a streak of lightning. The white shots of power barely touched Oroboris as he flew off, coasting along the ground.

Yerrbmot turned back around as Kageryu flew in, his snake-like body coasting in close to the smoldering dirt. He threw a pillar-like blast at the wizard, allowing it to be deflected as well. The wizard then turned immediately back around to throw his will against Oroboris as another blast rocketed down at him.

The wizard threw the energy aside, then turned back to where Kageryu had been. The wizard found himself staring at the board chest of the ninja. Yerrbmot looked up as Kageryu smiled down at him, standing just inches from the wizard's face. "Oh no." The wizard mumbled.

"*Oh yes.*" Kageryu grinned, drawing back on his katana.

Tiamat swung a tight slice at Livic, but the general blocked the sword with his arm, the metal plates of his armor instantly reshaping into a body-sized shield. The general countered Tiamat's swing with one of his own, slicing for the dragon's throat. Tiamat parried the slice, but Livic immediately caught him in the stomach with his shield. Knocking the dragon back, he swung overhead at the armored foe. Tiamat spun out of the way, slicing his sword underneath his arm, catching Livic across the chest with it.

The blow had little effect, however. Livic breathed through the pain and reached back, his shield turning into a flail. He whipped the spiked end at Tiamat, wrapping it around his neck and throwing him to the ground. Tiamat went with the throw, bringing his legs up as he went airborne, kicking Livic in the side of the head. The general shook off the kick, using it to give him momentum as he spun around once again. He brought his axe up to cleave Tiamat in two but didn't get the time.

Livic slid out of the way as Bahamut swung at him, using a sword identical to Tiamat's. As soon as the general was clear of Tiamat, the brown dragon threw himself forward, his body shaping itself into a crocodile-sized dragon, its head curving up from its nimble body. The general moved back away from the dragon, preparing to combat the new form.

Moving in next to him, Eminaf put her back to Livic's, her body racked with injuries. "I fear we may have bitten off more than we could chew." She confessed as she and Livic guarded against the Celestial Dragons.

"Where's Ecnilitsep when we need her?" Livic cursed. He looked from Bahamut, to Tiamat, to Leviathan, then bumped his head against the back of Eminaf's. "Well, we shall at least soften them up for her, won't we?" He said with a stoic smile.

"We're not dead yet." Eminaf said with a grin. "I have every intention of leaving their bodies to feed the crows." She said, turning her sword around, taking on a new stance.

The city streets were crowded, people bustling along here and there. Amongst them, a brown-haired boy walked down the street, a backpack strapped tightly to his shoulders. The boy had half a smile on his face, as if remembering a joke. Oblivious to the world, he unconsciously dodged the dreamy denizens of the city.

A pair of eyes caught his attention.

The boy looked up, seeing a pair of black, opaque sunglasses staring at him. They belonged to a man in a black trench coat, carrying a peculiar sword. He stared coldly at the boy. The people in the street parted, giving them a clear view of each another. The man wore black military boots and fingerless gloves. His entire body was covered in black, down to the three black stripes of paint across his face. He eyed the boy, his eyes narrowing behind those black sunglasses.

The boy's expression turned to one of utter fear as he turned and ran, trying to avoid hitting anyone on the street. He dodged this way and that, never hitting anyone but coming very near. The boy turned down a side street, pushing himself for all he was worth. He passed a café, his eyes scanning the glass. No one was coming to help him. No one could hear his screams for help. He stopped and banged on the glass. But no one came. No one turned to look at him. He saw familiar faces, his friends. Friends from distant, departed lives. Now, they ignored him. Now, they were unaware of him.

The boy turned to run again but before he could get past the café, the man in black was suddenly in front of him. The boy fell to the ground, trying hysterically to back away from the man. The man turned his dark attention to the boy, his face expressionless. The boy tried to get up, but the man reached down, grabbing the boy by his backpack straps and hoisted him up. With a powerful heave, the man sent the boy crashing through the window of the café, shattering the glass into a myriad world of sharp pain.

The boy landed hard, glass lodged in him at every point. He tried to move but the pain was too much. He couldn't move at all. With tears and screams of pain, he tried to brush the glass out of his bleeding skin. The pain threatened to overwhelm him but he forced himself to remove the glass, bit by bit. He pulled out a huge shard from his forearm, watching as the blood gushed out. The boy tried to grab the blood, tried to put it back in but couldn't. He turned his eyes to the door of the café, watching as the man in black walked in, heading straight for him.

A sound ruptured the barrier between consciousness and dream. Vincent's left eye fluttered open, his right swollen closed. His exhausted, blood-shot eye scanned the fuzzy world of his vision, searching for some sign of the sound's source.

The window in Vincent's hospital room was left open just a crack, a gentle breeze from the world outside billowing into the deathly room. The light wind from the twilight just outside floated into the white hospital room like a cemetery mist, moving the curtains in a deep slow motion. The wind pushed the stench of the slow death back, allowing Vincent the pleasure of a few last gasps of almost fresh air in the stale emptiness of his room.

"It doesn't have to end."

Vincent struggled against his broken and diseased body to see over to the corner of the room by the entrance. Sitting in a chair propped up against the door was Vincent's mirrored-image of an alternate. Sitting calmly and unobtrusively, Trebor leaned forward, his face half-cloaked in the dim light of the window. "It doesn't, you know?" He said with uncharacteristic honesty, looking Vincent straight in the eyes.

Trebor stood slowly, harmlessly. He watched Vincent's emergency switch, but his tortured twin made no move to grab the signal button. Trebor breathed out a small sigh and came to the foot of Vincent's bed. "All that time we've spent hating each other. All that time we've spent against one another and it comes to this." He ventured a light, sad laugh.

He looked down at the headset by Vincent's bed, as well as the cracked remains of the SkyFold glasses. "Pihc's gone." Trebor went on with a bit of a remorseful laugh, looking to Vincent again. "Ecnilitsep…got rid of him." He smirked. "So much for revenge."

Trebor moved around the bed, standing between Vincent and the window. The remains of the Vgm struggled to look up at the dark alternate. Trebor leaned over to lower himself down to eye level, as he looked imploringly into Vincent's gaze. "Vincent, it's no longer a matter of saving the magic in the world." He said sincerely. "It's about saving the world itself."

He took the last step to bring him right next to the bed. "Ecnilitsep's gonna destroy everyone. She's going to completely obliterate all life on earth. And there isn't anything anyone can do about it. No one can stop her." He could see in Vincent's eyes that the truth had registered.

"Except you and I." The alternate whispered.

Trebor reached out his hand, putting it right above Vincent's deformed hand. "I've lived the same way you have, with half my memories, with half my life." He said, having to chuckle at himself to choke back a tear. "You and I are so close, so much the same, no matter what you think. You think I stole your past from you." Trebor's voice was shaking, his long-restrained emotions coming to the surface. "Well, you did the same but you also stole my future." Trebor leaned down, coming so close to Vincent he could feel his weakened breath.

"Vincent, it's up to you." He whispered sincerely. "Do you want to be the knight you always dreamt of? Was what you said about doing everything within your power to save lives bull or did you really mean it, I mean really mean it? Because here's your chance to save everyone. Everyone!" Trebor nearly shouted, a tear falling down from his eye. "Please, Vincent. Please, let's do what we both know is right."

He held out his hand to Vincent.

With a tear in his eye and a prayer for his soul on his lips, Vincent took Trebor's hand.

Jim

CHAPTER 17

11th Hour Offensive

"Just DO whatever it is you do to make this go away."

—Colonel John Hall, Sgt Bilko

"I swear, not even two nights." Jim grumbled as he stepped off the plane into the multi-airline terminal of the tiny airport. Next to him, Dan and Emily walked, with Aria following behind. Jon strolled through the gate a moment later, chatting with the captain of the plane. As the four in front approached the concourse, they saw Chip waiting.

"Welcome back to the USA." He smiled, his arms crossed over his chest. "We're still waiting for Tim and Jessica's team to get here. Stay available." With that, he turned and walked off, leaving them standing in confusion.

"Um, okay." Dan called after him, tossing up his hands. "I wonder what's gotten into him." He mused under his breath.

"I don't know." Emily said with only half-hearted concern. "He doesn't seem his usual jolly self." She looked around the tiny single story concourse, taking note of the one fast-food stall. "Guys, I'm going to go find the rest of the group. Maybe I can find Vincent or Mich. They might be able to explain what's going on." She said, heading to their left.

"Good luck with that." Dan called. He took a bottle of Dr Pepper out from his denim jacket and looked around as well. "I'm going to go find something more interesting than that to do."

"I'm going to find something less interesting than that to do." Jim responded immediately, the two friends heading in different directions.

Aria was left standing in the middle of the concourse. She glanced around, pulling her loose white shirt close around her neck. As she did, Jon strolled up next to her, looking around. "Where'd the kids go?" He asked.

She turned back to him with a seductive smile. "I don't know but it does mean we're all alone."

"No." Jon said simply, taking off his duster. He folded it over his arms and looked back at her from beneath his cowboy hat. "You're not my type."

She smiled even deeper. "I can be whatever you want me to…"

"No." Jon said.

"I used to be irresistible." She said defiantly to him. "I once broke up a royal wedding between a princess and a legendary knight."

"Yeah, well, I'm neither, so maybe that's it." Jon said indifferently. He looked around the concourse once more, then took off to his right, leaving Aria dumbfounded.

"So that's the deal." Ben explained to the waitress dressed in a semi-tuxedo in the airline bar. Spinning peanuts around in the bowl with the slim salt shaker, he looked up at the woman and smiled fatalistically. "I'm here with my team to kill the aliens."

"I, I thought they were terrorists." The blonde-haired woman stuttered in awe, her serving tray held nervously over her chest.

"Yeah." Ben nodded sympathetically. "That's what they want you to think. But no, aliens." He looked away, sighing moodily. "And to think, today may be my last day on earth." He shook his head, taking a swig from his bottle of water. "I never thought I'd die a virgin." He lamented quietly.

The waitress poised herself to speak but as she did, Aria slid into the seat next to Ben. "Hello." The gorgeous woman smiled alluringly at the sniper.

"Hey, what's up?" He smiled back, moving closer to her. Without giving the waitress a thought, Ben wrapped himself around Aria, locking lips with her. The waitress stared on, amazed and appalled simultaneously. "Oh." Ben said, tearing himself away from Aria for just a moment, looking to the waitress. "Feel free to jump in whenever you want." He said to the server before turning back to the woman in his arms.

Shane twisted the steering wheel sharply to the right, the squealing sounds of tires echoing off the padded arcade walls. He twisted the steering wheel back into position and stepped on the gas pedal, the roar of the engine building in intensity as the race car on the screen shot forward past its opponents on the race track.

Jim strolled up to the game next to him, sliding in a quarter. “Hey, what’s up?” Jim grinned, hitting the start button as the two occupied the small corner of the seven-game arcade.

“Not much.” Shane said, turning the car again, the wheels squealing.

Jim looked over at Shane for a moment, then at the arcade machine. “Don’t they normally provide those sounds?”

“The speaker’s broken.” Shane said through gritted teeth, continuing to provide his own gear-shifting noise.

“Forgive me, father, for I have sinned.” Dan said, sitting innocuously in the confession booth. “It has been…well, I’ve never actually been to confession before.”

The kindly priest looked through the tiny window of the Insta-Confession booth inside the airport. “What have been your sins, my son?” Asked the priest, with well-rehearsed precision.

“Well, none that I know of.” Dan said, trying to think, screwing open another Dr Pepper bottle. “I’m really not sure if I’ve really sinned at all this last week or so.”

“We all sin, my son.” The Priest said through the screen. “But do not worry, the lord shall always forgive.”

“Oh, I know.” Dan said casually. “God and me, we’re buddies. It’s just, well, I’m probably going to die in the next couple of hours or so, so I thought I’d just be sure, you know, get this all out of the way and everything.”

“I’m sorry.” The priest stumbled, leaning closer to the screen. “Could you go over that last part again? You’re going to DIE in a couple of hours?”

“Maybe.” Dan said lightly, taking a swig from his bottle. “I don’t know. If everything goes as we planned it, then no. If it goes as it should, then yes. It’s kind of up to god, really.”

“What’s supposed to happen?” The Priest asked with morbid curiosity, swallowing hard.

“Oh, well, I’m going to go face up against the monster that’s attacking out in the desert.” Dan said, thinking still. “You know, it just occurred to me that this information might be considered ‘classified’ in some circles.” He thought about it for a moment. “Well, they’re not really circles that throw a lot of parties so I doubt I frequent them.”

"You're going to what?" The Priest exclaimed. "You're going to fight those terrorists? Why?"

"Well, I guess it's kind of my job." Dan shrugged. "I mean, yeah, I guess I could leave the group but it's too much fun. And, you know, I am staying at the warehouse and everything, so free food. And it was either that or go on my mission."

"What mission?" The Priest asked.

"You know, the one all of us are supposed to go on when we get out of high school." Answered Dan, chugging more Dr Pepper.

"I don't know about any…" The Priest's mind came to a stop. His jaw dropped. "You're not Catholic, are you?"

"No, I'm Mormon." Dan said, taken back the priest's brazenness.

"Oh. You're one of THEM."

"What do you mean 'one of THEM'?!" Dan replied, leaning towards the screen.

"Get out." The priest shot back, slamming the window shut.

Beth pushed open the bathroom door, shuffling blearily into the white-tiled room. She leaned on the sink and looked at her reflection, sighing. She pulled her pale blonde hair back, then let it fall around her face, considering her blueish-green eyes and pale skin with discontent.

"Beth?" Came a familiar voice. The girl turned around as Emily stepped out of one of the stalls, dressed in a fresh change of clothes. "Hey!" She shouted, practically jumping forward to embrace her friend. Beth hugged her back and smiled with relief. "Thank god." She half-laughed. "Are you okay?"

"Yeah." Beth answered with half emotion. "God, it's good to see you. We've been having all sorts of trouble since Chip left." She said.

Emily blinked. "Chip what? What happened?" She exclaimed.

"Chip side-stepped out of our hotel room to come back here." Beth said. "He just stood up and jumped through the mirror."

"Say what? Why'd he do that? I thought we couldn't, since it's too dangerous." The cheerleader nearly shouted.

"I'm guessing that's why he's got that cut on his head." Beth said. "He looks exhausted, too. So I guess it took a lot out of him. We had to make the arrangements to get here. Fortunately, Ben was able to hack into the bank and get us some money. Otherwise, I don't know how we would have afforded the tickets."

"Wow." Emily accepted. "I'm sorry to hear Chip, you know, did that but it does sound like him." She squeezed Beth's shoulder, then turned to the bathroom mirror. "I know what you mean about money problems. Fortunately Dan had one of the ATM cards so we could get the money for the hotel and the tickets. Coming back, we got a great deal." She almost laughed, walking over to the sink as she opened up a make-up pouch. "Everybody's flying out of the US. So we were able to get a plane all to ourselves for dirt cheap." She brushed some powder onto her face, then turned to Beth, holding the compact out to her. "You holding up okay?" She asked.

"As best I can." Beth sighed, looking more like her old, high school self. "Chip's been planning the whole time since we got here. He won't really talk. And something's got him spooked about Vincent."

"Why? What's the deal?" Emily asked. "I haven't seen Vincent. I assumed he was off with Ben or something. I saw Jared, but he's asleep by the terminal."

"Emily, Vincent's not here." Beth emphasized.

"What do you mean Vincent's not here?" Emily asked, turning around. But she suddenly got a coy look. "I bet he went with Jessica. There's no way he'd let her out of his sight."

"I don't know." Beth ventured, her voice sounding hollow. "Chip's awfully preoccupied. I think something might be wrong." Emily looked at Beth in the mirror, but didn't speak up. She looked back at her own eyes, seeing worry filling her gaze.

"I love empty flights." Tim said as he walked next to Michelle up the ramp into the concourse.

"That's just because you can stretch out over the seats." She argued.

"You're the one that took up an entire aisle for a nap." Tim argued. But as they came to the concourse, Chip was standing before them. "Good to see you, boss." Tim nodded. As he did, Michelle walked up and hugged Chip. The Vgm looked down uncomfortably at Michelle, then at Tim. "She got laid down south. She's feeling affectionate." Tim explained and was rewarded with a harsh hit on the shoulder from Michelle.

"Okay." Chip said as she stepped back. He looked at Tim. "Where's Jessica and Sophia?"

"Right behind us." Tim said, thumbing back to the airplane deck. "Mich and I got bumped up to first class."

"I thought you said it was an empty flight?" Chip asked, confused.

"Yeah, but they still draw the curtains." Tim grinned. "So how long have you been waiting? This was the closest airport we could find to Wikieup or however you pronounce it. I'm still amazed that we ended up at the same airport." He said with a grin.

"The miracles of emergency situations and the small number of international airports in the desert." Chip said with a humorless smile.

Tim looked down at Michelle but the girl waved her hand at Chip, barely getting his attention. "So what's the plan, Chuck?" She insisted loudly up to him.

Chip watched the rear doors for a moment longer, until he saw the form of Jessica and Sophia step out. With a solemn look, he hit the button on his headset. "All Vgms, online."

Tim looked back at Jessica as she came through. "Jessica, on-line." She said, motioning for Tim.

"Tim, on-line." He said, turning back to Chip.

Silence.

Tim's face slowly got cold. "Chip." He asked. "Where's Vincent?"

Chip looked at Tim for a long breath, then turned away. "We've got a lot to deal with in the next half an hour." He said as he walked away. "Come on. We're gathering at the baggage claim."

The gathered group of misfits stood near the baggage claim, the revolving tables as silent as the concourse itself. "This part of the US is evacuating. Every person who has family anywhere else in the country, or in other countries, is pretty much gone. They've cleared out of the line of devastation being wrought by Ecnilitsep, which is expected to cut right through the top portion of the state towards Santa Fe." Chip explained. "I've been in contact with Eric Comstock, yes the FBI agent who got us arrested, yes the FBI agent who saved our lives. He has arranged for a military pick-up to take us directly to the front lines."

Ben lifted his hands. "Question." He said, getting Chip's attention. "Um, Chip, that sounds like a really dumb idea."

"Well, I'm open to better ones." The Vgm said. "So far, the US military has not been able to put a dent in Ecnilitsep's forces. The death toll is mounting at an exponential rate, while she's only lost something like seventeen of three hundred 'Shees."

"What about Pihc?" Dan asked. "Or the alternates?"

"What I know is what I just told you." Chip explained systematically. "Eric's going to be arriving in a matter of moments and we're going to load up so he can take us about ten miles ahead of Ecnilitsep's march. We're going to dig in and prepare to confront her and whatever forces she's got."

"Are we going to get any military back-up?" Shane asked.

"No." Chip said. "But I've got a…"

"I want to know where Vincent is." Michelle cut in defiantly before Chip could go on.

A silent wave went through the crowd as Chip turned to her, a solemn look on his face. "Vincent's…" Chip's words choked in his throat and he had to swallow hard to speak again. "Vincent's currently lying half-dead in a hospital in Raleigh. He tried to take on Ecnilitsep single-handedly."

Jessica's hands flew to her mouth, fear flooding through her. Across the group, the effects of the news silenced everyone, the devastation shaking them down to their souls. Dan looked down in shock, while Beth fell against Tim.

"Why hasn't he healed?" Jon asked after a moment, the first to speak up.

Chip tried to speak, but found the words difficult. "I don't know." He shook off the uncertainty and was immediately back in charge. "We have to deal with that later. Right now, we deal with Ecnilitsep." He turned to the doors of the airport and started out. "Come on."

Jared looked over at Jim then yanked the whiskey bottle from the acrobat's hands. He took a heavy swig, swallowing hard. "Wow." He whispered. He took another long drink, then looked over at Jim. "Last charge of the VGM, huh?" The ninja asked rhetorically.

"Yeah." Jim said with a raspy voice, taking the bottle back to have his own swig.

Shimmering in the desert head, four huge black SUVs lumbered into the airport drive. There were no cars around to slow their progress as the giant vehicles pulled up to the front of the terminal, right next to the no parking signs.

As the caravan rolled to a stop, Eric Comstock jumped out of the lead hummer, his cell phone already in hand. But as he quickly dialed the numbers, his eyes were caught by the fluid motion of the doors opening, allowing the VGM to step out into the Colorado afternoon.

"Well, here we are again." Eric said, with a weak smile and a laugh. He looked ragged and worn, but his smile was genuine. "Are you guys sure you want to do this?" He asked, as if trying to make light of their seemingly impending deaths.

"I don't think it's a matter of 'want', Eric." Chip said, as the VGM circled around the FBI agent. "But we are willing. And ready."

"We're as ready as we'll ever be, anyway." Tim said, following Chip's response, getting a look from the VGM leader. "Let's just get this over with." He looked back to the rest of the VGM. They all seemed to share his sentiment.

"Intelligence reports Ecnilitsep's army less than half a day away from Yarnel, which may mean she'll make a turn south towards Phoenix." Eric said as he sat next to Chip in the backseat of the Hummer, with Beth between the two. In the front seat, next to the driver, Tim looked back in displaced interest. "Ecnilitsep's been tearing through everything in her sight. To make matters worse, her trio of alternates has launched a second offensive up north."

"The guys from the other night, in the armor?" Tim asked, getting a nod from Eric.

Chip was about to speak up, but then looked at Eric. "Where's my bag?" He asked.

"In the back." Called the army driver when Eric looked for an answer. "It's in the packing foam, just like you left it."

"Good." Chip nodded. He went back to the satellite feeds. "Any sign of Pihc?"

"Not that we've seen. Only S'ram. At least, we think its S'ram." Eric pointed at one of the pictures. "That's got to be S'ram. It's too big to be anything else."

"Yeah, but..." Chip stopped, staring at the series of pictures. "It looks like it's moving like Pihc." He sighed worriedly. "What are you doing about the northern offensive?"

"Canada's bringing most of their military to the border to help us evacuate." Eric explained. "But frankly, they've been stopped cold since last night."

"How?" Tim called over the roar of the engine.

"You haven't heard?" Eric gaped. The three VGM members shook their heads. "Guys, you're telling me you haven't heard about the dragons?"

Chip and Beth looked at each other. "Do tell." Chip prompted, trying not to smile. Eric pulled out more photos, handing them to Chip. He accepted them, immediately beginning to grin like a fool. "Kageryu delivers." He looked up at Tim, handing the photo to him. "Here you go. Something to put on your wall back home."

Tim took the photo, staring at the four shadow-impressions of the aircraft carrier-sized dragon shapes. "Great." He mumbled, staring at the picture, not sure what to do with it. "I'll put it next to my Star Wars poster." He handed the picture back to Chip, then a question hit him. "There are four dragons there. Where's the fifth?"

"Kageryu won't show up on a detection system." Chip sent back, like it was a matter of common knowledge. "Anyway, they seem to be keeping Ecnilitsep's boys busy. That means less to worry about for us."

"Yeah." Grumbled Tim, less relieved than the VGM leader. "That's a load off."

Jessica sat in the small middle seat, her head bent over her knees as her face rested in her hands. Her black hair was draped over her face, shrouding her from the world. Leaning forward from the back seat, Michelle tried to see through the thick strands, looking at Jessica. "You okay, Cameron?" She asked.

With a fast jerk, Jessica threw her hair over her shoulders, sitting up straight. She looked at Michelle with a tight-lipped smile and red-stained eyes. She tried to laugh. "No." She said simply. She looked about to speak for a moment, but then turned out the window, staring through her reflection.

Michelle sat back in her seat, a dumbfounded look on her face. She looked to Jared next to her, but the ninja just shrugged. "How have you been?" She asked.

"I've been good." Jared said, trying to speak as casually as he could.

"Really?" The girl asked, trying to keep the sound of voices moving.

"Yeah." Jared nodded, his head bobbing as he spoke.

"Getting these things on board planes these days is a bitch and a half." Jon said, sitting next to Ben in the middle seat, both of them checking their guns. The cowboy leaned forward to the two military men in the front seats. "Do you guys have any bullets you can spare?" The two men glanced at each other, confused, then the driver's aid shook his head.

"Wouldn't help anyway." Ben said. "Even with a guilded gun, you need silver bullets to hit Pihc."

"Good ole' werewolves." Jon said, spinning the cylinder of his revolver. He slid it empty into his holster, then turned around to the two girls in the back. Sophia sat in a dazed position, while Aria carefully moved closer to her. "Hey, Area." Jon said to the woman.

"Aria." She corrected.

"Yeah whatever." The cowboy said. "Please don't molest the catatonically frightened."

Sophia's head rose when she heard the words. She stared blankly at Jon, then looked down. "I'm not scared." She said in a cold voice. "Scared was what I was yesterday. I'm..." Her voice trailed off.

"Hey, Sophia." Ben said, turning around in his seat. "Jim was telling me a joke. What did one lesbian vampire say to the other lesbian vampire?" Sophia blinked at him. "See you next month." Sophia blinked again. "Wow." The sniper said, turning back around. "When Jim told it to Michelle, she nearly killed..."

Sophia's hand smacked Ben on the back of the head, his neon orange sunglasses flying off from the impact. "There we go!" Ben announced with a giant grin. He turned back to Sophia as she glared at him. "Disgusting, wasn't it?"

"Yeah!" She said angrily.

"Repulsive, misogynistic, demeaning?" He asked.

"Yeah!" She yelled.

"Good." Ben smiled, turning back. "You're back in the ring."

The girl glared at him for a moment more, then looked back at Jon. "If I had known the VGM was going to be doing all of this, I would have joined the swim team." She then closed her eyes. "And Aria, get your hand off my shoulder!"

Aria looked hurt for a moment, then turned away, pulling her arm off the seatback.

"Oh, the world owes me a living." Dan sang under his breath as he pulled the curved blade of his kukri across the whet stone. The sound of scraping metal echoed through the hummer. He whistled the refrain of the song, looking up at Jim as he dealt cards to the four passengers.

"Jim and Dan here spent most of their time drunk." Emily pointed out as she considered her cards, speaking to Shane. "You'd think they'd be happy about that at least." She handed one card back to the dealer. "I'll take one."

"I had a pretty good time." Shane said, accepting two cards. "I mean, given the circumstances and everything."

"Yeah, that whole escaping under threat of death." Dan said, accepting a new card and putting it in the stack of cards he had only looked at once.

"Which does beg the question why these guys aren't killing us?" Jim asked, motioning to the two drivers. "I mean, they're military right?"

"They're good military." Dan said as he continued sharpening the curved blade of his short sword. "Those were bad military."

"I think Tim said Eric talked them into giving us a chance or something like that." Shane offered up, shifting his cards from front to back.

"I'll call." Emily said, laying down her cards. The six, seven, eight, nine, and ten of diamonds. "Beat that." She said, gleefully.

"I'm out." Jim said, tossing his cards gently down into the middle of the middle seat. He leaned back against the window, disillusioned.

"Me too." Shane said also. He tossed his cards down like Jim had, but his stack of cards fell neatly in one pile.

"Come on, Hardin." Jim said to his friend, with a rooting face. "Tell me you've got a flush. Tell me I didn't just lose to her again."

"Oh, I've got a flush alright." Dan said, laying his cards down. "Right down the toilet." The two, three, four, five, and six of diamonds.

Emily picked up the cards with delight and was about to shuffle when she stopped. "What a minute." She said, thinking quickly. "That was two six of diamonds." She looked to Dan, who was drinking from a Dr Pepper bottle. "That's not legal." She half-heartedly accused.

Dan and Shane smiled, eventually chuckling. Jim grinned, his mouth getting wider until it turned into a full-blown laugh. "Legal?" The large acrobat chuckled, taking the pile of cards out of her hands and beginning to shuffle. "Evidently you've never played poker with Dan before."

The desert-camo hummer came to a fast stop, with the other three behind it pulling up into a close half circle. The doors on the giant metal machines opened up, allowing the members of the VGM to descend to their next battlefield.

As the group dropped out to the shimmering heat of the desert, they saw the sky. Black smoke rose up into the distance, a giant pillar of flames reaching into the sky. Even Ben was taken back by the sight.

"Ecnilitsep's forces are less than six hours away." Eric said, the only non-VGM stepping out of the hummers. "They're cutting a straight swath right through here and going through everything in sight."

"Ah, home sweet home." Jim finally said with a morose sigh.

"What about guns?" Ben offered, looking back at Eric. "Do we get any heavy ordinance to work with?"

"I've got a few clips worth of silver bullets." Chip said, placing the two handfuls of silver into Ben's hands. "Anything else won't work and you know that. If it's not gilded, then it won't be worth a damn against Ecnilitsep."

"Maybe not against her." Ben said, moving past the Vgm to the closest Hummer as he stuffed the bullets into his pockets. "But they might do some damage to a 'Shee or two or eight." He opened up the back of the trunk as the soldiers looked at Eric, unsure if they should stop him. Ben took out an M-16 and as many magazines as he could hold. "A machine gun and a pair of pistols. All a man could ask for."

"We've got to fall back." Eric said to Chip as the Vgm considered the devastation that was coming his way. "There's a gas station not far from here." He said, pointing up the deserted highway. "It's small, but it's got a phone and more importantly, it's not in Ecnilitsep's path." He turned back to Chip. "Assuming it doesn't get destroyed, I'll have a pick up waiting for a call."

"Waiting for the call?" Tim exclaimed as he joined into the conversation. "What if it is does get destroyed?"

"It's the best I can do, Tim." Eric said, imploring. "My command is limited. These men here are just volunteers. Try to remember that you're in a hot zone."

"Alright." Chip said, stopping the argument. "Enough. Eric, that'll be fine." He turned back to the hummer he had ridden in, opening up the rear. He gently pulled out a heavy, black duffel bag, leaving wads of packing foam in the truck. "We'll be alright. Just go and cover your ass. We'll deliver so the FBI doesn't fire you." He said, placing the bag very carefully on the ground away from the hummers. He started back towards the VGM as the vehicles came to life.

"Chip." Eric said, catching him on the shoulder. The Vgm turned his head around, surprised. "Good luck." Eric said genuinely, as he extended his hand. Chip looked down at the hand, then back at Eric. Finally, he reached out and shook Eric's hand unenthusiastically. He nodded to the FBI agent, then turned back to the VGM.

Chip waited until the four hummers had pulled off, then turned to the group. "All Vgms, on-line!"

"Tim, on-line."

"Jessica, on-line."

"Okay, kids." Chip called, the group gathering into a circle around him. "While in Raleigh, I grabbed some of our in-house explosives. Since taking on Ecnilitsep, Pihc, S'ram, three hundred something 'Shees and probably the alternates and the generals is insane, what we're going to do is isolate Ecnilitsep and deal with her solely." He said confidently. "Now, here's the plan." He began as he pointed into the rocky desert behind him.

Eminaf

CHAPTER 18

In Hell's Wake

"Your bargaining posture is highly dubious, but very well. I will provide you with a new body. And new troops to command."

—Unicron, Transformers the Movie

Chip knelt on the rocky surface, a video tape-sized metal box in his hand. He placed the box against the rock, holding it firmly in place as he hit the black button on the top left corner. A red light flashed beneath the button and a hard suction sound shot out from it. The light turned green, then disappeared.

Chip stood up, looking up at the VGM that stood on the ground down below him. He turned around to see Ben dangling upside down from a metal line that extended from his left hand as he set his own box. "***Okay.***" Chip said into his headset as he pushed the edges of his black jacket back down to his waist, the magic of his video game power echoing through his voice. "***That's the last of them.***"

"Now these bad boys are going to detonate in a shaped charge." Tim explained to the group as they stood in the deep recesses of the underground cavern, lit only by the ambient light that dripped down through the crevices in the rock like sheets through the dusty air. "The idea is that we're going to blow open a chunk of the ground above us, hopefully causing Ecnilitsep to fall down here. We will then engage her in three-man teams. Ben and Jon are going to give us suppressive fire in case any of her army decides to engage us as well."

"Um, Tim." Dan said, holding up his hand. He looked at the others as all eyes turned to him. "Is it just me or does it seem like a slightly questionable idea for us to be under the ground we're about to blow up?"

"Oh, it's not just you." Jon added from next to Dan.

"That's where the shaped charges come in." Tim said with some emphasis, getting frustrated. "They're going to keep all the debris from dropping down on our heads."

"Yeah, but those explosives were made by Ben. And Shane. And Shane's an idiot." Jim joined in.

"Hey!"

"So's Ben." Michelle added to Jim's argument, ignoring Shane's protest.

"For real." Emily came as well. "For all we know," She said, looking up while Ben rappelled down the stone wall. "He made them so they'll explode in the form of giant penises."

"No he wouldn't." Tim argued back.

"It wouldn't be the first time he made explosives that did that." Emily countered.

"Guys." Jessica said, stepping in front of Tim, getting their attention. "The explosives will be fine. They'll drop Ecnilitsep down in here, in that area." She said, pointing back to a large, smooth rock formation the size of a swimming pool. "Each team of three will fight her in thirty second intervals." The female Vgm explained. "The teams are Chip, Jim, and Emily. Tim, Dan, and Michelle will make up the second team while I'll be with Jared and Shane. Sophia, Beth, and Aria; you guys are going to be responsible for giving us cover as well as any support that maybe necessary. If Ecnilitsep begins to overpower us, you guys have got to find some way to distract her. Cast a spell, throw rocks, whatever it takes. But if she starts to get an upper hand that we can't handle, it falls to you guys to deal with her."

"Great." Sophia groaned, holding her stomach nervously.

"What am I supposed to do again?" Jon asked, waving his face with his hat.

As he spoke up, a small red platform crawled its way down the wall, carrying Chip. "***You and Ben are going to make sure no one else comes down the hole after Ecnilitsep.***" He said, jumping off the platform as Ben dropped the last few meters. "We ready?" He asked as he came up to Tim and Jessica.

"As ready as we're going to be." She sighed.

"Okay." He said, turning back to the group. He sighed and tried to smile. "I wish there was something to be said." But uncertainty turned into silence.

"Alright, kids." He said, rolling his shoulders as he took hold of his golden katana. "Take your places. Ecnilitsep will be on top of us soon."

The hot winds raked across the rocky desert, blowing sand into the ranks of the dark army. Ecnilitsep walked amongst her 'Shees, her army showing few signs of the constant fighting. With her scimitar drawn, she marched amongst the army, mindless of the cracked field of scorched red stone and rock they entered. Up above, the bright blue sky echoed with the screech of a hawk, while the crusty horizon showed no signs of life in any direction.

"***Almost there.***" Chip said into his headset, his eyes staring off into space as he leaned on the stalagmite. "***She's almost on us.***"

"What's he doing?" Jim asked, his arms crossed as he stared at Chip.

"He's using a power to see above the ground over us." Emily explained. "I think he's using Populous, but I'm not sure."

The rumble of the 'Shees spiky feet echoed across the dry earth. The rocky world shook subtly with their constant march. Moving amongst them, Ecnilitsep walked with a purpose. Around her, the 'Shees snatched and hissed, but she ignored them, focusing solely on her mission.

"***Now!***" Chip yelled.

As Ecnilitsep's armored boot placed onto the ground, a powerful rumbling violently struck the earth. The demon fell to her hands and knees as the ground around her crumbled. She tried to stand, but it was too late. The foundation of rock she knelt upon tilted and fell forward into the deep crevice that opened before her.

Ecnilitsep rode the rock down, leaping off at the last minute. She hit the ground hard, barely able to roll over the damage as the rock shattered against the denser stone. She struggled to her knees, then stood in the dusty air of the canyon.

From out of nowhere, Jim's feet slammed into her back, knocking her against a rocky wall. She bounced against the stone surface only to be sliced by Chip's katana. The steel blade cut deep across her throat, leaving blood across the sword's razor edge. Ecnilitsep grabbed her throat, but Chip swung again. Blocking the strike with her forearm guard, she caught Chip in the side with a hard punch and leapt away. Emily threw a ball of fire at her, but the giant moved too fast, leaving the fiery attack to land harmlessly against the stone wall.

The giant rushed away from Chip, snatching up her scimitar as she moved. She whirled around with the blade held ready; swinging at the attackers she felt closing in, forcing the VGM to leap back. Dan landed closest to her, drawing out his kukri. "*You did all this to face me?*" She hissed angrily, still clutching her throat as it healed. "*Well, here I am.*"

"Not for long." Dan said, leveling his kukri at her, its blade taking on a slight glow. He dashed at her, raising the short sword over his head. She readied herself for the attack, but just before Dan got there, a silver whip lashed out, wrapping around Ecnilitsep's scimitar, yanking it from her grasp.

Dan lunged forward, driving his kukri at Ecnilitsep's stomach. The woman swept her arm around just before the blade connected, narrowly deflecting the stab. Dan took the block in stride, spinning completely around, throwing his kukri into the sky. Dropping low, he locked onto Ecnilitsep's leg with all his strength, causing her to stumble.

As she fell back, Ecnilitsep turned onto her side, breaking her fall. Dan was ready. Shooting over her body before she even finished landing, the wrestler, spun around her head, grabbing it with his iron-hard grip. She tried to stand, but Dan spread his legs out behind him, holding her low.

As Dan held her, Jared leapt out from the shadows, his sword drawn and ready. He dropped towards Ecnilitsep but at the last minute, the woman threw all her strength against Dan, breaking free of his hold. She rolled out of the way, leaving Jared driving his sword just inches from Dan's face.

The ninja landed deftly, looking up at Dan with wide eyes. "You okay?" He asked. Dan looked down as the blade of Jared's sword stuck through the rock. Dan looked back up at Jared, his face pale. "Sorry." Jared whispered apologetically, not noticing Ecnilitsep's kick approaching the back of his head.

Ben dangled like a worm on a fishing line, holding the M-16 against his shoulder. He sent out a three-shot burst as one of the 'Shees moved over the hole, beginning to test the descent. The burst of noise and bullets sent the 'Shees skittering back from the edge, while others milled angrily nearby.

A few yards down the rope from him, Jon hung on, his own pistol drawn. "What are those things?" Jon yelled up at Ben.

"***Shridders.***" Ben yelled back, firing another volley of shots.

"What the hell are Shridders?" Jon called, firing a shot of his own, making a 'Shee's shoulder rupture with an explosion of corrosive acid.

"***Shit-critters.***" Ben called back down to him, shifting his weight on the rope to aim at the ledge directly above them. "***They're cannon fodder. They're called 'Shees, but they're basically just Pihc's shock troopers.***"

"They're pretty shocking, alright." Jon said, firing his pistol. The head of a 'Shee exploded back from the hole, it's green ooze spraying back onto the others, sending them bucking back in pain. "What are they?"

"***Ugly.***" Ben said, letting fly another burst. "***Any idea how the fight's going?***" He called down to Jon.

Jon looked down as Jessica was thrown into a pillar, her body nearly breaking from the impact. "The short answer is badly." He said grimacing with some sympathy. "The long answer involves profanity. Which do you want?"

Chip swung at Ecnilitsep with his katana but she parried it and riposted at his throat. The Vgm narrowly slipped out of the way of the strike but the giant didn't follow up. Whipping around, she swung at Dan to keep him at bay. Immediately turning back around, she caught Chip in the face with a hard elbow as he rushed in at her. His forward momentum continued as his head stopped cold, sending his body flying past the impact to crumple onto the ground.

Ecnilitsep flipped her sword over, driving her scimitar down at Chip. But before the blade could connect, the ground beneath her feet began to shake violently, bucking her off balance. The giant woman slammed her fist into the ground, instantly stopping its illusionary quake. She looked up where Beth stood, the girl's hands held as still as her petrified eyes. "*Your pitiful magic has no effect on me.*" She snarled.

"***Really?***" Came a voice. Ecnilitsep turned around just as Michelle leapt into the air at her, catching her with a rain of numbingly-fast spinning kicks while shouting "***Tatsu-maki-sempu-kyaku!***" The kicks sent Ecnilitsep falling back as Michelle landed, snapping her silver whip at the woman. "***Cause it sure looks like that fucking hurt!***"

Sophia grabbed Chip's left arm as Beth grabbed his right. The two girls threw their weight back, dragging him away from Ecnilitsep as she squared off with Michelle and Jared. Leaning him against a stone, Beth knelt in front of him, pushing his blonde hair out of his face. Chip's black, wrap-around glasses were cracked diagonally while blood poured from his brow.

Beth put her hands together, closing her eyes. "***Curaga!***" She said, passing her hands a few inches from Chip's face.

A sparkling array of light appeared around him and the blood stain on his skin faded from sight. There was a flutter of motion and Chip looked up. "Jesus." He cursed, spitting out a mouth full of blood. "She's fucking strong."

"She's stronger than Pihc." Beth warned. "Chip, we've got to…"

"Her sword."

Chip and Beth both looked up at Sophia as the girl glanced over her shoulder, just in time to watch Ecnilitsep throw Jim like a football before she turned to face Tim and Jessica. "You've got to get her sword away from her. You guys can take her if she's not armed but she's too good with her sword."

"Easier said than done." Chip said, struggling to his feet. He stood, twisting his head to the side to pop his neck. "Alright." He said, his commanding voice reappearing. "Sophia. I want you to move around the battlefield and start casting supportive magic on anyone who's about to engage Ecnilitsep."

"But I don't know how to…" She started.

"Yes, you do." Chip said emphatically, watching Dan grapple with Ecnilitsep's leg while Michelle and Jim tried in vain to land blows. "You just need practice and, well, now's the time. Use whatever you can think of. Healing magic, speed boosts. Anything and everything. Got it?" She nodded uncertainly. "Beth, I need you and Aria to, where is Aria?" He said, suddenly looking around the stony cavern.

"She's on the other side." Beth said, pointing through the fight, as the woman knelt down next to Tim, healing a gaping scrape across his entire left arm.

"Okay." Chip nodded. "She's playing battlefield medic. You do the same. Ecnilitsep's taking us apart and we've got to stay on top of her. Keep us fresh and we can do it."

"Right." Both girls said simultaneously.

"Okay. Go." He said, sending them both off. But before Beth could get too far, Chip caught her arm. Spinning her back to him, he grabbed her head, kissing her quickly. He pulled away from her, smiling with a wink, then burst back into the fight. Beth was left stunned, her cheeks burning a deep red.

"I'm out!" Jon yelled.

"***Here.***" Ben held out his spare pistol, dropping it down to Jon. The cowboy caught the gun and pulled the slide back, having trouble negotiating the weapon as he dangled under his own strength on the rope almost thirty feet above the ground. "***I'm out of spare clips.***" Ben yelled. "***Make those bullets count.***"

"What happens when we run out?" Jon yelled.

"***The 'Shees will probably swarm in here.***" Ben yelled, taking aim with his M-16.

"Can they do that?" Jon yelled. Ben shrugged casually, firing at one beast. The bullet ran through the monster's eye, rupturing out through the back of its head. Its whole body falling to the ground. Jon swiveled to see the other side of the giant fissure. As he did, a shadow passed over him. Ben and Jon both looked up as a form dropped past them, descending into the hole. "***Holy shit!***" Ben gaped, watching it land.

Landing with the force of an earthquake, a giant landed directly in front of Dan. The wrestler was knocked to the ground from the impact, barely able to keep from dropping his kukri. He looked up at the monster before him.

With tanned skin and black hair, the red and gold-armored figure stood tall, dividing the battlefield between the VGM and Ecnilitsep. At his waist, a familiar black katana waited, but in his hard eyes, a strangely familiar presence taunted the fighters.

"Who the fuck is that?!" Jim yelled.

Chip stared for a moment, then his eyes narrowed. "Pihc." He seethed, taking a new stance and raising his sword.

The figure turned to Chip with a smile. "*Oh no, Chip. Pihc is no more.*" The figure said, stretching out his arms, his massive frame dwarfing them all. "*I am Mars.*" He glanced over his shoulder at Ecnilitsep as she struggled to her feet. "*Get up.*" He said roughly to the woman, an arrogant smirk crossing his face. "*You're embarrassing me.*"

"Jesus, he's huge." Shane gaped in terror. "He's bigger than Pihc. Or S'ram."

"The bigger they are." Michelle said confidently, racing towards the newcomer. She rushed towards him as he turned to face Ecnilitsep. Michelle threw a fast barrage of kicks that ripped through the air, her leg moving faster than the eye could see. But Mars ducked back from the kicks, spinning low to sweep Michelle's legs out from underneath her. The girl hit the ground while Ecnilitsep vaulted over Mars to throw herself into the thick of the VGM.

Ecnilitsep landed with a swing, her scimitar splitting the group. The VGM scattered away, falling back behind the rocky stalagmites of the cavern. "What do we do now?" Tim called to Chip.

"Simple." The Vgm said, his eyes burning with rage. He threw off his black jacket and dropped his scabbard. "Free-for-all!" He screamed, throwing himself at the two giants.

Ecnilitsep whirled around as Chip rushed at her, slashing with her scimitar. Chip slipped under the swing, coming in close to Ecnilitsep, barely missing with his own thrust for her stomach. He came back around to stab her back but she passed her blade back over her shoulder to block the strike. The move left her front exposed to Jim who balled up into a tight sphere and fired like a cannonball into her stomach.

Mars grabbed Jessica's punch out of the air and sent her stumbling past him. He came back around to catch Shane in the face as the racer tried in vain to kick Mars from behind. Continuing to spin from the impact to Shane, Mars swept his leg high through the air and caught Jessica across the side of the head. The blow sent the Vgm flying, slamming her into a far pillar.

"I'm out!" Jon yelled. He pulled his arm back, throwing his pistol at a 'Shee. The monster's long tongue whipped out through the air, latching onto the weapon and pulling it into its mouth. "That's disgusting." Jon mumbled.

"***Don't do that.***" Ben yelled. "***These things are expensive.***"

"We'll, it looks like we're going to die." Jon said, looking down at the fight. "Things ain't going too well for the heroes."

"***Really?***" Ben said, turning to look inside. "***How bad can it...oooh.***"

Tim and Chip were thrown into each other, their bodies colliding in mid-air. Stopped cold by the bone-crunching impact, they collapsed to the ground as Mars and Ecnilitsep turned their attention to the rest of the Vgm. "This isn't going according to plan." Tim groaned, his face buried in the ground.

"It never fucking does." Chip cursed stoically, fighting against the pain to stand.

"Can't...breathe." Shane gasped as he leaned against the rock formation. Sophia pulled up his shirt to see a massive bruise spreading across his whole chest. She put her hands on the skin, but even the slightest touch made Shane tremble.

"Okay." She said, closing her eyes as she took a quick breath. She put her hands over Shane's chest, focusing. "Curaga!" She said.

Nothing happened.

Sophia rubbed her hands, then put her hands out again. "Curaga!"

Nothing happened.

"What's wrong?" Shane gasped, his breathing getting shallower.

"I never played Final Fantasy that much!" She shrieked fearfully.

"Than use something else." Shane fought, unable to shout.

Sophia's mind raced, but she held out her hand. "Okay." She said, closing her eyes. When she opened them, a large glass bottle sat quietly, a tiny glowing fairy inside. "***Here.***" She said, opening the bottle. The fairy flew out, darting around Shane. A high-pitched sound buzzed in his ears as the bruise visibly receded, his breathing getting easier.

The racer took a deep breath, then smiled up at Sophia, laughing. "Good job."

"Thanks." She said, just before the massive hand grabbed her around the face.

"*Here!*" Shouted Mars, effortlessly yanking Sophia off the ground. With the powerful torque of his body, she sent her small frame flying up above the rest of the fight.

"***Shit!***" Ben yelled. Jon looked up just as Ben dropped down onto his shoulders, making the cowboy struggle to maintain his grip. Leaping off Jon's body, Ben threw himself across the ravine just as Sophia reached the apex of her trajectory. Catching her in mid-air, Ben flung himself onwards, extending his free arm towards the rock face. A metal grappling hook shot out from his hand, biting into the rock face and letting him swing down to the ground with Sophia in his arms.

Jon watched the save, then felt the rope in his hands becoming thinner. He turned back to see the rope disappearing from view. "Son of a bitch!" He screamed all the way down to the ground.

Planting his foot straight into the small of Ecnilitsep's back, Chip knocked the giant forward, then charged at her. He dropped low, sliding underneath her slashing counter-attack and took her legs out with a fast sweep. Ecnilitsep hit the ground but immediately flipped back up to her feet, just in time for Jessica to move in; throwing a fast kick that caught the gray-skinned woman at the point of the jaw.

Mars rolled away as Michelle swung her whip viciously at the giant. He rose to his feet with his sword ready, then charged at the girl as she prepared to swing again. Michelle dropped her whip and thrust her hands forward, yelling "***Hydoken!***" A single blue fireball flew towards Mars. But the monster batted his hand at it, sending it back to its creator. Michelle didn't have time to get out of the way. She was slammed into the air by the force of her own replicated fireball.

"Sophia!" Jim yelled, pointing at a ridge on the ground between them and Mars. The girl disengaged from Ben, leaving him with a bewildered look. She rushed to the point Jim indicated as he ran to intersect her. She dropped to her hands and knees. She hit the ground as Jim placed his foot on her back, rushing past her and flipping into the air. He crossed the distance just as Mars turned around. Slamming into the giant with the force of car wreck, Jim knocked Mars to the ground.

The smoke from the impact cleared to reveal Jim lying on the ground, his eyes rolling around in his head. Behind him, Mars stood, disorientated momentarily but showing no signs of injury. The giant shook off the effects of the collision, then looked across the battlefield as Ecnilitsep grabbed Tim around the neck and threw him into Jon and Dan. Standing calmly with a confident smile, Mars summoned his dropped katana to his hand, then stalked back into the fray.

"I don't believe this." Eric said, rubbing his face as he stared at the computer screen's grim display. The highly advanced satellite imaging cleverly displayed an array of brilliantly confusing thermographic colors in a miss-matched dance of chaos. But every now and then, the colors flared into clarity, revealing the state of the war between the VGM and the two foes they faced.

"They're getting clobbered." He muttered, his mind returning to the matter at hand as he rubbed his temples. He took off his glasses, continuing to scrub at his eyes with the back of his hand. As he did, a tech called over to him.

"Sir, I think you had better come look at this." Called the aid. Eric lifted his head up, looking glumly at the tech. The soldier was seated at one of the numerous relay displays, staring at the screen nervously.

"I know that look." Eric said exhaustedly, even as he stood from his seat. "That's bad news." Still, he made his way across the army's mobile command center to the tech. "What is it?" He asked. "Because I know its bad news. Everything else today had been."

"I think you're gonna have to decide that for yourself." Said the tech, having trouble tearing his eyes away from the screen. The FBI agent leaned in to stare over the man's shoulder. As he did, he saw the full image on the screen. He closed his eyes tightly, reopened them, and stared at another screen, just to make certain of what he was seeing. He looked back at the first screen and saw the same thing.

"What is it?" Eric asked, leaning closer to the screen, as if the distance would help him to see.

"At first I thought it might be one of the, the UFOs that engaged the terrorists up north, but it's clearly got a human-like shape." He turned away, hitting a button on his display. "Command," Said the tech with a deep sigh, speaking into the microphone at his mouth. "We've got a bogie coming in at an altitude of approximately fifty feet above the desert surface, heading straight for the underground engagement site."

As the soldier said this, Eric moved even closer to the display, his eyes widening as he did. "Are those…" He asked, almost silently. "Wings?"

Another shadow appeared over the fissure. Tim leapt away from Ecnilitsep long enough to glance up through the crack in the rocky ceiling at the blue sky above. Through the mass of 'Shees that braved the edge of the rock formation, he saw a shape descending.

The angel collided with Ecnilitsep so hard and fast, Tim thought she had been hit by a falling moon. Ecnilitsep was sent skidding along the dried dirt, leaving a long canal behind her before she finally slammed into a stalagmite, cracking the rock formation. As soon as she was able to get up to her feet, the flying angel landed so close before her, he could have bumped her with his nose. For an instant, he loomed over the woman, his white wings spread out wide around her, his eyes piercing hers, penetrating deep into her impervious soul.

The angel's wings disappeared, fading away like the dawn driving away the night. And as the wings faded, the attack began.

The dark creature slammed his fist into Ecnilitsep's chest so hard, the metal armor that had protected her for all of her existence shattered completely. The shards of metal fell to the ground as the gray-skinned woman was knocked back by the blow. She tried to raise her arms to protect herself but the figure rushed at with her as she retreated, striking two fast blows to her stomach. When she lowered her arms to defend against more blows, he struck twice more to her face. Blood flowed freely from her mouth and nose as she tried to counter the third punch, parrying it in the air, wrist to wrist.

Mars tossed Shane aside and turned his attention to the new combatant that had appeared. The giant turned rushed towards the monster. As he did however, Jessica slammed into him, fire erupting from her fist as she shouted "***Boost Knuckle!***" The blow knocked Mars back a few steps and the Vgm danced back, readying her kitar. "***Keep Mars busy!***" She called, rallying the rest of the VGM.

Ecnilitsep caught her opponent in the side of the head with a hard punch but it turned with the blow, coming around with a sweeping kick that connected to her temple. The blow knocked her back and he flew in like water, decimating her with a rapid series of blows.

With a powerful shove, Ecnilitsep threw him away from her, then dove at the form, catching him around the waist. The monster fell back as she tackled him, flipping her over he landed, tossing her into the wall of the cavern. Ecnilitsep went with the throw and collided with the wall on her feet. She leapt off the cavern's wall itself and threw herself back at the creature.

The black-dressed angel caught her as she ducked low and dove to grab his legs. Wrapping his left arm in hers, he flipped her around, slamming her face-first into the ground. Drawing back his right arm, he slammed his fist down onto the back of her head, embedding her face in the rocky surface.

Mars side-stepped a blast of fire and caught Dan in the face with a hard punch that knocked him off his feet. He threw himself towards the monster on top of Ecnilitsep but as he did, Ben arrived from out of nowhere with a hard flip, catching Mars in the chin as he yelled "***Flash Kick!***"

The kick knocked Mars out of the air, but he was up on his feet instantly. As he stood, however, a silver whip lashed out from the rear of the fight, catching his right arm. Mars turned as Michelle and Tim both dug into the ground, yanking on the girl's metal whip.

From the other side, a leather whip slithered out, grabbing Mars' left arm. Chip and Jim both yanked on the replicated whip. From behind Jessica rushed in, throwing her hands at Mars' legs, a ball of ice colliding with the ground. He slipped on the slick surface, making it easy for Shane and Ben to both slam into him like linemen, knocking the giant to the ground.

The angel grabbed Ecnilitsep's arm, yanking her forward. As she was thrown off balance, he brought his other fist straight up into her hyper-extended elbow, violently bending it the wrong way with a heavy snap. With the elbow hanging limply, the monster yanked Ecnilitsep's arm over her shoulder as he raced by her. The muscles in her upper arm tore along the insert into the bone, blood spilling out from beneath the armor. The angel then smacked her with an opened-handed strike, slamming his palm into her upper back, the resulting crack echoing the shattered vertebrae he had just destroyed. In an instant, Ecnilitsep dropped to her hands and knees, her body going convulsing from the damage.

The angel leapt over her, grabbing her sword from its dusty resting place on the rocky ground, at the same time drawing out the black-bladed katana at his waist. He held the two swords together, raising them above his head and leveling the points down at her. The great beast paused to look her in the eyes and a flash of recognition came over her.

"*Trebor?*" She gasped, unbelievingly.

"Die by my hand!" The monster roared, as it drove the swords into Ecnilitsep. Their magical blades pierced through her as if she wasn't even there. The blades punctured through her chest, impaling her into the ground.

Trebor pulled his katana out of Ecnilitsep with a mighty yank, leaving her nailed to the rocky ground by her own scimitar. As the dark creature turned away, Ecnilitsep's lifeless body slid down against the blade of her own weapon, opening the wound the sword had created, spilling her noxious blood onto the dead ground she collapsed onto.

The dark figure turned across the cavern, his murderous eyes locking onto the stunned Mars, holding the edge of his bloody sword out to him. "Yours is the same fate, Pihc." The dark figure said.

Mars stared down at Ecnilitsep's body for a breath, then turned his eyes to the monster before him. He stood up, squaring his shoulders as the VGM cleared the distance around the two giants. "*Defeating me won't be that easy, Trebor.*" He pronounced confidently despite his sweating brow. "*To make such a mistake is to dance with death.*" Mars took a step forward, holding his own black katana out, it's blade aimed roughly at Trebor's heart. "*I'm not Pihc.*" He said, decisively.

The giant exploded at Trebor, closing the distance in the blink of an eye. Mars caught him across the face and knocked the dark figure back. Trebor went skidding across the ground, slamming his foot into the rocky ground to stop himself. But as soon as he came to a stop, Mars was there.

Grabbing Trebor around the waist, Mars slammed the figure against the stone wall of the cavern. He followed up with a hard cross to Trebor's body, rocking him violently to the side. Trebor threw a fast knee back at Mars, but the giant caught the attack and whipped him around, slamming him down to the ground.

"*I am not Pihc.*" Mars repeated.

"Maybe not." Trebor seethed, fighting for position against his foe. "But you'll die just the same." Trebor kicked up at Mars with both feet, knocking the warrior back. Leaping to his feet, Trebor shot forward at Mars and tackled him around the waist. Holding onto the giant, Trebor's back parted with power as the large, white wings shimmered into existence. With barely a flap, the wings lifted them both off the ground. Exploding out of the crevice, Trebor shot up into the sky, carrying Mars with him.

The VGM stood stunned at the edges of the cavern, staring up at the sky through the massive fissure. The shallow wind from the desert above rushed in, swirling the dusty remnants of the battle.

"Okay." Jim said, the first to speak as he looked over at Chip. "What the fuck just happened?"

Mars

CHAPTER 19

Clash of the Titans

> *"Oh my god! Is that man smiling? I don't believe it! You are dealing with a man that is, as near as I can tell, damn-near indestructible!"*
>
> **—Jim Ross, WWF Raw is War**

"Tonight, Phoenix, Arizona is in flames."

The reporter spoke between bursts of static, her disheveled appearance speaking volumes about the disaster that raged behind her. "All around," She continued, her tattered voice broadcasting her mounting fear. "Emergency crews try to fight against the growing destruction brought by these two figures." The screen flashed to a distant shot of two huge men, engaged in the bloodiest and most intense conflict that had ever been seen.

"And just who are these figures?" Continued the reporter. "All reports seem to indicate that one of these fighters is with the terrorist group that has been laying siege to the south-western portion of the United States for the past three days. The other figure's origin is completely unknown. All that is known, however, is that at this rate, by morning Phoenix will be nothing more than a pile of ash."

The tar-colored skies mixed with the plague of billowing smoke rising from the raging fires that crossed the city like a mad disease. Destruction and chaos was everywhere. Near the town's center, the fires were raging more intensely. The buildings there were ablaze as the destruction was brought anew. All about, the rubble and the carnage from the fighting was apparent, in spite of the heroic efforts of the emergency crews to minimize the damage.

Sailing out of a side street, Trebor collided with a car, the entire passenger side collapsing from the powerful impact. Broken glass covered him but he managed to rise to his feet, his red eyes remaining locked on his target. Mars stepped out into the street, his metal armor dented almost to uselessness.

Trebor stood with an evil smile on his face. Mars stopped his approach, preparing for the counter-attack. Trebor hissed like a feral cat, then reached behind him and grabbed the metal hood off the destroyed car. With a powerful yank, he tore the hood off the car and spun back at Mars, hurling the hood with all his might.

Mars dropped to one knee to duck under the thrown hood, not anticipating the projectile was a feint until too late. Trebor rushed forward directly behind the hood and planted a hard knee into Mars' face. The giant was knocked back up to his feet, where Trebor followed up with a fast cross directly to the monster's face.

Mars fell away, landing on his back. But as he landed, he wrapped his feet around Trebor's legs and yanked them out from beneath his foe. The armored giant rolled on top of Trebor, pinning one shoulder to the ground with his hand. With the other hand, Mars tried to hit Trebor as he had done. Instead, Trebor moved his leg and wrapped it over Mars' extended arm. Grabbing the arm that was holding him down, Trebor pulled back with his legs, spreading Mars' arms wide. With the opening available, he began to rain punches on Mars' face.

Only two punches landed before Mars slammed his fists together, knocking Trebor away. He took a second to gasp for air but in that time, Trebor returned to the fray. Hopping up onto his hands and kicking horizontally at the crouching Mars, Trebor connected with Mars' throat, followed by a kick with the other leg to his chest. The giant was knocked back onto the ground, where Trebor pressed his attack.

This time, however, Mars took the advantage. As Trebor tried to get on top of Mars, he maneuvered his legs around Trebor's left arm and head. Bending his body with surprising flexibility, Mars twisted forward until he could see the back of Trebor's head.

With all the force he could muster, Mars smashed the back of his fist into the base of Trebor's spine. The resulting crack seemed to echo across the destroyed street. Trebor's head bent sharply and unnaturally forward as he fell to the ground.

Mars stood and cast off his chest armor. He inhaled deeply, using the brief respite to catch his breath. In a few seconds, the telltale sound of bones resetting could be heard as Trebor's neck realigned. With a whip of his head, Trebor's neck went back into position, the bones, tendons and capillaries rejuvenating nigh-instantly. "*Let's go!*" Called Mars, ready to resume the battle.

Trebor's eyes opened with a flare of red power as he leapt to his feet. Before the giant was ready, Trebor wrapped his arms around Mars' waist in a powerful bear hug. Standing up, Trebor picked Mars up, preparing to slam him back to the ground. Mars, however, smashed both his hands into Trebor's ears, blood spewing from them.

Again, Trebor fell to the ground as Mars struggled to get his breath. He crouched over the collapsed figure, reaching for his head. Mars grabbed Trebor's hair, lifting him up by his head. Suddenly reversing the motion, he slammed Trebor's face into the pavement, cracking the cement. He lifted Trebor's head up again, ready to repeat the movement, but Trebor arched his back, slamming the back of his head into Mars' nose.

"Holy shit!" Yelled Eric, nearly dropping the phone he had just picked up. "You're alive?!"

"Yes, we're alive." Chip said morosely from the other end of the line. "No thanks to Acts of God."

"What do you mean?" Eric said, almost laughing and crying at the same time. "Jesus Christ, man. I'd be thanking God, Buddha, Ahla, Odin, Zeus, and anyone else I could think of if I was you."

"All fortune is a mixed blessing." Chip sighed into the phone, leaning against the half booth. "Just come and get us."

"Are you at the pick-up point?" Eric asked after a moment of exaltation.

"You know," Chip said, looking around him. The entire VGM were milling about in the parking lot of the only gas station for miles around, still standing in the midst of the destruction. "That's kind of a hard question to answer."

Dan sat down on the edge of the gas station's lot, rolling his right shoulder. He looked at his denim jacket, checking underneath the arm, seeing the large tear that wrapped around almost half the shoulder. Grumbling, he turned back to the endless desert around him as he pulled out a bottle of Dr Pepper.

Unscrewing the lid with one hand, he shook his head and sat back, considering the long shadows of the twilight on the empty gravel road.

"Hardin!" Came a shout. Dan turned as Jim sat down next to him, Michelle plopping down on the other side. "Mich and I were thinking about maybe hopping a bus or something and heading back to Salt Lake City. If we left before sundown, we could be at there in time for breakfast."

Dan looked out at the desert. "Hmmm." He said, blowing out of his mouth to bush up the brown hair that dangled down by the bridge of his nose. "But what about that Mars guy?" He asked rhetorically.

"We go see our parents." Michelle offered. "Or more accurately, your parents, since my parents hate me and then cross-over to wherever the VGM is at that point and we resume the battle."

Dan looked out at the desert. "Hmmm." He said. He started to nod his head, almost agreeing, then shook it. "No. We've got to deal with Mars and that super-Trebor thing."

"Yeah." Michelle said, yanking Dan's Dr Pepper out of his hand. She took a healthy swig of it, then handed it back. He accepted it, wiping the top off with his yellow shirt. "You do realize that uber-Trebor or whatever it was that mugged Pihc is probably the recombined Trebor and Vincent." She said with some worry as she stared at the twilight.

"Probably." Dan nodded.

"Wait, what?" Jim said, suddenly perking up. "Trebor and Vincent combined?"

"Yeah." Michelle said across Dan. "That big guy, the one that was so big, with the wings. That was probably Trebor and Vincent recombined."

"Combined?" Jim asked, still confused. "Jesus, if they could combine, why didn't they do that from the start?"

Dan and Michelle both turned to Jim, staring at him. "Are you really this dumb or is this just like an act?" She asked.

"A bit of both." He said, suddenly grinning.

"Spam." Ben said, looking at the fossilized food available on the ancient gas station shelves. "Canned Ham." He looked down at the second row, his eyebrows going up. "More spam."

"It's a miracle we survived." Sophia said, standing next to Beth with the doors to the soda coolers wide open, both basking in the air conditioned glory.

"For real." Emily said, reaching past Sophia to get a can of soda. "I just can't believe any of it."

"Believe it." Jon said, walking around her through the narrow aisles. He picked up a bag of chips, added it to the armload of junk food he carried in the crook of his left arm, then dropped it all onto the counter. "Here." He said to the man behind the counter. "I realize you've been working this position since you came out during the gold rush," Jon said to the ancient desert man. "But I don't suppose you take credit cards?"

"Cash only." The old-timer said in a rickety old voice.

"Cash?" Piqued Beth from the rear of the store. She looked at Jon, but the cowboy calmed her with a wave of his hand.

Jon rubbed his face for a moment, looking down at his stack of groceries, then looked at the old man. "How about this?" He offered as the others came around him, depositing their booty with his. "You let us have all this stuff and any two of these girls you want will kiss in front of you, right here."

Emily, Sophia, and Beth all turned slowly to Jon, glaring.

"Deal." The old man said, a giant smile appearing on his toothless face. The girls slowly turned to the old man in utter disgust. "But not them." He said, waving his hand dismissively at the girls. He pointed instead at Ben and Jon. "You two."

Jon's face went pale. He looked down at Ben, but the sniper had a look of utter disgust across his face. The two looked at each other, petrified.

Jared kicked the can with the inside of his foot, sending it skittering across the pavement past Shane. He pivoted to follow, but Jared was already driving towards Tim. The large mage stood ready at the small, broken plot in the pavement, his arms and legs wide to guard their makeshift goal.

Jared moved in quickly, kicking the can with a fast swipe of his foot. The can vaulted right into the air, coasting towards Tim. The mage swung in at it, slapping the can away with his hand. But as he did, Jared swept in from the other side, kicking the still-airborne can back towards the goal, knocking the tiny soda can over the hole and down the steep ravine to the desert below.

Jared and Tim stood at the edge of the pavement, looking down into the hole. "I guess that's game." Jared mumbled.

"I always looked basketball better, anyway." Tim said, turning from him.

"That's only because you're eleven foot sixteen." Jared chided.

"More like six-six." Tim said with a look. But they strolled over to Shane, who was left clueless. "So what do you guys want to do now?"

"I don't know." Shane said as a gust from the desert blustered past. "Keep busy? I don't know, but I just don't want to think about what happened a few hours ago."

"I don't think any of us do." Tim nodded solemnly. "Least of all me." He added under his breath, walking away.

Jessica kicked her legs over the step embankment, sitting on the edge of a short cliff behind the gas station. Letting her hair fall over her face, she slumped forward in the afternoon's burning light. In the distance, an eagle screeched, her head jerking up at the sound. But all she could see was the smoldering remains of Ecnilitsep's march.

"Penny for your thoughts."

Jessica looked over her shoulder in the single light of the building's rear street lamp to find Aria standing patiently behind her. She turned back to the desert landscape and snickered. "You did well today." The girl offered, a bitter tone in her voice. "You handled yourself almost like a true member of this team."

"I'd like to think I am a member." The black-haired woman said, braving a few steps closer towards her twin. "I'd like to think there's a chance that..."

"No." Jessica cautioned, glaring back at Aria as she jammed her finger at her. "Don't you even think about it."

Aria stared at her, a hurt look on her face. "Why do you hate me so much?"

Jessica turned back to the desert as the last vestiges of the sun slowly disappeared behind the edge of the horizon. "Because you're everything I hate about myself." She glared back at Aria. "You're everything that was evil."

"Because I got the addiction?" Aria demanded. "Because I got all the lust and desire and..." Tears sprang from her eyes. She turned away from Jessica but didn't run. "I can't believe that you'd hold our nature against me."

Jessica laughed painfully. "I guess it's in the nature of being an alternate." She said with a grim, humorless smile. "You can't like someone who's so similar to you. It goes against everything that makes humans human."

"But you and I aren't human." Aria said quietly, looking at Jessica. "Neither is Vincent for that matter. Not now. And deep down, he never was."

Mars was knocked back, allowing Trebor to roll onto his back. He turned to Mars, drawing back his massive fist. With a powerful blow to Mars' chest, he knocked the giant away, giving him the space to stand.

As Trebor rose to his feet, Mars rushed at him, swinging fast. Trebor threw both his hands up to block Mars' powerful punch, only to get slammed from the other side by Mars' left hand. Trebor fell to one knee, and Mars hammered the back of his head with punches. Again Trebor hit the ground.

"*You can't beat me.*" Mars said, yanking Trebor's head up again from a pool of his own blood. "*You can't beat me, Vincent. I'm too strong.*" He slammed Trebor's broken face down into the pool of crimson blood, then yanked his head back up. "*I'm too strong and too smart.*"

Trebor bucked up suddenly, throwing Mars from him. He stood, as Mars charged at him. Trebor rolled into the charging Mars, swinging his weight underneath him and threw him roughly to the ground. Mars landed hard, but as soon as he was on the ground, he rolled up onto the small of his back, driving his feet into Trebor's face.

Trebor was thrown to the ground as Mars stood. He slid in quickly, slamming Trebor across the face with a hard punch. Suddenly, he came back from the other side, with another punch, then he drove in low to Trebor with a punch to his stomach. Trebor doubled over and Mars grabbed his arms, trapping him underneath him. With a powerful thrust with his right leg, Mars slammed his knee into Trebor's stomach. Again, he leapt up, driving his knee into Trebor.

The third time, Trebor grabbed Mars's knee before it made contact. Holding onto the giant's right leg and left arm, Trebor snapped himself backwards, yanking Mars over him as he went. Pulling Mars over his head as he went, Trebor slammed the giant down onto the ground, both fighters landing hard, neither getting up immediately.

The dusty wind picked up from the road in the distance. "All Vgms, online!" Chip called into his headset. From out of the dust, four familiar hummers rode out of the desert nighttime. The four giant beasts came to a stop in the small parking lot of the antiquated gas station. The VGM gathered around them as Eric jumped out, a gigantic smile on his face. "Hey!" Chip grinned, walking past Eric. "Get us out of here."

Eric froze for a moment, then turned and looked back at Chip. "But, that, what about, the thing, and the other thing?"

"I wanna ride with two girls this time." Ben yelled, following Aria towards the back hummer.

"Then find another hummer because I wanna ride with Aria." Jim said, walking next to Ben.

The sniper considered Jim for a moment, then shrugged. "I guess you'll be okay, seeing as you fight like a girl."

"Better than being a prima donna like you, bitch." Jim said with a sarcastic glare. Ben turned to look at him, his eyes narrowing. Before Jim could do anything, the sniper tackled him.

"I want a shower." Sophia complained as she stepped into the second hummer.

"You and me both." Emily said from behind her, rubbing her eyes blearily. She looked behind her as Michelle started in. "Ground rule, Mich. No hitting on Sophia."

"But..." Michelle started.

"No." Emily said, her hand up like a school teacher. "No hitting on Sophia or I'll make you go sit with the boys."

Michelle playfully crossed her arms. "Fine." She pouted jokingly.

"I can't believe how lightly you're all taking this." Shane said to Jon and Dan as they waited for Jessica to climb into the third hummer. "I mean, Ecnilitsep's dead. Which is good. But Pihc is now Mars, which most everyone seems to think is bad. And then, well, Vincent."

"I think mostly we're not thinking about it." Dan said simply, rocking on his heels as Jon slid into the hummer. "That and a lot of us are too immature to really handle what's going on."

Shane nodded in casual acceptance. "There is that."

Tim and Jared watched the rest of the group load up, then he turned back to Eric. "What's the current state of things?" He asked, motioning for Jared to climb in behind Beth.

"Well, there's good news and bad news." Eric said, getting in the lead hummer as Tim slid in the door behind him. The hummer roared to life and led the way. "The good news is that Pihc, or whatever it is, has been stopped." Eric continued to say across Chip and Beth into the backseat where Jared and Tim sat.

"His name is Mars." Jared said up to Eric.

"Mars?" Eric said, thinking. "That's a pretty dumb name."

"Tell him that." Beth said, taking Chip's hand, holding it in her lap. He tried to smile at her, but he couldn't keep it up.

"Anyway, the bad news is that this Mars guy has been stopped in Phoenix."

"Then take us to Phoenix." Chip said, laying his head back on the seat. "Wake me up when we get there."

"Chip, Phoenix is practically non-existent." Eric warned. "That's the additional part of the bad news. Whatever that thing is, the thing that showed up, well, it and Mars or whatever he is have been slugging it out for the last couple of hours. The city's been pretty much laid to waste in just a few hours."

"We can imagine." Tim added. He turned to Jared. "We're going to need to coordinate some type of support plan. We can't directly interfere with the fight."

"Why not?" Jared asked, the conversation getting Beth's attention.

"Vincent won't let us." Tim explained. "He sees this as his fight. And with Trebor and he fused together, he just wouldn't be mad, he'd be dangerous."

"What's the worse that could happen?" The ninja asked.

"He could turn on us." Chip answered up from his closed eyes.

"Guys." Eric called, turning Jared and Tim back to him. "Do you know what that thing is? Is it one of Ecnilitsep's toys? And speaking of Ecnilitsep, what happened to her?"

"Ecnilitsep's dead." Chip grumbled exhaustedly. "That thing saw to it. Quite brutally."

"Where's the body?" Eric asked.

"It disappeared." Jared said. "It just kind of faded out of existence."

"What about the 'Shees?" Eric asked.

"We officially relegate that problem to you guys." Tim said, pointing at Eric.

The FBI agent stumbled mentally for a moment, then looked back at Chip. "Well, what about that thing killed Ecnilitsep?" He pressed. "I mean, give me something. How'd it do it? What is it?"

"It's Vincent." Tim said coarsely, staring at Eric. "That thing is Vincent and Trebor, recombined."

Trebor spun horizontally through the air, slamming his foot towards where Mars had been an instant ago. The earth-shaking impact slammed into a car instead, splitting the commuter vehicle in two. Mars slid narrowly beneath Trebor's attack, at the same time dropping to his hands. As Trebor turned to find his foe, Mars kicked his legs back like a mule, catching Trebor directly beneath the chin.

Trebor was knocked into the remains of the severed car, blood spilling from his mouth. As he hit the front half, Mars rushed up and slammed his right foot into Trebor's stomach. The car was knocked into a spin as the force from the strike sent Trebor past the rubble.

Trebor landed hard, skidding into the curb as Mars rushed to him. Planting his right hand on the ground, Trebor launched himself into the air, tackling

Mars around the waist. The force from the body spear knocked Mars into the spinning car.

Trebor stood, wiping blood from his mouth, glaring at Mars. "*Not bad, boy.*" Mars scoffed, as he came to his feet as well. "*But we've been at this fight for hours. The night has worn on and the sun will rise soon.*"

"This is the part where you remind me that I could join you." Trebor said, an evil grin. "You ask me to give up on my hopeless ideals."

"*There are two problems with that, however.*" Mars said, holding up his two fingers. "*One,*" He Said, dropping the index finger, leaving the middle finger extended. "*I doubt you really have that much idealism anymore. And Two,*" Mars said, closing his fist with a laugh. "*You never had the option of joining me.*" With the fist Mars had just closed, he threw himself at Trebor, slamming him across the face.

Trebor was knocked back, but used the impact to spin around, swinging his leg out to catch Mars across the face with the heel of his foot. The round house kick knocked Mars spinning into the air, but as Trebor rushed at him, Mars landed on his feet, ready.

The two collided with each other. Mars swung at Trebor's head, nearly taking the foe's head off. But Trebor ducked underneath, catching Mars in the side with a hard shin kick. He came around to the other side for another kick, but Mars kicked Trebor's leg out of the air and spun around, catching him in the stomach with his own kick.

Mars turned again, throwing a kick at Trebor's chest, but Trebor caught it. Mars bent his knee in, moving in close to strike at Trebor's face. But the rejoined alternate hopped back from the strike before kicking Mars' leg up, then redirecting the kick to catch Mars in the stomach. But as Mars's leg was thrown up, he threw himself into a tight circle and spun around to catch Trebor in the back of the head. Both kicks landed simultaneously, devastating the fighters and knocking them both to the ground, neither moving for several minutes.

The two lay on the ground. Trebor panted and gasped for air, blood draining from his mouth as Mars fought against his own pain and exhaustion to stand. But it was Mars who got up first. He rolled slowly to his knees, blood pouring from his mouth. He fought to get orientated, then crawled over to where Trebor lay. He reached down for Trebor's head once again.

But before Mars could grab Trebor's hair, a shot rang out through the night, the bullet zipping just inches from him. Mars' head snapped up, his eyes glowing a brilliant red. He moved suddenly, just in time to dodge the next shot from Ben's sniper rifle. Another shot sent Mars rolling farther away. As Mars dodged Ben's shots, Jessica and Tim positioned themselves for the run.

From the opposite side, Jim stood from his vantage on the roof of another building, pulling out a large machine gun. With chaotic accuracy, Jim laid down cover fire, drawing Mars' attention away with the harmless rain of bullets that scattered inches from Mars' form. While the giant was distracted, Jessica and Tim rushed into the street, grabbing Trebor's arms and dragging him to the relative safety of an alley.

Mars turned back around as one of Ben's shots didn't divert far enough and struck him across the jaw. The great giant's head twisted back, the gaping hole in his mouth already sealing up. He ran back over to one of the destroyed vehicles and grabbed the driver's side door of the car. The metal twisted and ripped as Mars tore it loose. With a powerful heave, he hurled the door into the air, where it slammed into the building Ben stood atop.

Trebor shook off the delirium that came from his wounds as Jessica and Tim tried to steady him. "Eat this." Jessica said, producing an energy bar from her jacket. She opened the wrapper, handing it to Trebor. He looked at the bar, then to Jessica. "Come on." She ordered, glancing back towards the entrance of the alley. Trebor looked at her once more, then devoured the bar instantly before accepting the water bottle Tim carried.

"Mars keeps trying to take you to the ground." Jessica said, as Trebor drank. "You've got to try and force him to stand up and fight. He's too much of a grappler for you."

"We'll see about that." Trebor sent back with a harsh stare.

"Damn it, Vincent, this is no time to get arrogant." She said, getting an even harsher glare. But she took a breath and continued. "Try and get him above street level, maybe onto a building. Up there, you can jump around and move more freely. You're more agile than he is. You're also more comfortable fighting on your feet. Force him to follow you. Make him fight your fight."

"That's the last one." Tim said, as another shot rang through the air. "We've got to go." Tim looked into what used to be his younger brother's face and touched his shoulder. "Hang in there, Vincent." The hulking mass glanced at Tim, nodded, and took a deep breath. Tim turned and started running away from the raging fires. Jessica turned to follow Tim.

"I'll win." Trebor promised, his words stopping Jessica. She turned back to him, the emotions on her face alien to Trebor.

"Come on, Jessica." Tim called, from the other exit of the alleyway. She turned to Tim, but as she did, Trebor's hand reached up, holding onto Jessica's shoulder. She looked back at him again. He tried to speak but nothing came.

"Please come back," Jessica said to Trebor. She looked towards the exit of the alley that led to Mars, then back to Trebor. "Please come back, Vince." She said, leaning close. "Now do what you're here to do." She reached out to touch his shoulder but her hand withdrew on its own. She disappeared into the destroyed night.

Trebor stood, flexing his hands powerfully. Mars stepped into the mouth of the alleyway. Trebor spun around to him and leapt out of the narrow space, swinging at Mars. His right fist swept narrowly past Mars' face but the warrior giant moved away from the blow. Trebor continued his airborne spin, coming around completely to catch Mars across the face with his left leg.

Landing in a wide, low stance, Trebor rushed at Mars, throwing a fast kick for the giant's body. Mars deflected the kick and moved in with a hard strike meant for Trebor's sternum. But Trebor slipped his hand in around Mars' arm, stepping past him. With a fast torque over his hip, Trebor slammed Mars to the ground, cracking the sidewalk and shattering the remaining glass in the windows nearby.

"Hey." Came a voice. Chip turned and looked up from the computer screen as Eric sat down next to him. He handed the Vgm a soda, then turned to the monitor. "I see you've seen the news." The FBI agent said, noting as the army officers and FBI agents around them rushed about, packing up materials. Chip nodded. "The fight's coming this way. We're evacuating."

"There's nothing more we can do here, Eric." Chip said stoically, leaning on his hand as he watched the monitor.

"Well, the plan right now is for us to get you back to Raleigh." Eric said. "We've got a chopper or a plane or something waiting at the base. It'll fly you straight in to RDU."

"So this means the military doesn't want to kill us any more?" Chip asked, glancing back at the government agent.

"They've got their hands full." Eric shrugged. "Besides, they were grasping at straws with that one to begin with."

"And we're just supposed to be okay with that." Chip said, looking back at the screen. On the display, he watched as the satellite feed followed the brawl between Mars and Trebor.

"When's the last time you got any sleep, Chip?" Eric asked.

Chip chuckled. "You sound like Beth." He rubbed his eyes, yawing a bit. "I can't remember. At least a few days ago." As he spoke, the monitor screen went dead. The two looked up as an army officer grabbed the screen and took it with him. Chip stared after the man. "We were watching that!" He futilely yelled.

Eric chuckled under his breath, then stood up. "Come on. We've got to go. We'll leave this between Mars and Trebor and deal with the victor when it's done."

Chip stood up with sore motions, groaning with exhaustion. He stared where the screen had been, then turned defeatedly after Eric. "Trebor doesn't stand a chance." He pronounced in grudging acceptance as he walked away.

CHAPTER 20

Retreating to Ground Zero

"When two parts become whole, a hero shall be born."

—Narrator, Fist of the North Star

The rain felt like razors, burning Trebor's skin, melting away his aggression. Up above in the dark sky, the floating clouds brought by the destruction of an entire city and its surrounding areas rained down on the city, quenching the fires and driving out the intense heat, a heat that had kept Trebor warm.

Woken up just moments ago by the first tears of rain to fall, he laid half-alive in the street, staring up at the clouds. Defeated. Around him, the effects of the night's carnage were clearly visible. The remains of the battle that had waged over city blocks and across neighborhoods, had leveled buildings and devastated entire portions of the city, left the population center in ruin. In the end, the city was left destroyed, beyond any hope of salvation.

"I remember." He whispered, his chapped lips barely moving as he stared dreamily up at the sky. "I remember...seeing clouds like these." He breathed out slowly, the gentle, constant rain sprinkling down on him. "Beth and I sat under clouds like these, just before I moved." He blinked slowly, staring into the rain. "And, and then Mich and I, we, we hid under a tree, in the park by the school." A bitter-sweet smile came to him. "The rain felt so...so pure."

He closed his eyes, driving out the thought of the rain. "I won't stain those memories," He said with weak determination. "With this humiliation." Trebor didn't stand up.

The frog-shaped helicopter skimmed through the air, leaving the smoky night far behind. Inside, the remains of the VGM straddled the unforgiving benches meant for military officers. The entire group was passed out, still recovering. Chip and Eric sat near the front of the transport vehicle. Beth lay with her head in Chip's lap, while the Vgm stroked her almost-white hair. He looked up at Eric. "We're not going to Raleigh." He said, breaking the silence.

The FBI agent glanced up from a PDA, a confused look on his face. "What?" He asked, his voice a whisper to keep from waking the rest of the VGM.

"When we get to RDU airport, you were going to take us back to the warehouse." Chip said, not looking away from Beth. "Don't. We need to go to Wilmington."

"Wilmington?" Eric said, still confused. "That's almost an hour and a half east, on the beach. Why there?"

"Eric," Chip said in a tight tone, looking over at the agent. "Mars is not as rational as Ecnilitsep or Pihc. I've seen that personally. I don't know what he's got up his sleeve but I will bet you anything that he's going to come after us. And if he remembers anything from his life as Pihc or S'ram, then he knows that the VGM's home is in Raleigh. But since Pihc never knew about the warehouse, which probably means that a guy like Mars will just tear the entire city apart until he finds us. And if he remembers the attack in May, from Pihc's memories, then he'll really know how to take the place apart."

"I, I see your point." Eric nodded. "But why the beach?"

Chip looked forward, breathing out. "We have a second base in Wilmington." Eric's eyes went wide. "Jessica, Vincent, and I are the only ones who know about it. If Mars and his boys are going to hunt us, then they'll follow us there and avoid Raleigh. And there, they'll have to fight on new territory." Chip leaned back and smiled quietly. "Besides, it's Wilmington. They get hit with at least five or so hurricanes a year. I assure you, they know how to clean up after a disaster."

"But what about Vincent?" Eric asked. "I thought you guys were hoping...Since he survived and all."

Chip took a deep breath. "Vincent, Trebor, whoever, will know about the base. If he comes to Raleigh and finds us gone, that'll be his next place to look."

Eric looked from Chip, then out the front window. "Okay." He nodded. "When we get to Raleigh, I'll make the arrangements."

Mars stood on top of the desert hill, sighing as he wiped sweat from his brow. He stared up at the orange horizon as the last stars of the night disappeared, a sense of wonder coming over him. The dark blue panorama above was slowly catching fire as the sun once more ascended into the sky.

The giant stood atop the small hill with his thick arms crossed over his chest, deep in thought. "*To be or not to be.*" He said slowly, a grin spreading across his face. "*That is the question.*" He paused now, as his own thoughts sweeping through the fading mind-control and the confusion wrought by Ecnilitsep control. "*I stand at the threshold of destiny, once more able to affect the very course of all existence.*" He turned around slowly, still staring at the dawning sky.

"*On one hand,*" He said, looking at his powerful left palm. "*I can crush the VGM. I could take them away from this place, so that this domain may once again rest peacefully; so that nothing would disturb it. But on the other hand,*" He said, his right palm rising into view. "*I have a war to be waged, against a foe I do not even fully remember, whose name is just beyond the edge of my memory.*"

Mars looked out to the horizon, the wind sweeping across him. He reached up to the shoulders of his reformed armor, letting the flawless form fall away. Standing now before the world, his chest bared, he glanced behind himself at Pihc's black katana that rested in the hard ground of the desert.

"*I am the instrument of existence.*" Mars finally continued, looking back at the sky. "*I was created so that others might exist. And I must destroy, so that others can be born. The choice is clear.*" He said, with a grim nod to the horizon.

"*Whoever is a foe to existence is a foe to me. And as such, in order to protect all that is, I must destroy those who would endanger existence. And it is the VGM who is more immediately the danger.*" With a grin, Mars turned back to the slumbering sword. "*And so, I step once more into the glorious future, prepared to do battle and defeat those who, willingly or unwittingly, would bring the wrath of nothingness. I shall slay the foes of life and presence, wherever and whoever they may be.*" He smiled confidently. He held his hands wide as his grin turned into a triumphant laughed. His deep, powerful voice echoed amongst the silent hills and the disappearing shadows.

As his laughter died away, Mars looked beyond the horizon, seeing the glittering lights of a distant city. "*And I shall take the final battle to the VGM's doorstep.*"

"I have to admit." Jon said as he walked next to Chip, the large mass of the VGM behind them on the sidewalk. "It was awfully nice of the military boys to drop us off two-something miles from this second base of ours."

"I asked them to." Chip said. "I don't want them know where it is."

"But they've got satellites and stuff." Jon said. "They're probably tracking us right now." As he spoke, Beth looked up from where she was holding Chip's hand, glancing at the sky.

"Maybe." Chip shrugged. "But I doubt it. I think they've got bigger things to worry about." But as he spoke, he turned a corner in the street and stopped. The rest of the VGM stopped around him, staring apprehensively into the space beyond.

Breaking off from a tiny side-street of the main road, a dilapidated car lot stood quietly. Amidst the cracked pavement that had more gaping holes than actual parking spaces, grass and weeds punctured through the rubble of cement. And in the very middle of the concrete black hole was a large, two-story building with faded white paint and boarded up windows.

"How very retro, man." Shane said, marveling in disgust at the sixties styling of the building.

"It was cheap. You try finding a giant warehouse available for rent in this town." Jessica defended, coming up next to Chip. "Speaking of which," She whispered to him. "We're almost out of money in our account. We needed to go back to the warehouse so we can make a withdrawal from the chest."

"What chest?" Beth perked up.

"The one full of gold that January gave us." Chip explained as he breathed out, staring at the car dealership. "We'll deal with that tomorrow. We've got emergency food supplies here. We eat that, or send Ben and Jim and anyone else with less-than-spotless morals out to steal us some food."

"Chip, what are we going to do about Mars? And Vincent?" Jessica implored.

"Jessica, I don't know." He said, staring back at her. "I've been trying to come up with a plan but I just..." He sighed as he looked away. "I'm working on it." He said, making his way towards the dealership. "Everyone." He called. "Get situated and dig in. We're going to be here for at least a few days."

"Here, in Tetanus Alley?" Dan gawked, still marveling at the lot and the line of dying beach trees that surrounded it on three sides.

"I still can't get used to this place." Jim said, as he stood next to Ben and Shane. The three stood at the edge of the parking lot, each holding sodas. "I mean, who knew?"

"Well, when it's Chip, I think it kind of went without saying." Ben said.

"Yeah, but a VGM base 2.0?" Shane asked, looking over his shoulder at the converted car mega-dealership. The rundown almost-white building stood at their backs, its squat appearance an eyesore hidden just behind the bustling businesses on the main street.

"Hey, redundancy means safety." Ben shrugged. He took another swig from his soda and stared out gloomily at the tall, spindly trees blew in the salt water wind. The sniper tilted his head a bit, letting himself become fixated on the trees.

Jim looked out at the trees, then at Ben. "You okay?"

"No, I'm not." Ben said without his usual humor. "My best friend since middle school is…" He stopped. He looked down at his almost empty soda and tossed it into the parking lot. "I'm going to find something stronger." He grumbled, heading across the parking lot. Jim and Shane glanced at each other, then rushed after him.

Chip stood on the roof of the auto shop, staring at the afternoon sky, marveling at unusually deeper blue. Chip took off his black jacket, draping it over the side of the giant store. Looking down, he could see the ground far below as Ben, Shane, and Jim headed out across the lot towards the street.

Chip reached into his pocket, producing the familiar silver pocket watch. He turned it over in his hands, a wave of nostalgia making him smile bittersweetly.

"Everything's ready." Jessica's voice came from the stairs that led down into the store. "Emily and Sophia aren't too thrilled to be sleeping on cots in one big room with everybody else but I think they'll survive." She stepped out onto the roof and stared at Chip's back. When he didn't turn to her, she stuck her hands into her jacket pockets and swayed slightly as she slowly approached him. "I, uh, I stowed the bag with the explosives and everything in the cooler. Hopefully the cold will protect them from the temperature and the humidity. And maybe it'll protect our little surprise from being felt by Mars."

Chip didn't say anything as Jessica hopped up onto the roof's edge next him, sitting just a few feet away. "I've got to admit, I'm worried about you." She said, her feet dangling over the side. "I was wondering what could drive you, of all people, into seclusion."

"Just thinking." Chip said, lightly. "Planning, really." He continued after a moment. "Trying to get everything in the right frame of mind." He said with a pointless hand motion and a bad smile.

"If you think too much, you'll go batty." Jessica pointed out with a bit of a smile.

"Then distract me." Chip said, with a bit of a grin. "Tell me your secrets."

"My secrets?" Jessica laughed. "Good grief, Chip. Secrets are what the VGM is founded on." She glanced at him but even behind his SkyFold sunglasses, the seriousness in his eyes was evident. Jessica just chuckled again. "My secrets aren't all that interesting. Besides, you've got just as many as I do." She looked at him, returning his intense gaze. "You kept Pihc a secret from the VGM, along with Crossworld. You kept Jon a secret from all of us."

"You kept being an alternate secret." Chip countered, looking away.

"That's just my point." Jessica said as she looked back out over the parking lot. "We've got secrets on top of secrets. Neither you or Jon will tell any of us what the deal is between the two of you and Pihc and S'ram, why you two look so much like the two of them."

"Well, you won't tell us what the deal is with you and Aria." Chip countered, turning now to Jessica. The two stared for a moment, then held out their fists. With three quick shakes, Chip held out two fingers while Jessica held her hand flat.

She laughed stoically, falling back. She laid her head on her hands and stared up. A single white cloud sailed by on the blue ocean of the sky. "Once upon a time," She said, her voice drifting lazily like the cloud above her. "There was a little girl. That girl lived with her father and all of her brothers and sisters. They were happy and content until one day the oldest son and the father got into a fight." Jessica sat up, staring off in the distance, as if watching the events of her story transpire before her.

"Because the fight went on for so long, all the brothers and sisters eventually got caught up in it, siding with either the father or with the son. But, ultimately, the father won. And all the children who had sided with the son were thrown out of the house and told never to come back."

Jessica pulled in on herself, tucking her knees under her chin. "And so the little girl was thrown out of the house. She started to wander, trying to find a home. She found a beautiful castle, one she thought she could call home. But it was attacked and the country fell to the attackers, and the little girl had to run away again."

Jessica took a deep breath, the memories fresh in her mind. As she sighed out, the wind picked up her hair, drifting it off away from the ocean. "After running for a long time, she was caught by a demon named Pihc. The demon held her until she managed to escape to the nearest world. Knowing Pihc would find her, the little girl hurried to tell anyone that could hear her about the demon, to help her. But only a few children could hear her. So, she touched their lives, helping them or showing them a different part of the world, so that one day, they would come together and help her escape." Jessica smiled with tear-filled eyes as she stared up at the sun. But her smile faded, the vulnerability returning to her expression. "The demon did find her." She whispered, her voice barely louder than the wind around her. "He captured her again and he tore her in two. One part of her he kept, while the other part, he allowed to escape."

The silence was heavy. Neither looked at the other. Up above, the single cloud floated away, leaving the deep blue sky empty. Finally, Chip nodded. He stood and turned away. "Your turn." Jessica said weakly up to Chip after awhile, looking back to him with a sad expression. "Tell me your story."

Chip sighed, then looked up at the sun, as it began its afternoon path. "Maybe some other time." He whispered, staring at the sun. "We've got work to do." He turned away, startling Jessica as he headed for the stairwell.

"Chip," Jessica sighed sadly. "Come on." He turned around to her, looking at her through his icy sunglasses. "This is your game. Play by the rules."

"You sound like Vincent used to." Chip laughed a bit.

"And he was right!" Jessica accused, standing up. "You started this."

"That's right. And I'm finishing it." Chip said. He looked back at the stairs, then turned to Jessica. He walked back to her, picking up his jacket. He stood over her, his shadow half-obscuring the sun. "Look, Jessica," He said with some trouble. "My past is one you know." He said as he held out his right arm over her, his shadow covering her eyes. "You know all about it."

"I don't know that much, Chip." She implored. "Remember, Aria has half of my memories. I don't know where you're from or your real name, much less how you relate to Pihc."

"Pihc and I were enemies, are enemies, whatever." He said with an exhausted tone. "We've never been nor will we ever be anything more." He turned again.

"That's a lie!" Jessica called, stopping Chip. "You and Pihc look too much alike, act too much alike, for there not to be something."

"There is something, Jessica." Chip said, not turning back to her. "But I'd be lying if I said I knew what it was. It's, it's just a hunch. A half memory that I'm not even sure is mine." He slid his arms into the jacket, shrugging it on over his gi. "Come on. We've got work to do." He made it halfway to the stairwell.

"All Vgms, on-line." Came Tim's voice.

Chip dug his headset out from his jacket pocket, sighing. He glanced back at Jessica who was getting hers out as well. "Chip, on-line. What's up?"

"We've got, uh, just come down here." Tim finally said.

Chip looked at Jessica, but she shrugged. The two went down the stairwell into the wide, cot-filled room that was the entire second story of the auto store. Waiting in the center of the quiet room was Tim.

Trebor stood behind him.

Chip and Jessica paused at the bottom of the stairs. Chip's eyebrows went up, his body not moving. "There are a lot of things I thought you would call us down here for." Chip said as Jessica gasped behind him. "That wasn't one of them."

Tim look back at Trebor, ready to speak, but the hulking mass stepped forward. "Help me." He said simply to the two, his voice soft from determination and loss. "Please."

Chip blinked, totally taken back by the appearance. He closed his eyes tight, then opened them again quickly. Trebor was still there. "Wow." Chip said after a moment. "I didn't think I'd see you so soon."

"Or at all, I imagine." Tim said, coming around Trebor, putting his hand up on his brother's shoulder. "He wants to complete the rejoining." Tim explained. "He wants to get whole."

Chip rubbed his jaw, still struggling to accept what he saw. He breathed out. Finally, with a shake of his head, he looked at Tim. "Do the others know?" He asked.

"Only Michelle and Jon." Tim explained. "They're keeping a lid on it for the moment."

Chip nodded. He looked back at Trebor. He leaned a bit from one side to the other, trying to get a handle on the larger version of Vincent. He looked back at Tim. "What can we do?"

"I don't know." Tim said, his eyes dancing between Chip and Trebor. "But I know that they both want a reckoning. And this is going to be their chance."

Trebor made a hate-filled sound, but Chip tried to ignore it. He turned to Tim. "I don't want to be a naysayer here, but we know very little about alternates, even less about rejoining. I mean, if they've rejoined, do you know why he's so damn big? Shouldn't they be, I don't know, back to normal?"

Tim looked up at his brother, then to Chip. "Chip, their mass and psyche is connected, but not reintegrated." He tried to explain. He glanced back at Trebor, but the large figure just watched quietly, listening. "I, I can't think of a why to explain it. But if you had a knife and all the patience in the world, you could physically divide Trebor's molecules from Vincent's. That's why he's so big. And the same is true for his mind."

"So both Vincent and Trebor are in there?" Jessica asked, coming around Chip. She stepped before Vincent, shock in her eyes. "What's it like?" She whispered to him.

"Hell." He whispered back to her.

Chip finally dropped his arms. He looked past Jessica to Tim. "Do you know how to get them to rejoin?" He said stalwartly.

Tim looked at Jessica and Trebor. "No." He said cautiously. "But I do think I know what will be involved." He stepped around Jessica, getting Trebor's attention as he came in front of him. "Do you understand what's going to happen, Vincent? Trebor?" He asked, getting a strange look from the figure in front of him. "This is going to be dangerous. I don't completely know or understand what's involved, but I do have an idea about the danger. If you don't put your egos and your emotions aside and do what you both have to, then one or both of you is going to end up dead."

"So be it." Trebor seethed, his civility visibly straining behind his eyes.

Silence fell into the room. Tim turned back to Chip as did Jessica. The Vgm prepared to speak but no words came. He just breathed, crossing his arms. "So what do we do?" Jessica asked, the first to break the quiet.

"I don't know." Tim said, looking at Trebor, studying every facet of the giant. "None of the books at the Raleigh warehouse have any information on rejoining; just alternating. And since we don't have those books, it's going to be doubly hard."

"What about Beth?" Chip offered. Tim and Trebor both looked back at him. "She's read those books backwards and forwards. She's practically got them memorized." The Vgm offered. "She can help."

Tim thought for a moment, then looked at Jessica. "Get Emily and Michelle and Beth together." He said. He turned back to Trebor, looking into his brother's eyes. "We'll take care of this." He said with a comforting look. Trebor just stared back at him as if not understanding.

The door to the farmland gas station swung open and Livic stepped out, carrying three coffee cups in his hands. Dressed in his armor, he ignored the looks of the local farm boys who were filling up their tractors. "Here." Livic said, handing Yerrbmot one of the fragrant cups. The wizard accepted the warm cup and slowly inhaled its fumes. Livic then handed the spare cup to Eminaf.

"What now?" The female general asked. "Our army is destroyed by the dragons and we can't locate Ecnilitsep or her army."

"We must retreat back to Pihc's castle." Yerrbmot maintained. "We'll wait for Ecnilitsep there."

"You don't think the VGM could have…" Eminaf left unfinished. "They're formidable foes, but not her." Livic was about to answer.

"*And where have you three been?*"

The trio turned around in the parking lot as Mars walked towards them, a small smile on his face. Carrying his armor over his deeply tanned shoulder, dangling it from the sheathed katana, the giant walked comfortably in the Midwestern afternoon. "*I've been looking for you for almost a day.*"

"We were defeated." Livic explained with an embarrassed tone. "Tiamat and his brothers showed up and devastated our army, although we dealt them more than a few injuries." He waited for a response, but Mars just kept listening. "What of Ecnilitsep?" He asked.

"*Gentlemen,*" Mars said with a surprisingly jolly expression on his face. "*There's about to be some major changes in the way we do things around here.*" He said, laying down his armor and sword, smiling at their confused expressions. "*I can see you're confused. Let me assure you that I have every intention of striving for the same goals that Ecnilitsep had set forth. Only I plan on actually achieving those goals, rather than wallowing in the mire of failure like she did.*"

The three generals looked at one another, uncertainty racing through them. "But where is Ecnilitsep?" Yerrbmot asked, hesitantly.

"*Ecnilitsep is…no longer with us.*" Mars answered, grinning just a bit. "*The rejoined Trebor has seen to that.*" There was a long silence. The three generals stood in shock at the news.

"So, who's in charge now?" Eminaf asked, deftly. The other two generals looked harshly at her.

"*I am.*" Mars answered, his grin fading slightly. "*Or wasn't that obvious?*" Eminaf swallowed hard, but Mars just laughed to himself.

"Where will you be leading us?" Yerrbmot asked, stepping apart from the other two. "How will things be changed?"

"*Oh, you'll see.*" Mars said, looking up at the sky, his smile growing. He looked past the generals to the group of farm boys watching the exchange. "*If you have something to say, say it. Otherwise, keep your eyes to yourselves.*" He accosted them. They all scrambled suddenly; hurriedly trying to make up something to pretend they could go back to doing. "*We shall first deal with our foes, here and now,*" Mars said to the generals, turning his eyes back to the trio. "*And rid this world of the VGM. I can not help but see them as our single largest threat.*"

"What of the Shadows?" Yerrbmot asked.

"*Shadows.*" Mars repeated, looking at the wizard general. Something inside the back of his mind twitched, but he could not recall it. "*They will wait.*" He spontaneously decided. Livic and Yerrbmot shared concerned looks. "*However, I need you to do something before we pursue the VGM any longer.*" Mars said, turning to Eminaf. "*I want you to collect all the items on this list.*" He said as he handed the female general a small piece of paper.

The general looked over the list, the words puzzling her. "What are these?" She asked, staring at the list.

"*Find them.*" Mars said, looking past his conversation with Eminaf to the other two generals as they tilted their heads in unison to look over her shoulder. "*There's a town not far from here. Go there and retrieve all of these things. Take them back to the castle, then meet up with us at the VGM's home city.*"

"Mars, I don't even know what these are, much less where to find them." The general protested.

"*Then use your imagination, my competent general.*" The giant said with a confident smile, walking past her. "*And hurry. I don't want the VGM to live one day more than can be helped.*"

"These suck." Michelle said as she sat on the floor, shoving the book she had back into the tiny, communal pile.

"These are all we've got." Emily said, picking up the book Michelle had thrown. "We've only got a stock of the most major esoteric manuals here. This is an auxiliary base, after all."

"They don't even have a book on blood magic." Michelle protested.

"That's because nobody does." Emily countered, flipping the pages. "You're probably one of a hundred people on the planet that can use it."

Michelle just shook her head. She reached for another book, but stopped. She looked at Emily, following her eyes as she read. "I can't believe you're taking this all so casually." She said, staring at the girl.

"I think I'm just numb." The cheerleader cast down, focusing on her reading. "I think if I stopped to actually think about what was going on, I'd be pissed beyond words."

"You and me both." Beth grumbled next to her friend.

"Okay." Tim called from the far side of the pile, leaning against the wall, his long legs spread out around the modest stack of books. "Let's start over. What exactly is rejoining?" He said with his eyes closed. Beth moved to speak up, but the mage went on. "I mean, it's not summoning because no other spirit is involved. So it must be ceremonial."

"And it's high magic because it involves preparation and stuff." Emily finished. "Which means it should be within the realm of our school of magic."

"I think you're on the wrong track." Beth spoke up with surprising authority. The other three turned and looked at her. "You're both thinking about how to go about alternating a person, and not focusing on the effects of an alternation."

"But how would focusing on the effects of alternating help us with a rejoining?" Emily asked.

"You don't need to study how to shoot a gun to learn how to fix a gunshot wound." Michelle supported, nodding at Beth. "I think I see where you're going."

"Right." The pale girl said. "Understanding the mechanics of alternating someone isn't important. You need to be dealing with uber-Trebor's body being literally the mass and mind of both Trebor and Vincent. And they're fighting each other for dominance."

"But what is the rejoining then, if not one winning dominance?" Tim asked.

Beth was about to speak, but her mouth just hung open for a moment. "I don't know." She humbly admitted after a moment.

"Well, maybe it's like a car with two steering wheels." Emily spoke up. "And there's a wall between the two of them. And rejoining is just opening up that wall, letting them actually talk and stuff. I don't know."

"I think you guys are complicating this." Michelle said, sitting back as well.

Tim looked over at her, confused. "What do you mean?"

"I mean, his mind and soul are pretty fragile." The girl said, making a motion back towards the rear of the cot-strewn room where Trebor could be heard milling about. "I mean, in theory, he and Trebor could be torn apart again if we could figure out what first triggered it. So if they can fall apart so easily, it makes sense that they could confront each other easily."

"I don't see how that makes sense." Tim said.

"Tim, you're thinking about this like a scientist." Michelle explained, leaning towards him. "Think about it like a mystic. Sometimes, things find ways to work, not work because of the way things are. If Trebor and Vincent are meant to be rejoined, getting them to do that will be easy. So, what will it take?"

Emily and Tim blinked at each other.

"Unconsciousness." Beth surmised, getting a nod from Michelle.

"You mean like falling asleep?" Emily asked.

"No." Tim said, realization slowly dawning across his face. "You mean like a coma." Michelle nodded. "But that would involve drugging him." She nodded again. "But that won't work." Tim said. "His anatomy's too adaptable. He'll metabolize any drug or narcotic we put into his system."

"Tim," Emily said with a smile. "With all the societal lowlifes and magical types in this group, I'm confident we can concoct something that will knock his ass out."

"But where are we going to find someone with the chemical knowledge to make it?" The mage asked.

"Okay, Jim." Chip said as he stood before the rotund acrobat. "It's time we put that chemistry major to good use."

"Um, I'm only in general ed classes right now." Jim said hesitantly. "I am a freshman, after all."

"Yeah, but we need drugs which we figure its right up your alley." The Vgm said definitely. "We need a magical concoction that will send Uber-Trebor upstairs into a coma."

Jim blinked at him for a moment. "Oh." He said sarcastically. "Is that all?" He sighed and looked back at Dan, Ben, and Jared where they sat, playing cards. He sighed and turned back to Chip. He put his five cards in the Vgm's hand. "I'm up by ten bucks. Have me up by fifty by the time I'm done."

Chip looked down at the cards as Jim walked off, then turned to gawk back at Jim. "Against Dan? Are you kidding?"

Jessica slid the blade of the razor-sharp pocket knife across Aria's pale skin, drawing a slender line of red blood. "Why are we doing this again?" Aria asked as Jessica held the woman's forearm over the plastic fast food cup.

"Jim needs the potency of our blood to act as a catalyst for his formula." The Vgm answered. She looked at Aria. "We're going to drug Vincent so that he and Trebor can rejoin."

Aria's eyes went wide with fear. "Jessica." She whispered breathlessly. "There's no way that he can survive that."

Jessica sat down next to her on the curb of the sidewalk that ran around the building. She placed the racing promotion cup between her knees as she pushed her black hair away from her face. She put the pocketknife to her own skin, flinching a bit as she sliced through her own skin. "I know." She whispered. "But if there's a chance at all..."

"But there isn't." Aria protested. "Jessica, no one has ever survived a rejoining."

"Pihc did." Jessica said honestly, staring at Aria. "And I for one am willing to wager that Vincent is stronger than Pihc."

Trebor stood at the window and watched as the last lights of the sun disappeared below the horizon. Staring out over the flat beach terrain of the city, the giant watched the world shift casually into ambient night. An anger came over him as he watched the darkness spread from the horizon, bringing the first evening street lamps to life.

A sound came from the door. Chip stepped into the small room, holding a fast food cup with some caution. "Vincent." He said softly. From the window, the giant turned his head, his red eyes glowing. "Drink this."

Trebor accepted the cup, looking at the thick soupy liquid inside. "It's going to induce a coma." Chip explained as he stood before the beast. "It'll facilitate your and Trebor's...final rejoining." Trebor looked at him, a worried appearance in his eyes. At the door, Jessica and Tim waited unobtrusively. "The VGM's going to call it a night soon." Chip said, cautiously. "But we're going to stay up with you."

"Don't worry." Tim said from the doorway.

"We'll be watching over you." Jessica offered with a kind smile.

Trebor looked at the three again, then down at the cup. "I wish I could have seen the moon rise." He said to himself. The great form took a deep breath, then held it. With a fluid, controlled motion, he lifted the cup to his mouth and drained the contents.

CHAPTER 21

Reunification

"Now the world is gone,
I'm just one
Oh God help me!"

—Metallica, <u>One</u>

"Do you think this is safe?" Jessica asked, as she and Chip stood in the narrow doorway of the office that had become the infirmary where Trebor now slept on a pair of cots pulled together. His muscles twitched and jerked as his large body fell over the sides in every direction. His eyes fluttered against the deep sleep that had taken hold of him.

"Safe?" Chip scoffed humorlessly, eliciting an annoyed look from Jessica. "Hell no. This is probably going to end up nothing short of tragic."

"Let me guess, the possibility of that solution Mich and Jim put together being real is negligible; the chances he's going to come out of this alive are slim to none; and he's under a time restraint to get finished by the time Mars gets here." Jessica said sarcastically.

"About that, yeah." Chip nodded, leaning against the doorframe.

"So when does it start?" The woman asked, crossing her arms. "How's this whole thing supposed to work? Psychologically, I mean."

"According to Beth, in order for the two of them to rejoin completely," Chip began with a sigh. "They must reconcile all the troubles they've had. Everything that's happened in Vincent's life that has caused him to hate Trebor must be dealt with, face to face, with Trebor. And vice versa, I guess."

"So they're just going to fight it out until they come to a stand-still?" Asked Jessica.

"No, that's the point they're at now, a stand-still." Chip corrected. "What happens now is they must finish the reckoning, once and for all. They can't just fight about it, they have to resolve it. Neither one of them can really run from the other now. They have to face every issue, every troubling problem that separates the two of them."

"And when they're done with that?" Jessica asked hesitantly.

"That's the tricky part." Chip conceded. "It's not just a matter of beating one into submission, morally. Trebor can't just convince Vincent into dormancy, or the other way around. To do so would cause the dominant one to manifest, while the other one remained in the subconscious."

"I thought that was kind of the point. For Vincent to drive Trebor back into his subconscious." Jessica asked.

"If Vincent wins, he'll be burying Trebor deep down inside of him but he'll be the same person he has been since he and Trebor separated. He'll be the emotionless asshole that we've all come to know and love." Chip said calmly, as Jessica started and stared at him. "The problem with that is that Trebor will still be somewhere inside of him, trying to get free. You'll be dealing with full-blown multiple-personalities, with the ever-present danger of Trebor resurfacing." Chip shrugged and looked back at Trebor as he bucked from the dark dream he inhabited.

"If Trebor wins, well," Chip went on. "He'll turn into a gray husk, like Brenard or Yadiloh." He looked down, away from Trebor, his eyes hidden behind his glasses. "The original soul, Vincent, can not be complete by just driving the alternate into dormancy. Just the same, the alternate, Trebor, can not remain a conscious and complete creature if the original dies, which would be the only way Vincent would fall into submission."

"So either way, he's not going to be the real, true Vincent?" Jessica mumbled, sorrow filling her voice.

Chip moved hesitantly to speak. "Not entirely." He said finally after several attempts to choose his words properly. "If, and this is a big damn 'IF', Vincent and Trebor can come to a mutual understanding, a true coexistence, then it's just possible that they will rejoin completely, reforming into the Vincent that existed before Pihc alternated him."

"What are the odds of that happening?" Jessica asked, morosely.

"Oh, hell." Chip laughed. "I can't think of a hyperbole strong enough to demonstrate how unlikely that is. If anyone else had presented me with the possibility of performing this little whacked-out procedure, I would have told them they were crazy."

"Then why did you agree to let Vincent do it?" She asked.

"Well, we already know he's crazy." Chip chuckled a bit. "But, I guess, I trust him." He smiled as a small flash of hope crossed his face. "I know Vincent very well. Better than maybe anyone else, including himself."

"I don't know." Chip went on after a moment. "Maybe he can't do it. Vincent and Trebor have caused each other a lot of pain. And on top of that, few people have ever felt the hatred and agony that Vincent's known. Then again, few people of have the determination and the raw sheer force of will that Vincent's been able to muster in his life." Chip laughed again. "I don't know if it's really even possible. But if anyone can pull off this miracle, it's gonna be our boy there."

The city streets were crowded, people bustling along here and there. A brown-haired boy walked down the street, a backpack strapped tightly to his shoulders. The boy had a half smile on his face, as if thinking of something funny that had happened earlier. He was oblivious to the world, unconsciously dodging the dreamy denizen's of the city.

A pair of eyes caught his attention. The boy looked up, seeing a pair of black, opaque sunglasses staring at him. They belonged to a man in a black trench coat with a peculiar broadsword at his side. He stared coldly at the boy, the people in the street parting, giving them a clear view of each another. The man wore black military boots and fingerless gloves. His entire body was covered in black, even the three black stripes of paint across his face. He eyed the boy, his eyes narrowing behind those black sunglasses.

The boy's expression turned to one of utter fear as he turned and ran, trying to avoid hitting anyone on the street. He dodged this way and that, barely missing the other pedestrians. The boy turned down a street, pushing himself for all he was worth. He passed a café, his eyes scanning the glass. No one was coming to help him. No one could hear his screams for help. He stopped and banged on the glass but no one came. No one turned to look at him. He saw familiar faces. Friends from another life. Now, they ignored him. Now, they were unaware of him.

The boy turned to run again but before he could get past the café, the man in black was suddenly in front of the boy. The boy fell to the ground, his heels kicking against the pavement as he backed away from the man. The man focused his dark attention onto the boy, his face expressionless. The boy began to rise, but the man reached down, grabbed the boy by his backpack straps and hoisted him up. With a powerful swing, the man sent the boy crashing through the window of the café, shattering the glass into a myriad world of sharp pain.

The boy landed hard, glass lodging in him at every point. He tried to get up, but the pain from the shards of glass was too much. With tears and screams of pain, he tried to brush the glass out of his bleeding skin. The pain threatened to overwhelm him, but he forced himself to remove the glass, bit by bit. He pulled a huge shard out of his forearm, watching as the blood billowed out like oil. The boy tried to scoop up the blood, to put it back in, but couldn't. He turned his eyes to the door of the café, watching as the man in black walked in and head straight for him.

The man came to stand over the boy, pushing aside his black trench coat and reaching for the sword that rested at his side. The black sword waited with a blue crystal set in its pommel. The man drew the sword, its mirrored blade reflecting the boy's horror-filled eyes. He turned the sword towards the boy, its arrowhead tip aimed right between his eyes.

Trebor threw a fast punch, barely missing Vincent's face. The dark Vgm parried the blow and countered with a fast strike to Trebor's stomach. Trebor jumped back as best he could in the tiny kitchen of Vincent's house in Salt Lake City.

Trebor kicked at Vincent as he landed, but Vincent kicked Trebor's leg first then spun around, back fisting Trebor to the face. The alternate spun with the blow, kicking Vincent across the face with a roundhouse, knocking him onto the lit stove. "I hated you!" Trebor roared as he grabbed Vincent's hair, pushing his head towards the red-hot burner. Vincent tried to press away, but Trebor pushed down even harder. "You took everything from me!"

"You?!" Vincent growled as he fought against Trebor's strength. With a sudden reverse of motion, Vincent spun around, trapping both of Trebor's wrists in his left hand. He threw Trebor up against the refrigerator, holding his hands still. He slammed a low elbow into Trebor's stomach, then stepped in with a teeth-rattling uppercut to his chin after releasing the alternate's hands. "You were the monster that killed all those people! You were the one who wanted to kill, to destroy, to do anything we could to hurt anyone we could find!"

"Yes!" Trebor yelled back at Vincent, his ferocity stunning his foe. "I was the one who had the balls to realize what I really wanted!" Trebor took a step towards Vincent. "And what I wanted was what you wanted!"

"No!" Vincent yelled back, his strength wavering.

"Yes!" Screamed Trebor. "Admit it. You wanted the rest of the world to feel the pain you, we, felt."

Sophia sat with Tim in the front space of the auto shop, a notepad in her hands. Drawing across the pad with a piece of charcoal, the girl sketched away as Tim sat next to her on a customers' waiting bench, pouring over the small collection of old books.

"Well, that explains the terrorist attack." Tim said out of the blue, closing the book he hadn't been reading.

Sophia looked up, somewhat startled. "What, what do you mean?" She asked.

"A few years ago, there was this big terrorist attack outside of Durham. A lot of people died; there was a lot of property damage and such. It was really tragic." He explained in the darkness of the dusk, his voice distant. "Following it was kind of a hobby of mine, like others followed the Unabomber. After joining the VGM, I guess I kind of assumed that it was Pihc who did it. I guess now would make sense that it was Vincent as Uber-Trebor."

"Uber-Trebor?" Sophia tried to say. "That thing that he is now? The big thing from the desert?"

"Yep." Tim half laughed. "I still can't believe he rejoined with Trebor. I mean, that had to be hell for him."

"Yeah." Sophia nodded. "Paying the ferry man twenty pieces of silver and everything."

Tim smiled callously. "Vincent always did have a thing for silver." He mumbled to himself.

Vincent was lying on a stone altar, his hands and ankles held tight by silver ropes. He struggled as best he could, but with the red eyes of an innumerable host of faceless monks on him, he could do little. The huge room he was held in was constructed of red stone, archaic symbols painstakingly handcrafted on each stone. The room radiated a dark heat as a light from high above drifted down like unholy feathers onto Vincent.

Only 14, the young boy's mind struggled with the horror he faced. He tried to scream but the sound was drowned out by the chants of the dark, formless monks. But then from within the endless hosts, a great darkness appeared. Vincent watched in horror as the monks parted, making way for the darkness.

Standing in a black robe with silver designs was the largest man Vincent had ever seen. With gray skin and white hair, the man held a black katana ceremoniously in both hands. He slowly made his way to the altar, turning the katana very carefully in his hands so that the long, slender blade pointed down. The figure chanted along with the faceless monks, his eyes glowing a murderous red.

Vincent tried to scream again but no sound escaped his mouth. The dark one raised the sword, holding the point just above Vincent's heart. With a deep cry, the man shouted out for all of existence to hear, "***By my will, Awaken!***" The blade was driven down.

Right before the blade punctured Vincent's skin, he made a last bid for life. Summoning up all his strength, Vincent called out "***Believe in the Lord and the power of his might!***" On Vincent's forehead, a tiny blue cross burned into existence. The blade stopped, held in place by a blue field of energy. Vincent repeated the saving words over and over, trying to will the sword away.

But the power failed him.

The blue cross flickered out of existence and disappeared from his forehead just as the dark blade plunged into his chest. Vincent's body convulsed against the power, his mouth opened wide in a silent, agonizing scream of pain.

"I was everything you ever wanted to be!" Trebor yelled, as Vincent backed onto the mat. Alone in the VGM's giant training room, they two were encased by the light of the full moon as it shone in through the high windows. "I was all the emotion, all the drive. I was everything you wanted to be, but refused to admit."

"You were madness!" Vincent yelled, as he hunched up, backing away from the alternate. "You were murder!"

"Because that's what you wanted." Trebor yelled back. "You wanted to be dark. You wanted to be evil. Because that's what we are. You wanted to kill and destroy and hurt. You wanted it. It was your very nature."

"I never wanted that! Never!" Vincent yelled, flailing at Trebor with a weak punch. He dodged easily around it, catching Vincent with the palm of his right hand. Vincent went down, blood pouring from his mouth.

"To deny what we really are," Trebor said, dropping his knee into the back of Vincent's neck, pinning him to the ground. "Is to hold everything back." Trebor leaned close, whispering into Vincent's ear. "We are anger. We are hatred. We are evil."

Vincent threw Trebor off with a sudden buck of his hips, the dark alternate sprawling on the sand of a playground. All around, the children played, oblivious to the fighting pair. "All the pain I felt was because of you, because of your anger." Vincent accused.

"It was yours first, you idiot." Trebor yelled. He stepped forward, planting a fast kick into Vincent's side, then spun around, kicking Vincent's head with a fast roundhouse. Vincent narrowly rolled with the kick, using the force of the kick to fuel his own spin. He came back around with a roundhouse kick of his own, landing it full force against Trebor.

Trebor slammed his foot into the ground to stop his spin and kicked back at Vincent. The Vgm grabbed Trebor' leg out of the air and threw him to the ground. Trebor crashed down, immediately rolling away. "You're right." Vincent said, not following Trebor. "You're right." He repeated, stunning Trebor. "You did embody, at least in part, what I thought I wanted." He said, his voice sounding strangely calm, his eyes unflinching behind the SkyFold glasses. "You were the evil that lived in my heart." He admitted.

Trebor stared at Vincent for a moment, then glanced around as if expecting an ambush. "Is this a trick?" He asked hesitantly, not letting his guard down. "Are you giving up?"

"No trick." Vincent said honestly, standing up straight, wiping the blood away from his mouth with the back of his gloved hand. "But it doesn't mean I'm giving up either."

Jessica sat with her knees tucked in underneath her chin as she watched. Trebor convulsed and kicked, bucking against his fevered dreams. As his kicking subsided, she reached out to touch his forehead. It burned against her fingers, sweat pouring off his skin. She squeezed his hand, hoping.

If he survives this, he is mine.

Jessica didn't move, even as anger crossed her face. "Leave him alone." She threatened to the distant voice. "I won't let you take him." She spoke with a dangerous resolve, her eyes burning with the intensity that carried in her voice.

He is mine. Said the voice in the silent room, almost gleefully at Jessica's insistence. **I have the contract. I have his word. If he survives, he is mine.**

Jessica said nothing. She simply watched over Vincent.

Vincent fell back onto the wet grass, his rail-thin body covered in blood.

He dropped down onto his chest, breathing raggedly. When he looked up at the parting clouds and the stars up above, his eyes blurred, exhaustion taking its toll. Pain and death filled him, stealing away his mind and his will.

Against his will, his eyes traveled over to the space next to him, seeing the twin lying there. Nearly identical to Vincent, but with long black hair and healthier frame, he was Vincent's darker half. He was Trebor.

Vincent rested on the wet grass as the clouds swirled and thundered, threatening to rain. He panted and sighed, unable to catch his breath. With a great effort, he grabbed a handful of grass and pulled himself towards his twin. He pulled again and once more, until he was right next to Trebor.

With a sudden lunge, Vincent collapsed onto Trebor, fighting to straddle the unconscious alternate's chest. Wheezing from the exertion, Vincent grabbed Trebor's throat, pressing his two thumbs into the image of himself. "I hate you." Vincent muttered painfully through his gasps for air. "I hate you." He said again. Inside his mind, the words echoed, gaining strength. "I hate you. I hate you. I hate you. I hate I hate I hate I hate I hate hate hate hate hate hate HATE HATE ***HATE HATE HATE***!"

A grassy field stood in the shadow of a snow-capped mountain. Around the far reaches of the field, the thick tree line acted as a barrier against escape. There was no way out now for either of them.

Vincent stood across from Trebor, their eyes locked on one another. Hatred and fury was held tightly in check. "We can't keep this up." Vincent called, the strong wind drowning out most of his voice.

"Well, we have to do something. Otherwise, Mars is going to win for sure." Trebor sent back, nervously fingering his katana handle from beneath his crossed arms.

"Exactly. We lost to Mars, Trebor." Vincent said, taking a few steps towards his target. "Mars will always win if we stay like this."

"You mean even if we're at our strongest?!" Trebor exclaimed in shock. "Vincent, are you crazy? We are at our strongest. This is it, Vincent." Trebor threw his hands out, motioning to the scenery. Even as he spoke, a front of dark clouds rolled over the sky, darkening the wilderness. "This is rejoined. This is the most we could ever have hoped for. This is it. This is as far as we can go. This is the final stage in our reunification, of who we are."

"This isn't it, Trebor." Vincent said harshly. "This isn't the end." Trebor lowered his arms, still staring, still anxious. Vincent simply stood in the wind, his reserve holding him steady. "If this is the ultimate level we could ever hope to achieve, then I don't want anything to do with it. This isn't strong enough. It's not even close. We could never beat Mars like this." For a second, Trebor looked like he was falling apart. Vincent knew this was his chance.

"Our only hope lies in finishing this." Vincent reached out with his hand. "This can be our final death, or our final destiny, Trebor. We have to finish rejoining. Once and for all."

Trebor's face suddenly contorted in irrational rage. "NEVER!" He screamed, suddenly roaring as if he was in pain. Tears exploded from his eyes as he almost convulsed in agony.

"Trebor, get a hold of yourself." Vincent rushed up to the staggering Trebor, grabbing him by the shoulders. "Trebor, it's our emotional friction that's kept us from being able to effectively fight Mars." Vincent yelled into his face. "You and I may be physically and mentally together, but our souls are still unaligned."

"But we're the same!" Trebor cried back. He pushed Vincent away, jumping back from his twin. As he landed, the ground shook and split. A fiery pit opened between Trebor and Vincent as the mountains and trees disappeared into endless darkness.

"No!" Screamed Vincent as the ground cracked and fell away, leaving the two on pillars apart from each other. "We ARE the same soul, the same spirit. Your heart IS mine, Trebor. Your life IS mine. But we can't be truly rejoined as long as this friction remains!"

"Then we'll never rejoin." Trebor shouted, angrily. "Because I'm not going to die!" Trebor turned away from Vincent, jumping to a pedestal away that had been behind him. Vincent took a deep breath, summoning up his own strength and leapt after the escaping Trebor. "I know what you're trying to do, but I won't do it!" Trebor screamed, as he jumped from pedestal to pedestal. "I won't!" He got a running start and he jumped down into the fiery pit.

Vincent watched him fall until Trebor disappeared. "Damn it." He cursed. But even as he looked around for another option, his heart sent his body into motion. With a quick jump, Vincent dropped down into the pit also.

As Vincent fell, the fiery light transformed into a cool glow. Suddenly, the crevice and the fire disappeared. In its place was a watery realm. In a wave of confusion, Vincent was spun around and around, unable to keep his bearings.

A strange light appeared beneath him as he floated in the cold water. He flailed about, trying to swim up, but no such orientation existed. Everyway he moved, it felt like he was falling deeper into the abyss.

Gradually, Vincent saw a glowing aura of light that shimmered with an unearthly presence. As he neared it, the light began to grow more brilliant. With a bit of exertion, Vincent turned himself in the water and began to swim towards it. He moved forward at an astonishing rate, much faster than seemed possible.

As he approached the light, the shapes within the glow coalesced. Like mercury drops flowing into one another, the silver images formed into the shapes of buildings and a ground. The closer Vincent got, the more pronounced the shapes became. Soon, a small city stretched out before him as he descended towards a silver palace.

The gothic architecture fused with a strange Greco-Roman styling that gave Vincent an uneasy feeling. The strange, silver palace was deserted, but still seemed to feel like a living thing, a place of ancient and hidden things.

"Trebor!" Called Vincent as he looked around. But his darker half was nowhere to be seen. "Trebor! Come out and face me!" Vincent called, still looking about at the great silver capital. "Stand and deliver, you coward!"

"Shut the hell up!" Came a voice from behind a pillar. Vincent raced towards the pillar that lined a huge city square, but when he got there, there was no sign of Trebor. "You just don't get it!" Came Trebor's voice, shouting from a pillar opposite the one Vincent had stopped at. "You just don't seem to understand that no matter how many times you 'kill' me, I'm just not going to die."

"We'll see about that." Growled Vincent, his hatred getting the best of him. He held up his bowie knife as Trebor stepped out from the pillar.

"We already have." Trebor said, an evil smile crossing his face as the glinting blade of Vincent's bowie knife flashed at him from across the square. Behind the two foes, the silver city and the golden light faded away, until the only thing that remained was the circular ground they stood on. "The darkness of our soul has clouded and poisoned us, Vincent." Trebor said, taking a demonstrative look around. "You always thought I was the destructive half, if we can be divided so cleanly, but the fact is, you were the destructive half."

A red light began to emanate from the barriers of the distant edge of the ground. As the light arose, it cast shadows around five figures in the darkness. Figures suspended in the air. "This is our destiny, Vincent." Trebor said, his smile still assured as he looked around. "This darkness has consumed us, but we can control it."

As Trebor said this, the center of the circular field opened up, a single sword rising up through it. A sword whose blade and handle alike were completely black, its shape resounded in Vincent's mind. It was the sword he had dreamt about so many times, the sword the black-clad hunter had aimed at the boy.

"What is that?" Vincent asked hesitantly to Trebor, motioning to the sword.

"You don't know?" Trebor exclaimed in disbelief. "Impossible. You have to have seen it before."

"I've seen it." Vincent admitted. "But I don't know what it is."

"You don't know about the Black Sword?" Trebor exclaimed, in utter disbelief. "I thought for sure you remembered that, at the very least. You had to have"

"Sorry to disappoint you." Vincent said, without emotion. "But this still isn't getting us anywhere."

"Quite the contrary." Trebor said, recovering his composure. "I'm trying to get you to see why you and I can never be rejoined." Trebor reached to his side, drawing his black-bladed katana. "There can be only one mind in this body and soul. Only one who controls our fate. We can either learn to live in this disharmonious union, or…" Trebor held his katana up in his stance, letting his silence and gesture speak in place of stating the obvious. "What's it gonna be, Vincent?" He challenged. "You or me?"

"If you do this, Trebor," Vincent warned, at the same time, taking up his own stance. "I'll win."

"We'll see, pretty boy." Trebor smiled. In a flash, he launched himself at Vincent, his katana raised at his side. Vincent waited patiently, his knife held ready. Trebor closed the distance quickly, swinging powerfully at Vincent's neck. But the Vgm simply wasn't there to be hit.

Sidestepping Trebor's blow, Vincent slid around the dark image of himself, slashing his twin along the back with his bowie knife. Trebor used the momentum of his swing to spin around, trying to disembowel his foe. Vincent hinged with the slash, narrowly avoiding the blade. At the same time, he dropped his knife and grabbed Trebor's hands with his right hand. Spinning like a top, Vincent punched Trebor along the face, then continued the motion to roundhouse kick Trebor in the jaw. The dark figure was sent hard to the ground. "It doesn't have to be this way." Vincent called to Trebor, as the dark monster struggled to his feet.

"It's one or the other!" Trebor screamed, thrusting at Vincent. Vincent sidestepped and riposted at Trebor's elbow, knocking the sword free. At the same motion, Vincent dropped low and grabbed Trebor's ankle. With a powerful yank, he pulled Trebor off balance. As the alternate fell to the ground, the bricks of the circle opened up, allowing Trebor to fall through.

Vincent moved fast and jumped through the hole, not letting Trebor get away. Back in the water, he swam towards the fleeing Trebor, grabbing him by his ankles. Trebor spun around in the liquid and swung at Vincent. He slid narrowly around the strikes, finally grabbing Trebor's right arm and pulling it to the side. With a fast motion, he slammed his positioned elbow into Trebor's neck, knocking him farther into the water.

"It doesn't have to end with one of us dying." Vincent said, hanging close to Trebor, as the alternate tried to swim away. "We can find our own peace together. One of us can't die. We both have to live."

"I don't believe you!" Trebor screamed, tears now flowing from his eyes. They approached another golden light and Trebor made for it. Vincent had trouble keeping up with his alternate but managed to stay close.

Trebor pushed through the immaterial barrier between him and the open air of the golden light. Once inside, he began to free fall in some incomprehensible direction. Vincent pushed through the barrier an instant later, following after Trebor. As he punctured the barrier of the light, the water from the outside realm began to ebb. But as his body cleared into the open air, the water continued to cascade off of him, streaking along the form of two wings from his back that weren't there.

"We can't coexist." Trebor shouted, as Vincent closed in on him. "The darkness in our souls is too great. Pihc chose us because of that. No alternate can ever fully rejoin!" Vincent shot down at Trebor, grabbing his arms and stopping his fall.

"Then we'll succeed where no one else ever has." Vincent yelled back, from behind his elusive foe. "We'll both live through this, Trebor. We have to."

"NO!" Screamed Trebor, trying in vain to fight against Vincent. As Vincent fought to hold Trebor still, the image of Trebor faded to transparency for a brief instant, revealing the silhouette of a small boy. But it immediately disappeared. "No! NO!" Trebor continued to fight. "You're lying! You're trying to end me!"

"Trebor." Vincent said in a calming voice that slowed the fighting until it stopped. "Trebor, neither of us has to die." He said clearly. Trebor stopped fighting entirely, blinking through tears. "If this is going to work, then neither of us CAN die." Vincent released his hold on Trebor and the two floated together, the terrified Trebor gazing at Vincent. "We can rejoin completely." He said honestly, holding out his hand. "We can be just like we were before Pihc ever came into our lives."

"How?" Trebor whispered plaintively, tears brimming in his eyes. Vincent smiled slightly, holding out his hand farther. Trebor looked at Vincent's hand, then his own. Slowly and unsure, he reached out and took Vincent's hand. "I don't want to die." He finally said, crying now.

Vincent smiled peacefully at Trebor. Reaching up to the alternate's chest, Vincent pushed through the physical barrier that had once separated the two. He pushed through Trebor's body, reaching down to into the core of his being. Vincent's hand cradled the delicate center as he and Trebor moved close to one another.

"You don't have to die…" Vincent said sincerely, smiling confidently as he looked Trebor in the eye. Slowly, Vincent's hands both passed through the physical barrier of Trebor, reaching out and taking hold of Trebor's whole body. Gently pulling him close, the two pulled into each other, their physical forms melding slowly, as if into pure light. "Neither of us has to die." They both said, their voices speaking in unison. "We'll live on…" They said, Vincent and Trebor's voice joining into one. "I'll live on." Came the unified voice. "I don't have to die to be reborn."

The light in the bathroom seemed bright. Even though the light was dim by normal standards, the incandescent bulb sent him back, receding into the darkness. It took a few moments before he could stand the brilliance, but as he slinked into the tiny room, the image opposite him caught his attention.

In the mirror was a familiar face, but one which was changed. A more defined visage of life and death, the face stared back with a tired intensity that seemed impossible. A look of dismay stared back at the image as he moved his hand over his face. The body in the mirror was frail, but beneath the skin was a brewing strength.

"You look like shit."

Vincent turned around to see Chip in the doorway. "Looks like you did it, Vincent." Chip said with a small, but relieved grin.

"That remains to be seen." Vincent said with half a smile, turning back to the mirror. "I've lost so much weight." He said, considering his shirtless form.

"It'll come back." Chip said, reassuringly. "Just take it easy for a couple of days."

"Yeah." Vincent said, laughing as he considered his reflection. He was about to speak, but turned instead. "Do I even have a couple of days?" He asked with a yawn.

"Don't worry about that. Everything can wait." Chip said with a cautioning tone, watching Vincent in the mirror. "Don't get overzealous. One day at a time."

"Yeah, yeah." Vincent said, looking in the mirror again. "What did Jim give for my chances?"

"Chances?" Chip asked. But he suddenly chuckled. "Oh. I think he was giving you twenty to one."

"Did you put me down for five? I was good for it." Vincent said. He leaned in close to the mirror. "Have my eyes always been blue?"

"Yes." Chip spouted out, laughing. Vincent looked back at him in the mirror, smiling also. "I know Jessica's going to be happy to see that."

Vincent's attention perked up. "See what?"

"Your smile." Chip said. "She didn't leave your side the whole time. You may have noticed her passed out in there."

"Yeah." The dark Vgm nodded. "I didn't have the heart to wake her. It's so late and she seemed so peaceful."

"Yeah, she's really pretty when she's asleep and not talking." He chided. "God, she annoys me sometimes."

"To each his own." Vincent mumbled.

"I suppose." Chip ventured. He turned back to the figure in the mirror and appraised him for a moment. "I must say, I expected a bigger change."

"What do you mean?" Asked Vincent with a weak chuckle. "A third eye, perhaps?"

"Not exactly." Chip said, taking a step into the tiny bathroom. "Just that you look the same as you did before. Just a bit lighter." He said, thumping Vincent in the stomach. Vincent simply grinned a chuckle, then turned back to the mirror.

Chip shook his head, which caught Vincent's attention. "What?" He asked, but Chip said nothing; just smiling. Vincent went back to his reflection. "I think you're right." He said, after a moment. "I should at least have grown some facial hair or something."

"Exactly." Chip pointed out. "Although I think a beard's a bit over-rated. Maybe a goatee." Vincent gave Chip a strange look in the mirror without turning to him.

"Whatever." He cast aside. Then he stood up straight, coming to just a hair's breadth shorter than Chip and snapped a salute. "I'll see what I can do." Chip couldn't help but laugh. Vincent turned back to the mirror, continuing to stare at his reflection for a few more minutes. Somewhat satisfied, he stood up again and turned to Chip. "I think I'm going to get something to eat, then head back to bed." Vincent said, with a sigh. "I'm exhausted."

"Good idea." Chip said, leading Vincent out. "Good night, Vincent."

"Yes it has been." Vincent smiled, heading downstairs. "I'll see you in the morning."

Chip watched the younger Vgm walk silently through the darkness, then turned away with a smile.

In the main space of the auto shop, the debris-littered floor was mostly cleared by the traffic of the day. Metal pipes ran overhead, while the fragments of the passing years had been pushed against the boarded up windows and filthy walls.

On bare feet, Vincent stepped with quiet caution out into the darkness of the room, walking over to the wall. He glanced over his shoulder at the stairwell leading upstairs, then grabbed up a thin metal pipe the length of his arm, feeling its weight in his grip. Laying it across his shoulders, he walked into the center of the dark room.

In the echoing space of the auto-dealership, Vincent took the bar at one end and held it out in front of him like a sword. He positioned his feet, moving them into a relaxed, but ready position, while keeping his eyes focused on the tip of the metal pipe.

With a slow motion, he stepped forward, pulling the sword up over his head, then smacking it down at the air in front of him. But the heavy weight of the metal pipe jerked him forward. It smacked down onto the cheap flooring of the lobby, cracking the tile it landed on. Vincent pulled the sword free and listened for feet on the stairs, waiting.

Satisfied when he heard nothing, he turned to face the stairs, taking up the same sword position again. He gritted his teeth and flexed his hands, his eyes still focusing beyond the blade of the sword. He breathed out slowly, his forearms flexing to keep control.

Stepping forward with a fluid, restrained motion, Vincent again lifted the makeshift above his head, then slammed it back down in front of him. But this time, he was able to keep the sword from striking the ground. Turning back around, he focused beyond the tip of the sword, sweat appearing on his brow. But even as he forced his breathing to slow, he looked beyond the blade. With a faster step and a quicker motion of his arms, Vincent slide forward, moving like a panther, raising the sword. The blade swished through the air, only to be yanked back into position.

Vincent turned back again, his eyes locked beyond the blade. As he felt the breath move in and out of his lungs, a pleased look appeared in his eyes. A small smile curled on his lips as he focused on his chosen task.

Yerrbmot

CHAPTER 22

One, If by Land

"All right, listen up everyone! I want you to calmly file towards the exits. That's it, that's it. Nobody runs, just walk. Single file. That's it. Now if we just stay calm, no one's gonna be harmed by the huge bomb that's gonna explode any minute."

—Nordberg, The Naked Gun 2 ½: The Smell of Fear

"*What does it say?*" Mars asked, as Livic and Yerrbmot read over the front page of a newspaper as they turned from the smashed newspaper machine next to the double doors of the antiquated mountains grocery store. Dressed in their armor, with weapons plainly displayed, they walked calmly, perfectly at ease. Meanwhile, the ancient man behind the single counter in the grocery store watched through the window with utter awe while in the empty parking lot, the three warriors communed.

"It says that a city on the coast, Wilmington, is being evacuated." Livic explained, handing the newspaper he carried to Yerrbmot. In his other hand, he carried a steaming cup of coffee.

"*Sounds auspicious. Where is this 'Wilmington' in relation to the VGM's home city?*" Mars asked, looking off as he tried in vain to remember the layout of the state.

"It's on the farthest, most eastern portion of the province, on the coast." Yerrbmot said, studying the newspaper.

"State." Corrected Livic, without turning from Mars. "It's the 'state' of North Carolina, not the province."

"*Regardless.*" Mars said, getting his generals' attention back. "*What does that evacuation mean in regards to our plans?*"

"Well, the report says that a 'chemical spill' is proving deadly to humans." Yerrbmot said, pointing to the front page beneath the picture of the clogged interstate. "So, the entire area needs to be evacuated and 'cleaned'."

"*That's starting to sound suspicious.*" Mars said again, scratching his chin. "*Sounds like a cover-up.*"

"Cover-up?" Asked Livic. "Why do you say that?"

"They're hiding the truth." Yerrbmot said, handing the newspaper to Mars. Mars took it, immediately handing it to Livic, who handed it to Yerrbmot. Yerrbmot read the story again. "This smells like a trap."

"Then the VGM is most likely preparing to engage us there." Livic added, also considering the newspaper. "There, instead of in the capital." He thought about that for a moment. "Why in the world would they do that?" He pondered aloud, his voice heavy with confusion. "What possible advantage would being in that city give them over being in Raleigh?"

"*Wilmington's a port town. It's on the ocean. The water might be able to afford them protection.*" Mars said, thinking. "*The 'Shees can't swim. Neither can we in our armor.*"

"But the oceans are dangerous." Yerrbmot responded, shifting the newspaper to the hand that held the staff so he could take a sip from his cheap plastic coffee cup. "Masters and the VGM can't be that ignorant."

"*Maybe he is not, maybe he is. Who is to say?*" Mars said, scratching his chin. "*It's hard to tell sometimes.*" The two generals laughed.

"Water's never been very good to us." Yerrbmot mused, as the laughter subsided. "I'm hesitant to attack, or defend, around the ocean."

"*I'm not fond of it, either.*" Mars said, grumbling.

"Understandably so." Livic nodded. "Part of you spent a great deal of time in that Ocean Palace."

"To make matters worse," Yerrbmot said, getting everyone's attention back to the matter at hand. "This area of the ocean, near this city, Wilmington, seems like it might be a weak point. I would have to consider the lines of natural magic that run over the city and that area, but it looks like the barrier of reality may already be at the breaking point."

"How?" Livic asked, more worried than the other two. "How is it weak?"

"*That doesn't matter.*" Mars said decisively. He swallowed his uncertainty and stretched back his shoulders, standing up fully to tower over his generals. "*The VGM have decided the battle will be in Wilmington. So be it.*" He looked at his generals. "*To Wilmington we shall go.*"

"We can not just charge in there, Mars." Livic said carefully. "We no longer have an army of 'Shees with which to work. Our army was decimated by the celestial dragons. Yours was sadly left scattered across the desert. And I'm sure they've been hunted down."

"*Once Eminaf returns, the four of us alone could decimate that town.*" Mars posed confidently.

"Yes, but it would take time, and energy. Both of which will need to be focused solely on the VGM."

"Additionally," Yerrbmot cautioned, looking up at Mars as he stood next to Livic. "It's dangerous to confront the denizens of a domain so drained of magic with what they know to be impossible. We were capable of that previously because of Ecnilitsep's magic and our absolute destruction of everything to see us. Unless you're prepared to destroy the whole city the moment we're within sight of it, then…"

"*The people of this nation have already seen us, and the 'Shees.*" Mars protested.

"On television, or whatever they call it. These people live in a world of fiction and make-believe. To see it on television is one thing. It's distanced, distracted, false, even if they know it to be true." The wizard general maintained. "Mars, when Pihc made his move on this earth half a year ago, he prepared endlessly. And when he finally moved, it was surgical and concise. But we don't have the luxury of time or preparation that Pihc did."

The muscular giant took a deep breath, his hands resting on the pommel of the katana at his waist. He pushed his impatience down and turned to the two generals. "*Then what do you suggest?*" He asked with only slight agitation.

"Let us collect Eminaf in Raleigh, then we quietly maneuver into Wilmington." Livic explained. "While the VGM looks for an army to come charging over the sand dunes we sneak up on them from behind and take the fight to them, personally."

"*Just us four?*" Mars asked, a small grin appearing on his face.

"Just us four?" Yerrbmot said, less than pleased with the idea.

"Just us four." Livic nodded. "Three of us are more than capable of stealth." As he spoke, his green armor became strangely gelatinous and shifted around his body, reforming slowly into the shape of a white t-shirt pulled across his muscular frame. Complete with hefty work boots and stained jeans, the gray-haired general suddenly looked like a casual farmhand. "We can sneak in unnoticed. And we can take the VGM. It's either this, or we charge in, just us four, and try to raze the city to the ground. Unless, of course, you want to wait long enough to grow a new crop of 'Shees?" He posed, making the giant stare at him. "I didn't think so." He glanced at Yerrbmot, then back to Mars. "Granted, stealth hasn't been our forte so far, but I assure you, we can do it." He added.

Yerrbmot opened his mouth to protest, but before he could speak Mars exclaimed loudly. "*I like it.*"

The police cruiser crawled through the neighborhood streets, just yards from the shore. Blaring over its loudspeaker, a message echoed in the early morning sunlight just over the buzzing of cicadas. "A state of emergency has been declared. A dangerous chemical spill has occurred within Wilmington city limits. Please tune to local media for information on evacuation procedures. Repeat, a state of emergency has been declared."

The voice repeated mechanically, waking the city's few permanent residents as they stepped out of their stilted houses into the October morning to listen to the warning. The police car kept slowly down the single-lane street, spreading its frightening message.

On the tall bridge that led off the islands of the beachfront property, the lanes were clogged. Both inbound and outbound lands had been converted into one long road heading away from the town.

Honks and beeps drowned out the calls of the native wildlife as the population of the coastal center struggled to escape from the news reports and repeated, automated warnings of the dangers that crept up on them.

"What the hell are you doing up?" Chip asked as he strolled into the break room-turned-kitchen. Jessica was at the small table in the dilapidated white room, slumped over a coffee mug half-full of something that smelled powerfully alcoholic. "It's seven in the morning." He continued, while digging futilely through the cabinets, getting visibly more frustrated with each new disappointment. "Do we have anything to eat?"

"It doesn't seem that way." Jessica grumbled, turning back to her mug.

"You didn't answer my question." Chip said, finding a box of cereal. He opened the top and poured a few shakes into his mouth. He stopped when his mouth was full, chewing just enough to be able to speak again. "Wha ar u doiin up dis earry?" He managed to get out through the corn flakes.

"I could ask you the same thing." Jessica sent back, without reservation. She looked up at Chip, who stared back with a greater intensity. Finally, Jessica turned to him and they both held out their hands. They shook their fists twice, then opened them; Jessica's into the shape of a pair of scissors and Chip into a closed fist of a rock.

"Damn." Jessica mumbled, turning back to her glass. "I was up with Vincent." She said, ignoring the exaggerated consternation that came from Chip.

"You were what?" He nearly shouted.

"Chip, keep your voice down." She bit back at him. "Everyone's asleep and I'm in no mood to be yelled at this morning."

"What the hell were the two of you doing?" Chip pressed. A thought suddenly entered his mind, slowing his complaint.

"Sadly, no." She said, anticipating where his mind would go. "I was training him." She said with some pent up aggression. "I woke up at about one or so this morning and he was gone. I looked for him and I found him out there, doing push-ups."

"And so you decided to help him push himself after everything he's been through?" Chip again nearly shouted.

"Chip!" Jessica said, the force of her voice rather than its volume finally making it through to him. After a moment, he backed down slightly, leaning against the counter of the kitchen. "Chip, you have to admit it. You wouldn't take this whole thing lying down and neither will Vincent." She said, her voice low, for both the hour and the words. "He's got one thing on his mind now and that's Round 2 with Mars. He's not going to stop until either he beats Mars or he's dead."

"So you're going to push him when he needs to be recovering?" Chip said, his volume replaced with a calmer tone.

"Chip, you can't tell Vincent to not do what he's spent his whole life doing. Since he was first in the VGM, he's trained to fight Pihc. Now, in his mind, Pihc is Mars. So he's gearing up to do the very thing he's lived and breathed for years. And that's fight. And in order to do that, he's got to get ready. And being ready means training."

"Jessica, in a couple of days, that might be close to feasible. But right now…" Chip tried to counter.

"You and I both know that Vincent doesn't have a few days." She dismissed with a wave of her gloved hand. "Mars is gunning for us. Even if Eric can evacuate this town and get the civilians out of the way, Mars'll still be here tomorrow, if not sooner. Vincent knows that and he's going to be ready." Chip tried to interject something, but Jessica kept talking. "Now we can either help him to get stronger, and maybe have him back on the lines against Mars, or we can try and keep him from it, and run the risk of him hurting himself in the process."

"Jessica, he's going to strain himself too quickly, either way." Chip tried.

"I'm not sure of that." She countered weakly as she turned away. "Say what you want Chip, but he's going to fight Mars when he comes. We can either fight him and try to keep him from doing what comes natural, or we can help him be ready." Signaling the end of the conversation, she turned away from Chip, looking sleepily back over the table.

"This battle with the VGM, at Wilmington." Yerrbmot said, as he walked with Mars and Livic along the roadside. "This threatens everything Ecnilitsep worked towards."

"*Which was the safeguarding of reality.*" Mars nodded. "*Then explain to me why she was never able to accomplish it?*" He asked rhetorically.

"She had to fight three foes." Livic said calmly, walking just behind Mars. "Don't you remember? She had to battle Htead, her creator. She had to battle Tiamat as well, and occasionally his brethren. And they, least of all."

"*Least of all?*" Mars asked, one eyebrow going up. "*Least of all what?*"

Livic stopped and looked up at Mars. "You honestly don't remember?" The green-dressed general asked. He looked at Yerrbmot with stoic concern.

"*Remember what?*" Mars asked, looking between the two.

"The Shadows." Yerrbmot said. "You don't remember the Shadows?"

"*Apparently not.*" The giant said. "*I admit there is something to that word, but it's nothing more than a chilling thought.*"

"It's more than a chilling thought, Mars." Yerrbmot warned. He looked around the warm late autumn day, thinking. "The Shadows are the agents of the Oblivion. They are the foes that we, with Ecnilitsep, have faced for countless ages. They are the reason we strove for so long and so hard to safeguard reality. They would devour all that is in an instant if they could."

"*All that is?*" Mars asked. "*What are they?*"

"They are," Yerrbmot tried, unable to find the words. "The Oblivion incarnate."

"Have we got anything?" Ben said, flopping down in the corner of the large communal office space. She and Dan sat in front of the small television, flipping through the channels manually.

"Not a thing." Dan said, twisting the dial of the tiny black and white television. "All we get are the local channels, and even they're coming in all fuzzy."

"They're nothing but evacuation reports anyway." Sophia grumbled. She sat up frustrated from the TV and looked at Dan. "I wish we had something to play."

"Well," Ben started with an innocent look. "Since the city's pretty much evacuated, I suppose if an enterprising individual was interested, they could..."

"Stop." Dan said, shaking his head, not even looking up at Ben. "Just stop."

"What?" Ben said. "I'm just saying..."

"Stick to ganking booze with illegal IDs." Dan maintained adamantly as he continued to work on the television. "There will be no pillaging."

As he spoke, Jim came into the room, two large burlap sacks in his hands. He looked at Dan, then to Sophia and Ben. "What?" He asked. He glanced down at Dan, then at Ben. "He said no, didn't he?"

Vincent sat with his back against the tree. At the edge of the dealership parking lot, he rested with closed eyes, his black katana laid across his knees. He breathed in the warm smell of the coast's salty air and the fresh scent of the spindly trees as they swayed in the dusty, sun-drenched breeze.

Vincent opened his eyes to see Emily standing in front of him. He smiled at her, not moving. "How can I help you?" He asked.

She smiled, her shadow cast directly below her. "It's so odd to hear you like that again."

"Like what?" He asked, his smile not completely gone.

"I don't know. Alive. Emotional. Like you were back in high school." She said. "It's, I don't know, it feels right, to see you smile."

"Beth said the same thing earlier today." He said to her. "She said 'familiar', but you know."

"Is that what you're doing out here?" She asked, coming to sit down on the edge of the pavement. "Looking for the familiar?"

Vincent smiled. "There's something very restful about leaning against a tree. Something..." He stopped himself, chuckling. "And how are you Emily?" He asked.

She laughed as well. "I feel terrible. I want a shower, some new clothes, anything to feel clean again. I bet I look awful."

"No, you don't." Vincent smiled. "You don't look like anything but a princess."

'I'm sorry.'

Emily's head jerked back. Her vision was clouded, shadowy images appearing before the real world. She held her head, struggling as images superimposed over themselves over her sight.

She saw a room, beautiful and extravagant, with blue and silver everywhere. But fire crawled across the walls, while the shadows themselves seemed alive, seeming to seep out from the corners of the world, seemed to reach out. She saw a knight, her once-betrothed. He was kneeling over her. Behind him, the entire room was covered in darkness. "I'm sorry, it's the only way." He whispered with forced emotionlessness.

Emily pushed away from Vincent, her eyes shaking fearfully. "What's wrong?" He asked, moving to stand up.

"Stay away." Emily called, pushing herself to her feet. She backed away from Vincent, emotions running through her mind. "It's, it's nothing. Just, just stay away." She said, backpedaling away from him. Vincent watched her leave, confused.

"So what do you think?" Shane asked with a loud burp. He took another sip from the can of soda in his hands, then looked over at Tim. "Think she can make it?"

In front of the two, Michelle was bent over, carefully pacing the strength of her arm as she swung the full can of soda like a bowling ball, her eyes locked on the ten standing cans of soda a few parking spaces down from them. But as Shane got ready to ask Tim again, the tall mage bent his head over just a bit as Michelle stepped forward to bend over into her throw. Shane tilted his head as well.

"Are you guys staring at my ass again?!" Michelle charge with a violent shout, not taking her eyes off the cans in front of her.

"No!" The two chimed innocently in unison, their heads snapping back upright.

The glass doors slid open for the woman dressed in purple, form-fitting armor. With her saber at her side, she stepped into the giant toy store hesitantly. Overhead, an overly cheerful version of a Top 40 song played just loud enough so it couldn't be tuned out. All around, the white shelves and bins held a vast array of toys for all ages and interests, while posters hung from the ceiling to advertise still more toys.

Eminaf looked at the woman at the register next to the door, the woman's eyes staring in surprise. "Honey?" The woman said, smacking her gum. "You one of them cos-playahs?

Eminaf stared at the woman for a moment. "Sure." She finally said, walking over to the red counter. "I am in need of the items on this list." The female general said, handing Mars' list to the woman.

The woman behind the register took the list and looked it over for a moment, nodding her head. "Mm-hmm." She finally decided, handing the list back to Eminaf with a bored look. "'Lectronics. Over there." She said, pointing lazily over her shoulder at a small sectioned off space on the other corner of the store.

Eminaf looked over at the section, then to the woman. With a sigh of annoyance, she walked towards the area.

"All Vgms, on-line."

"Jessica, on-line."

"Tim, on-line."

"Vincent, on-line."

"Okay, kids." Chip said, as he stood before the rag-tag group in the front of the car shop. "Eric has pulled his last strings to help us out. As we speak, the last vestiges of Wilmington's population are being evacuated under the guise of a chemical spill."

The leader of the VGM paused as he paced to one side of the group, considering the tall trees in the area as he tried to think. "That being the case, we've got a pretty free run of this place until tomorrow morning. And we're going to need it because all reports indicate that Mars is on his way and will be here sometime tonight."

"Is this going to be another all-out battle like at Crossworld?" Ben asked, raising his hand. "Because if so, I need to run back to Raleigh and get more guns."

"What we've got right now is what we've got." Chip said with only a small touch of sympathy. "And before you guys, and by you guys I mean Ben and Jim, decide to run off pillaging, it should be noted that we've already concocted a plan."

"Is it a good plan or one of our usual crackpot schemes?" Michelle asked, raising her hand as well.

"Somewhere in between." Chip explained without missing a beat. "Tim and I have located a spot that we think may be able to isolate Mars and take him temporarily out of the fight."

Silence.

"I'm sorry, come again." Dan piped up.

"The plan is," Chip explained with careful words as he came back to stand directly in front of the whole group. "We are going to engage Mars, his generals, and whatever alternates may still be working for him, at the city's center. There's a parking deck there that's four stories tall, that we're going to drop onto Mars, leaving him isolated and giving us time to deal with the generals and the alternates."

"Drop it?" Beth asked with some concern.

"Yeah." Tim said, nodding his head sarcastically to show his lack of enthusiasm for the plan. "We've got some explosives left over from the little jaunt in the desert and they're expiration goes out at midnight, so we figured, you know…"

"Um, question. What about the 'Shees?" Jon asked, ignoring Tim.

"If there are any left, which is unlikely," Chip explained. "The FBI is going to station what military force they've got handy to stall them. We are only going to concern ourselves with Mars and his crew."

"So, let me recap." Jim offered up. "We're going to lure Mars and his boys, which is something like seven guys now."

"Three now." Vincent chimed in. "Eminaf, Livic, and Yerrbmot are the only ones that are going to be with Mars now. Brenard, Cye, and Yadiloh have gone renegade."

Silence.

"That's new." Chip said, turning to Vincent. "They left?"

"Yeah." He nodded. "They didn't support Ecnilitsep, and left after Pihc was forced to rejoin with S'ram."

"And you know this from…" Chip asked, putting his hands demonstratively together. Vincent nodded. "You know, this is something you could have offered up in the meeting."

"Chip, right now I'm lucky to remember my own birthday." Vincent tossed back. "Cut me some slack, will you?"

"So, Mars and his three goons." Ben tossed in between Chip and Vincent. He seemed to think it over for a minute, then shrugged. "We can do that." He said with some confidence, getting some strange stares from those around him.

"How long until Mars gets here?" Emily asked, her arms crossed. "And once he does get here, how are we going to get him into the parking deck and then drop it on him? And once we do that, how are we going to deal with the generals? And once we deal with the generals how are we going to deal with Mars afterwards?"

"That was like seven questions." Jim protested, raising his hand childishly. "She should have to wait her turn."

"We're going to lure Mars into the parking deck the way we always control the fights." Jessica offered up.

"Which is to say with absolute confusion and not a small bit of improvisation." Tim finished.

"As for the generals," Vincent spoke up. "We're going to hope that they can be done in the same way the alternates are, which is with their own weapons."

"But what about Mars?" Emily asked. "Are we planning on stealing his sword and using that?"

Chip smiled. "Not exactly. We've got a little surprise." He turned subtly to Vincent and nodded. The dark Vgm turned around to the car shop's door and pushed it open, drawing out the opened bag which held once held explosives. Reaching inside, he pulled out a long shape wrapped in a military blanket. "We're going to use this." Chip said, as Vincent unwrapped the olive drab covering.

The VGM all started as the dark Vgm held up Ecnilitsep's scimitar.

CHAPTER 23

Anything That Can Go Wrong

"Where are you gonna be,
When It all comes down?
What are you gonna do,
When it all comes down on you?
I'll be sitting on top of the world,
When It All Goes Wrong Again!"

—Everclear, When It All Goes Wrong Again

In the far distance, the sun was setting into the Atlantic Ocean. The orange sky of flame sent long shadows across the city as silent winds blew sand from the beach across the empty roads. In the far distance, a screen door slammed in the wind while the perpetual sound of the crashing waves wafted through the desolate city on the salt-stained air.

"Any word from the dragons?" Tim asked, as he held an ohm reader to the detonator. When the reader went wild, he started to screw in the red and black wires.

"None." Chip said, leaning against a red sedan that Tim worked next to. "Eric said after the generals finally disappeared, they kind of skedaddled in a hurry." Chip poked his upper lip up with his tongue, checking his gums in the windows of the SUV across him.

"But they won." Tim considered academically as he checked his work.

"Allegedly." Chip said, tapping into the microphone of his headset. "The fight did go on for like eight hours or something. Just the five of them against the generals and whatever little tricks they had up their collective sleeves." He tapped the microphone again. "I think I need some new batteries."

Tim turned on his haunches, looking up past Chip at the large four-story parking deck of solid concrete. "You know, property damage follows us everywhere we go."

"Better a parking deck than the entire planet." Chip said callously, glancing fatalistically down at Tim. "Besides, I hate to say it Pierce, but we've got nothing that can stop Mars. Not unless the entire group jumps on him. And even then…"

"We'll make it through." The mage said, standing up. "All Vgms, on-line." He called into the microphone.

"Chip, on-line." Said the fighter next to him.

"Jessica, on-line."

"Vincent, on-line."

"Ben, on-line."

Tim rolled his eyes. "Ben, you're not a Vgm. You don't get to talk."

"Can we use that excuse on him every time he opens his mouth?" Came Dan's voice over the network.

"Shut up, Dan." Came Ben's shout. "I cut you. I cut you bad."

"You couldn't cut the cheese at a baked bean convention." Dan retorted.

"Oh, so that's how it's gonna be." Ben came back. "It's on now. It's on."

"Oh kids." Came Vincent's voice in a mockingly paternal tone. "I do so hate to interrupt your little shenanigans, but there are some very powerful people coming to kill us."

Tim covered up his microphone and shook his head at Chip. "You know, I think I liked Vincent better when he didn't have a personality."

"He's just getting used to being able to use sarcasm again." Chip said with a cheap smile. "Cut him some slack."

"Right." Tim called, releasing his microphone. "Okay, everyone. Do we need to go over the plan again?"

"No." Came a cacophony of intentionally childlike voices over the headset.

"Alright then." Tim said, looking down at the detonator switch. "Then we're officially ready to go. Eric said a satellite image put Mars and his boys less than thirty miles away." He looked over at Chip. "That means they could be here any minute, so stay on guard." Tim slid his headset down to the back of his neck and sighed. "You realize that the chances of all of us surviving a second encounter with Mars are practically nil."

"You can't think about that, Tim." Chip said stoically, popping his neck. "We'll just do the best we can." He said, stepping away from the mage. "We'll see who's standing when it's all said and done." He added, heading off into the sunset.

Mars climbed a few steps up the sand dune, looking around the squat downtown that spread out with the coast just a few hills away. "This is Wilmington." Livic said from behind the giant. "The VGM should be here somewhere, no doubt waiting for us."

"They are such elusively painful foes, aren't they?" Eminaf said in the back, behind Yerrbmot as she considered the durable, but shoddy materials of most of the buildings. "I wonder how they plan to defeat us?"

"*All that matters now is finding them, and then doing what we do.*" Mars attested, his armor shimmering in the dusky starlight. "*Of course, we have to actually find them.*" He allowed under his breath.

"That's not going to be that hard." Livic said, as if distracted by something.

"Yeah." Eminaf went on. "They're right over there." She pointed up the street to where Ben and Michelle were sitting on top of a city bus, watching the sunset. Ben put his arm around Michelle's shoulders, which she immediately removed.

"*Very well.*" Mars grinned humorously, cracking his knuckles. "*Let's begin.*"

As the giant headed towards the bus, Livic stepped forward, putting his hand out to stop Mars. "Hold on." The general said cautiously as he stepped back to take in the whole picture of the downtown area. "There's just two of them."

"And?" Yerrbmot asked from the middle of the four.

"That makes them bait." Livic said, just before a loud pop caused his face to vaporize.

Mars and the two remaining generals turned as Ben stood on the bus, holding the pistol at a slight angle in his hands. The smoke from the barrel obscured his eyes, but the wide smile on his face was evident. "*Eminaf.*" Mars said in a hard tone. "*Kill him.*"

The female general leaped into a sprint towards the bus, but Ben didn't lower his gun to fire again. As the woman charged past the first square of the city block around the parking deck, a shadow appeared from nowhere. Vincent tackled Eminaf, lifting her off her feet with the impact. Slamming her into a telephone pole, he bent her nearly in half. With the female general down, Tim and Sophia rushed out to join Vincent.

"It is an ambush." Yerrbmot shrieked in terror. But as he turned around, he saw Jessica and Emily rushing towards him.

"*Excellent.*" Mars grinned, drawing his massive katana with a deliberate gesture.

"You say that now." Came a voice from behind. The giant turned around just as both of Jim's feet slammed into Mars' face, sending him crashing against the parking deck wall.

Livic stumbled unevenly to his feet, holding his head. When his eyes opened, Chip stood in front of him, with Shane and Beth flanking him. "The VGM's leader." Livic said, twirling his axe out from behind his back as his left forearm guard turned into a wide shield. "I could not have hoped for such a fight."

"Well, I do like to play requests." Chip smiled as he held his katana up close to his face.

Livic lunged at Chip, hacking with a fast attack towards his head. Chip ducked out of the way, slicing at the general's abdomen, striking his armor and sending out a flash of sparks. The two turned back to each other, their weapons ready. "And with whom am I warring?" Chip asked, as the tips of both their weapons hovered inches from each other while Shane and Beth kept their distance. "You're with Mars. That much I got." The Vgm said.

"I am General Livic." Said the green-clad warrior with a cordial smile. "I am your death."

"You know, I've heard that so much." Chip said with a shake of his head, stepping back just a few feet. "And to date, no one has ever made good on it."

"Well then, I am pleased to be the one to finally deliver." The general said, taking up a new stance, holding the axe blade by his face. "Shall we?" He asked.

"Oh, let's." Chip said with a smile, just before throwing his hand forward, a burst of power in geometric shapes flying from his palm.

"Stay down!" Tim said, punching Eminaf in the back of the head. As he did, his hand struck the lip of her armor. The sound of a bell chimed as Tim reeled back, clutching his hand painfully. The female general came up with a fast haymaker to the mage's jaw, then she turned around to Sophia. The girl stood in the general's sight, her eyes as wide as a deer's caught in headlights.

"You poor, little thing." Eminaf said, her voice taking on a melodic, maternal tone. "All alone in this dark world of chaos and combat. Here." She said, extending one hand to Sophia, while the other readied her saber. "Let me end your suffering."

Like a shadow, Vincent slid between Sophia and Eminaf, a familiar, cold expression on his face. Eminaf stepped back from the fighter, then looked up at the cut on his brow. "You're not healing as quickly as you used to."

Vincent's hands came up, reading the familiar black katana. "And you won't heal fast enough."

Yerrbmot watched as Mars and the other two generals fought against the VGM. He looked from one to the other, then spotted Mars as he threw Jim like a javelin. He gripped his staff with certainty, ignoring the sweat on his brow and took his first step towards the fight.

"Bang."

The wizard froze as Jon pushed his hand cannon into the back of the general's head. "You look like a 'Frank' to me." Jon said, as Dan and Jared stood ready behind him.

"My name is General Yerrbmot, of Ecnilitsep's armies." Yerrbmot answered, his head held high even as his voice shook.

"Well, it's official then." Dan said, gulping the last bit of Dr Pepper before he drew out his kukri. "I hate him."

"Step in line, Hardin." Jon said, glancing over his shoulder at the wiry wrestler. In the instant Jon looked away, Yerrbmot spun around, knocking the silver weapon away. He turned to finish the spin and slam his staff into Jon's side, but the biker's massive hand caught Yerrbmot around the neck. The grab stopped the general in a heartbeat, his staff falling to the pavement.

Jon's lip curled up in violent anger as he slowly lifted Yerrbmot off the ground by his neck. "Don't do that again." Jon said clearly, as Yerrbmot continued to rise up.

"***Flash Kick!***" Screamed Jessica, leaping into the air as her leg came within inches of Mars' chin. Mars bounded back from the flip, then threw himself toward the girl, his powerful right hand colliding with Jessica's back as she flipped over. She went flying into the side of the city bus, the windows rupturing outward from the impact.

The giant burst forward, slamming into the bus with his shoulder, pushing the giant vehicle up onto two wheels, throwing Michelle from the top as the bus rocked to the side. He then ducked down as Ben came around the front, his pistol firing indiscriminately.

Mars torqued back, then with a powerful swing, threw his black katana at Ben. The sniper jumped to the side, still firing with his gun while the sword whistled through the air. The bullets from the shots flew fast and true, but Mars ducked away from the shots, mindless as the bullets ripped through the thin metal frame of the touring bus.

Like a giant stick of dynamite, the bus exploded in flame, covering the entire street with a burning inferno. The combatants across the streets were knocked off their feet as the buildings caught fire, the entire block immediately igniting like a fuse. The flames flew up into the sky, as if paying homage to the already orange hued dusk clouds. The flames grew, dwarfing the tallest buildings in the city as the bus was sent into the air.

The bus flew up, almost to the third floor of the parking deck, before it reversed direction and plunged back to earth. Landing hard and solidly, the bus simply collapsed in on itself, shattering and erupting into a mass of destroyed pieces.

"Oh my god!" Screamed Beth, as the explosion ripped through the small engagement area. She looked around, her petrified eyes locked on the flames on the opposite side of the parking deck. "What was that?"

"That was Mars." Livic said, lunging at Chip. The leader of the VGM parried the lunge easily, then spun around, slicing for the general's neck. The gray-haired man narrowly slipped out of the way of the swing, then tried to riposte with a fast stab for Chip's shoulders. But the Vgm parried the attack, slicing for Livic's hands, hitting the armor plating the protected him.

"You're friends are dying, Masters." Livic said through gritted teeth as he backed away from the katana-wielding Vgm.

"No, they're just standing there doing nothing." Chip said, sparing Shane and Beth a harsh glare before he turned back to Livic. "The only one around here that's dying is you." He bit out, pressing against the general. With a quick thrust, Chip let the general block his sword, only to come up around, slamming his fist into Livic's face, covering it in blood and knocking him to the pavement.

"Maybe loading that thing with explosives wasn't the best idea." Ben said to himself.

"You think?!" Screamed Michelle from the other side of the street. "When I get my hands on you…" But Michelle never finished. For even as the fires burned with a hell-bound intensity, there was movement from within.

Michelle crawled along the sidewalk, cursing as the pavement rose in temperature. Still, she made her way from the block that had been turned into an inferno, turning back to see the flames. "I hope Jessica got out." Ben said, dropping the magazine in his pistol. "I didn't see where she was."

"I think she was…" Michelle's voice trailed off, her jaw dropping. Ben looked from her to the flames before them. His jaw dropped also.

Rising from the fire like a beast out of hell, Mars drew himself to his full height, towering over the pair. Looming over them, the giant stepped out of the fires, his armor unscathed. "*I'm not sure what you hoped to accomplish.*" He said, closing his fist tight, the sound of the tendons stretching echoing through their ears like the bloody screams of tearing flesh. "*However, it should be plain to see now, that you simply can not beat me.*"

"We'll see." Michelle yelled, lashing out with her silver whip. Mars sidestepped the slash and charged at the girl. She dropped to one knee and whipped at Mars' knees, the blades of her silver whip clinking as they flew. Still, the giant leapt nimbly, flipping in the air, his feet poised to land where Michelle crouched. Ben pushed Michelle out of the way, rolling in the opposite direction. He came up, his twin pistols ready. All he saw was Chip.

A fast kick to the stomach and another to the side of the head knocked Mars back, sending him stumbling towards the inferno. Jim suddenly raced up, leaping into the air, twisting horizontally, both his feet catching Mars in the chest. The giant was thrown over the concrete divider to the parking deck, landing hard between two cars. On the asphalt, he came to his feet instantly.

"Ben, get into position. Shane's by the elevator." Chip yelled to the sniper, then turned to the parking deck. He leapt over the barrier, landing just an instant before Mars' punch connected right into his chest. Chip went down, immediately, gasping in pain.

Mars stepped towards the downed Vgm, but as he did, a silver whip wrapped around his legs, pulling him off balance. He pivoted around to swing at Michelle, but she carefully ducked under the tree-leveling blow. As the giant moved, Dan swept in, catching him in the side with his kukri. The slash caught Mars off guard and turned him again, just as Jim rushed up along his side. Leaping up, the acrobat grabbed hold of the back of Mars' head and yanked him forward, knocking him out of the line of cars and into the middle of the parking deck.

Jim rolled away from the giant, letting Dan move in. Catching Mars around his knee, Dan tripped the giant onto his shoulders. With all his strength, he stood up with Mars across his shoulders, then bucked up to throw the giant over himself, over the row of cement blocks into the inner-most lane of the parking deck.

From the side, a ball of ice flew at Mars. The giant stepped back as it hit the car, freezing the door and the roof. He turned to see Jessica standing on the hood of the car next to him, bloodied and bruised, but still alive. With a powerful forward kick, Mars smashed the entire front side of the car and sent the car skidding, knocking Jessica off.

Mars turned back to Chip, just as the leader of the VGM leapt into the air. Spinning quickly, Chip rained down kicks on Mars yelling "***Tatsu-Maki-Senpu-Kyaku!***" Mars managed to remain standing, blocking the barrage of kicks, until Chip was done. As the Vgm landed, Mars reached out with lightning reflexes and grabbed Chip around the neck with one hand. Lifting Chip into the air, Mars held him high, preparing to hurl him to the ground.

"**Fall Down!**" Came Tim's voice from behind Mars. The giant's legs buckled a bit, but they didn't move. Still, the uncertainty of the spell gave Chip the space he needed to get free of the grip. Holding onto the monster at the shoulder, Chip flung himself down in a wide arm, kicking Mars' knees out from under him.

Mars dropped to one knee, but slammed his elbow back instinctively, knocking Chip away. He turned back around, with Jessica slamming into him with a hard straight kick. Mars knocked the kick out of the air with his arm, countering the attack with a hard punch to Jessica's stomach. She went down. Mars tried to get back up to his feet, but Dan stopped him.

Tackling Mars around the leg, Dan used all his strength and leverage to throw Mars back, Dan hoisted Mars over his hips and threw him down to the ground, at the base of the 'Up' ramp of the parking deck.

"Mars!" Eminaf shouted, rushing for the parking deck. But as she did, Jared dropped down on her shoulders, driving his katana in through the side of her neck into her body. The female general fell instantly to her knees, then collapsed onto the ground.

Jared landed in a roll and came up to see Jon catch Livic's axe in mid-swing. The larger fighter glared down at the gray-haired general, then yanked the axe violently to the side, dragging the unwilling general with the pull. "Looks like you've got everything in hand." Jared yelled to Jon.

"You ain't kidding." Jon said, suddenly breaking his grip with the axe as he grabbed the collar of Livic's arm. The general barely had time to gasp before Jon flattened his face with his fist.

Dan grappled Mars' leg, but the giant dropped to his knee, pinning Dan's arms against his thick legs. The huge fighter held up his right fist to level Dan with one blow. But as his arm rose up, Jim threw himself past Mars, hooking the giant's arm with his own. Spinning on the seemingly-immovable arm, Jim whirled back against Mars and slammed his knee into the base of the giant's neck. The blow knocked Mars onto all fours.

Dan rolled out from underneath Mars and came up as Jim landed. "Jim!" Dan called. The acrobat rushed at Dan and leapt into his cupped hands. Dan dropped back, using his fall to help throw Jim into the air. As Jim sailed over Mars in a spin, he stuck his leg out along the vertical axis, spinning it like a buzz saw. And with the force of a hurricane, Jim connected with the kick right onto Mars' neck. The giant was driven down into the ground, face first.

"GO!" Screamed Chip, with a wave of his katana.

Shane hit the gas on the car he had hotwired, the tires screaming before gaining a hold on the pavement. Mars barely looked up in time to see the headlights just before the car collided with him. Shane angled the impact to scoop Mars up onto the car's hood. Throwing the car into a higher gear, he squealed up onto the second deck. The giant rolled his head around to Shane, preparing to punch through the windshield at the driver, but Ben leaned out of the passenger's side, shooting Mars rapidly in the chest.

Mars endured another turn onto the third level, then grabbed the car by the door, tearing the giant piece of metal free it skidded to a halt. The giant nearly fell off the car, the door in his hands. Dizzied by the drive, Mars was unable to follow Shane and Ben as they raced for the edges of the parking deck.

Mars threw the car door ahead of them, the metal piece knocking a chunk of pavement out of the pillar next to them. Ben and Shane turned around as Mars stalked closer. Ben glanced at his gun, then at Shane. "Go!" He shouted. Shane turned back to the edge of the parking deck and climbed up onto the edge of the barrier. Ben held up his pistol. "All Vgms, on-line!" He shouted into the headset as Mars stalked closer. "Get ready!"

Shane looked out into the night wind and closed his eyes. A second later, a black and red rocket sled appeared on the edge of the divider. The rear of the jet erupted with flame and threatened to shoot forward. Shane glanced back at Ben as he stepped onto the sled. "***Ben, come on!***" He shouted.

"Go!" Ben yelled again, his eyes still aimed at Mars, the pistol leveled calmly even as Ben's eyes shook.

"*It won't work.*" Mars taunted as he stalked closer. "*It won't work, Ben.*"

"Wanna bet?" Ben asked just before pulling the trigger.

Mars dropped to his knees. His body fell, his head split open and spilling out onto the pavement like an overripe melon. "We're clear!" He shouted as he jumped out through the open space of the parking deck. Dropping into the open night air, a cloud burst around Ben, a raccoon tail and ears sprouting out of his body. The tail began to flutter and spin, slowing his descent.

Michelle watched as Ben and Shane disappeared out of the parking deck. She then looked down across the street and held up her hand. "***Now!***" She shouted, dropping her hand. Just as she did, Dan rushed up behind her, grabbing her close as a purple sphere appeared around him.

"Fire in the hole!" Came the Aria's voice over the headsets.

Nothing.

Tim blinked, then looked back at a building a street over, at the woman hidden in the top-most floor behind the windows. He watched her frantically hit the switch again.

Nothing.

On the parking deck, Mars shook his head, slowly rising to his feet as his mind came back to him, his eyes suddenly glowing with a burning dark red. He stepped up to the cement divider of the third story, staring down at Dan and Michelle and the VGM beyond them. He held out his hand, his black katana flying to his grip. He locked his eyes on the pair and moved up onto the divider itself, posed to step off into the world below.

"No!" Vincent screamed. He frantically looked around, then rushed at the base of the parking deck. As he neared it, a red and white cartoon-like mechanical dog appeared in front of him. Leaping onto the dog's back, a spring shot up, throwing Vincent into the air. Mars barely had time to see him before he was tackled at the waist, sending both flying back into the parking deck. The blow slammed Mars into a minivan and left Vincent dazed on the ground.

"Chip, it's beeping!" Came Aria's voice. He turned around to see her duck down behind the windows of the building she hid in. Chip's eyes narrowed, then went wide. "Fire in the…" Came her voice over the headset.

Hell exploded out from the lower half of the parking deck.

A concussive wave of heat shot from the first floor as the force of the explosion shattered everything glass within the square. The VGM and the generals were sent flying off their feet, while cars and even trees were sent colliding against the surrounding buildings.

After the fire shot out like the breath of a dragon, the sound of debris slammed into existence. The weakened supports groaned and then began to crumble. The deck's lower levels gave in and the whole structure collapsed.

The first two levels gave away with the third following. It buckled, but held. The smoke and heat dissipated, revealing the top two levels of the parking deck still standing, though uncertainly, on the rubble of the first two levels.

"Shit!" Chip yelled, staring at the deck. "It didn't blow up completely."

"Yeah, but it should still hold Mars." Shane said next to him. "I mean, it should, shouldn't it?"

"If it won't," Came Dan's voice over the headsets. "Then Vincent will."

"What?!" Chip roared, hitting the button on his headset. "Vincent's not…"

"Maybe you didn't notice the delay." Jim called. "Vincent knocked Mars back inside. He was inside when it detonated."

"Oh Jesus." Chip groaned, his face pale.

Amidst the piles of smoking rubble, there was movement. A few pieces of debris were thrown back as Mars rose up from the remains of the parking deck floor. He steadied himself uncertainly, looking around. The third level had remained mostly intact, having simply fallen onto the second level and all the vehicles inside it. But the perimeter was filled with devastation as the concrete dividers had fallen inward. He looked up, considering the climb.

"Mars."

The voice was clear. There was no hint of emotional distress in it as the name echoed through the empty and destroyed parking deck. The giant stopped and straightened his wide back, a small smile tugging at the corners of his mouth. Behind him, nearly the entire length of the parking deck away, stood Vincent. The giant warrior turned to the Vgm, his smile widening.

"*Well, well.*" Mars said, taking a few steps towards Vincent. "*The prodigal child returns.*" Mars laughed, his grin growing. "*Back for 'Round two', I imagine. Or rather, back for another session of beatings.*"

"Talk all you want." Vincent said, clearly and confidently, his dark voice meeting Mars' cruel tone head on. "You'll find that I give as good as I get." He mimicked Mars' strides, opening and closing his fingerless gloved hands as he walked. "Tonight is a night you're not going to forget."

"*It's already a night I'm not going to forget.*" Mars allowed as he continued to smile, closing the distance between Vincent and himself to about twenty feet. "*It's soon going to see the end of the VGM, and it's about to see the end of you, boy.*"

"We'll see about that." Said Vincent, holding up his hands in a relaxed, but ready stance.

"*Hmm.*" Chuckled Mars as he tossed his katana away and holding his arms out in his own fighting stance. "*We'll see, indeed.*" He took a few quick, cautious steps, clearing the distance to within a few feet.

Vincent dropped low while Mars was taking the last step. In an instant, he threw himself off the ground, rocketing himself towards Mars. The giant's foot hadn't even touched the ground when Vincent made impact.

Vincent planted his shoulder right into Mars' solar plexus, driving straight into his rib cage. Mars was knocked up into the air by Vincent's force. As he landed, Vincent wrapped his arms around his waist, holding onto him, even as the two slammed back into the pavement.

Mars tried to get to his feet, but Vincent held his grip. As Mars got up to one knee, Vincent reached one arm around and under Mars' lifted leg and flipped him over, slamming the giant down onto his back. Mars took the fall, scissoring his legs on Vincent's arm. Grabbing the vulnerable arm, Mars rolled over, trying to pull Vincent's arm out of its socket. Instead of resisting, the Vgm went with the roll, pulling out of Mars' hold halfway through the spin.

The two came up, fists ready. Mars drove in, swinging for Vincent's head. Vincent ducked back, allowing just a tiny bit of space between his head and the strike. Mars swung again, this time at Vincent's stomach. Vincent danced back a step, maintaining a minimum distance from his foe. Mars swung a third time again at Vincent's head, but he slid to the side, parrying Mars' jab. With his other hand, Vincent snaked up Mars' arm, trapping it with his fingers at the elbow. With a fast circular motion, he smashed his fist into Mars' exposed ribs.

Mars roared as he jumped back, the punch to the nerve cluster causing his muscles to spasm. He tried to move away, but Vincent pressed on, slamming his shin into the side of Mars' hip. Mars tried to grab the kick, but Vincent moved too quickly. Mars' leg gave out and he dropped to one knee.

Vincent moved into position, throwing a hard forward kick at Mars' head. He reached up to grab the kick, but Vincent hinged at his knee at the last second and the kick dropped to the ground. Mars' hands followed after it, leaving his head exposed. Vincent spun around, catching Mars with an impossibly hard roundhouse just as the giant realized the feint.

Mars was sent flying into the air, spinning twice before he hit the hard pavement. Vincent dropped back into his stance, ready for more. But Mars was up in a flash, faster than Vincent expected. In a second, Mars had cleared the distance and threw for Vincent's head. Vincent blocked the blow with his left arm, but the sheer force of the strike knocked him off balance. As he skipped to the right, Mars pivoted around, sweeping his legs out from underneath him.

Vincent landed on his hands, flipping away to his feet. Mars rushed in to follow the flip, but Vincent was ready. As he landed and Mars closed in on him, Vincent jumped up, bringing both his legs up around Mars' neck. Wrapping his feet together behind his head, he threw himself out to the side, while Mars continued forward. Using the sideways momentum, Vincent spun around Mars, flinging the giant into a parked van. The resulting impact nearly tore the van in two.

Vincent rolled along the ground after hearing Mars' collision. He came up to his feet with a quick breath. The air didn't even get in. Mars slammed Vincent's back with a hard kick, knocking him into the pavement. Vincent skidded along the ground, leaving a trail of blood as his flesh was racked off by the broken concrete. Vincent tried to roll with the impact, but it did little good. When he finally stopped, he came up fighting.

Vincent threw a fast hook, but Mars dodged it, sliding into Vincent's blind spot. He planted a precision strike to Vincent's kidney, then reached up with his other hand, grabbing Vincent around the neck with the crook of his arm. The giant reached up with his other arm, closing the gap around Vincent's neck.

Vincent was jolted back to awareness by the chokehold as Mars locked it into place. Using the leverage of one arm against the other, Mars held Vincent firmly around the neck. The Vgm tried to gain some type of advantage with the hold, but he couldn't. He flailed his arms to try and hit Mars in any weak spot he could, but he couldn't land any worthwhile strikes. Vincent threw his head back to head butt Mars, but Mars interrupted him, head butting him in the base of his skull before he could build up any momentum.

"*There.*" Hissed Mars with a trickle of blood from his mouth as he held Vincent by the neck. "*Now that I've got your attention, let's talk.*" He squeezed his arms together a bit more, stopping Vincent's flailing. "*Vincent, you are about to die.*" The words were spoken clearly and concisely, not as a threat, but as a statement.

Mars braced for a struggle from Vincent, but there was none. Vincent simply held onto Mars' arms, trying to force them open. "*I just wanted to make certain you knew that.*" He nearly whispered into Vincent's ear. "*I wanted to make certain that you understood that, no matter what, you knew who it was that killed you.*"

Vincent's vision was beyond blurry. He tipped over, taking Mars with him. The giant let him fall over, keeping the chokehold strong. "*Chip Masters, the VGM, the demon, all of them. They are all going to follow you to Hell.*" He leaned in close, whispering into Vincent's ear. "*So, die by my...*"

Vincent's foot managed to push itself between him and the pavement. With a powerful motion, he threw himself and Mars back up to a standing position. Vincent grabbed Mars' arms with a renewed vigor as he tried to get some air. "*Give it up, Vincent.*" Mars laughed jovially, squeezing harder. "*It's no use.*" As he said that, Vincent reached back behind his head, feeling for Mars' head. "*Oh what now?*" The giant scoffed, moving his head over Vincent's shoulder to rest against Vincent's head. Vincent's hands felt along the base of Mars' shoulders and reached up, following his neck. "*What in the world are you trying to reach?*" He whispered into Vincent's ear.

"***I...***" Came Vincent's raspy and hollow voice. Airless, it sounded little more than a death rattle. "***...will...***" Suddenly, his hands grabbed Mars' head, holding it in place next to Vincent's head. "***...not...***" Vincent's fingers inter-laced behind Mars' neck as he pushed off the ground just a bit. "***FAIL!***"

Vincent yanked his feet out from underneath him, dropping to the ground and dragging Mars along with him. When Vincent hit the ground, Mars' neck landed directly on his shoulder, stunning him and knocking him back.

Vincent was up in less time than it took him to inhale. Before Mars had even started to recover, Vincent plowed into him with the most powerful punch he had ever mustered. Knocking Mars back against another car, Vincent planted a hard punch to Mars' stomach, then another to his face, directly into his nose. Faster than Vincent had ever moved before, he landed punch after punch after punch against the defenseless Mars, simply raining devastation on the giant. Superhuman recovery had been replaced by inhuman determination as Vincent let emotion drive his fists.

Finally, when Vincent's arms refused to hit any more, he reached up and grabbed Mars by the collar of his armor and grabbed his belt at the same time. With the force of a single exhale, Vincent spun around, dragging Mars with him. Their momentum threw Mars into the side of a car. The resulting impact buckled the car against the debris-strewn concrete, totaling the vehicle entirely.

Vincent dropped away from Mars, taking precious seconds to catch his breath. He bent over, gasping as sweat poured off his face. In only a few seconds, he heard Mars moving.

The giant warrior stood up from the impact against the car; glass still lodged into the wounds on his face and chest. Dislodged by the force of the impact, Mars's left eye pulled itself back into its socket by the power of his regeneration, revealing his harsh glare as he stared down at Vincent with pure hatred. He reached up and undid the shoulder clasps of his armor. With a demonstrative gesture, he tossed the chest plate aside. The heavy metal clanged against the cement, throwing up sparks as it slid a few inches.

As soon as the plate hit the ground, Mars jumped forward from the car, racing towards Vincent. Vincent stood his ground, timing the distance. Ten feet from Vincent, Mars leapt into the air, letting his momentum carry him. He chambered his leg, preparing to catch Vincent in the head with an aerial shin kick, one that would take Vincent's head off when it landed. But as soon as Mars launched the kick, Vincent dropped to the ground, rolling forward on his shoulder. Mars let the kick fly, his momentum carrying him past Vincent. Vincent stopped halfway through the roll, pushing himself off the ground with his hands. He drove his feet straight up, catching Mars between the legs.

Mars landed on his feet, but stumbled to the nearest car, holding his groin. Vincent didn't give him a chance to recover. He slammed the back of Mars' knee with his shin, knocking the giant onto his knees. This time, Vincent wrapped his arm around Mars' neck. However, Vincent slid his free hand under Mars' shoulder, catching the giant's arm inside the choke itself.

As soon as Vincent locked the hold, Mars jumped back from his place on the ground and threw himself into a smoking pile of debris. Vincent wasn't ready for the move and was smashed against the door of a huge truck. Mars slammed him again, then slammed his head backwards, knocking Vincent free.

Vincent landed on his feet, but Mars spun, back fisting him out into the driveway of the parking lot. Vincent slid to a standstill, just as Mars snapped a fast kick at him. Vincent blocked the blow with a kick of his own, then he sent his leg up higher, catching Mars in the stomach. Mars took the blow, letting it meet with rock-hard muscles ready for the strike. Vincent, undaunted by the defense, dropped in and slammed his fist into Mars stomach. Mars took that blow and plowed both his fists into Vincent's shoulders, driving the Vgm to his knees as if he was a stake.

Mars lifted his hands again, but Vincent planted his hand on the ground, ready to tackle Mars again. Mars saw the move and dropped his hands, reaching for Vincent. Vincent leapt forward, just as Mars grabbed him around his neck. Going against Vincent's momentum, Mars lifted Vincent into the air, to the extent of his own arm reach. Holding him almost twelve feet high, Mars smiled as time seemed to slow and he watched as Vincent's expression turned to one of absolute horror as he grasped what was about to happen.

Turning the motion around, Mars twisted about, literally throwing Vincent down onto the roof of a parked car. The glass shot out like bullets as the entire car collapsed in on itself from the impact. Smoke and liquids spewed out as the wheels were thrown off the axels of the car and the entire superstructure of the car caved in.

Mars stumbled away from the decimated vehicle, blood pouring from his mouth. Out of breath and exhausted, he leaned against the concrete wall next to the car and stared at Vincent. There was no motion; no breath or pulse. Mars wiped blood from his mouth, then sweat from his brow. Slowly, a smile crept across his face.

"*Heh.*" He tried to laugh, barely even able to speak as more blood come out. "*Die, boy.*" Mars finally succeeded in laughing. "*Die by my hand.*" He smiled, pushing away from the wall. As he walked away from Vincent's body, he tossed back "*Remember everything I am and I still beat you.*" Mars headed back into the smoking debris of the parking deck, disappearing as he made his escape.

Vincent lay motionless on the top of the car, blood pouring from his body. But with a sudden jerk, he inhaled, his body shifting just a bit. His eyes flickered and opened, burning with a strange determination. He tried to move, finding it hard, but not impossible. His body creaked and groaned, but it obeyed him, painfully moving as he pulled himself to consciousness. "Remember, Mars," Came Vincent's breathless voice, hatred filling the words. "It took everything you had to beat me."

CHAPTER 24

Two, If by Sea

"Our situation has not improved."

—Dr. Henry Jones, Indiana Jones and the Last Crusade

Mars collapsed into the waves of the beach, blood spilling from his mouth as he struggled to breathe. Sitting up on his knees, he lifted his head up to the starry, moonless night, a sharp smile on his face. "*That kid really messed me up.*" He half-laughed.

He turned his head back towards the lights of Wilmington, gazing at the pillar of smoke that rose from the destruction of the parking deck. He tried to get up, but his exhausted body still wavered. Standing in the ankle-deep water, he closed his eyes, feeling his regeneration.

"*Mars.*"

Mars' eyes snapped open. He looked slowly to the right, down the line of the beach. Standing nearby just beyond the curl of the nighttime waves, was a figured dressed in a simple white robe, holding a golden staff. The giant's eyes narrowed as his gaze flashed deep red. "*Htead.*" He whispered angrily.

Chip landed hard on the destroyed ground of the parking deck, his golden katana drawn and ready. His eyes quickly scanned the area, searching for any sight of Mars. But with just a quick scan, his eyes fell onto the final sight of the battleground. "Vincent!" He yelled, desperately sprinting to the car where the body lay.

The dark Vgm rolled over to Chip, holding his finger up to his lips. "I'm trying to take a nap. Dick." He whispered groggily.

"Jesus, what happened?" Chip said, quickly appraising Vincent's injuries as well as the damage that surrounded him.

Vincent lifted his head up just enough to look at his beaten body, then looked back at Chip. "Was that, like, a rhetorical question or was there more coming?"

"Shut up and come on." Chip chastised as he grabbed Vincent's arm and helped him lift up. "How's it feel to not be immortal any more?"

"Oh I'd say I'm still at least a little bit." Vincent said, sitting up. He stopped and coughed violently, a mouthful of lumpy blood spitting out. "Otherwise, I think I'd be a lot more dead." He said sickly. He sat up fully, shaking the glass from his hair. "By the way, what's the rush?"

"The generals disappeared during all the chaos of the explosion and we can't find Mars." Chip said. "Come on. We need to either find them or evacuate."

"Evacuate?" Vincent asked, rubbing his head. He swallowed with some effort. "Why?"

"You didn't feel it?" Chip asked. Vincent shook his head. "All the more reason you should be panicking. Something big's happening."

"Define something big." Vincent said, letting himself be pulled out of the crater on top of the car. Shredded paint and metal fragments fell off his back as his joints popped agonizingly with movement. "Oh, Jesus." He groaned, sitting up with a loud pop coming from his lower back. "I don't think I've ever felt this bad in my entire life."

"You may be about to feel a lot worse." Chip warned, already moving back towards the top of the parking deck. "Come on."

"Right. Right." Vincent said, pushing himself off the top of the car. "Coming on." As he slid, the jolt of landing woke him up. He stood up slowly, recognition rushing across his face. He looked back at the front of the parking deck, to where the bus was still smoking with flames rising up to the sky. "Fire." Vincent said, his eyes narrowing. He looked around at the sky, seeing the motionless clouds. "The wind." He whispered, his voice distant. "The wind, the absence of the wind, is a harbinger of…" He turned to Chip as the Vgm waited at the edge of the parking deck. "Chip." He called, his tone frantic. "Where's the wind?" He called hysterically.

Yerrbmot stopped cold.

Eminaf and Livic skidded to a halt, both turning back to him. The wizard general looked away, his eyes slowly widening in fear. He looked at the two generals in front of him, then glanced down a row of trees in the small downtown beautification project. The trees sat quietly, undisturbed by even the slightest breeze. "No wind." The wizard said cryptically.

"What did he say?" Livic asked to the female general next to him.

"Something like 'no win'." Eminaf responded quizzically. "I think he's giving up."

"I said no wind." Yerrbmot snapped back at her. His face drained of color as his voice rapidly beat with his breath. "We're by the ocean and there's no wind?" Eminaf and Livic turned simultaneously towards the trees, the absence of movement finally registering with them. Both their eyes grew fearful. "They're here." The wizard breathed in terror.

"*What are you doing here?*" Mars asked, his eyes locked on Htead.

"*I have come to seek my creation.*" The ancient-looking man said, the gray skin of his face contrasting with his hair that shifted prismatically to a new shade or color with the slightest movement, while the white robe was lined with gold and platinum designs that also shifted and altered. "*Now that you are free of Ecnilitsep's domination,*" The figure said, his ageless face a mixture of boredom and contempt. "*It is time for you to resume your place by my side.*"

Mars stared to smile. "*No.*" He said clearly.

Htead showed almost no sign of response as he stared at Mars. "*I do not have interest in your childish disputes.*" The ancient figure said up to the giant. "*The war with the Shadows can suffer no more divisions between my creations.*"

"*Your creations?*" Mars asked.

"*Yes.*" Htead said simply. "*All that is was created by me.*"

"*And the Shadows?*" Mars asked, almost condescendingly.

"*They are what is not.*" Htead retorted angrily. But as he spoke, his head began to turn, facing the ocean.

"*That doesn't answer my question.*" Htead charged Mars, drawing out his katana. "*What are they?*"

The robed figure turned back to Mars, his eyes taking on a deep red glow of their own. "*What are they?*" Htead asked, staring at Mars. "*You don't remember?*" He said rhetorically with a slow tone.

"*I don't remember a lot of things.*" Mars said with a cruel voice as he took a step towards Htead. "*But I remember enough.*"

"*Clearly not.*" Htead responded stoically with a condescending air. "*If you remembered 'enough', then you would remember the Shadows.*"

"*What are they, Htead?*" Mars threatened, anger and violence filling his voice. "*What are the Shadows?*"

Just as those words escaped his lips, a disruption of existence rushed through the beach. Mars' head whipped out towards the deepest of the ocean. And out amongst the silent wind and the starlight-drenched waves, he saw it.

A space opened up, like a black hole on the ocean, three-dimensional and yet not there at the same time. It pulsed as if alive, and then surged towards the land like the first rays of a dark sun from beneath the ocean's surface.

"*What they are, Mars,*" Htead answered, turning back to the giant with a morose look. "*Is here.*"

APPENDIX

Video Game Magic

Video Game Magic, the system of powers that the VGM uses, is based on directly replicating powers seen in video games. The replication's power is based off the individual's inner spirit (or Chi). This Chi-based power is quite different from the two major schools of magical thought; casting (wizardry, using elemental forces to affect the world) and summoning (witchcraft, calling upon spirits to affect the world).

Given the vast array of video games, the VGM have at their disposal a theoretically limitless arsenal of magical powers. However, the strength and effectiveness of the video game magic is directly related to the inner strength of the individual using them, as well as other more logistical constraints, not the least of which is the familiarity with the game power that is being replicated. Other drawbacks include the concentration required, the use of any activation words, the exhaustion associated with using any form of magic, as well as the height of the caster determining the realm of effectiveness (beyond that range, the usefulness of most video game spells diminishes quickly).

Credits

As homage to the video games that helped inspire this story, actual video game powers are used and referenced throughout this book. Their use is in no way a challenge to the trademarks or copyrights of their respective holders.

The video game powers are listed in order of their use, as well as the game of their origin and the company that published them.

Chapter 04:

Storm Tornado	Mega Man X (Capcom)
Cure	Final Fantasy III (Square Soft)
Teleport	Mortal Kombat II (Midway)
Top Spin	Mega Man III (Capcom)
Phantom Double	Ninja Gaiden III (Tecmo)
Ashura Senku	Street Fighter Alpha 3 (Capcom)
Flying Kick	Mortal Kombat (Midway)

Chapter 05:

Flash Kick	Street Fighter II (Capcom)
Storm Tornado	Mega Man X (Capcom)
Firaga	Final Fantasy III (Square Soft)
Electric Thunder	Street Fighter II (Capcom)
Fireball	Street Fighter II (Capcom)

Chapter 09:

Magic Cape	Legend of Zelda III: Link to the Past (Nintendo)
Ice Blast	Mortal Kombat (Midway)
Titan's Mitt	Legend of Zelda III: Link to the Past (Nintendo)
Teleport	Mortal Kombat II (Midway)
Rolling Attack	Street Fighter II (Capcom)
Super Leap	Super Mario Brothers 2 (Nintendo)
Radiant	Dragon Warrior (Enix)

Chapter 10:

Electric Thunder	Street Fighter II (Capcom)
Tanuki Suit (Stone Form)	Super Mario Brothers 3 (Nintendo)
Invisibility Potion	Super Castlevania IV (Konami)
Magnet Boots	Strider (Capcom)
Blizzaga	Final Fantasy III (Square Soft)
Magic Missile	Final Fantasy VII (Square Soft)
Exit	Final Fantasy (Square Soft)
Exit	Final Fantasy (Square Soft)

Chapter 11:

Wall	Final Fantasy (Square Soft)
Wall	Final Fantasy (Square Soft)
Wall	Final Fantasy (Square Soft)
Flash	Final Fantasy V (Square Soft)
Rolling Shield	Mega Man X (Capcom)
Crystal Ball Roll	Street Fighter II (Capcom)
Rising Tackle	Fatal Fury (SNK)
Jaguar Kick	Street Fighter Alpha (Capcom)
Gravity Inversion	Metal Storm (Irem)
Air Hurricane Kick	Super Street Fighter II (Capcom)
Dragon Punch	Street Fighter II (Capcom)
Candle	Legend of Zelda II: The Adventure of Link (Nintendo)
Scan	Final Fantasy III (Square Soft)
Freeze Ray	Super Turrican (Seika)
Sleep	Final Fantasy III (Square Soft)

Chapter 12:

Sonic Boom	Street Fighter II (Capcom)

Chapter 14:

Rolling Shield	Mega Man X (Capcom)
Spinning Bird Kick	Street Fighter II (Capcom)
Cannon Drill	Super Street Fighter II (Capcom)
Firaga	Final Fantasy III (Square Soft)

Chapter 15:

Electric Thunder	Street Fighter II (Capcom)

Chapter 18:

Magnet Boots	Strider (Capcom)
Bionic Arm	Bionic Commando (Capcom)
Item-3	Mega Man 2 (Capcom)
God-Sight	Populous (Bullfrog)
Fire	Final Fantasy III (Square Soft)
Grappling Hook	Rygar (Tecmo)
Quake	Final Fantasy III (Square Soft)
Hurricane Kick	Street Fighter II (Capcom)
Curaga	Final Fantasy III (Square Soft)
Lightning Kick	Street Fighter II (Capcom)
Rolling Attack	Street Fighter II (Capcom)
Magic Bottle/Fairy	Legend of Zelda III: Link to the Past (Nintendo)
Bionic Arm	Bionic Commando (Capcom)

Fireball	Street Fighter II (Capcom)
Boost Knuckle	Fatal Fury (SNK)
Flash Kick	Street Fighter II (Capcom)
Leather Whip	Castlevania (Konami)
Ice Blast	Mortal Kombat (Midway)

Chapter 23:

Basic Attack	Totally Rad (Jaleco)
Flash Kick	Street Fighter II (Capcom)
Freeze Ray	Mortal Kombat (Midway)
Hurricane Kick	Street Fighter II (Capcom)
Item-2	Mega Man 2 (Capcom)
Raccoon Leaf	Super Mario Brothers 3 (Nintendo)
Rolling Shield	Mega Man X (Capcom)
Rush Coil	Mega Man 3 (Capcom)

978-0-595-36874-7
0-595-36874-3

Printed in the United States
36256LVS00003B/51